The Incredible Adventure
and Other Interstellar Excursions

IN THE SAME SERIES

The Incredible Adventure
and Other Interstellar Excursions

Translated, annotated and introduced by
Brian Stableford

A Black Coat Press Book

ISBN 978-1-61227-859-9. First Printing. May 2019. Published by Black Coat Press, an imprint of Hollywood Comics.com, LLC, P.O. Box 17270, Encino, CA 91416. All rights reserved. Except for review purposes, no part of this book may be reproduced or transmitted in any form or by any means, electronic or mechanical, including photocopying, recording, or by any information storage and retrieval system, without permission in writing from the publisher. The stories and characters depicted in this novel are entirely fictional. Printed in the United States of America.

TABLE OF CONTENTS

Introduction

This anthology assembles three novellas of *roman scientifique*, each of which attempted in a different fashion to accommodate their human characters to a cosmic perspective, partly in order to explore imaginatively and illustrate the size and complexity of a universe in which the Earth is merely one tiny mote of matter among billions, and partly in order to suggest how we might or ought to react philosophically to that awareness.

The first features the invention and employment of a spaceship capable of traveling faster than light; in the second, the Earth is moved out of its orbit in order to become an interstellar traveler itself, eventually reaching the star Vega; the third features the development of a system of interstellar television, which provides its protagonist with a means of investigating life on twelve different planets scattered throughout the galaxy, in search of a possible key to human happiness.

"L'Incroyable aventure de Paul de Lembergen" by Louis Forest, here translated as "The Incredible Adventure," was initially published in four parts between the 1 July and 15 August 1902 issues of the periodical *La Nouvelle Revue*, then under the direction of Pierre-Barthelémy Gheusi.

Le Triomphe de l'Homme by François Léonard, here translated as "The Triumph of Humankind," was published in Brussels by A. Kemplen in an undated edition, probably in 1911.

T.S.F. avec les étoiles by Paul Gsell, here translated as "Wireless Communication with the Stars," was published in Paris by La Nouvelle Societé d'Édition in 1930.

"L'Incroyable aventure de Paul de Lembergen" was not the first story about faster-than-light travel to appear in France, and appears to have been heavily influenced by Camille Flammarion's *Lumen* (1866-69; in book form 1872; revised 1887), in the course of which the eponymous disembodied soul, liberated from the shackles of matter, explores several consequences of traveling faster than light, including that of being able to intercept light reflected from Earth many years in the past and, by adjusting his relative velocity, being able to view events occurring there in reverse. Like Lumen, Forest's far traveler is drawn to the battle of Waterloo, but does not need to comments on the edifying sight of Waterloo viewed in reverse, as a miracle of resurrection rather than slaughter, because he has already made the point. Instead, he goes on to a fanciful account of the subsequent career of Napoléon I.

Forest's version of such viewpoint-juggling, however, moves the idea of hyperluminal from the context of metaphysics to physics, in making its hero the inventor of a material vehicle capable of carrying passengers anywhere in the universe, and he devotes considerable attention to hypothetical physical and psychological effects of the experience of approaching and transcending the velocity of light. Although he is writing a comedy, which ventures more than once into deliberate absurdity, there is nevertheless a measure of scientific method in his literary madness. If the story remains, as its title blithely admits, incredible, there is nevertheless a careful sanity in measuring the incredibility in question.

In particular, Forest neglects to address some of the objections that might be raised to Flammarion's notion of interstellar sight—the fact that maintaining continuity of vision would require the observer to travel in a circle several light-years in diameter in order to match the Earth's axial rotation, to be able to see through clouds, foliage and roofs, and to be able to identify individuals and evaluate their actions from a perpendicular viewpoint—but he does make a tokenistic attempt to recognize such problems, and there is certainly evidence of a rational conscience at work throughout his story, alongside the defensive flippancy of its comicality.

The truly original aspect of the incredible adventure, however, is not so much the invention of the starship, and the extrapolation of the notion, unusual as those imaginative feats were for its time, but the eventual decision of the protagonist, Paul Lembergen, as to how to carry his personal adventure further—a narrative move that very few works of speculative fiction have ever replicated, and which still retains a certain shock value today.

Although extraordinary and idiosyncratic, however, Forest's exercise was not out of keeping with the spirit of its time; "L'Incroyable aventure de Paul de Lembergen" is contemporary with Alfred Jarry's *Le Sûrmale* (1902; tr. as *The Supermale*), published by the press associated with the innovative Symbolist periodical *Revue Blanche*, the example of which undoubtedly had some influence of Pierre-Barthélémy Gheusi's editorship of the *Nouvelle Revue*, a much more experimental periodical while he was in charge than it had been under the tenure of its former proprietor, Juliette Adam. Jarry was in the process if inventing the mock-science of pataphysics and a fiction appropriate to it, and Forest's novella can easily be viewed as paradigm example, alongside Jarry's novella.

The author of "L'Incroyable aventure de Paul de Lembergen," Louis Nathan (1872-1933), who employed the pseudonym Louis Forest for all his journalistic and work literary work, was responsible for one other significant item of *roman scientifique*, the remarkable melodrama *On vole des enfants en Paris* (tr. as *Someone is Stealing Children in Paris*)[1], first published as a feuilleton serial in *Le Matin* in 1906. The novel offers a day-by-day account of an investigation by the police and newspapers reporters of a strange series of events as if they were happening in parallel with their reportage—a narrative strategy that could not have the same effect when the story was reprinted, in abridged form, as a book in 1909.

The author might have produced further ventures in the genre, but most of his work for newspapers was never reprint-

---

[1] Black Coat Press, ISBN 978-1-61227-252-8.

ed in book form and no detailed bibliography of it exists. Forest was most celebrated during his lifetime as a political activist, first making a name as an ardent Dreyfusard, and later taking up an idiosyncratic position on what might be characterized as the "liberal right." His relentless quest for originality, clearly exhibited in both of his known items of *roman scientifique*, isolated him from established political parties, but made him a more interesting and appealing thinker, especially in retrospect, than his more orthodox contemporaries.

Nothing is known for sure about the author of the second novella, *Le Triomphe de l'Homme*, except that his signature appeared on another futuristic novel, *Le Conquête de Londres*, allegedly published in 1919, although there might have been an earlier edition. His birthdate is indicated as "1883?" in bibliographical references that contain no other information, and *Le Triomphe de l'Homme* certainly seems to be a first novel by a young author, which might have been written several years before 1911, as its account of air travel in the far future does not seem to take much account of developments that occurred in the early days of actual air travel.

As to what became of the author, if he was a real person and not a pseudonym, we can only speculate, but synoptic accounts suggest that *Le Conquête de Londres* was written before the Great War, whenever it was actually published, and might well have been a posthumous publication based on an unfinished, or at least unrevised, manuscript. Its appearance in 1919, therefore, if that actually was its first publication, does not provide evidence that the author had survived the war, and might be suggestive of the probability that he had not.

Whatever the facts might be of its precise authorship, *Le Triomphe de l'Homme* is a much less sophisticated work, in literary terms, than the stories that bracket it herein, but that does not make it any less remarkable as a work of vaulting imagination. It is utterly implausible—the author has an extremely casual attitude to the laws of motion and matters of celestial mechanics—but that is not the point of the exercise, which is to describe the adventure of the planet in its interstellar journey, and the future of humankind as a result of that displacement.

As with Paul Lembergen's decision as to what to do with his epoch-making scientific discoveries, the reaction of the physicist Neick to his hypothetical discovery, and that of the scientific community of which he is a part, is so startling that it has rarely, if ever, been replicated in the annals of speculative fiction, but that is not a bad thing in the context of imaginative adventurism, and it certainly helps to add a paradoxical irony to the novella's title.

Seen as a *conte philosophique*, *Le Triomphe de l'Homme* is extremely open-ended, the narrative voice maintaining an oddly compromised objectivity in its commentary, especially when the storyline has no other viewpoint left to issue even the most tentative of judgments on what is happening, but that too is not necessarily a bad thing.

That distanced objectivity does, however, make an interesting contrast with *T.S.F. avec les étoiles*, which hammers its message home in no uncertain terms in a final chapter whose argument deliberately echoes, albeit in a light-hearted manner, one of Plato's best-known dialogues.

The story is, in essence, a boisterous comedy in a vein not unlike that of "L'Incroyable aventure de Paul de Lembergen"—and, indeed, one of the strange planets examined by means of interstellar television is one where time marches backwards, producing visions and comments similar to these featured in Forest's novella—but the tone of its satire varies very markedly as the angst-ridden protagonist, the aptly-named Jacques Lagité, seeks an answer to his own self-defined existential predicament by examining a series of exemplary societies.

The narrative swings from amiable absurdity to scathing caricature with a casual ease, but also produces a sharp poignancy in several places where its slippery velvet glove is removed, in order to issue a challenge to the reader's thinking, and the iron fist beneath is revealed in all its intellectual and emotional brutality.

Paul Gsell (1870-1947) is remembered today primarily as a critic, whose book *L'Art* (1911), recording his discussions with the sculptor Auguste Rodin, remains in print. He also made copious records of his conversations with another of his friends, the writer Anatole France. Rodin is mentioned briefly in *T.S.F. avec les étoiles*, but the literary influence of Anatole France's satirical novels is far more important, in terms of the novella's cavalier narrative strategy and skeptical rhetorical standpoint. Gsell had written at least one previous work of *roman scientifique*, the similarly satirical *L'Homme qui lit dans les âmes* (1928) (tr. as *The Man Who Could Read Minds*)[2], but as with Louis Forest, there is no detailed biblio-graphical account of his copious writings, so he too might have produced further ventures. At the beginning of his career he published a brief visionary fantasy, "Pierre Paquery" (1893) in *La Nouvelle Revue* before Gheusi acquired the mag-azine; he might well have read Louis Forest's novella in the periodical's pages, and remembered it.

As in the case of the starship in "L'Incroyable aventure de Paul de Lembergen," Gsell's invention of "astral wireless" is not without precedent in *roman scientifique*. The invention and employment of such a technology is featured in some of the vignettes reprinted in *Pour lire en automobile* (1901) (tr. as *The Mysterious Fluid*)[3] by the journalist Paul Vibert, whose satirical tone and attitude has something in common was Gsell's, but Vibert merely sketches the notion and a few of its corollaries in brief pieces written for daily newspapers, and Gsell's elaborately organized extrapolation of it provides a far more satisfactory analysis, the comedy of which does not de-tract from its intellectual discipline and underlying serious-ness.

---

[2] Black Coat Press, ISBN 978-1-61227-860-5.
[3] Black Coat Press, ISBN 978-1-61227-020-3.

In several respects, *T.S.F. avec les étoiles* is a story very much of its time, not only because it is an imaginative product of a particular phrase in the development of radio broadcasting, but also because of its constant preoccupation with the threat of a more destructive repetition of the Great War. In the latter regard the story echoes the macabre tenor of a great deal of interbellum futuristic fiction, and the black humor of the account of the planet of the Forgetful is only unusual in its conciseness, as is the cynical account of the collapse of civilization on the doomed planet Grul.

The novel does, however, make a serious attempt to transcend the preoccupations of its day in order to address eternal questions, and the breath of its imagistic spectrum enables it to do that, while it relative coherency supports the rare conviction of its conclusion. Characters who set out to find the secret of happiness in *contes philosophiques* usually fail to find it, merely learning resignation, and Jacques Lagité is privileged in that regard, although not all readers will be able to sympathize with his ultimate acquisition, for a variety of reasons, any more than Paul de Lembergen's friends were able to sympathize with the not-dissimilar happiness that Louis Forest had permitted him to discover.

As well as with being familiar with the methods and attitudes characteristically deployed in the rich tradition of *contes philosophiques* following on from Voltaire's classic *Candide* (1759), Paul Gsell was certainly familiar with the specific example of Anatole France's novella "La Chemise" (in *Les Sept femmes de Barbe-Bleue et autres contes merveilleux*, 1909), which features a similar search for happiness in a different hypothetical framework. He might well have planned and executed his interstellar tour with the bold aim of attempting to take the quest one step further than his friend and mentor had been able to do; whether he succeeded or not is for the reader to decide, but it certainly worked to his advantage to have the vast stellar universe available as a hunting-ground rather than the narrow confines of Earth.

If that expansion of scale rendered Gesell's exercise, like its two predecessors, less plausible in the eyes of many readers, that is simply one of the costs of employing *roman scientifique* as a literary genre, and the fact that all three of the novellas in the present assembly were damned for it in their own day and slipped quietly into literary oblivion provides a telling illustration of the fact. All three stories are heroic endeavors nevertheless, and now that the cosmic perspective is much more solidly and abundantly established in the arena of modern media mythology, it is much easier for readers to appreciate their pioneering boldness and to sympathize with their defiant idiosyncrasy. Literary antiques they might be, but that adds to their value rather than detracting from it.

The translation of "L'Incroyable aventure de Paul de Lembergen" was made from the copies of the relevant issues of *La Nouvelle Revue* reproduced on the Bibliothèque Nationale's *gallica* website. The translation of *Le Triomphe de l'Homme* was made from copy of the Kemplen edition, and that of *T.S.F. avec les étoiles* from a copy of the 1930 book published by La Nouvelle Société d'Édition.

Brian Stableford

Louis Forest: *The Incredible Adventure* (1902)

This is the story of Paul de Lembergen.

His father, enriched by the exploitation of Cuban sugar, arrived in Paris one day in order to obtain treatment for his diabetes.

He was a handsome man with a caramel complexion, sweet speech, honeyed laughter, a candied gaze and fondant gestures. He put his son in the Lycée Louis-le-Grand and hastened to consult a Parisian physician highly reputed in Havana for once having saved a famous creole who was not ill.

Paul's father was a widower.

The doctor did not cure his malady but he cured his widowhood by enabling him to marry his elder daughter, Georgette Vaudois.

The old Cuban died three years later, leaving his wife with two children. Honorine Vaudois is Paul's fiancée, and the sister, fifteen years younger, of Georgette. By his marriage, therefore, Paul will become the brother-in-law of his late father and the brother-in-law of his stepmother, who will become the mother-in-law of her sister, who will be, in her turn, the daughter-in-law of her sister and the daughter-in-law of her late brother-in-law. The children of Paul's father, in addition to being, so to speak, the brothers of their uncle and the nephews of their cousins—if Paul has any sons—will also be the brothers-in-law of their aunt, while Paul's children (still hypothesizing a fertile union) will be the grandsons of their late uncle and the nephews of their grandmother.

At the lycée, Paul was immediately considered to be a phenomenon. The headmaster was obliged to employ serious threats to prevent the physician attached to the establishment making a report to the Académie on such an interesting case.

The young native of Havana had entered the class on the fifteenth of October, not knowing French and completely ignorant of its syntax, and knowing nothing about our history. By the following first of January, he was first in French composition, having developed admirably the subject: "A son writes to his mother describing the Musée du Louvre." Paul had never set foot in the celebrated galleries, and had only heard vague mention of them. That sufficed for him to beat all his comrades.

He continued in the same vein.

He was never seen with a book in his hands; he never worked during the hours of study. He did not learn his lessons, finding that he had no need to write his assigned work, catching flies or sleeping voluptuously while others were scraping pens or engraving *amo, amas, amat* in the lobes of the brain while poring over Latin grammars.

In spite of that inveterate idleness, however, refractory to any punishment, and his somnolent appearance, he knew everything, better informed than anyone else. From time to time, when the whim took him—not very often—he amused himself by astonishing his professors with the vivacity of his mind and the clarity and surety of his science. He was either null or perfect.

One day, as a pupil in the third form, he found half a page in the courtyard torn out of a book by a bigger boy preparing for his baccalaureate. He scanned the few mud-stained lines, a dozen phrases of an abridged memento of a summary of a manual of a treatise in philosophy, in which there was question of the Kantian theory of judgment. A week later, in a drawing class, he scribbled in black pencil around a head of Cicero copied from his bust, a dissertation on the opinions of the moralist of Königsberg. He had almost finished when the study-master, a graduate in philosophy, seized the paper and, after having read it, declared enthusiastically that the argument was a masterpiece of logic and a model of ingenious reflection, possessed of excellent coherency.

Paul's work was communicated to the headmaster. The headmaster showed it to the professor of philosophy. The professor of philosophy wanted to make the acquaintance of the young prodigy. In the conversation, young Lembergen corrected an error on the part of the old scholar on the subject of Herbert Spencer.

"You've read Herbert Spencer, then?" asked the professor.

"No."

"But where the devil do you get everything you know?"

"I don't know anything," Paul de Lemebrgen replied, phlegmatically.

After having failed the baccalaureate once and received it, at the second attempt, with the unanimous congratulations of the professors, Paul de Lembergen hesitated at first between several careers.

Being rich, he would have been able to follow any dream, as a rentier.

He did not want to do that, and bought, successively, a factory making strong-boxes and an establishment of horticulture. Then, one morning, he sold both businesses and went to enroll in the history course in the Faculty of Letters. As a student, he lived extravagantly, sometimes associating with cutthroats, burglars and hooligans, dirty clients of the Parisian dens of vice to which the police take foreign princes, and sometimes frequenting the most refined, elegant and aristocratic milieux. He was only seen at the Sorbonne very rarely, which did not prevent him finishing first in the final examinations.

After a year in the provinces he was appointed as a professor of history at the Lycée Condorcet in Paris. All of that exceptional intelligence and all of that abnormal instinctive knowledge of everything concluded, therefore, in a banal career in education.

For three years, Paul de Lembergen was a model professor, a symbol of universitarian conscience, regularity itself. A few months ago, he fell madly in love with his sister-in-law, to whom he had not previously paid any attention.

Almost all his leisure time was occupied with absorbing labor of which no one had any knowledge except for his fiancée. Although temperamentally over-excited, Honorine was not talkative, especially when it was a matter of Paul. A large shed, constructed in the courtyard of the house in Neuilly in which Lembergen lived, served him as a mysterious laboratory.

No one knew anything more about his studies. If anyone asked: "How do you spend your time between those diabolical planks?" he replied: "Bah! Everything and nothing," or: "Patience! Perhaps one day I'll tell you things that aren't banal."

We didn't insist, in spite of our curiosity, for it would be easier to extract milk from a locomotive than to make such an obstinate man talk.

We met up almost every evening in his drawing room, Guy de Rommelle a former cavalry lieutenant who had handed in his resignation in order to trade in postage stamps, Siegmund Bergmann of the *Berliner Lokalanzeiger* and I, whom my parents had destined for the notariat and who had fallen into literature. When midnight chimed we left, and on the way, we took Honorine home to the Boulevard Péreire.

The day before yesterday, as we were going home in that fashion and a frightful nocturnal squall was curbing our heads and searching our cloaks, Honorine seemed to me to be very nervous. Among remarks, half of which the wind carried away, she said to me:

"Oh...Paul...the brain of a god!"

Here begins an extraordinary story.

Paul de Lembergen, after having arranged the chess-pieces, sat down on a sofa, stuffed his pipe, lit it, and became meditative.

Paul de Lembergen's pipe resembles its owner. He has the custom of saying: "I wouldn't sell it for a hundred thousand francs, and it cost me two sous." No one has ever offered the hundred thousand francs, so that declaration never engages its author; it only signifies that he loves his pipe.

It is a simple clay pipe. The bowl is fitted to the slender stem at an obtuse angle. When Paul de Lembergen reflects he does not lower his head like everyone else; in the contrary, he raises it, and it makes an angle with his thin, long body equal to that of the bowl with the stem of his puffer. We have measured it. Furthermore, the heel of the pipe, bisected, appears to be the little brother of Paul de Lembergen's nose. Around the mouthpiece, where his teeth rest, our friend has personally wrapped a precious thread that winds tightly in artistically-knotted spirals. Since he once broke both wrists while trying to stop an enraged donkey, he wears bracelets from the origin of his hands to the mid-point of his forearm, woven with the same thread as that of his pipe.

That is not all.

The name Paul de Lembergen sounds Germanic. His ancestors were, in fact, Swabian. In 1430, one Hugo von Lembergen acquired a certain reputation when it was discovered that he had successively murdered his eight wives, in the fashion of Bluebeard. The Lembergens are otherwise undistinguished by history. In 1698, Ulrich von Lembergen, condemned to be hanged for I know not what crime, escaped and ran away to Havana, where he married a creole. Gradually, as a consequence of several marriages made locally, the German blood was greatly diluted in the family. It is only enounced any longer by the eyes, which are obstinate in remaining blue. Thus, Lembergen has a mat complexion, brown and warm, comparable to that of his pipe where it is not wrapped up.

Those physical resemblances between Paul de Lembergen and his pipe are trivial compared with the psychological resemblances.

Psychological! Do pipes have a soul, then?

I do not know whether all pipes are thus endowed, but one could swear on one's honor that Paul de Lembergen's has one. Sometimes it has a placid character, of slow, measured, even painstaking reflection, sometimes it gets hot and bothered to the extent of becoming scary. Sometimes its smoke rises sagely and calmly; sometimes it emerges volcanically in acrid and precipitate swirls.

Like his pipe, Paul is ordinarily dull, his imagination tranquil, to say no more. He is not talkative, absorbed in his dreams without sudden starts, and his speech does not shine, But when he gets excited, when he is pushed, he is transformed. Then his forehead lights up, his eyes shine, and he become eloquent. He stupefies his audience with the strangeness and the violence of his speech.

Just like his pipe.

His pipe seems frail. One would think that one could break it by blowing on it. But steel is no more resistant. Several times, it has fallen on the floor; one thought it would be smashed but on examination, one could not see a scratch. Paul de Lembergen, apparently paltry, almost ill and feverish, is solid and hard, as strong as Hercules.

Just like his pipe.

Is there any need now to explain at greater length why our friend values his pipe so much? We know that he has two amours: Honorine Vaudois, the strange girl with the yellow garnet complexion, and his pipe.

You will, therefore understand our fear when, yesterday evening, *after having put on his red beret*, Paul started to laugh—oh, laughter that made us feel ill, nasty and savage laughter—and declared to us: "Messieurs it's eight thirty-five. At eleven forty, I shall break my pipe."

In popular parlance "to break one's pipe" means to decamp, to bid the company farewell, to pack one's bags, to swallow one's tongue, to kick the bucket, to turn up one's toes, to pop one's clogs, to pass over, or to unscrew one's light-bulb—in a word, to die.

Did Paul intend to commit suicide?

He surprised that question in our eyes, and hastened to explain: "Don't worry, I'm not speaking metaphorically or figuratively. I really will break my pipe—the pipe I hold between my teeth, which is smoking its last smoke at present, at eleven forty."

Guy de Rommelle, Siegmund Bergmann and I looked at one another. I also tried to read some sentiment in the face of Honorine Vaudois. The young woman was smiling, and did not appear to be afraid.

Siegmund Bergmann leaned toward me and murmured in my ear, so close that he tickled me with his breath: "Note that he has his red beret on."

For some time, our friend had abandoned himself to violent crises of excitement every time he camped on his head a sort of crimson wool beret that his fiancée knitted for him. He had complained one day of neuralgia, and Honorine Vaudois had claimed that she could cure him by means of warm headgear. Paul did not lend credence to that vulgar remedy for long, but as the hat came from the woman he loved, he had hung it on the wall, on the nail supporting a trophy of Cuban weapons. The sofa on which he habitually reposed during our evening meetings was placed directly beneath that bellicose ornament. Paul only had to reach out his hand to seize the cap. It happened quite often, therefore, that without any precise intention, he stretched out his arm, initially to tap with his index-finger a few times on the butt of a rifle, and then to take the red cap mechanically in order to amuse himself by slipping his little finger through the mesh of the knitting, while one of us read aloud harmonious and incomprehensible verses or exposed lengthy theories of social regeneration.

Frissons of anxiety vibrated in the nape of our neck when Paul de Lembergen toyed with the red beret. That headgear produced such extravagant effects on him!

When he was coiffed with it, he became extraordinarily animated, and said crazy things. Was it not insensate to want to break his pipe, such a dear pipe, so well cared for? He could have announced his intention to murder Honorine Vaudois and we would not have been more anguished.

The mysterious influence of the red beret made me tremble.

"You're going to break your pipe, then?"

"At eleven forty."

"You no longer love it, then?"

He threw his arms toward the heavens to attest his amour. "I still love it. The sacrifice will cost me."

"It doesn't draw any more, then?"

"As well as in its finest epoch."

"Then why?"

"Ask Honorine."

The young woman smiled: a unique, exquisite smile, silky and pale...

People who lack imagination might claim that, since there is no silk in the eyes, and no color in a gaze or in an expression of sentiment, a smile can nether be silky nor pale. So much the worse for them. I'm not telling this story for them. I don't care about them.

Words with a golden sound glided through the pale and silky smile.

"It's a vow," Honorine Vaudois explained.

"A vow? What is this enigma?"

Paul de Lembergen stood up and went to stand in front of the fireplace, like a young man about to deliver a monologue. With an abrupt gesture, he covered his left ear with the red cap.

"My friends, my friends," he said, staring at the circles of moving light that the lamp designed there, "I'm little known to the public; I've never attempted to attract the world's attention to me. I am informing you that I've had enough of that obscurity, enough of repeating the same course every year to different cretins, enough of being only a tranquil universitarian, while I sense a fulminating genius palpitating within me, thoughts seething within my skull, a single one of which might turn the globe upside-down. I shall tell you, since you're my friends, that in a week, the name of Paul de Lembergen will be famous throughout the entire world, and curious women will be striving to discover the secret of my gaze in my photograph, displayed in showcases.

Siegmund Bergmann whispered to me: "Delusions of grandeur."

"I fear so."

After a time of repose, Paul de Lembergen continued, increasingly animated: "I have, in fact, conceived a theory of the world that..."

"That's it," Guy de Rommelle interrupted. "He's mad. You're mad, my poor Paul. Tomorrow, I'll take it upon myself to send you to Doctor Calamardini. A few cold showers will be salutary for you. A new theory of the world! That's a well-characterized madness. It's thus that a large number of mental illnesses permit the first diagnosis of derangement. Aren't you Jesus Christ as well? It only lacks you presenting yourself as the savior of your contemporaries and the awaited messiah! Or, what might perhaps be even better, jump on the first train departing for a mountainous country, and go to repose in the isolation of a serious altitude. My word, I'm not joking. You're worrying me with your theory of the world..."

"Perfect, perfect!" replied Paul de Lembergen. "Among the ineluctable laws that support my theories, I've listed the following: every person to whom I explain my discoveries will begin by thinking me unhinged. If my other predictions are verified with the same exactitude, I shall have nothing more to do than rub my hands. That's all right, that's all right... but grant me two minutes before cutting off my speech.

"I have, I tell you, conceived a theory of the world that no other philosopher has ever imagined. My doctrine is a universal key, which will transform the sciences—or, rather, the science, for there is only one science, divided arbitrarily into independent parcels by human weakness. I'll spare you all the ideas that have preceded mine on the subject, those of Democritus, Epicurus, Lucretius, Gassendi, Descartes, Leibniz, Kant, Copernicus, Kepler, Newton, Laplace and a hundred other metaphysicians or physicists who have, more or less, by different routes, sought to explain a part of the mystery, or the entire mystery, of the universe. Nor will I recount to you the incredible chain of reasoning that I've forged. I've been working for more than ten years, and I certainly couldn't expose that long labor to you even if I talked for a week without stopping. Let it suffice for you to know that, departing from the essential quality of the molecules of matter, which is to attract one another in direct proportion to their masses and in inverse proportion to the square of their distance apart, and also departing from an original theory of the ether, which has furnished me with the laws of elasticity and capillarity, and departing, finally, from the theory of waves of light and that of the identity of electromagnetic waves and light waves, after Maxwell, I've obtained results so new and so compelling that you'll soon bow down almost to the ground, calling me 'dear master.' My friends, I'm not content with theoretical estimations or calculations on paper, even though they can fulfill the glory of a man. I've constructed apparatus with my hands that will crush you with astonishment, veritable machines to render the impossible possible..."

Siegmund Bergmann has a methodical mind, which never runs two ideas at once. He attempted to canalize, so to speak, Lembergen's divagations.

"What relationship is there between these famous machines and the execution of your pipe at eleven forty?"

"This: my work was already complete five years ago. It has already been five years since all my calculations were finished, all my theories fully demonstrated, five years since my apparatus as almost ready. I say 'almost' because, by virtue of a veritable satanic persecution, one single difficulty among the ten thousand that I've overcome, resisted my efforts. The obstacle appeared to me to be insurmountable. I've stayed awake all night searching for the solution to the last problem that stopped me. Discouraged, I was about to send everything to the devil when I got engaged. You know that, in order to relieve the migraines caused by the continual tension in my brain, Honorine made me a present of the red beret. Bless the day when I received that gift! The red beret, by the warmth it maintained in the forebrain, by the more ardent blood that it caused to rise to my head, multiplied my intellectual strength tenfold, and one evening, at eleven forty...

"You'll remember that Sunday evening. I sent you telegrams telling you not to come to the usual meeting. Well, that evening, drunk on genius, thanks to the red beret, I discovered the means of breaking the infernal obstacle by which my life was poisoned..."

"But what about the pipe! The pipe!"

"I'm getting to that. To whom did I owe the definitive success? To Honorine. Without her, would I have thought of covering my head, in the house, with a woolen hat? I wanted, therefore, to prove my gratitude to her. 'Beloved fiancée,' I said to her, 'for the victory that I owe to you, tell me the secret wish of your soul, the wish whose realization would give you the most pleasure, the wish that you haven't yet dared to reveal to me, which you're keeping for the supreme moments of intimacy; later. I swear to satisfy it.'

"Honorine replied to me immediately: 'Don't smoke anymore; the smoke upsets me, and I only tolerate it here for love of you.'"

Lembergen's words had immediate effects. Siegmund Bergmann snatched from his mouth the cigar that was embalming the whole room, and crushed the lighted end under his heel. Guy de Rommelle spat on his cigarette to put it out. For myself, I put on a pretence of not having understood and hypnotized myself to model round eyes while drawing on my superior caporal. In truth, women can't imagine how indebted to me they are!

"Now, my friends," said Paul de Lembergen, "no longer smoking is the equivalent for me of having a leg amputated, if not two...but after all, I had promised, and I had to keep the promise. However, as the sacrifice seemed painful, I asked for a few days' grace in order to get used to the idea of renouncing the dearest of my habits. As a deadline, I fixed for myself the fifteenth of September at eleven forty in the evening. At that moment it will be exactly a month, to the minute, since, poring over my retort, emotional and anguished, I saw the birth of the miraculous material that will open the world to me…

"Oh, my friends, those thirty days have passed, for me, like those of a condemned man for whom the scaffold is waiting. Nevertheless, the last week has been lighter, and has gradually suggested to me a new principle, which is giving me today one of the greatest joys of my existence. I have reflected on the notion of 'sacrifice.' I have ground it down, alloyed it with all known philosophies, and I have finally found that the highest human sentiment is that of sacrifice. A sacrifice for another, in full consciousness, coldly, with a full awareness of the harm one is doing to oneself, is a nobility of divine essence. No other quality of the soul can claim more beauty. The man who sacrifices himself thus finds the highest place above animality in the pure realm of intelligence…

"I love Honorine. 'Love!' The word has been galvanized. I only employ it for want of a better and superior term, impregnated with a thousand nuances with which I would like to dress the vocable. I love Honorine. Now, veritable love, not the vulgar passion that we are accustomed to admire, cannot be understood without the spirit of sacrifice. Sacrificial love surpasses banal love as a mathematical verity surpasses a political verity. It is transcendent in essence, while the other is only material or human in essence. I wanted to raise myself up to sacrificial love. And that's why, after having considered that settlement as a misfortune, I shall soon break my pipe…gladly!"

When Guy de Rommelle emerges from his calmness, he extends the arch of his eyebrow and his monocle falls out. The stamp merchant coughed in an artificial fashion to attract our attention. "Ahem! Ahem!"

One can attribute to "Ahem! Ahem" an *ad libitum* meaning. I divined that the noise signified: "He's definitely out of his mind."

Undoubtedly Paul de Lembergen understood it thus, for he shrugged his shoulders impolitely.

"Your theory," commenced Siegmund Bergmann, "has the fault that..."

He did not get any further.

Honorine had risen to her feet and traversed the room.

She placed her little finger on the dial of an Empire clock and remarked, while looking at her fiancé: "Paul, it's eleven thirty-nine and twenty seconds."

"Ah!"

Our friend drew another five or six rapid puffs from his pipe; then he emptied out the ash and contemplated, tenderly, the little instrument that had so often kept him company like a living being.

"My poor, poor pipe!" he said.

"It's eleven forty," replied the implacable young woman. "Let's go!"

Paul de Lembergen approached the fireplace, and with a dry click he rapped the head of the pipe against the marble. We heard a *tock*, but he pipe did not break.

Paul recommenced the experiment. The pipe remained entire.

Our friend examined it carefully, and murmured: "That's extraordinary! I took so many precautions not to break it! It's made of stone!"

A third, more violent attempt had no more result. Not only did the pipe not suffer from it, but no splinter was detached from it. It remained entire, integral, in Paul's quivering hands.

"Bizarre! Bizarre!" said Lembergen, his eyes illuminated by anger.

For the fourth time he tried to annihilate his pipe; for the fourth time, the impact had no effect,

"Damn it! Is it bewitched?"

Then we witnessed a frenetic and ferocious combat. His fingers clenched upon his adversary, the force of whose inertia overexcited him, Paul gave himself entirely to that passionate and novel duel.

The battle was terrible.

The pipe was obstinate in living. Paul threw it against the marble twenty times without breaking it. In order to give himself more energy he accompanied his gestures with frightful oaths. He shouted, exasperated by the resistance, becoming redder than his beret. Long droplets of sweat ran down his cheeks. His cravat was unknotted, his neck flexed like an accordion.

We were oppressed, spectators of a captivating struggle. The pipe moved us to pity. Its stubbornness in not dying inspired admiration and compassion in us.

"Leave it," begged Siegmund Bergmann, who admits murderous wars in his capacity as a politician, but is moved by the death of a fly. "Leave it!"

"No...no...I want to be...I will be...the master," cried our friend, foaming at the mouth, his eyes bulging. "Understand that if I don't succeed in taming it, it's the end of my happiness...of love...oh, bitch of a pipe!"

He tried once again—in vain—to vanquish it.

Breathless, his breast heaving, he paused for breath, and to reflect.

"Do you believe that it's very intelligent to exert yourself like this?" asked Guy de Rommelle. "And for what purpose? For an almost incomprehensible whim. You don't want to smoke any longer? Throw the pipe into the street, or the river. There! What's the point of giving yourself all this trouble, when the solution is so simple?"

"Stamp merchant, your mind is limited," replied Lembergen, in a dull voice. "Do you know what the religion of symbols is? Do you know that...?"

He did not complete his thought. His face was illuminated by an idea. He bent down, put the pipe on the floor, placed himself directly against it so that it was in contact with his shoe, straightened up, as stiff s a Prussian soldier insulted by his corporal, held his breath, raised his right foot and struck down with his heel. A pile-driver is not more precise, nor more forceful.

Immediately, the pipe was smashed. The central part formed a little heap of fine powder. The pipe had ceded once and for all, as if, finally resigned, it had released all its molecules and consented definitively to the dissociation of its being.

Paul de Lembergen took possession of the handkerchief that Honorine was holding in her hand and mopped his brow.

"Finally," he sighed. "Now I can hope for a happy future. I believed, in being unable to break the pipe, that nature was against me, and forbidding me forever the sacred and superhuman domain of sacrifice.

"You have the philosophical tally-ho," muttered Guy de Rommelle.

Paul de Lembergen poured himself three glasses of water, which he drank almost without pausing for breath.

When he was refreshed, Paul de Lembergen turned toward his fiancée.

"Honorine," he said, "since I've been strong enough to vanquish myself without difficulty, why don't I try my machines immediately? I feel marvelously well. I have a clear and logical mind. Do you want to?"

"Of course. What about these messieurs?"

"These messieurs, if they're not damp chickens, will go with us, in order to witness my strange conquest."

Bergmann and Rommelle consulted me with their gazes. I replied, in the same language, that it was necessary to accept Paul's offer, in order to help our friend avoid the dangers to which his mental alienation might expose him.

"Well, are you with us?" demanded the madman.

"Certainly."

"Bring your hats and cloaks, then, and come."

Paul picked up a lamp in order to light our way, and conducted us into the shed where he was accustomed to shut himself away in order to work.

"Well, you've increased the height of the building," observed Siegmund Bergmann, his gaze measuring the walls that were vaguely illuminated by the nascent moon.

"Yes, I needed more space and height for my experiments." And, turning the key in the entrance door, "Paul de Lembergen added: "Messieurs, the present minute is inaugurating the most important moments of your life."

We might have been skeptical, and we might not have believed what our friend said, but we were impressed nevertheless by his assurance and the confidence of his affirmations.

Already, Guy de Rommelle was yielding. I asked him: "What do you think?"

He replied: "Who knows?"

It was, therefore, with a certain pensiveness that we crossed the threshold of the shed.

"What's that machine?" exclaimed Bergmann, who had gone in first.

Almost all the space between the walls was filled by an immense ball about ten meters in diameter, whose gleam resembled that of the dorsal scales of a mackerel.

"This sphere," Lembergen replied to us, turning up the light as far as it would go, in order to enable us to embrace the vast proportions of the giant ball, "is an apparatus that I've baptized the 'radiomobile.' Oh, I don't have any godfatherly self-esteem, and if that name displeases you, you can choose another. I made up the word by taking account of one of the most interesting properties of the machine, that of moving by means of the action of luminous rays. The materials that compose it are all new. The twelve metals composing it are not part of any known series, and each one is an original discovery. I designate them as metal A, metal B, metal C, and so on. As I've already told you, I don't fatigue myself finding topical denominations. The other materials, similarly unknown, of which all the accessories and interior instruments are made, have never been obtained before, and as popular language is naturally unaware of them, it's sufficient to classify them by means of chemical formulas. Spare me, then, unnecessary questions to which I can only respond by means of a vocabulary with doesn't explain anything to your inferior intelligences. Content yourselves with the few characteristic details that your minds are, in my judgment, capable of digesting. My ball..."

"You've lost it, your ball," I interrupted, a trifle ruffled by the disdainful tone in which Paul was talking about our intellectual capacities. I humbly admit however, that my joke was bad taste, out of place and dishonest. But what do you expect? I have a rather slow repartee. Responses full of wit always occur to me a quarter of an hour later, while the coarse remark arrives right away. It's an infirmity. I deplore it. I also deplore having said to Paul de Lembergen, before the sphere the color of mackerel scales: "You've lost it, your ball."

I regret it all the more because he hadn't lost it at all, as the rest of this story will prove. For my excuse, I'll add that I still didn't believe in our fried's inventions.

Paul de Lembergen simply interleaved between "my ball" and the continuation of his speech, the word "imbecile." I am too modest not to declare here that the epithet I question was destined for me. It embarrassed me at first because of Honorine. I nearly tried to pick a quarrel, but only nearly. After all, Paul and I had been comrades for too long not to be able to overlook a few insults.

So, he said: "My ball...imbecile...is already something very curious by virtue of its construction, which merits filling twenty sessions at the Académie des Sciences. However. let's not waste and more time admiring the outside and go inside..."

"Go inside? How? I don't see any door..."

Paul de Lembergen took a little stone out of his pocket, a sort of opal, which he pressed against the all of the sphere. Immediately, a round piece of the wall was detached in order to give us passage, like a slice of melon detached from the fruit, which remains adherent to the fruit at the inferior extremity, rotating on a little thread of pulp.

"Oh!" said Bergmann. "One might think we were in the home of a conjurer."

A plank rose up to the interior of the globe, two meters above the ground, if one can say that a gray and vitreous matter can form a plank. An eight-step stairway permitted access to it. We climbed up in single file.

"This chamber doesn't resemble any other, does it?" asked Lembergen.

And, indeed, it defied description, as much by the glittering reflections of the walls as by the oblique ceiling and the furniture of a sorcerer. At the back there was a small sideboard, and in the middle, a table, surrounded by five three-legged stools. Apart from the sideboard the table and the tripods there were a hundred objects of strange form, to which it was materially impossible to give names and attribute uses. There were contorted utensils that would have sickened the imagination of an alchemist.

"My friends," said Paul de Lembergen, "You find yourselves now in the most ingenious machine in the world. I only have to open the mobile roof of the shed that contains the apparatus, to manipulate these two fluorescent handles—above all, don't touch them without protecting your hands with the protective gloves that you'll find in the sideboard—and the radiomobile will rise up into the air and take me wherever I wish, at whatever height I wish, at whatever velocity I wish"

Siegmund Bergmann, Guy de Rommelle and I had made the decision not to exchange any more reflections and to remain silent. We were suspended between the idea of the madness of our friend and the mysterious dread of the unknown.

"We shall now, if you wish," Paul continued, "try out my radiomobile. But before then, if one of you is scared, let him get down."

No one budged.

"Good," said our friend.

He left the sphere and we soon heard a rolling sound. Paul was making the mobile roof of the shed slide.

I leaned out of the opening of the globe. Above the walls of planks I saw two of the stars of the Great Bear scintillating. A fresh wind was blowing. The lamp went out. We didn't budge, our hearts constricted by that obscurity.

Lembergen came back after five minutes.

"Oh!" he said. "The air current has blown out the lamp. Bah, too bad—we'll be able to see clearly enough soon; it's not worth the trouble of lighting it again."

Our friend moved about in the darkness. I listened to him coming and going, shifting and activating things, a sound like a squeaky axle ripped our ears. And suddenly, a light illuminated the chamber, a green floating light that was not emitted by any luminous body, a glow like the one that flickers in Crookes tubes.

Paul de Lembergen, leaning over a lever, his hands gloved in black, seemed phantasmal to me. He was wearing his red beret.

The machine jumped like an elevator moving off too quickly.

"We're off."

Guy de Rommelle murmured anxiously in my ear in order to reassure himself: "We need a good dose of intrepidity to expose ourselves like this to the experiments of a madman. In this order of discoveries, very serious and very knowledgeable men have broken their backs. I confess that I'm trembling a little for my skin, for it's my own, I'm fond of it, and I find it excellent and precious. However, it's undeniable that we're rising, so Paul's invention isn't entirely a pipe-dream. Anyway, come what may! I've made my will and disinherited those who were hoping for my succession."

Siegmund Bergmann, as a good journalist, kept quiet in order to engrave his impressions more deeply in his memory.

Paul de Lembergen monitored the functioning of the apparatus tranquilly. The radiomobile was now flying through the air soundlessly, without any jolts, by virtue of an inexplicable and hidden principle.

Sitting on our stools, embarrassed by the strange light that rendered us pale, we remained still, slightly stupidly, waiting for I know not what before speaking, which didn't arrive.

"How long is it since we left?" asked Paul de Lembergen, abruptly.

"Twenty minutes," replied Bergmann.

"Very good! I'm going stop, then."

The machine slowed down gently. We soon had he sensation that the radiomobile was no longer moving, that it was floating in the air, immobile.

"We're above Reims," said Lembergen. "How well my instruments obey me! The globe is maintaining itself in perfect equilibrium! A child could maneuver my levers."

He was absorbed in the admiration of his work. Guy de Rommelle woke him up.

"It's taken us twenty minutes to travel from Paris to Reims, then?"

"Yes."

"And we wouldn't have been perceived while we were moving at that speed!"

"Certainly. Because the machine is hermetically sealed, we're breathing air artificially renewed by that apparatus in the corner to the left. We're in a sort of round shell that..."

"You've discovered the dirigible balloon, then!" cried the stamp merchant.

"The dirigible balloon!" repeated Lembergen, his tone full of scorn. He added: "The dirigible balloon is an significant toy by comparison with my radiomobile. I have other ambitions than making an omnibus float over human heads."

"Are you certain that we're over Reims?"

"Mathematically certain. You've been able to observe that I haven't cast a glance outside, and yet, knowing the speed and direction imprinted on the machine, I can certify to you, firstly, that a city is asleep beneath us; and secondly, that the city in question is Reims. I can even affirm, so much faith do I have in my calculations, that the machine has stopped on a line that, represented by a plumb line, would fall thirty meters from the cathedral. The demonstration is easy."

He lifted a lateral frame. We looked into the void. The night was too dark, in spite of the crescent moon. We could only perceive blackness beneath us, with isolated points of vacillating flame.

"It's a little like the monkey shown a magic lantern," exclaimed Bergmann, trying to hide his emotion with a little joke. "I can see something, but I can't distinguish anything."

"Wait," said Lembergen. "Take these telescopes."

He distributed long tubes of white metal to us, with zigzag bends.

"This is a telescope?" queried Guy de Rommelle, astonished, with the expression of an invalid inspecting an unknown medicine.

"Yes, a new and powerful telescope. Its properties are almost miraculous. It approaches all objects to ten meters, no matter how far away they are, even if they're millions of kilometers away. It also permits one to see in the dark. Don't believe me, believe your eyes. Pay attention. I'm going to circle the machine slowly around the cathedral. When I say 'three' I'll press these buttons, and... and you'll see what you'll see."

I held the irregular tube against my eye.

"One, two, three..."

I was struck by a splendid vision. Bathed in a violet light, the cathedral was before me, very close. The details stood out in full relief.

We were mute with admiration.

"Well, what do you say to that? asked Paul, triumphant.

"You're a magician..."

"Oh!" cried Honorine, transported by enthusiasm. "The cathedral has never appeared to me so majestic and so beautiful. How everything is harmonized in that magical light, the perforations and the jumble of stones. Look at the princes guarding the towers and the triumph of Mary, Jesus and the Church. There are the months, the arts, the sciences, the virtues and the vices, sculpted by pious artists. And then the forts of Damascus and blind Saint Paul, Saint Michael and the demon, Judas disemboweled. Then virgins, birds, Magi, crosses, Jews, apostles, horses, kings, soldiers, angels singing and killing, evils, crows pecking out eyes terrified women, laughing children, men shouting, old men weeping; Abraham immolating a very little Isaac facing Saint-Memmius of Châlons, Saint Simon of Soissons and Saint Sixtus, and further away, Saint Remy, Saint Celine, Saint Nicasius, Saint Florent and a thousand others; all the passions, all the compassions, all the mourners, a crowd praying, appealing, dolorous or blessing."

Honorine's voice sang a hymn while we filled our eyes, avid for the spectacle of the cathedral seen thus through Lembergen's telescope, from two thousand meters above the earth, by night.

The silenced embarrassed us. Honorine understood that it was necessary to accompany our living dream again with the sound of her words.

"Look also," she said, "at the monstrous rhinoceros, the mouth of the gargoyle that is taking on ivory tints. Look at that lacework to the left, which glides along an arch like flowing frost...and sinister Goliath collapsing before David, brightened by yellow fires, kings of France draped with light..."

"I'm turning the machine," said Lembergen. Look at the skeletal structure to the left of the north transept. In spite of the shrinkage and the narrow street, my telescope allows the recitation of the epic inscribed on the wall...and better than from below, everyone can find one of his sobs there, one of his dolors, one of his dreams, and the interminable collision of contrary wills."

"Isn't the ogive reminiscent of the harmonious movement of arms that are knotting the joined hands of desperate and sincere sinners?" said Honorine? From here one might think that the ogive is praying... All around, climbing the steps under the arch, are the apostles, the foolish virgins and the virtuous virgins. The apostles remain grave...the dishonest virgins are advancing lamentably. The sage virgins are going toward the Lord, tranquilly. They're carrying lighted lamps, and the brightness of the flame in less pure than the gaze of their eyes. And then the orchestra of angels; they're singing. With their trumpets they're accompanying the psalmodies, calling humans to the Last Judgment, and in the imperious summons you can already hear the mildness of pardon...for those who believe and those who love without believing, the material foreheads are meditating, the fixed eyes shining, the motionless lips stirring and the inert breasts exhaling violently for the phrases of triumph...aren't they?"

Our gazes followed Honorine's lyrical descriptions. We could have remained thus for hours, fascinated.

But the inventor became impatient.

"That's enough," he said. "Let's not waste any more time. You're certainly not at the end of your astonishments."

He pressed the ivory buttons once again, and the cathedral faded slowly into the darkness, and then vanished.

Bergmann shook our friend's hand vigorously. We congratulate you," he said, warmly. "You're a great genius."

Insensible to that eulogy, Paul de Lembergen did not take the trouble to thank him.

"Now," he said, "I ask you to assure me once again of your consent to the journey that we're about to undertake. We shall have to contend with unknowns such that my anticipations might be thrown out by one that has escaped me. I've calculated all the obstacles of physical and chemical laws to the utmost limits of the possible, so I think I've set aside all mortal risks. I'm taking Honorine—that says everything. Nevertheless, some mischance might be contrary to me."

"After what you've already shown us," declared Guy de Rommelle, "who wouldn't follow you to the end of the world?"

"In fact, it is a matter of going to the end of the world..."

"Ah! The end of the world?" The audacity of the stamp merchant was suddenly chilled, for he went pale and added: "Perhaps that's a bit far."

Lembergen smiled with pity and continued his explanations.

"We arrived over Reims in a few minutes, but at that speed I had to reduce considerably the propulsive power of the motor agents—which is to say, luminous rays. Scrupulous experiments have already been carried out to determine whether light is a force in itself. All have failed, except mine. Through a lens shaped in one of the new substances I mentioned to you, I concentrate and transform the rays in such a fashion that I make use of them as a mariner utilizes the waves. They carry us, they drive us. If I allowed the machine to travel at its whim, we would rise toward the stars at the same velocity as light."

"But that velocity is enormous!" yelped Guy de Rommelle.

"Enormous? Pooh! No, two hundred and ninety-eight thousand kilometers a second."

"You think that two hundred and ninety-eight thousand kilometers a second is trivial?"

"Trivial, indeed. It's necessary not to judge the number with the mind of a pedestrian who, by walking briskly, covers his mere league and a half in an hour, nor even with that of the mechanic of a express train who thinks that he is 'burning up the track.' Humans are veritable tortoises beside natural forces in movement. By comparison with the formidable extent of known worlds and the even more considerable one of unknown worlds, a velocity of two hundred and ninety-eight thousand kilometers a second is perfectly insignificant. There is a star visible to the naked eye whose light takes sixty-three years to reach us—which is to say that it is about sixty billion billion kilometers above us. The fixed star closest to us after our sun is thirty-three thousand and three hundred million kilometers away. Truly, in the context of those spaces, luminous rays, with their poor ten billion, seven hundred and twenty-eight million kilometers an hour are mere dawdlers. But enough of theoretical considerations! Let's return to the two hundred and ninety-eight thousand kilometers a second. In the time that a train takes to go from Paris to Versailles, we could go around the terrestrial meridian twelve or fifteen thousand times."

"A fine record," I murmured.

"Then...you want to launch us...with that rapidity...through the ether?" stammered Guy de Rommelle, in whom fear and astonishment produced phonetic difficulties.

"Yes, progressively."

"But...but...but...but that's insane," stammered the stamp merchant.

"What's insane about it?" replied Paul de Lembergen. "I'm not advancing anything that I can't prove at will. My dear Guy, to give you a little courage, would you like a drink of champagne? I've brought ten bottles."

"No thank you," replied Guy de Rommelle. "Flies have fallen in the salad bowl..."

"What did he say?" asked Bergmann, opening his eyes wide. "Repeat your last words."

Guy made a despairing gesture. He pointed at his forehead, and then introduced the index finger of his right hand into his mouth and howled: "The inkwell has turned the menagerie upside down!"

From that moment on and for five minutes, Guy de Rommelle did not pronounce a single rational word or phrase. When anyone addressed him, his movements, his gaze and his facial expression indicated that he had understood, that precise ideas and images had awakened in his intelligence, but the poor fellow, in spite of the efforts that made him pull his temples, was no longer master of his vocal cords. They no longer obeyed him, and were out of order. He extended all his willpower to express his concepts, but the proffered sounds had no relationship with those he had the intention of emitting. In brief, his mind was sane, but his throat had gone mad.

It took us some time to take account of that abnormal malady. It was doubtless caused by the struggle of the sentiment of the terror of the unknown with the sentiment of the thirst for knowledge. That combat between the Guy who wanted to recoil and the Guy who wanted to advance provoked in the former officer the nervous aberrations that alarmed us momentarily.

When the trouble had calmed down, Paul resumed his discourse.

"So, the radiomobile will permit us to travel distances that no man has yet attained. Today, for our first trial, we won't attempt to reach the stars; we'll content ourselves with gliding between them, and, at a certain moment, observing the earth with our telescopes.

"Invincible gastronomy!" whimpered Guy de Rommelle.

We were hanging on the inventor's lips. I pinched Guy to make him shut up. He was annoying us with his divagations.

"Pay attention!" said Paul de Lembergen. "I'm setting forth..."

A terrible shock shook the radiomobile; Guy de Rommelle fell on Bergmann, who, in order to steady himself, grabbed the pocket of my jacket.

Guy rubbed his shoulder. "Hurrah for the anemone!" he cried.

I gave him a shove. "Will you hold your tongue?"

Paul de Lembergen, attentively following the oscillations of a long needle suspended in front of him, counted: "forty thousand kilometers a second...forty-eight thousand...fifty-three thousand...sixty-six thousand...eighty thousand...a hundred thousand...a hundred and twenty-seven thousand...a hundred and thirty thousand...a hundred and thirty-five thousand...a hundred and sixty thousand, a hundred and ninety thousand...a hundred and ninety-nine thousand..."

"Look, Paul, look," said Honorine.

The walls of the ball in which we were enclosed had just turned red.

"Don't pay any attention to it," replied our friend. "It's the effect of our friction on the ether. There's no danger...two hundred and three thousand...don't be frightened...two hundred and ten thousand…by translations of color…two hundred and twenty thousand…and brightness…two hundred and twenty-two thousand…of the sphere…two hundred and thirty thousand...two hundred and thirty-five thousand...two hundred and forty-one thousand…two hundred and forty-two thousand…"

An astonishing thing: I divined as he spoke those numbers the next figure that he was about to pronounce. I also remarked that, by virtue a kind of suggestion, Honorine, Siegmund, Guy and I had a certain tendency to imitate Paul's movements.

Lembergen continued, in an altered voice: "Two hundred and fifty thousand…two hundred and sixty thousand…two hundred and seventy-two thousand…two hundred and eighty-one thousand…"

The solemnity of the moment contracted my diaphragm. I was torn by violent hiccups…

In the intervals of the crisis, a singular noise beat in my ear. It was the sound of my heart, but a double sound, as if I had two hearts. I listened, and I soon perceived that my hearing had sharpened phenomenally, and that the second heart was that of Siegmund Bergmann, my neighbor to the right.

I leaned toward him in order to communicate the observation to him.

"That's curious…"

I interrupted myself. All five of us, at the same moment, had just made similar gestures. Siegmund had leaned toward Guy, Guy toward Paul, Paul toward Honorine and Honorine toward me. Siegmund and Honorine had also said: "That's curious!"

Naturally, it was with one voice that we repeated the old familiar cliché: "Great minds think alike!"

"And then they separate!" cried our friend Paul, whose face was creased by anxiety.

"What's the matter?" implored Honorine, mildly. "Why that anguish in your expression? Are you no longer confident?

Do you fear a hitch? But what does a snag matter, since I love you?" She embraced him tenderly, and added: "Darling."

Whoever has not heard that young woman murmur the word "darling" will be eternally ignorant of how love sings.

Paul had stopped the machine abruptly. We were floating again.

"Siegmund," he said, imperiously, "tell me, quickly, what phrase you had on your lips after "That's curious.""

"I can hear your heart beating," the German replied.

"Why, me too!" Honorine cried, looking at me. "Except that I was thinking *votre coeur* and not *ton coeur*."

"Me to," I added. "I was about to express the same thought."

"With *ton coeur* or *votre coeur*?"

"*Ton coeur*."

"These coincidences are amazing, all the same," declared Bergmann.

"Yes, yes, terribly terrifying," said Paul. "What about you, Guy?"

The stamp merchant stammered, lamentably: "Child of Bohemia..."

The inventor shrugged his shoulders and muttered: "We'll have to take him back if this goes on."

Lembergen sat down on a stool then, put his head in his hands, and started to reflect. We waited, ill at ease.

Finally, he decided to speak. "Friends, I foresaw all that a man can foresee; I took account of all the givens of the problem—but how could I have obviated unknown inconveniences? That's why I have no remedy to hand for the mental effects of extreme velocity. We have flown at a rate of two hundred and ninety-eight kilometers a second for a brief moment, and during that blink of an eye we observed, thought and spoke in an identical fashion and made identical gestures, or very nearly...except Guy, who's still rambling and doesn't count. You'll divine my hesitation before an eventuality that..."

"In sum, what do you fear?"

"That, by virtue of a bizarre cause, velocity causes us to lose our personality, obliges us all to think and act alike, as if we no longer had any but a single brain, a single nervous and muscular system, like puppets whose strings are being pulled with a single thrust by something superior to us."

"The rapidity of our velocity might have resulted in..."

"Yes, and the phenomenon can already by observed, on a reduced scale, on Earth. Examine two drivers traveling at sixty, seventy or eighty kilometers a second. They resemble one another, body and mind, garments and attitude. Both are leaning forward, with no other idea than looking at the road, no other preoccupation than the automobile and future obstacles. They're no longer men with various conceptions, different judgments, more or less vivid imaginations, their own gestures...

"Speed dries up the very source of originality within them. In consequence of the same law, the faster human beings go, in steamships or railway trains, the more they lose their particular customs, local fashions, regional habits...speed is the great unifier of the world. What is astonishing about the fact that, in our hyper-rapid voyage, we felt the maximum influence of that principle of nature?"

While he was speaking, the walls of the sphere, which had become crimson, had faded to a dark red.

"Are we condemned to go back down?" I asked.

"We could go up more slowly," said Bergmann, "as we did at the beginning of the ascent, for example?"

"Are the chickens asleep in the salt?" asked Guy, who was definitely not deprived of his insanities.

Paul de Lembergen reflected momentarily, and then said: "Go back down! Rise slowly! Certainly, that's easy. But what becomes of my capital experiment then? The thing that interests me most! It would be necessary to renounce *history in reverse*."

"History in reverse?"

Our friend did not reveal to us the secret of those mysterious words. An inspiration took possession of his mind.

"The great danger," he went on, "of no longer having any but a single thought for five persons is no longer being able to control good sense mutually. Imagine that, for a brief moment, the idea came to us all to open the frame and throw ourselves out into the void. Who would prevent us from carrying out the action? We'd find ourselves in circumstances so abnormal, so eccentric, that any suggestion is possible. Perhaps, however, there's a remedy for the situation. It's perilous, but now that I've shown you what I can do, you'd be very cowardly to oblige me to return to the Earth, to waste this beautiful night."

"We'll follow you," cried Bergmann, with the fine gesture of an operatic hero.

"I haven't told you everything," said the inventor, "because I didn't want to stun you by revealing too many miracles at once. Luminous rays are elastic by nature, and compressible. It's possible to enclose them in accumulators of a sort, and thus store forces of which no engineer has ever dreamed. If I release those rays under the radiomobile, they would act in the manner of monstrous springs, and, delivered, we would be launched into the ether at a velocity even greater than that of ordinary light. I can, in consequence, make the machine travel much faster than two hundred and ninety-eight kilometers a second. I can attain billions of billions of kilometers in the same time. I had the intention of reaching that extreme rapidity little by little, by degrees, without and shock or abruptness, as a train increases its speed. But I judge now that there's no means of advancing so sagely. It will be necessary to pass from a velocity of three hundred thousand kilometers a second to that of billions almost instantaneously. And...well, we'll be shaken, and at risk of a few disagreeable sensations."

"But why that feat of strength?"

"In order to remain for the least possible time in the zone of median velocity in which our mental faculties are subject to a common law. You know the proverb: extremes come into contact. That truth merits better than being a popular maxim, for it's one of the great axioms of matter. Our machine won't be melted by the heat generated by its friction against the ether because, with its unimaginable rapidity, it will attain, before being volatilized, the limit of eighteen thousand degrees, at which heat becomes cold. Reasoning by analogy, I believe that, by dint of acceleration, we'll succeed in neutralizing by means of velocity the mental effects of velocity itself."

"The rascal is worth the broth," remarked Guy de Rommelle, with a sly expression.

"That cretin won't leave us in peace!" I exclaimed, beside myself, and I added, threatening the stamp merchant: "If you wag your tongue again when Paul is talking to us, I'll throw you out of the window."

"Pleasure always has charms," he replied.

Bergmann shrugged his shoulders. He was about to speak when he saw that Honorine had something to say to us.

"Messieurs," she said, "would you be kind enough, once and for all, to assure Paul that, whatever enterprise he can conceive, we shall stay with him, in order to support and encourage him?"

"Of course, Mademoiselle," Siegmund Bergmann and I replied, in chorus.

As for Guy, he whispered: "Rocambole..."

But I did not let him finish, and stuck my right palm over his mouth, vigorously. He said "Oof!" and shut up.

"Now, my Paul," said Honorine, "you have no more scruples. Forward ho! Don't worry about us. We're your slaves."

Oh, that excursion! It will remain in my memory eternally. Bumped, jostled, knocked down, rising to my feet again, knocked down again, shaken and jolted, we were like seeds in a winnowing-tray. The machine advanced by prodigious bounds and the rattle of a machine-gun. I saw thirty-six thousand candles.

"Finally," cried Paul de Lembergen, "we've passed the dangerous interval. It's over. Relax. You didn't suffer too badly?"

"I have a bloody nose," declared Honorine, whose garnet hair had come undone.

"I've sprained my wrist," observed Siegmund Bergmann.

"I've broken my braces."

"I sell tambours,"[4] announced Guy de Rommelle, whose face was ornamented by a superb black eye.

Paul made no attempt to console us. "Bah!" he said. "War is war. Oh, if I could open the shutter, you'd see a fine march-past of stars. In a minute, though, I'll be able to show you something very curious. But first we need to suffer the point of fusion by cold. Anyway, it's beginning..."

The machine, which had passed through all the shades of red, brightened to a fulgurant white, and a radiant and unusual light set the sphere ablaze..

Oh, that light! We were splashed by it, filled with it and traversed by it. Our translucent vertebral columns allowed phosphorescent marrow to shine, through which we could follow, with the naked eye, the flux and reflux of neural forces. Our ganglions appeared like inexhaustible rockets.

And everything in us and everything on us and everything around us was the light, was in light. We breathed in, we breathed out, we ate and we digested light. We spoke, we gazed, we acted and we thought in light. Clothing, skin and bone, we were pure radiance; we were mingled and confounded, radiance and light. The blinding splendor of the environment reverberated superbly through our "selves." We were resplendent with magical gleams that emanated from other majestic fulgurations, to which our own aural florescence sent back sparkling magnificence.

And the colors!

The fires of diamond, the curve of rainbows and the play of the prism are opaque darkness compared with the new chromatism that we perceived in our hectic flight through the worlds. Millions of colors other than the primitive seven undu-

_____

[4] The French term for a postage stamp is *timbre*, so this phonetic near miss is a sign that Guy is getting better.

lated, unexpected tints, enchanted iridescence. The exquisite freshnesses and shattering violences of unknown tones...

Damn it! Damn it! I have, in rage, broken on this piece of paper the seventh pen between my fingers, clenched by the impotence to describe.

The indigence of the language is atrocious when one collides in one's brain with the absolute impossibility of expressing ideas that do not approach any idea yet expressed, of depicting scenes such as the gray matter has never reflected. The frightful torture! I sense within me fantastic modes of luminous intensity that I cannot translate because of the stupidity of the dictionary. They want to come out, and they can't. My skull is the jail of superhuman images that I shall have to keep imprisoned there forever. I shall be obliged to seal up within me, in spite of myself, marvelous secrets that I am burning to reveal, and which will remain there, prisoners enchained by formidable invisible and immaterial things.

Is it necessary to forge new words framed in ancient terminology? But my language won't be understandable and will seem macaronic...

So: the bath of albatriform light was supershadowed by similistellar maculochromatics, blinding paroxystic fuliginosities. Oh, the poetry of figurant lucipetant beams—from the Latin *petere*[5]—caecoficient seminations, emollient inferior zones of refracted aurorigiornocrepucular coruscations, inspiratory and divinely photopsical reverberations!

Paul de Lembergen lowered the lever of progression, in order to let us breathe a little before exposing us to new astonishments that might have been fatal to our reason.

We were breathless with ecstasy and admiration. My blood was circulating so rapidly that I felt all my veins and

---

[5] To seek or to beseech. The note was necessary in case French readers thought the "pet" part of the improvised word derived from the French term for a fart.

arteries dilated by the fascination of the incomprehensible, by the reaction of the inconceivable.

"Ha ha!" cried our friend, examining on the back of his hand one of the good God's creatures that had departed with us. "Will you still call me a rider of chimeras?"

"No."

He blew upon the tiny creature. It flew away and settled on the astrakhan hat that Honorine was wearing.

"But I can announce other, greater surprises," he said, "other, more unexpected emotions. We're going...we're going...but before explaining to you the marvel that's waiting us, it's necessary that I know whether you're definitively convinced. Does any shadow of a doubt still remain in your minds?"

"No."

"Have you set aside any supposition of trickery?"

"Yes."

"No afterthought is weighing upon your intelligence?"

"None."

"I suppose that the hours are definitively dead when you considered me to be a madman?"

"Yes, yes," I exhaled.

"You'll no longer look at me with the eyes of pitiful pigs, then," he said, smiling, "if I declare to you that time has hair?"

Siegmund Bergmann breathed: "No, no."

There was merit in that response. Some people become ill with laughter. In the same way, Siegmund Bergmann was suffering physically from accumulated bewilderment.

Personally, I had reached the point of believing anything. The proposition that time might be hairy didn't astonish me at all. Paul could have declared to me that they will wears a corset, that the ideal is apple-green, that one can pave the streets with abstractions and that poetry belongs to the family of batrachians, and I would have broken the bones of anyone who might have denied that the will wears a corset, that the ideal is apple-green, that one can pave the streets with abstractions and that poetry belongs to the family of batrachians.

Paul had inspired in us a faith capable of all illogicalities, the faith that admits that A equals not-A and that thirty-six thousand zeroes are worth more than one: unchecked, unrestricted, unattenuated faith; the faith that kills the denier of the apple-green ideal as well as the more timidly impious individual who grants, under the torture of red-hot pincers, that the ideal really is green, but only spinach-green.

Guy de Rommelle continued to understand everything without being able to oblige his lips to follow his thought. His eyes indicated that he wanted to say: "Paul, time has hair, I believe it gladly," but is mouth pronounced: "Oh, how nice it would be to have a beer."

Paul de Lembergen burst out laughing. "You're real mugs!"

I looked at him, bewildered. "Why?"

"Because you're capable of bending your reason to believe for a single second that time might have hair."

"But since you told us so!"

His hilarity was redoubled. Honorine Vaudois hid her nose in her handkerchief in order to dissimulate her mocking gaiety.

"You're no longer capable of recognizing an absurdity, then? You know full well that time doesn't exist, that it's one of the forms of our mind. How can something that doesn't exist be hairy, or frizzy, or even bald? Think about it. Is duration capable of being hairy?"

I examined Paul de Lembergen eye to eye. Was he joking or speaking seriously? I had the impression that he was trying to determine, by joking, whether we were ready to learn other implausible facts without going mad.

"Yes," I relied. "Don't try to get a rise out of us, to put one over us. I know your game. Time has hair, I'm firmly convinced of it."

This time, Honorine could no longer hold it in. She bit her handkerchief six times and was shaken by a convulsive gaiety, the fits of which redoubled after pauses.

"Strange, strange!" remarked our friend. "Well, that's humanity for you! When someone raises a prodigious and novel idea, the entire world turns against him; he's blessed by God if he isn't locked in a padded cell. But once he has, by a rare good fortune, embedded his influence and succeeded in imposing his imprint on other brains, he will henceforth be the master of everything; one will believe the most monstrous howlers, by virtue of the principle that truth only has two roots and lies a thousand. All fanaticisms have that origin...

"Come on, come on," he went on, turning to me. "Get a grip, old chap. Give yourself a jab of the spur to reawaken your common sense; be able to recognize the difference between a reality of false appearance from a real falsity. I was making fun of you in pretending that time has hair, and I'm not making fun of you in demonstrating the contrary. Word of honor!"

I was humiliated, less convinced by Paul's tirade than by Honorine's convulsive laughter.

"That's all very well," I said, "but explain the phrase that you used just now: 'You'll no longer look at me with the eyes of pitiful pigs, if I declare to you that time has hair?'"

"I wanted to bring you, by means of an image, to understand the spectacle that is going to delight your eyes. Listen to me carefully: the luminous rays that depart from the Sun, the Moon and the stars, and come to strike the Earth, aren't absorbed by our planet. They're reflected into space, they return to the ether. That's why we can affirm that, if Mars or Saturn has inhabitants, they can contemplate our globe as we can contemplate theirs. Those luminous rays issued from our soil flee into the sky, into space, until they're reflected in their turn by some star encountered on their route. When I walk in the street, the rays that enable you to see me rebound from me, and if, billions of kilometers above, someone possessed an eye powerful enough to collect the light emanated from my body, he would perceive me without difficulty.

"My telescope, which I call 'the duplicator of the luminous source,' aimed at any point of the globe, permits the leisurely contemplation of everything that is happening there. Take, for example, the Eiffel Tower such as it was last Monday, at nine o'clock in the morning. At that moment, luminous rays were disengaged therefrom that are in the process of traveling though the sky at a speed of two hundred and ninety-eight thousand kilometers a second. With the radiomobile, I can catch up with those rays and match their progress. If I observe them then with the duplicator of the luminous source, I will see the Eiffel Tower at nine o'clock in the morning last Monday.

"But what happens if I increase the speed of my machine, altering its course obliquely in order to follow the rotation of the Earth and not lose sight of the tower? I shall overtake the light springing from the iron colossus at nine o'clock in the morning last Monday, but I shall catch up with the luminous rays departing from the tower at five to nine, ten to nine, quarter to nine and half past eight. The more I accelerate my speed, the more we are able to observe the light that once illuminated the Eiffel Tower, which is definitively dead for our brethren down below. The radiomobile and my telescope permit us, therefore, to see past events at will.

"Yes, as we draw way from the Earth more rapidly than light, we will rediscover, as we progress, the scenes that it reflected to minutes ago, an hour ago, yesterday, the day before, last week, last year, ten years ago, a century ago, and so on, in rays that are traveling through space. But as we will first encounter the rays that departed most recently, it follows that with my apparatus we will perceive past events not in the order in which they succeeded one another but in the inverse order. Picture a guillotined man; we would see his head emerge from the basket, reconnect with the trunk; the blade would rise up again; the condemned man would stand up and be taken back to prison, and we would only witness his crime after his execution.

"For a man who lived in the fashion in which you could see him living in my telescope, the past would always be the future. If he said 'I was,' that would signify 'I will be.' To employ an audacious locution, you would see time brushed the wrong way…I had that comparison in mind, and was led by it to tell you that time has hair, in order that I could enable you to imagine it brushed the wrong way, Hence the misunderstanding. Do you get it?"

"Very nearly."

"Have you ever seen a session of cinematography in which the operator made the celluloid strips wind backwards?"

"Yes...I laughed a great deal on seeing swimmers emerge from the water head down, diving backwards to land on their feet."

"That's it—the world will appear to you thus."

"I'd rather look at the stars," declared Guy de Rommelle. "The Earth I know well enough."

"Hey! Guy has recovered his good sense."

In fact, the stamp merchant had suddenly recovered the ability to guide his vocal cords.

After congratulating him, Paul added: "My dear Guy, we'll examine the stars another time. I've only adapted my telescopes to the terrestrial atmosphere."

Lembergen opened the inferior shutter and gave us the twisted telescopes again.

A peasant who hears a phonograph for the first time could not be more amazed than I was in looking toward the Earth. The telescope revealed to me clearly an area of about five hundred square meters, in which I could distinguish all the details, and the coming and going—or, rather, the going and coming—of human beings. First I saw a boat emerging from the port of Hamburg, behind its propeller; the wake was in front and the smoke was going into the funnels.

"Look at Paris," exclaimed Paul de Lembergen, giving a slight twitch to the fluorescent handle. "We're above Montparnasse cemetery...look...oh, if all those who are afraid of death could put their eye to this telescope, what a warmth they would feel in her hearts and how cheerfully they would march through life.

"Thanks to the strange reversal of things and movements that we're witnessing, everyone is coming back to life, and we can contemplate an incessant and vast resurrection. Funerary monuments are disappearing, each stone going to rejoin its quarry. Gradually, the dead are emerging from the tombs. Follow that cortege advancing backwards, accompanying a coffin to the house in mourning. The sinister box is taken upstairs and laid on the floor of the dead man's bedroom. The nails spring forth, sucked out by the hammers and are replaced in the tool-box. The lid is removed. Men lift up the corpse and carry him backwards to his bed. Now he's breathing, deagonizing, lamenting, coming back, vomiting up the prescribed medicaments into the pharmacist's bottles, eating...eating in a singular fashion, for the aliments are extracted from his mouth to become whole vegetables and entire lamb chops on fishes, and although the fashion of nourishment might seem uncomfortable, he recovers his health...

"The more meat, bread and wine he draws from his mouth, the healthier he becomes, becoming youthful and courageous; the more he recovers his appetite for life, the more he is rejuvenated...and around him, everything grows younger too; his children shrink, to the point of disappearing, and we're now at his wedding. As soon as he is married he becomes a fiancé, a bachelor. A little later we find him a young man, then he regresses to childhood and we see him re-enter his swaddling clothes as a nursling.

"In the meantime, the flowers that served for his mortuary wreaths return to the florist, and then the gardener. They unfade and gradually return to their stems in order to live their vegetal existence, from the blossom to the bud, to the shoot to the buried seed, to the fresh seed, and, continuing to unlive and to be unborn, contrary to natural laws.

"Direct the telescope where you will; you will find new subjects of astonishment everywhere. But one discovery, above all, is capital for historians. We can follow with our eyes all the great politicians and reconstitute events with the actions of the celebrated men. Look, I can see Thiers in conference with Maréchal MacMahon. Finally, we can know the truth about the past—the whole truth! We shall no longer be reduced to trying to extract particles of it from deceptive books, the memoirs of liars and suspect witnesses. It will be possible to write history if one could see it—and we shall, in reality! How many errors it will be possible to correct!"

Before all the immensity that was unfurling before us like a scroll of parchment, Guy was only attracted by one tiny and mediocre particular point, which interested him prodigiously. It sufficed for him to see himself live backwards. That spectacle electrified him.

"What does the agitation of other men matter to me?" he said, enthusiastically. "It's indifferent to me to rectify history. Even if the events of the past are not as they are recounted, leave them out of charity, deceptive and false. People believe them to be true, so they are; the task is inhuman and the work cruel, to want to redress so many judgments considered as definitively acquired. A searcher has the right and the ability to discover one or two errors, but he would be an antisocial and wicked individual if he claimed, even if he were a thousand times right, to reform all the opinions to which our brains are habituated.

"How much more alive and more instructive it would be to see oneself again, to contemplate each of one's actions again, as an impartial and quasi-disinterested spectator, to obey, in that original fashion, the Socratic principle: *Know thyself*. It's extraordinary! I can see myself a week ago, then days ago. What! It's already a week since I sold the engravings to the Grand Duke of Luxemburg! How amusing it is, how amusing to contemplate one's existence! As time passes, my memories no longer accord exactly with the events that file past my telescope. How much one doesn't know! If I couldn't see myself with my own eyes, I'd swear that it was a matter of a stranger. Bah! I remained flat on my belly on a chaise longue for four hours! When? I no longer recall. Oh yes—it as the morning I had myself purged. I read half a good book like that, Maeterlinck's bees. Oh, the purge is producing its..."

"My dear fellow," said Bergmann, impatiently, "avoid descriptions, especially before a lady."

"Pardon me."

Guy strove to keep his impressions to himself. Nevertheless, from time to time an explanation burst forth from his lip, when he found himself in the presence of some salient fact of his life.

"Thunder of Brest! What am I permitting myself there...? Oh, but I'm a little rogue! What! It was me who...? Now I'm an officer again... Yes, Colonel, No, Colonel... True. I find myself a lieutenant, with my monocle. Uh oh! Shocking...! My word, I make myself blush! Saint-Cyr...the lycée... Well, good day Zinc Can...Zinc Can is the nickname a schoolmaster... What a vile brat I was, nasty and talkative! My first pair of trousers...I'm being born!"

Guy is the first person, since the beginning of the world who has been able to say, in the full meaning of the phrase: "I'm being born."

The radiomobile was rising at billons of kilometers and second. We are all, now, passionately watching the reconstruction, reversed in time, of the great events that weighed upon the fate of nations. We followed thus Napoléon III, Louis Philippe, Charles X, Louis XVIII and Napoléon I.

Tacking between the stars, Lembergen was taking us at such a velocity that we were the spectators of ten years in an hour. Naturally, the details escaped us, but the ensemble was sufficiently interesting to merit the painful fatigue of focusing with an energetic attention of sight on the fluttering of events. When we were at Waterloo, Paul slowed the machine down, and said to me:

"I'll give the luminous rays that we've overtaken time to catch up with us. In that manner we'll see, on the spot, the story of Napoléon on Saint Helena, which we've just seen backwards, for the last luminous rays encountered in our ascension will naturally present themselves first, in the order in which they were emitted.

"Afterwards, we'll redescend slowly. Thus, we'll be able to reconstitute the emperor's life chronologically, from his final battle to his death. It seems to me, in passing, that we might have sensational revelations to make on that subject. Take a pen and paper from that cupboard, then; you can write to my dictation."

That note, drafted by me during the first celestial voyage and destined for the Académie des Sciences, will be a document of signal value. It will be deposited piously in a museum. I carried out the instruction, only too glad to associate myself as a scribe with a work susceptible of traversing the centuries. I waited for a minute, the pen between my teeth.

Paul regulated the operation of his instruments, and soon, his eye applied to the telescope, he dictated to me the following implausible story:

NOTE
For a History of France rectified in accordance with the eye-witness evidence of Paul de Lembergen

The most firmly established facts of history are often pure lies. The events that have transpired in France, for example, in the last three centuries ought, according to general opinion, be sheltered from fundamental errors on the part of chroniclers, in view of the number and importance of the documents. The alteration of details, it is thought in the literate public, does not affect the fundamental accuracy. Even if the fabric is light, the weave, at least, remains solid.

That confidence, unfortunately, is unfounded. My new system of historical investigation by direct observation has permitted me to observe, visually, that certain notions considered as irrefutable are, in reality, audacious deceptions.

That preamble is indispensable before daring to write here—such an idea seems devoid of sense, so extravagant does the truth seem—that Napoléon the First did not die on Saint Helena.

Thanks to an unusual combination of circumstances, and a few machinations, perhaps unique in the annals of the world, it proved possible to deceive the public, the English government and the kings associated in order to maintain the Emperor of the French in exile: that is what I want to summarize in this paper.

It can be admitted that the Memorial of Saint Helena is an almost reliable source, from the return of Napoléon to the Élysée, after Waterloo, passing through the events of the *Bellerophon*, the sojourn in dock at Plymouth, the navigation aboard the *Northumberland*, the disembarkation on the island, the sojourn at Briars, the establishment in the miserable residence of Longwood, until 27 June 1816.

On that date, one reads at the head of Las Cases' journal: *The rats, a true scourge fir us, etc...Impostures of Lord Castlereagh...French heirs.*

At the same epoch. General Baron Gourgaud wrote in his memoirs of Saint Helena:

Tuesday 25. Boredom. Boredom! Wednesday 26. Ditto. Thursday 27. Ditto. Friday 28. Ditto. Saturday 29. Ditto. Sunday 30. Great boredom. One day, the Emperor said to me: "Henri IV never did anything great; he gave 1,500 francs to his mistresses. Saint Louis was an imbecile. Louis XIV was the only King of France worthy of that name."

The most penetrating intelligence would never be able to divine, from reading those documents, similar in tone and appearance to those which precede and follow them, that at that moment, Napoléon, under the name and with the papers of his domestic Santini, succeeded in escaping on a brig.

The ship set sail on 30 Jun and departed for Brazil, but a tempest drove the vessel back all the way to the Cape of Good Hope. Napoléon had to disembark, denuded of all resources. Not wanting to make himself known to his enemies, he went inland and received hospitality from a Dutch farmer established in the midst of negroes, in the exact spot occupied today by the Simmer and Jack gold mine.[6]

To his profound amazement, the Emperor perceived that his host, lost in the African expanse in the company of his family, his Bible and this livestock, had never heard mention of Napoléon. Delighted by an ignorance that secured his retreat the enterprising Corsica decided to establish himself in the neighborhood, on free land. His secret hope was to gather the scattered and disunited farmers of the South African territories and create an Empire to take back the possessions of his eternal enemies, the English. A few months sufficed for him to organize an estate, albeit rather primitive, destined to hold the indigenes in respect and to purge the land of the wild beasts that pullulated there. Subsequently, he married Ruth Dewet and took the name Napoléon Dewet. Six children were born from that union.[7] That situation, in consequence, rendered Napoléon bigamous, since he was not divorced from Marie-Louise.

Soon after the Emperor's departure, Comte Las Cases went to the Governor of Saint Helena, the famous Hudson Lowe, and told him about the fortunate escape. At first, the

---

[6] Simmer and Jack Mines Ltd—which still exists—was founded in 1887 by August Simmer and John Jack shortly after the discovery of gold in the Witwatersrand.

[7] Forest's readers would have been familiar with the name of Christian de Wet, a general who fought the English, along with his brother and his three sons, in the Second Boer War; after the publication of the present story he went on to have a successful career as a politician before turning to armed rebellion again in 1914.

Englishman flew into a very comprehensible anger, but then he listened to the advice that Napoléon's confidant gave him.

"You Excellency," said Las Cases, "has just allowed a prisoner to escape, on whom the entire world has its eyes, for the guard of whom it disposed considerable resources and more than sufficient forces. I don't have to predict the resounding disgrace that awaits Your Excellency; the prophecy is too easy. In those conditions I have the honor of proposing a pact to you, which will simultaneously ensure your tranquility, your fortune and your renown, and favor plans the objective of which I do not have to reveal to you."

It was agreed, in consequence, that the disappearance of the former sovereign would not be revealed, that Santini, whose papers the Emperor had taken away, would play the role of Napoléon, and that Hudson Lowe would sign, ostentatiously, ferocious dispositions incompatible with the just pride of the fallen prince. In that fashion, the rumor could be put round that, not wanting to submit to the shameful demands of the English governor, Napoléon—i.e., Santini—preferred to shut himself in his room and not to see anyone any longer. That explanation authorized an excellent argument for use with French, Russian and Austrian commissioners who came to disembark on the island and asked to visit the celebrated prisoner. In the confidence of the subterfuge were Maréchal Bertrand and his wife, Madame de Montholon and her husband, General Gourgaud, the valet de chambre Marchand, Doctor Barry O'Meara and, naturally, Santini.

To what motive were those individuals obedient? Simply to the orders of the Emperor, who had departed with secret designs. He had recommended that nothing should change in the habits of Longwood until the day when he relieved his friends of that order. Thus, Las Cases imagined a continuation of his journal; Gourgaud and O'Meara continued to write memoirs that were henceforth entirely fantasized. If the English government had taken possession of their papers, the seized manuscripts would not have raised any suspicions. The complicity of Hudson Lowe, in any case, facilitated a strangely difficult task. In Europe, three members of the imperial family were aware of the affair: Napoléon's mother, Princesse Pauline and Cardinal Fesch.

Unfortunately, Santini fell ill, and that hitch rendered more difficult the active lie to which Napoléon's friends lent themselves devotedly. After O'Meara's departure, Doctor Antomarchi was summoned from Europe to try to save the false Emperor. The most devoted cares were futile. Santini died. In order not to disobey the Emperor, the French of Saint Helena had to announce Napoléon's death. It was, therefore, Santini who was buried under the famous willow, and it was Santini whose ashes were pompously repatriated in 1840. And it is the tomb of the obscure Santini, in a pious frame, that is exposed to popular admiration under the magnificent vault of the Palais des Invalides.

As for the real Napoléon, who had become Napoléon Dewet, he could not leave South Africa until two months after his "death." Having arrived in Europe, he hastened to depart for Rome, where he had himself recognized by his relatives. As it was impossible, under pain of tarnishing imperial glory forever, to make the bizarre confession of a false death that had agitated the entire terrestrial globe, the conqueror as persuaded to keep quiet. Weary, fatigued by action, he accepted without any argument the capital of ten millions that the Bonapartes gave him.

That great intelligence was to conclude lamentably. After the death of the King of Rome, Napoléon, known by the name of André Martin, first went to reside in Germany, where he lost his fortune. He attempted, during a journey to France, to reclaim his title and his rights, but the police imprisoned the man who claimed to be Napoléon for a year in Charenton. Released because he appeared to have recovered from his madness, the Emperor did not attempt to recommence such a perilous experiment.

As he had conserved the papers of his former domestic Santini, he ended up acquiring, in the quality of the Emperor's faithful companion on Saint Helena, a place in the Invalides.

By a prodigious twist of fate he was charged with guarding "his" tomb, and for some years, as a tremulous and weary old man, Napoléon I, Emperor of the French, showed "his" ashes to curious English tourists visiting Paris.

Having terminated that chapter of history, Paul de Lembergen allowed me thirty seconds to get my breath back; I had writer's cramp, he had dictated so much.

"It's very necessary," he said, "that I add certain considerations for the members of the Académie des Science; so add these few lines:

"I have deposited this summary of a new history of Napoléon with the secretariat of your high assembly in order to have the envelope unsealed on the day after the verity of my physical and mathematical calculations have been universally recognized.

"I estimate, I fact, that the historical conquests rendered by my inventions, are of an importance no less great by virtue of the progress of civilization. It is therefore urgent to attract public curiosity, as soon as possible, to an accessory discovery of this value.

"I hope that the attached document, although very brief and written in the fever of a first observation that is certainly incomplete, will demonstrate to the most skeptical the capital interest that there is in re-founding world history by means of the direct observation of luminous rays overtaken in space. Paul de Lembergen."

Paul had scarcely finished speaking when he precipitated himself upon a sort of manometer.

"Uh oh!" he exclaimed.

"Is something broken?"

"No, no, but our provision of respirable air is exhausted. It's time to go back down."

At the peak of emotion, I advanced toward our friend. "You're a great man," I cried. "A very great man."

I would have liked to find something better, all the more so as Bergmann had already said a few words of the same sort, but the very excess of my admiration paralyzed my rhetoric.

"Yes, yes, I know," he said. "I know that no mind has ever equaled my genius. I'm conscious of my value. The future is mine, as vast as my immeasurable ambition. I want all glories, all honors, and I shall bend the world to my victorious will."

"Pay attention!" Paul ordered. "I'm closing the shutter...look out! Hold hard. Ah! Honorine..."

"My friend?" queried the young woman.

"I've forgotten, as I had promised you, to warn Dr. Vaudois and my domestic. I've only just thought of it."

"Oh! Papa must be anxious!" she exclaimed, very pale. "Let's go home quickly."

"Yes...look out! Look out!"

Oh, that fall! What a fall! Frightful...and again, the light became impossible to describe...perhaps a hundred thousand billions of billons of kilometers a second, perhaps more. My head explodes when I think about it. What a fall...! What a fall...! I can still feel a hollow in my stomach. Guy had seasickness.

A bizarre phenomenon! We made the vertiginous trajectory while adhering by our hair to the ceiling of the radiomobile, with our legs in empty space. We marched on our heads, feet down; I was like a ludion fixed to its glass bowl. We only recovered our normal attitude gradually when, a little above the moon, Paul de Lembergen attenuated the velocity, in order to soften the impact that would have broken us against the ground.

The inventor pulled a lever violently. The sound of the radiomobile changed immediately. The whistle changed into a purr.

"We're in the Earth's atmosphere," said our friend. "I'm slowing down. There...there...there...there...Paris... Sapristi!"

A shock caused the machine to quiver.

"I steered badly," added Lembergen. "We've bumped into the wall of the hangar."

The sphere swayed in order to recover its equilibrium, and stopped.

"What! We've reached our goal already?"

"Yes."

"I'd be exaggerating," affirmed Guy de Rommelle, "if I said that I was sorry."

"Oof!" Paul de Lembergen yawned. "I've had enough of conducting this instrument."

He pressed his ring once again to one of the walls of the ball. The slice of melon that served as a door fell away, in order to let us pass.

The exterior of the globe had changed. It was no longer the color of a mackerel's scales; it was the color of cooked *ris de veau.*

The voyage had lasted scarcely twenty-four hours.

We were very tired, Bergmann, neurasthenic, an eternal moaner, was whining about his leaden hat. Guy, having touched one of the fluorescent handles after removing his protective glove, had burned the fingers of his right hand. For myself, my mind was none too clear; I was like a convalescent at the troubled moment when, his legs in cotton, he begins to reconnect the ideas that illness has put out of joint.

Lembergen and his fiancée seemed exhausted. Honorine was asleep on her feet. Paul was peering ahead of him like drunkard. He emerged from the machine and left he shed without closing the door.

In the drawing room we were greeted by the clamors of Ali, the Arab domestic. He would not have made more noise if he had perceived specters on his eiderdown. The previous evening he had informed Dr. Vaudois of our surprising disappearance, and they had both hastened to inform the police. They were searching for us everywhere.

"Leave us in peace, imbecile!" replied our friend, terribly grumpy.

63

We sat down in armchairs. Five minutes later we were all asleep.

I woke up about midnight, in order to lie down full length on the carpet, with my head buried in a plush cushion. Honorine was asleep, leaning on Paul, snoring softly. I also saw Guy de Rommelle, who was sticking compresses on his fingers made of slices of potato dipped in vinegar, by the light of a candle, and pulling faces.

The morning was still indecisive, neither day nor night, when Honorine got up suddenly, exclaiming: "I'm hungry!"

That declaration opened all eyelids. It responded so perfectly to our state of mind that each of us deemed the exclamation fortunate and welcome. Paul therefore went to wake Ali, who soon brought us an entire ham, a glazed beef joint with carrots, Alsatian gherkins and preserves. We ate with an excellent appetite, and Sigmund Bergmann swallowed two jars of quince jelly under the pretext that he had had too much emotion during the journey.

We were emptying the ninth bottle of champagne when eight o'clock in the morning chimed. We drank toasts to the glory of Paul de Lembergen and his union with Honorine. I even made a little speech, very well-turned, in truth, to beg the master of masters not to forget his faithful friends tomorrow, "in the bosom of his grandeurs."

Paul thanked us, and dismissed us in these terms:

"I would like to believe that it isn't my champagne that is agitating the fibers of your eloquence, and that it isn't in the wine that you've finally discovered the truth. I therefore welcome with pleasure the felicitations of serious and reasonable men who treated me as a madman a few hours ago. It proves to me that my good sense has been recognized, or that, although insane, I have succeeded in making proselytes. Both hypotheses delight me. In the former case, I'm assured with regard to my mental faculties; in the second case, you're preparing a joyful life for me, for you know that the madder one is, the more one laughs.

"But in either case, the hour doesn't permit lingering in long dissertations; I'll put off a more complete expression of my satisfaction until this evening. It's time for you to go home and rest from the new fatigues that a feast so appropriately washed down must have awakened.

"Until this evening, then, after dinner. We can discuss together the best ways and means of informing people of my discoveries and making use of my exceptional genus. But while awaiting the results of our council, I recommend you to silence. Don't breathe a word of our voyage. It's important that the great secret is revealed to the world with precaution and method. Until this evening!"

Each of us returned to his own home. In the afternoon I went to see my sister. Oh, how hard it is to hold one's tongue when one has a mind full of such curious memories! I had to make up a story to excuse myself for not having come to lunch with the family the day before, as I had promised. I was clever enough to make up a story that was not entirely to my honor, so my sister believed me and did not ask any searching questions. In the house I was obliged to take my poodle for a confidant.

"Hey, Monton, your master had a fine excursion without you. You master visited the stars and saw history backwards..."

Etc., etc.

The worthy beast wagged her tail. Perhaps she didn't understand me. I gave her a biscuit.

Naturally, Siegmund Bergmann, Guy de Rommelle and I were punctual at the rendezvous. Without having made any agreement, we had dressed up. Siegmund was wearing a maroon colored suit that gave him the air of a Russian prince dressed in Paris. Guy was wearing a dinner jacket. More simply, I only had my black jacket, but my collar was a centimeter higher than my everyday collar, scratching my skin, and I was shod in varnished boots that were too tight.

Our entry into the drawing room interrupted a very animated conversation between Paul and Honorine.

Paul was as cheerful as ever; contentment dilated his skin; his gaze was laughing and sunny.

Oh, good evening, good evening!" he cried. "Have you recovered from your spree? For myself, I had a two-hour nap this afternoon."

Honorine was also expansive, blissful rather than joyful.

We were very serious. Before the inventor of genius who has initiated us first into his fantastic discoveries, we felt ourselves becoming timid. Dazzled and fervent, we were embarrassed in confrontation with him, like the comrades of Lieutenant Bonaparte received at the Tuileries by the Emperor Napoléon. The evident superiority of Paul crushed us and defamiliarized us. Was he not going to be a celebrated man tomorrow, world famous, marking his passage in history as a giant leaves tracks on his route?

The triviality of his language shocked us. We were astonished, as if seeing a prince in court dress amusing himself trampling in the mud.

In his capacity as a German, a worshiper of hierarchies, and more wounded in consequence than Guy or me by that lack of formality. Siegmund Bergmann remarked aloud: "Oh, how you talk!"

"What! What!" said Paul, exaggerating the vulgar accent. "Oh, my brothers, what faces! But what's wrong then, O nightcaps?"

"I beg you to think," implored Guy de Rommelle, in a heartbroken tone, "that certain situations in life necessarily demand special modesties. Think about the high destiny that awaits you, the great honors, the respect, the enthusiasm and the incense with which you will be surrounded; think that tomorrow, you will be a sort of Majesty, a…"

"I shall be nothing at all."

"What?"

"I shall be nothing at all."

"But…"

"Nothing…"

"…as soon as our first…"

"…at…"

"…communication to the Académie…"

"…all."

"…des Sciences, your name will make all the rotations of the globe turn. And molten lead will be crushed in thousands and thousands of inky rollers to print, thousands and thousands and thousands of times: *Paul de Lembergen.*"

"At all."

"After all, haven't you recounted your splendid hopes to us yourself? Your prayers? You can realize the dreams that no longer seem to us to be chimerical…we're sure and certain of that now."

"I shall only realize one single dream, my friends," declared the inventor, "and it is incomparably superior to all those that I have been able to conceive before today. Do you recall my theory of sacrifice in love at the moment when, while my heart was lacerated, I went to break my pipe in order to please Honorine? That idea has grown within me. During our reckless voyage, I was increasingly troubled by it and solicited by it, and now it has expanded; it is mature; it possesses me entirely."

Paul de Lembergen unhooked his red beret and put it on.

"How calm I remain, in spite of this coiffure! Are you not astonished by that? For I've finally found complete equilibrium, perfection, the ultimate discovery to which humans tend. There is nothing superior to the superior amour. Now, I am within reach of that unique felicity. Parted from a pipe, broken reluctantly, I am arriving at the supreme goal, which humanity might only attain in millions of centuries, in the same way that it might yet need millions of centuries to recommence and ethereal voyage like ours.

Applause, honors, glory and fortune…I renounce them. I am sacrificing them to Honorine. I only want to live for her; I want to spare her the inconvenience of being the wife of an excessively celebrated man, whom the world will snatch from her. Tomorrow, I shall burn all my papers. All my laborious calculations, all the miracles inferred from my precious observations, all the deductions that would have astonished the world by virtue of my frightening capacity for reasoning, will go up in smoke toward the sky. I shall break my machines, my apparatus, in such a way that the most sagacious mind, after mine, will be unable to deduce my genius from the debris. I shall reduce to dust the strange substances of which I have made use, and scatter them to the winds. I shall live henceforth alongside Honorine. Like a peaceful bourgeois who cares for plants, happy in the sunshine, sad in the rain, who knows how to wait for death without attracting, by an unforeseen gesture, the attention of the world, or even his neighbors, to his very humble personality. Admit that my disinterest is not banal, and that, in moral value, it is at least as rare and as fantastic as my concentrator of refraction or my radiomobile!"

What a thunderbolt! We remained mute for a moment, frozen as if by horror. Lembergen's tranquility terrified me more than his excitement of the previous day had made me shiver.

Paul had leaned back, his head lying on the back of a low armchair. Behind him, Honorine, pale with emotion, was contemplating him, radiant and enamored, her blue eyes in his blue eyes. He was inspiring himself with that gaze, and his throat was animated with lyrical and tender vibrations.

"I intend," he continued, "to elevate myself thus to the highest moral summit that humanity can attain: absolute sacrifice. I am giving my fiancée more than my life. And if you see some pride in me, it is because I am still imperfect in spite of my efforts."

He forgot out presence and was only talking now for Honorine.

"Beloved fiancée," he said, "accept this present. No jeweler will be able to put a monetary value on it, no notary will be able to find the gibberish to insert it in a contract. It is imponderable and subtle, and yet, it is a marvelous present of amour."

She linked her arms around Paul's neck like a necklace. Her transparent skin formed a nacreous frame from our friend's brown complexion.

"A coquettish and frivolous woman," she sighed, "who received in a single basket all the stones with which intoxicated kings have adorned their favorites, would be less happy than me. I am the beneficiary of an unprecedented and superb renunciation. Let the goddess descend from the heavens who could ever boast of an equivalent propitiatory sacrifice! You are a superhuman and magnificent hero and I shall not share you with anyone. You are a hero for me alone. When we go for a walk in the Bois de Boulogne, passers-by will perhaps say of us: 'They seem to love one another very much,' but no idler will ever discover our unique and fabulous bond. We will be, in appearance, people like everyone else, but our enjoyment will be precisely to disappear, unknown, in the crowd, while knowing ourselves to be exceptional, quintessential and sublime.

Guy de Rommelle, furious, interrupted that duo.

"Mademoiselle," he cried, anger allowing his monocle to fall out, "permit me to express my opinion to you frankly. The gravity of the circumstances will excuse the vivacity of my words. Add, then, to all the grandiloquent epithets with which you ornament your discourse that of 'superlative egotist.' Assuredly, Paul has the right to burn his papers and his machines, to immolate himself for you, invoking I know not what bizarre and ridiculous ideal...but as for you, by what right do you accept that disinterest? You seem to me to be audacious and overweening when you associate yourself with your fiancé for qualifications of which only he is worthy; and you, Mademoiselle, I have the great regret if informing you, are neither exceptional, nor quintessential, nor, even less, sublime. You are simply an extravagant young Parisienne, spoiled by reading romantic novels, ferociously egotistical and... and...and..."

He searched for a word. Siegmund Bergmann, having found it, pronounced: "Autolatrous."

"Autolatrous, that's right. And hard and wicked too, for the advancement of all humankind will be arrested by you at the moment when the thinking world is perhaps about to take an immeasurable step toward progress and, in consequence, toward happiness.

Without rancor, Honorine protested: "Oh, Monsieur Guy, don't judge me badly. I don't want to pride myself on any extraordinary virtue. I know what I'm worth and I know that I'm a woman. I don't seek to magnify myself vainly. I was once told the fable of the frog and the ox. Paul loves me. My great ambition is to annihilate myself henceforth to the point of confounding myself in him. When I say: 'We are sublime,' believe me that I measure my part in that sublimity precisely. I consider myself to be a negligible quantity: in myself, nothing; as an integral part of Paul, everything. He also merits the adjectives for whose employment you reproach me. Add zero to a million and it will still gives you a million, and yet you will have performed a mental operation in order to aggregate two different terms. Thus, in proportion to my fiancé, I am mingled, confounded in him. We are one and we are two; or, rather—excuse the wordplay—since that plural appears to you to be singular, Paul is one and he is two, for he is him and me. So, as I have no other will than his, no other soul than his, by what influence could I prevent him acting in accordance with his taste?"

Paul de Lembergen thanked her with an enthusiastic murmur of the lips: "Sister fiancée!"

Bergmann muttered in German: "*Unsinn!*"[8]

Guy de Rommelle rummaged nervously in his orbit with the frame if his monocle.

"Sophism! Miserable sophism!" he complained.

For myself, I groaned: "Stupidity! Lamentable stupidity!"

"But damn it, Mademoiselle," exclaimed Guy de Rommelle, "Have you not reflected, then? It seems to me that

---

[8] Nonsense.

your vanity is following a false route, if I might express it thus."

"Explain yourself, Monsieur Guy."

"In consenting to an abnegation that, for my part, I declare imbecilic, you're renouncing yourself certain joys that, I sure you, are worth being experienced. Ha ha! The wife of a dignitary of all foreign and national Orders, the wife of a scientist of worldwide acclaim, the wife of an individual before whom emperors and kings will bow down. Ha ha!"

"Yes," replied Honorine, "I confess that it requires a certain strength of mind to reconcile myself to deliberate mediocrity when I have only to reach out my hand to pick the finest fruits of a prodigal fortune. With an ordinary conception of life your reproaches and your objurgations are unassailable. It would indeed be advantageous and agreeable to become the wife of a scientist as celebrated as Paul could be, the most illustrious and the most eminent of all. His radiance would reflect on me, that is certain. All women would envy my fate, and there is, in general, no happiness sweeter than to be the object of universal jealousy. But I would be unworthy of being Paul's companion if I too did not elevate myself to the idea of the sacrifice as soon as he has conceived it."

Lembergen, still lying in the armchair, raised his arms, and Honorine, still standing behind him, enlaced her fingers with those of the man she loved. He murmured: "Dear, dear beloved fiancée."

And she, leaning forward, caressed the inventors forehead with her lips, in a silent kiss: "Darling!"

Then they contemplated one another again, at length, as if their eyes were communicating a discourse too beautiful to be spoken.

The amorous words had perfumed the room. Their odor insinuated itself into the fibers of our being, anesthetizing momentarily our determination to raise objections, our desire for contradiction. Our nerves quivered, touched most sensibly. A tear rolled under Guy's monocle.

They remained thus for a good four minutes, in that intimate exchange of gazes.

"Now," exclaimed Paul, suddenly, turning toward us, "I have an important service to ask of you. Thanks to me, you have witnessed an unforgettable spectacle. I beg you, in return, and for the pious motives that you know, not to tell anyone about my discoveries or the wonderful voyage; to make a formal engagement with Honorine and me never to reveal it. You would not want, by your indiscretion, to undermine or diminish our special happiness. Your word of honor, Guy?"

The stamp merchant made a grand gesture. For a second I had the hope of seeing his monocle slip—which is to say, of witnessing a categorical refusal. The circle of glass oscillated frenetically, but then it calmed down. Guy was vanquished.

He replied, in a whisper: "I give you my word of honor."

"Your turn, Siegmund."

The German, although a good journalist, allowed himself to be drawn by the example. "My word of honor," he articulated, very emotional.

Then Paul de Lembergen inclined in my direction.

"And you?"

Me?

I fled. I slammed the door. I tumbled down the stairs. I ran through the streets. I went home. I lit my lamp. I put on a velvet jacket. I prepared fifty sheets of paper; I filled my inkwell. I placed half a cold chicken to my right, and to my left a glass of water sharpened with a finger of cognac, and an open pack of cigarettes in front of me. I kicked my dog, who was begging for a caress. I enveloped my limbs in a fur blanket, and I wrote, while eating, drinking, smoking and digesting…the story of Paul de Lembergen.

François Léonard: *The Triumph of Humankind* (1911)

PART ONE

I

"Too poetic!" said Neick, placing an amicable hand on Dionel's shoulder. "You're too much inclined that way; far too much... You almost forget, in embellishing the darkness of history, that this century is richer and more beautiful..."

"I don't go as far as denying the beauty of our life, but..."

"You see? I'm no longer your age; I've grown old, but I still have enthusiasm."

"I don't doubt it."

"Do you know what the great theme of my interior life has been? Shall I tell you the slow and methodical evolution to which my thoughts and dreams have been subject?"

"I can guess..."

"To begin with, I loved, exactly as you love, vanished splendors. A few years later I enjoyed the light hour in which we live..."

"And now you're thinking about the future?"

"That's the best thing, I've found."

"However, some people have devoted their entire lives to the study of archeology."

"But do you believe that a science of that sort can ever be as exciting as the clear beauty of a mathematical verity launched in the conquest of the unknown? Oh, if you wanted to follow me..."

Neick's voice was trembling slightly; his eyes were gleaming with a strange flame, and his entire being, thickset but still supple, was vibrant, as if ready to bound toward some glorious adventure. In a flash of thought, Dionel understood all the labor of that human life; he saw the old man's physiology harmonize with the vibrant complexity of the scientific apparatus that was all round them, to the farthest depths of the room, colliding in an artificial, delicate and precious life with the various rhythms of their faint clicking.

For a moment, he fell silent, forgetting his own dream in confrontation with a dream that seemed to him to be greater. But Neick went on, in a calm voice: "Believe me, your thought is condemning itself by remaining the slave of a dead civilization, all the more so because the humankind you're studying was still barbaric."

"But so passionate! And so beautiful!"

"But so distant! So imperfect! Still full of ignorance, and red with human blood. Under the reign of force, life couldn't be, and wasn't, anything but a vast battlefield..."

"Yes, but what a lesson for us! The seeds of all the virtues of our present society were found there, alongside all the extinct faults of our race. Amid the pools of blood of the massacres shone the glorious dawn of the science that has since saved the world."

"But how much dust overlies all that!"

"It's up to us to lift it, in order that the treasures that it hides aren't lost. Thanks to what we're doing, the thought of today can reach back to its origins in a wing-beat."

"How many other civilizations already overlay the one about which you're passionate! What a long process of swarming human crowds! What myriads of dreams and efforts!"

"Almost ten thousand years. But it's under an immense tide of dead things that the most marvelous memories are sometimes hidden. It's in that remote epoch, in the tragic shadow of the Christian era, that human beings first became conscious of their grandeur. It was then that science emerged, young, strong and flamboyant, from the darkness. It was then—in the twentieth century most of all—that the old bestial humankind discovered a god in itself, once captive, which it was liberating gradually. Have no doubt about it, that's worth some ardent labor, and the spectacle of that ancient life, which is growing more resplendent in my mind every day, has a great part to play in my present happiness. Don't you think so?"

Sketching a vague gesture, Neick had headed toward a portal veiled by heavy curtains; Dionel, his nephew, had followed him while pronouncing the last question, but it remained unanswered. The two men were already subject to the habitual suggestion of the place in which, once again, they were about to experience a radiant vertigo.

It was a circular chamber with bare metallic walls. In the gloom, several astronomical telescopes, edged with reflections, outlined their motionless forms. In the silence, there was a cold, grim solemnity, and the tubes aimed toward the infinity of the sky seemed intent on fascinating with their fixed eyes a formidable dream. Obedient to the old man's mute invitation, the young man approached the first ocular without saying a word, and was suddenly wonderstruck. Before him, in the dark blue circle that was clearly outlined, two stars were shining, one white and the other very pale. To see them thus, suspended in velvet space, one might have thought them two pearls motionless in a jewel-case; and Dionel, whose quivering thought had suddenly been dazzled, could scarcely retain a cry of admiration.

"Those two stars," said Neick, "are the ones designated by the unique name of Rigel."

"In the constellation of Orion?"

"Yes. They seem to the naked eye to form a single star of the first magnitude, but in reality there are two suns with numerous satellites. Displaced northwards, they only entered into our celestial hemisphere a hundred and ten years ago, but already, since then, they've gained almost half a degree of elevation above the horizon relative to our eyes. Some star still unknown is attracting them. In a few centuries no doubt, they'll be visible from here on the other side of the Milky Way. Thus, everything moves, including our system; everything is just dust in motion, swarming atoms in the living organism of space, in the disconcerting complexity of the universe."

Again, Dionel looked at the stars; his heart was hammering; a surge of joy filled his breast.

With a gently amiability, his host explained to him the movement of the two stars, quoting figures and opposing the grandeur of those worlds to the infimal smallness of the terrestrial globe. All that, added to the magic of the spectacle, excited Dionel's imagination, but, while opening avid eyes, he remained silent, as if all the words of his thought could not suffice to exteriorize his impression.

Neick touched a small lever. Immediately, the telescope was elevated by a few degrees, following one of the meridians of the cupola, and offered to the young man's curious eyes the white mist of the Milky Way. What a marvel! In an accumulation of luminous jewels, the dust of stars, confused at first, flowed and separated, and gradually became more precise, like adamantine flowers in an opaline pollen. Mysteriously impelled by occult forces, they circled in foamy waves in the heart of the immensity, drawing their light tresses through the calm depths of the azure. A green-tinted nebulosity, gliding over a broad sheet of white light, was reminiscent of a crown of fine grains brushing the robe of a invisible goddess; all around, like golden bees and blue damsel-flies, other flames seemed to be fluttering, and amid all those harmonies, all those corollas, all those wings, heavy globules of light trembled, which, in spite of their apparent smallness, were enormous suns.

"How beautiful it is," Dionel murmured, without taking his eyes off the celestial spectacle. "How beautiful it is! And we still know so few things, by comparison with all those magical, inaccessible distances."

"Patience," said Neick, with a malicious smile. "Our dreams already visit the sumptuous gardens of the ideal, and collect magical beauties there at the whim of our fantasy. Later, it's not impossible that science will show us even more..."

Dionel gazed, only half-listening, trying to imprison the vertiginous sensation of the infinite within a concrete idea.

Suddenly, however, he was extracted from his ecstasy by the complex sound of a motor humming a few paces away from him. Without fully understanding what was happening, he perceived the purr of helices, and then an abrupt metallic clink, and shortly thereafter, an exclamation.

Less distracted, Neick had rushed to one of the large glazed bays of the great hall and had opened a door abruptly. In front of him, on a terrace bordered with dense rose-bushes, a great metallic bird had just stopped, bringing its black wings together vertically.

Already out of the nacelle, a tall, thin man with an expansive face cried on seeing him arrive: "I've had a narrow escape, my dear Neick!"

"An accident?"

"Almost."

"Nothing serious?"

"Fortunately, no, but it wouldn't have taken much..."

"A collision?"

"A funny story, which I must tell you..."

They went inside.

The newcomer, who had just flown some distance in the dark, was dazzled momentarily by the lighting in the hall; he stopped. Neick turned a commutator, and the light immediately turned from white to blue and became milder.

Dionel having approached the newcomer, Neick hastened to introduce them to one another.

"My friend Berlois...my nephew Dionel..."

They shook hands. They sat down, and chatted about various things. After an exchange of questions and news, Berlois began to recount his aerial adventure.

"Yes, I've made quite a long journey today, involuntarily and in rather odd conditions. This is how it came about: at about four o'clock, when I was in the region of Tannus, I was suddenly cared away by an unexpected squall; I resisted, opposing all the force of my electrostryge[9] to the wind; I increased my speed, changed the inclination of my wings, and I was already turning south-west, victoriously, when I plunged, by virtue of a maladroit maneuver, into the Rhine valley. On the river, traveling at precisely three hundred kilometers an hour, was one of those large suspended trains that transport merchandise, and only stop at the sea."

"You collided with it?"

"I felt a shock, it seemed that I was choking, and, by virtue of an instinct of self-preservation, I opened the oxygen tank automatically."

"A fall?"

"At first, I didn't realize what had happened; a few minutes later I realized that the electrostryge, having been drawn toward the train by the action of the air, had stuck to the last wagon as if to an electromagnet."

"And then? How did you get out of it?"

"Still a prisoner, but traveling fast, I floated like that for two hours, following all the bends of the river, provoking multiple cries of astonishment as I passed by. In order not to be killed I was lying down in the bottom of the nacelle, and I arrived at the port safe and sound, like a parcel.

"You had a narrow escape."

"Yes, indeed; but one of the electrostryge's wings was broken; it had to be repaired before I could set off again, and

---

[9] This neologism is a trifle odd. In French the noun *stryge* comes from the Latin *striga* and means witch, but it seems more likely that the author has in mind the Danish verb *stryge*, from the old Norse, meaning stroke or caress. The author subsequently makes the point that the language spoken by the people of his future era is a composite of disparate old languages.

that was another full hour lost. That's why I'm late; excuse me."

He uttered a loud burst of laughter, which almost caused the danger he had run to be forgotten. His two interlocutors smiled, and Neick, turning to his nephew, said to him ironically: "That's a story that the people of the twentieth century would have found very implausible."

"They didn't know then about suspended trains and electrostryges," added Berlois."

"Pardon me, but trains already existed of the same kind as those of the Rhine, on the Wipper,"[10] the young archeologist corrected. "As for electrostryges, it wouldn't be astonishing if the people of that century had possessed them, as we do."

"But primitive apparatus, in proportion..."

"I agree. The people of that time didn't know the vertigo of speed."

"In comparison with our century, they knew hardly anything," Neick concluded, laughing. "And would you believe it, it's for those people that my nephew is neglecting to interest himself in the great problems of today."

"You've admitted to me that at my age you had ideas similar to mine; so..."

"Yes, but that was in order for my example to serve you to reach sooner a goal identical to mine, toward which you're advancing in spite of archeology, in spite of yourself and in spite of everything."

"In that case, I'll arrive there; what does the detour mater?"

"I believe he's right," said Berlois. "Detours have a charm that I can't appreciate; nothing is worth as much as that.

---

[10] The reference is to the Wuppertal Elevated Railway built between 1897 and 1903, running for about thirteen kilometers above the River Wupper (known as the Wipper in its upper stretches) for about ten kilometers.

I'll even make one this evening if you like. Where do you live?"

"47-22-14 and East 1-12-28," Dionel replied.

Having made a note of the figures, Berlois stood up. Knowing that it was pointless to attempt to retain his friend for longer, Neick escorted him to the terrace, where the somber wings of the electrostryge were outlined against the sky. On the horizon, the luminous roofs of scattered houses, sculpted into facets like sapphires, emeralds and rubies, were scintillating magnificently; above it, in the placid air, large bird-like forms were passing from time to time.

The weather was already mild, although it was only April, and the roses of Algeria, which were wilting there, filled the shadows with a soft voluptuousness.

Berlois and Dionel took their places in the nacelle; Neick shook their hands for the last time, and then retreated a few steps. The motor began to vibrate, the wings lowered, and with a supple twitch, the apparatus launched forth into the night.

The old man followed it with his eyes until it had disappeared completely, and then went back into the hall. He headed for a large blackboard, on which algebraic equations were aligned. For a moment, he remained pensive; then he tapped a keyboard with a feverish hand and, making the unknowns leap from one polynomial to another, he pursued his problems.

II

The next day, Berlois, waking up at home, was surprised to see broad daylight where his eyes had only expected, as usual, to encounter a pale dawn gleam. He rubbed his eyes and reached out toward an electric distribution panel placed beside his bed...and he felt himself gently carried away again by his dream, between the green banks of a great river, brushing in turn mountains, waves and clouds. It was exquisite; a mild intoxication seemed to soften curves and distance objects, annihilating the anguish and vertigo of the previous day. Beneath him, almost indistinct, the landscape was gliding, in which humans were clinging to the verdure like insects.

Suddenly, a shrill whistle cut through the air.

The sleeper had an abrupt sensation of reality, and, darting a glance at the widow, he distinguished very clearly in the sky the oblong form of the great Northern Company dirigible *Lofga*.

"Eleven o'clock!" he murmured, astonished.

He got up and headed for the bathroom. A quarter of an hour later, fully dressed, he went down briskly to the dining room.

As he finished his meal, he received a visit from Dionel. They had promised one another the day before to visit some newly-discovered ruins; that prospect interested both of them keenly, so they set forth without delay.

The elevator, with its customary obedience, deposited them in accordance with their desire at the third subterranean pillar of the city, in front of a fan of open bays in which red lamps scintillated at intervals. They took their places in a light and comfortable vehicle; by applying the trolley to one of the numerous rails suspended from the ceiling, and then commanding a gear mechanism by means of a small lever, they caused a container of striated glass—a radium tube—to rotate slowly. After a few seconds of immobility, during which the two travelers swiftly buckled the straps of the safety belts designed to retain them within the cushions, they tilted a second lever, linked to the front wheels, and the vehicle immediately began sliding along the rail.

"The ruins that I mentioned to you yesterday," said Berlois, "must contain many documents precious for you, my dear friend; we should arrive there soon enough to permit us to consult them at our ease, before the invasion of numerous visitors."

"Will we be the first?"

"I hope so; the discovery only having been made late in the evening, only a few privileged individuals will have been warned, as we were, via the Hertzian waves; most people will probably be unaware of it until the distribution of the daily films at six o'clock this evening. In any case, I'm glad to observe, in that regard, that today's public is content to look at finds of that nature without routinely pillaging them, as they once did. That's one more proof of the superiority of the contemporary world, as your uncle would say if we had the pleasure of seeing him with us."

"Yes, but it wasn't the crowds that once pillaged discovered treasures; it was a few scholars who displaced everything—without thinking that their removal destroyed, by virtue of that very fact, their greatest value of evocation—in order to make absurd collections."

"Egotists?"

"No exactly. Thos collections served for public education and were exhibited in special buildings.

"Which were called, I believe, museums?"

"Indeed. In any case, in those primitive times that was almost necessary. People being unable to travel rapidly over the surface of the globe, it seemed practical to educators to gather together the marvels of history where the great number of individuals were assembled—which is to say, in the small areas of cities."

"And they did that to the detriment of those who lived much closer to the ruins themselves, in the genuinely evocative regions? What sacrilege!"

"But think of the ignorance and poverty of the ancient inhabitants of rural regions; remember that the historical or artistic value of things was negligible in their eyes. You'll admit with indulgence that the gold in question, offered by the intellectuals of cities in exchange for the recovered works was bound to impel the mass of vulgar appetites to the profanation of memories."

"But what a barbaric mentality that reveals! Frankly, it's far better to be alive today."

"On condition of studying the past; it's only the comparison that permits us to appreciate our present good fortune."

"Perhaps, although personally, I only find in the study of history the brutal satisfaction of a keen curiosity, and hence one more pleasure in the passing moment. I don't know whether, from the point of view of pleasure, we're exactly in tune. But there are egotistical joys, without repercussion, that only last for a flash, and which…look, like the fact of seeing trembling, in that passing red flame, a rapid white radiance."

"I, too, sometimes felt that intense joy. Recently, an old Spanish text, all lyricism and color, delighted me."

"You've learned dead languages?"

"A few. The universal language that we speak is a composite in any case, and French, Italian, German and Russian idioms, for example, contain in their ancient and picturesque brutality the typical seeds from which the luminous forms of our present words have emerged. And how admirable, too, are the depictions of life conserved under the dust of old books! To judge in accordance with the authors of those vanished times the fever of the slow disaggregation that preceded, in the twenty-first century, the destruction of aristocracies, the very intellectual chaos, so to speak, ought to have a flavorsome charm.

"Remember that millions of brains, scarcely emerged from their age-old lethargy, were experiencing then, for the very first time, the enthusiasm of discovering one another. Civilizations, so various in that epoch, were encountering one another, reciprocally dazzled, at the crossroads of the world. Commerce, although slow and at the price of long efforts, was transforming and gradually fusing mores and customs, bringing new ideas along with new products, mingling the ice of Norway with bright tropical fruits, the elegance of Japan and the glory of France. Imagine the voluptuous astonishment that those people who had conserved, in spite of the ambient disturbance, vibrant hearts and clear sight must have felt, at the surprise of those contrasts. Also, what names of great artists that century has left us!"

"They were the last of antiquity."

"And that's explicable. Once that astonishment had passed, Europe, and then the rest of the world, found itself facing a gigantic treasure, still largely unemployed and un-comprehended. Art had only savored the superficial aspects of it; it was science that elucidated its mystery. Hence, a long period—about four centuries—in which only the names of a few illustrious scientists, like Jeulindo, Psamm and Knargof stand out; that was the basis of a new era."

"Yes."

"Even more sumptuous..."

"Quite different, simply; for, in comparing the centuries, one takes account both of the apparent diversity and the real equivalence of their glory. Humankind was wrong, it seems to me, always to think that it had arrived at a summit of power, a maximum of glory. You remember the noise that was made last year by the artificial creation of amoebas?"

"Garfman's discovery? I should think so. It was a revolution..."

"Evidently, it appeared extraordinary, at that moment, of a nature to leave the trace in history of a great upheaval."

"But..."

"And yet..."

"But it explained the secret of life."

"So be it..."

"It made humankind a demiurge, a creator rivaling eternal forces."

"So be it; but has that, in our epoch, more relative importance than already-distant discoveries such as oil, radium and X-rays? Think of the upheavals that must have been provoked in past centuries by the employment of each new force understood and dominated, of the naive astonishment and pride surrounding each human conquest. When Christopher Columbus discovered America, for example, it modified the life of old Europe far more than many a scientific discovery at which we marvel today. And if you want to go back to antediluvian epochs, think about the first voluntary creation of fire, and the importance that must have had. In many respects, all

84

centuries are alike, but we're always infinitely more astonished by what we see ourselves, and that's why, aided by our vanity, we always think that we're realizing the maximum of possibilities."

While conversing this, Berlois and Dionel followed with their eyes, on a luminous panel placed in the front of the vehicle, the delicate progress of a platinum needle, the inclination of which indicated the number of kilometers they had traveled.

"We're nearly there," said Berlois, lowering with an abrupt gesture the metal bar placed to his right. "In a moment we'll be breathing the open air. Look, the lamps are already becoming more precise."

For a few minutes, the purr of the brakes rendered any conversation impossible; the bloody claws of the light became, in their clearly discernible bulbs, fixed scarlet balls, and they were able to distinguish, along the white walls, the cool rigidity of oxygen tubes.

They stopped.

At a signal transmitted by a simple electric bell, Monsieur Daxwone, the tenant of the house under which the two travelers found themselves, hastened to send one of his mobile landings down to the third subterranean corridor. Then he welcomed Dionel and Berlois cordially, who had been unknown to him until that moment, and took real pleasure in being able to inform them on the subject of the excavations undertaken the day before not far from his dwelling.

"It's in the property of my friend Torwarg," he said, "that the ruins have been discovered. Workmen deploying a large perforator of the Plo system were digging out a new well there from the sixth gallery when the sounding apparatus suddenly brought a fragment of a cornice back to the surface and the debris of a statue. You can imagine the tumult that ensued. The possibility of soon finding the mysterious riches of a disappeared world stimulated general curiosity."

"And people set to work?"

"Torwarg, who had been warned immediately, proposed replacing the perforator with the electric dredgers from his estate, but he only had seven of them, which wasn't sufficient. The news spread for several leagues around, and requests made for help. Then there was a truly admirable spectacle. Automobile dredgers of all forms and dimensions arrived from all directions. Every minute brought the beauty of a new effort from distant and anonymous sympathies. Like living beings finding their battle order in serried ranks, the dredgers took up their positions near the well, rubbing their metallic limbs with a martial sound. Twenty workmen were sufficient to control them, to position them and insufflate them with an active, buzzing soul. A few minutes later, disposed in a great fan, they were seen scratching the earth impatiently and throwing the products of their labor into their reservoir-wagons."

"Don't you think," Dionel put in, "that the artificial power in question is both strange and magnificent? Humans create metal monsters; those monsters are terrible, after all; they could destroy, kill and vanquish, but humans master them; their brutal strength is tamed merely by the impetus of thought; they become passive servants, while still redoubtable, both gigantic and obedient."

"That's what renders the joy of being human intoxicating," added Berlois. Then, addressing their host, he said: "You've lived a few grandiose hours there!"

"In twenty-five minutes the work was concluded, and a few hectares of the ancient surface of the world were offered once again to the radiance of the sun."

"But the ruins?"

"Only a single building was discovered, a sort of vast palace, very well-preserved but surrounded, for a distance of five hundred meters, by not the slightest vestige of civilization. That's why Torwarg judged it unnecessary to continue the excavations. The palace in question is in a strange style, and seems to have belonged to some great leader of the barbaric people who presumably lived, many centuries ago, in the same country as us. But I'll hasten to show it to you; it's not far away and the route is quite beautiful."

So saying, Daxwone indicated with his gaze a sunlit road among fields of roses and violets. All three smiled at the joyful thought of following it, without haste, like barbarians, glad to be alive, and chatting.

The walk was exquisite; it lasted an hour, but the hour seemed short. Finally, the three men perceived before them a quadrangular excavation about a kilometer wide, and twice the height of a house in depth.

For a moment, Dionel remained nailed to the spot; his temples were hammering as if to burst, and the ardor of his soul was shining in his eyes. O marvel of marvels! A dream realized! That proud construction, with slender and noble columns, in pure and clear detail! That frieze, still so broad in its broken line, reminiscent of the clear sweep of a divinely extended wing, so simultaneously strong and gentle did it seem in its serene harmony. That fronton! Those caryatids! Those archivolts! All that magic born of stone and suddenly surging before him, he recognized, having admired it for a long time in his mind.

The horizon trembled.

Around the motionless mass, Dionel saw an entire resuscitated people surge forth in the sunlit solitude.

Oh, how moving a ruin could be!

Now he devoured it with his eyes; he sensed his soul fill with ardent admiration.

Berlois and Daxwone were there, two paces away from him, but they did not know what he was thinking, what he would like to say about that world, to cry to every horizon.

With an instinctive impulse, he drew nearer, and, extending his hand toward what all three of them were gazing at, he cried triumphantly: "I recognize it! It's the Louvre! We've rediscovered Paris!"[11]

_____

[11] Since the publication of Joseph Méry's account of "Les Ruines de Paris (1844, reprinted several times in slightly different versions; tr. as "The Ruins of Paris" in *The Tower of Destiny*, Black Coat Press, ISBN 978-1-61227-101-9) the idea

III

In his laboratory, Neick was pensive.

The weather that day was overcast, and a laziness floated in the air.

Scarcely attentive the scientist regulated by force of habit the slow and revelatory displacement of a disk of barium platinocyanide amid the strange efflorescence of green vapors imprisoned in a series of crystal tubes.

From time to time, in the silence of the room, a faint sound like the buzz of a bee recalled the presence of some milliampmeter, a fragile, almost living mechanism, which could not be distracted by the caress of the breeze, the first ray of sunlight or human thought.

But Neick was distracted.

A healthy sensuality scattered in nature gradually infiltrated his mathematical preoccupations and obliged him to savor the perfume of spring.

He opened a window; all of nature smiled at him, and the silence redoubled.

For more than a quarter of an hour, almost forgetting everything that was not the primordial joy of sensing that he existed, Neick, immobile, watched the pale cotton wool of a cloud dissolve on the horizon.

Suddenly, however, a new fever filed the laboratory; it was six o'clock, and the pearly voice of bells announced the daily news broadcast.

At a rapid pace, the old man went toward the apparatus; with a nervous gesture he rectified the position of a few needles, slowed the progress of a few gears and immobilized the platinocyanide disk completely. Then he headed for a large

---

of future archeologists excavating the ruins of the city had become one of the stock themes of *roman scientifique*, recapitulated in numerous speculative stories, most of them satirical.

opaline screen on which the multiple and rapid synthesis of all human communication had just appeared in luminous stenograms. One initial flash almost straight and horizontal, signified Mathematics; another, an oblique zigzag, signified Astronomy; other varied gleams, in the form of circles and various angles, slow or rapid curves, with different frissons, translated by turns the words Physics, Chemistry, Biology, Sociology, and so on.

For each of those sciences, a very simple mechanism permitted the reader to arrest the symbol, and beneath it, immediately, other stenograms were aligned, representing the habitual divisions of that science. At each synthesis of thought an arrest was possible and, by means of a further release, one could then cause to surge forth, in the middle of the screen, firstly an explanatory text and then a cinematographic reproduction of recent events relative to the chosen subject.

Neick, curious about astronomy, caused the living spectacle of several recent observations made by astronomers to appear before him. One that interested him above all was the spectral analysis of a very small star, scarcely visible, in the region of Eridanus. The photograph had been taken last night in one of the most renowned observatories in southern Africa, and the experiment had been brilliantly carried out by the famous Vax.

It resulted from the analysis that the distant atom of force and light in question was composed of substances absolutely similar to those of our own sun, combined in the same proportions, which almost permitted the conclusion that out there, a few trillion billions of kilometers away, a system was in motion almost identical to our own planetary archipelago, with globes similar to Venus, Mars, Saturn and so on, and—a more troubling enigma—perhaps one similar to the one we inhabit, with continents, sea, plants, animals and humans.

For a long time, Neick, savoring subtle thoughts, interrupted the reading of the magical and impassioning screen; but amid the apparently logical charm of his reasoning, one question loomed up, cold, insoluble and deceptive: was the universe simple and numerable, or infinitely complex? Was the astral ambience, which we call improperly the void, which is merely a milieu propitious or hostile to certain combinations, the same around that star as it is around us?

Could nature repeat herself, yes or no?

The scientist, tormented by that unanswered question, followed at hazard the audacious leaps of his suppositions, but every time their frail scaffolding was erected, a fog enveloped them, and he sensed them crumbling.

O weakness of reasoning, which is daring, but nothing but smoke!

In order to extract himself from that dolorous intoxication, Neick touched an electric button situated at the left-hand corner of the screen, and from a new series of titles he chose the word History, which immediately gave way to its subdivisions; those were followed by the names of auxiliary sciences connected to it, but Neick was still thinking about the incomprehensibility of infinity when the word Archeology appeared. Mechanically, he immobilized it; immediately, he saw a text appear in the middle of the screen, which he did not read, and then the ruins of Kamstown, so many centuries old, on which people had been working for several days in order to save their grandiose beauty from collapse.

The luminous illustration of the newscast took Neick's viewpoint through all the streets still existent of the ancient capital of Australia. Its houses, in the pure style of the twenty-third century of the Christian Era, displayed the splendid surge of their fourteen or fifteen stories, in an ornamental debauchery of sumptuous architecture, in a dazzling mixture of gold, crystal and marble, entirely populated by legends. The ensemble, as bright in outline and in memory as in the scintillation of its raw materials, was animated, thanks to the imagination of the spectator by the innumerable and sumptuous barbarian processions that life had once precipitated there from battle to battle, and from glory to triumph, ever more terrible and prideful.

Only the laughter of the crystal, the nobility of the marble and the majesty of the gold had resisted the assault of the years; the people, from century to century, had mingled their dust.

Following new thoughts, the scientist forgot for a moment the star that the famous astronomer Vax had exhibited. But the light of the screen paled, and abruptly, the elation of the dream gave way to the cruel disquiet of science. The man, obsessed once again by the grim unknown, was suddenly afraid of his solitude, and in order to escape it, he summoned new scenes of light into the penumbra.

A vast denuded plain appeared, under the pale sky of a country that he seemed to recognize. On the horizon, the cupolas of houses glittered that he had seen before, and the trees, aligned along the roads, seemed to him to have a familiar aspect. However, he did not recognize the vast plateau the color of freshly-labored earth, nor, in the middle of it, the tall and bizarre construction surrounded by a swarm of electrostryges airplanes and airships of every sort, in a buzzing and tumultuous swarm. Others were arriving from all directions. What the object of that general curiosity was, Neick still did not know, although all of Europe might be talking about it.

At that moment, someone knocked on the door. Without having made any response, he divined that the door had opened and he sensed in the shadow the silhouette of a mischievous child looking at him. He turned round and asked the newcomer if he had already heard mention today of what he newscast was representing; but the child started laughing, and took from his pocket some twenty minuscule films, threw them on a table, laughed again, more brazenly mocking, and then fled.

Somewhat vexed, Neick examined the twenty-two films one by one, placing them in a special fitting of the lamp. They all showed the same spectacle as the newscast, but seen from distant angles; he imagined himself thus making a tour of the ruined palace and penetrating into it, mingling with the crowd. Nevertheless, he regretted not having paid more attention, a little while before, to the text on the screen. He reproached himself for his habitual distraction, feeling old and almost unhappy.

But voices collided with his windows. He ran outside. They were bearers of news who were all proclaiming the same thing: "The ruins of Paris have just been discovered! The ruins of ancient Paris, the voluptuous city of Kings!"

The the old man tilted his head and asked himself, in all sincerity, whether the serious knowledge of dead things might not contain, after all, more joy than the science of her future alone brought him.

IV

The electrostryge rose up.

Berlois darted a glance at the mercury and observed that it marked 2,800 meters. With a calm precision, manipulating the levers governing the elevation and direction of the vehicle by turns, he arrested the ascension. The apparatus, immobilizing its great wings and retaining the breath of its motor, yielded meekly to the caress of the breeze and hovered, borne gently in a north-easterly direction.

After the rude and mathematical audacity of the ascensional journey, Berlois now savored the restful delight of the spectacle of which he had come so high in search.

Beneath him, an immensity of fleecy whiteness hid the surface of the habitual world almost completely. Only something like a patch of verdure could be seen in the hollows of the moving cotton-wool hills, like life appearing here and there in the midst of a dream, divinely softened by an unreal distance.

In the east, among the fantastic forms of a multitude of heavy clouds, like several chains of superimposed mountains rolling toward some unknown gulf, in the interstices of the snowy summits, soft gorges and blue-gray abysses, yellow rays burst forth, melting in order to be reborn, struggling against the magical ideality of the décor. But gray galloping masses, dragging behind them large and undulating shadows, mounted an assault on the mountains and repelled the golden enemy.

Under the white sea, at times, a pink lava inundated the ground, sliding in violet fringes along imprecise verdures. The islets of life, marvelously iridescent, triumphed in a fleeting gleam, crying the glory of colors; then, suddenly faded and shredded in a light mist, they were lost in the milky tide.

But the warrior clouds, the grim valkyries clad in night, gradually retreated under the torrential avalanche of powdered fire announcing the sun's approach. There was soon a crackling of light, a red surge rearing up over the crests of that suspended wave. Like a heavy cart bounding over suddenly-resplendent ruts, the star appeared, in a miracle of gems; and amid the opaline foam fringed with ruby glints and speckled with ocher, topaz and copper, unexpected rays sent from cloud to cloud collided in fans, rockets and rainbows.

From one minute to the next, the general aspect of the cloud modified its magical deployment and scattered its multicolored sheets in flames, in necklaces, in butterflies or pearls, collapsing her in silent torrents, here in retinues of shadow and crimson, to all the horizons.

In that superhuman décor, Berlois' dream bounded in pursuit of bright forms, clung tightly to their dying splendors, savored the vertigo of seeing them disappear, then being reborn with them, to the right or the left, ever new, multiple, young and varied, in the pantheistic intoxication of his enthusiasm.

Non-existent in that eternity, two hours passed without him perceiving them. Only the need to proclaim his joy to others made him think of terrestrial life, the time that had gone by, and the necessity of returning.

He brushed his burning forehead with his hand as if to wipe away the voluptuous anguish of his dream; he regained possession of all his thought, regulated the march of the shuddering motor, and prepared for the descent.

Everything dazzled the electric bird flapping its wings in a soothing rhythm.

The clouds soon brushed him with their diaphanous mist; the earth reappeared beneath him, profound and vast, sumptuous and inundated by the luminous morning.

Berlois consulted the barometer; the mercury was rising in its glass tube.

O fresh and young laughter of nature! Glory of the sun on light foliage! Breathing deeply, inhaling every breath like the passionate ardor of a universal amour, Berlois drank the joy scattered in the splendor of the world.

Already, beneath him, like brightly colored flowers, round roofs, sheets of water and metallic circles were outlined. A moment later, he was able to recognize bridges, aqueducts, towers, spires, meadows and woods. As he came closer still, moving precisely amid rapid flocks of engines of light and brilliant forms, there was the roaring rush of enormous beetles made entirely of metal, and the silky glide of large commercial balloons and divinely suspended airborne houses. Then there were, at the tops of Menave towers, the trills of various sounds, and blue sparks at the height of Almor needles, and the constant exchange of telegrams between a thousand various spires.

It was necessary to beware of the highways of great aerial traffic, to watch out for the passage of lepibolides, to avoid Wemmer currents, to think of the security of others as much of his own, and reconquer all the mastery of habitual life. With a sure hand, Berlois commanded the steering-wheel; all the joy that had filled his brain a little while before seemed dead and forgotten.

He headed toward his dwelling, a tall bright building that he could distinguish in the distance, its roof bristling with a host of metallic darts.

On the way, the movement became less and less intense; he had an abrupt desire to escape that animation; with a clear, slightly irritated eye he fixed the white terrace on which he wanted to arrest his flight, and with a single bound, his nerves taut, he flew toward the goal and reached it.

When he found himself in the large familiar room, alone and tranquil, far from external noises, he saw again in a dream the reality of his ascent. His nerves calmed down completely, his joy became more measured, more internal and more subtle, his memory harmonizing its enthusiasm before a sort of wisdom more compatible with life.

Berlois became truly himself again—which is to say, insouciant, skeptical and slightly mocking. Around him, the softness of the sumptuous furniture seemed, by the evocation of other delightful hours, to want to charm the present moment. Berlois lit a cigarette; observed the swirls of smoke for a few seconds, and then reflected and estimated himself to be the most fortunate of men.

In the same way as Neick and Dionel, he belonged to the elite of society—which is to say that, according to contemporary conventions, he represented a intellectual wealth, a useful quality of thought and action well above the mean; with regard to the crowd, he was one of those who could, when circumstances demanded it, direct it. He even thought that it would be easy, given the faculty of comprehension of each unit of that mass, the desire of each of them to realize great and beautiful things, and the practical power of solidarity.

Oh, everything that it would be possible to do...!

The smoke of the cigarette strayed in spirals, stopped momentarily, and started again in a pale swirl, a blue thread.

But what was the point of domination?

What was the point of occupying the summit of a hierarchy?

Until now, although hazard had placed him there, Berlois had scarcely cared about it. His happiness consisted, above all, of forgetting his own merit, of mingling, obscure and unperceived, in all the splendors of active life, superb and rich, splendid and audacious. To see the world, nature and human beings! To see everything! To be intoxicated by the spectacle! To aspire via the eyes all the effort, all the life and all the wellbeing of others, to mingle them with the fortunate richness of his own brain; to watch, to learn and to know; to augment every day the indestructible treasure of his soul, and, without stopping at any marvel, to go from one to another recklessly.

A curiosity was in him, but it was rapid and sharp, all superficial caprice. That is why the profession of informer, so adequate to his character, had impassioned him for a long time. Every day, in his work-room, where innumerable metallic wires translated into ringing bells, signals and stenograms the news collected throughout the world, he spent long hours interesting himself in everything that was transmitted, scattering his soul, feeling every fiber of the apparatus vibrate within his heart and following along each thread, each needle and each wire a thought marching toward the unknown.

But what he preferred, in spite of everything, were free excursions in the air, the voluptuous anguish of speed, struggling with the savage intoxication of danger, the new décors and incessantly renewed spectacles of nature. In the early morning he often fled in an electrostryge or lepibolide all the way to the Bosphorus, Norway or Africa in order to watch a sunrise. What did distance matter, with good engines? He forgot human beings.

Then, returning to them, sympathetically, he amused himself with them, finding them simultaneously comical, strange and divinely beautiful.

All his friends seemed to him to be slightly illogical, in various ways, but they all had his sincere affection. Did not each of them represent a special conception of life?

In Neick, for example, it was the strange that transported him. Living almost isolated. He was passionate about an arid science, vertiginous but cruel, full of hope but of a verity, so to speak, abstract, inaccessible and certainly deceptive.

His nephew, on the contrary, directed his joy and enthusiasm into the contemplation of the past.

But both of them pleased him; both of them responded to the constant intoxication of his curiosity...

Berlois shook the ash from his cigarette; he was astonished to have been without news of the two friends in question for more than a month, and promised himself to render them a visit as soon as possible. He checked the time, and hastened to head for his work-room.

V

A mass of information, arrived from everywhere and already registered, awaited him there. He took cognizance of it, filtered it, and then, reuniting via a slender copper wire all the received items whose news warranted publication, he put them in contact with the telegraphic transmitter specially destined for *Western Europe* correspondence.

Western Europe was one of the eleven great global journals, and Berlois, a participant in all that gigantic work with all the force of his minuscule individuality, could not help feeling a little pride every time he sent some important message to the central bureau.

Today, that was the case; the harvest was rich, precious documents were abundant from all directions. At every moment new Hertzian, Wingallian and Corid vibrations arrived, immediately translated into sound, light and script, or into designs, immediately sorted, classified and sent to the journal.

In spite of his role as a minor intermediary, however, Berlois, the devoted servant of that distant and prodigious intellectual Minotaur, sometimes savored the plenitude of his own power. Was he not the first to know the scattered thought of a large part of the world, the first to see scintillating, in suspended glass bubbles, the reflections of all new spectacles? For as long as he wished, he could delay, for his own pleasure, the miraculous flight of an entire swarm of ideas. But altruism puts into the heart of the man who practices it a joy similar to triumph, and Berlois was voluntarily altruistic.

Understanding the grandeur and the beauty of life, he loved his fellows for all that, each in accordance with his destiny, they brought to the earth of the multiple happiness that was united every day with his own joy in living. Like a drop of water, is soul reflected the multicolored and joyful scintillation of all other souls. He took account of those myriads of reflections found in himself, of his reciprocal utility for other happiness, of an entire complex and marvelous tangle.

Every item of news, collected from a distance by the miracle of the apparatus, also impassioned him by virtue of the prodigy of a journey scarcely traced in space but directed by humans to their purposes. At every minute, along a wire or vibrating freely in the air, a phrase arrived, mysteriously faithful, launched and registered by various procedures, offered to him in his office; docile, he tapped a keyboard discreetly, and murmured a name; pretty, the item rendered itself visible in a bubble of light.

Berlois hastened from one to another, and in spite of the ticking of the clock, time passed rapidly, beating its wing around him.

Suddenly, his labor was interrupted by the curt and slightly brutal ringing of advertiser A, which was in communication with the ground floor. Divining from the violence of the appeal some unfortunate event, Berlois opened the door and lent an ear, but scarcely had he penetrated into the next room than he saw a crazed old man launch himself toward him. After a few seconds he recognized Neick, in spite of the latter's extraordinary gaze, his wild gestures and incoherent exclamations, and his utterly unkempt appearance.

Pressed with questions the old man only replied with imprecise phrases; a joy was divinable in him, mingled with anxiety and fever, impatience and curiosity. Suddenly, he seized his interlocutor by the hand, looked into his eyes, hesitated momentarily, and then asked him, in a tone that was by turns suppliant, hopeful and almost commanding: "Will you permit me? It's necessary for me to transmit the news, to question the world, to undertake the realization of my project; it's necessary for me to take your place for a few hours, to dispose of all your apparatus, to be in communication with the thought of others, with their science and their will, in order ask for their aid, to explain to them why I want, why it's necessary, to attempt the adventure...oh, I'll convince them! But I need to take your place. Don't refuse me that, I beg you. Don't refuse me!"

"But the *Western Europe*..."

"I'll alert the journal."

"What will your text be?"

"It will be more beautiful than ever."

"But what about the films..."

"What films?"

"Those of the transatlantic tunnel catastrophe, which I was in the process of transmitting..."

"It's certainly a matter of catastrophe!"

"Millions of readers want to be informed. It's a grave event. The journal will be lost!"

"On the contrary...you'll see! You'll see!"

So saying, Neick had launched himself toward the workroom, and had already taken possession of one of the phonic cornets of the Wirs transmitter in communication with the central editorial bureau, and shouted: "Stop everything! Stop everything! Details will follow! Hurrah! Only put out a single title: *The Conquest of the Universe*."

Believing his friend to be mad, Berlois tried to stop him, but the latter turned round. He struck such a supremely dignified pose and had such a gleam of triumphant lucidity in his eyes that Berlois was subjugated.

"You think I'm mad?" said Neick, in an ironic tone. "Yes, mad, don't you? And yet, if you knew how certain I am now of that conquest...! If you knew what a grandiose goal humankind is able to attain, what a dream it will be possible to realize! Oh, poor friend, let me be...you'll see. You'll see!"

He went to a small table, where a luminoscope was slumbering, regulated the delicate mechanism, and spread throughout the world, by that means, the luminous translation of the words: *The Conquest of the Universe*."

For an instant, he remained motionless.

Perhaps he could see in the distance, thousands of kilometers away, other luminoscopes, similar to that one, translating the registered phrase into clear stenograms, and perhaps he could see, leaning over their little tables, pensive human faces like his own.

At that moment, Berlois could not explain his own impression, but Neick seemed to him to be an extraordinary being, full of the unknown and superiority.

Then Neick headed for the Gann multiplicator, whose innumerable silk threads rose up in vertical tresses, light and parallel, toward a mat copper dome bristling with fine needles. On the distribution scale he displaced the cursor as far as the words 'Scientific World.' With a brisk finger he caused the keyboard of titles to slide, lifted the clapper of the bell, set the registration disk in movement, and waited.

There was a minute of solemn silence, while Berlois gazed at Neick, admired him, and dared not question him.

Finally, the bell rang.

Neick, whose voice was now being registered, multiplied and distributed, live, into all the scientific bureaus in the world, spoke.

"To everyone, fraternal greetings! I, Neick, here present, at 45° 8'12" North latitude and 1° 20' 13" East longitude, humble servant of humankind, propose to everyone the following..."

A murmur palpitated in the resonators. Neick smiled, fell silent for a few seconds, and then continued slowly, stressing every syllable:

"The irregularities of the oscillation of the Earth on its axis having recently been explained by the formation, under the terrestrial crust, of enormous and mobile masses of pyrriline, and the present location of the most considerable mass having been observed at 87° 5' 14" south latitude—which is to say, a distance from the South Magnetic Pole greater than ever, which explains the slight variation in the present oscillation—it would be sufficient to establish a high tension current between that mass of pyrriline and the magnetic pole to disorganize completely the harmony of the telluric currents, in order to project our planet out of its orbit and to..."

The end of the sentence was lost in a tumult of interruptions; all the resonators were vibrating at the same time, launching indignant monosyllables and disapproving phrases toward the old man, stormily intermingled, among which the words *cataclysm, destruction, inutility, consequences, folly* and *catastrophe* were repeated with a hostile frenzy.

Neick, standing up proudly, disdained that avalanche of antipathy and went on, even more loudly and more clearly than at the beginning:

"For four centuries, the great dream of all great minds has been raised up, like a challenge, toward the blue profundities of space: humankind entire has desired, and still desires, today more violently than ever, to know the universe. I have found the means to do that; I am submitting to your thought the result of an entire life of science, hope and effort, and, although each of you has had, like me, the desire for that grandiose adventure whose realization I am finally rendering possible, you cry to me: 'Folly!' and you do not listen to me? It is doubtless fear that has seized you by the throat and is commanding you to this supreme and risible recoil.

"What does the danger matter?

"We know almost all the secrets of our globe; soon—as soon as our curiosity senses that it is impotent before the abysms of infinity—we will crush under the weight of our own fear the glory of our minds. Whatever the obstacles might be to our thirst for knowledge, our primordial duty is still to go forward, forever. Humankind cannot stop. The horror of the void is lying in wait for us, as if for a prey and it will kill us as soon as we become cowardly or hesitant.

"Think that, outside of our little world, other marvelous worlds exist. Think of the complete triumph of humankind, finally rendered greater than natural forces, directing the globe we inhabit, in spite of the sun, through infinite space. It is grandiose, and it is no longer a dream; it is sufficient to establish an electric current between the two points that I have indicated to you. It is sufficient to unite our efforts in that direction, and, minuscule as we are on our atom of a planet, we can finally take our place among the dominating powers, we will do something at our own whim in the universe, and we will be great!"

Again the resonators quivered, but this time, with a murmur of approval.

Neick continued.

In order to explain the possibility of success, he launched into a longer algebraic demonstration, aligning from memory formulas, equations and polynomials, showing in a clear and neat fashion the disequilibration of forces that could result from the strong and abrupt but mathematically foreseen oscillation of the Earth on its axis. He spoke about its mass, magnetic currents, the atmosphere and tides; he spoke about everything, at length and victoriously.

And gradually, emerging from the mystery of phonic apparatus, the acclamations rose into a murmur, into a rumble, and into a thunder of enthusiasm. A thousand voices united in a formidable "Hurrah!" The cause was won.

It was only then that Berlois perceived, above the *Western Europe* transmitter, the green flame indicating an urgent request for communication. He ran to it and seized one of the acoustic cornets, from which emerged, immediately, a rush of urgent nervous questions. He scarcely listened to them and, mad with joy, he howled his response: "Yes, it's true! Announce the conquest of the universe!"

VI

Every day, Dionel had returned to the ruins.

The day after their discovery, he had communicated to the journals a study entitled *Ancient Cities*, on which he had already been working for a long time and which he had finished feverishly, under the spur of the intense emotion that he had just felt. Paris seemed to him to revive with a fabulous and distant life: amid the empty shadows of the great plains of antiquity, it scintillated, buzzing like a beehive, outlining enormous ramparts in the night garnished with perfume-burners; sculpted towers and domes of solid gold insulted the stars in its name, and the tumult of human life unfurled there in savage and splendid frescos on terraces staged between marble colonnades under suspended awnings.

Paris impassioned Dionel, mingling with its historical education all the occult power of a superhuman poetry.

One day, still subject to that uplifting domination, the young man had stopped not far from the ruins and, sitting on a grassy mound, he was copying out a few notes that he had just made inside the palace.

A sound of light footsteps, like a rustle of leaves, caused him to raise his head. A woman passed by, bracing the supple harmony of her body beneath sparkling fabrics.

Dionel followed her with his eyes for a long time.

She went around the ruins, sometimes stopping before the beauty of a bas-relief that she examined.

As long as her presence lasted, Dionel only looked at her, and felt happy; never, it seemed to him, had his artistic soul experienced such joy in the contemplation of an rustling and harmonious dress; he gazed at it, as at something fragile, ephemeral and pretty beside the giant, massive and eternal Louvre, as he would have gazed at a flower alongside the Egyptian pyramids. He did not even think about amour, but a sensation of enervated melancholy invaded him as soon as he no longer saw the gracious silhouette. He strove to think about something else.

The next day, returning to see the ruins, he was anxious at not being able to find the unknown woman again right away; he perceived the importance that she had acquired in his life, in spite of him. It was then, while his imagination was striving to see her again, as he had the day before, that he acquired the certainty of a very distant memory. In the shadow of the past, a new form as born; it was apparently another woman, and yet he recognized her. Where, then, had he seen her? Imprecise and troubling, that image obsessed him delectably. He tried to recall it; he cited names, but he could not fix in his memory the moving depiction of his former joy.

Where, then, had he seen that mysterious beauty, that dream, that goddess, that attractive and enigmatic woman? Where, then, had he spoken to her? And yet, he had encountered her one day; he had said banal things to her; perhaps he had shaken her hand. At present, he did not understand how that had been possible, without the vertigo that illuminates and the confession that enchains having followed it.

Around the vague regret of having brushed happiness thus without recognizing it, other imprecise regrets were grouped: a thousand joys lost, a thousand possibilities disdained by life, were illuminated in a total of new hopes, but how many shadows there were over their distant origin! That woman, he loved! He had always loved her! Why had he not told her so much sooner?

He felt an abrupt shock in his heart when he saw her emerge from the enormous palace, not far away from him; she appeared even smaller, and more beautiful, and gentler in the bright freshness of her dress under the somber vault of the portico; her astonished image smiled, and it seemed to Dionel that it was the first smile of the world that was being offered to him.

He approached her.

Already, she was looking at him with a benevolent emotion. She recognized him, and saluted him with a gracious nod of the head.

Abruptly, he remembered. He saw again, magically, the gardens of Plogerelle inclining their clumps of illuminated shade over Lake Garda; he saw, again, on a delightful spring evening, the festival of gondolas dotting the tranquil water with a thousand fiery garlands; he remembered a boat touched, a few words exchanged, a blurred silhouette in the night behind a cape florid with magnolias. He also remembered, word for word, a banal conversation in a vast white drawing room starred with golden chandeliers.

So, it was Psyllene! It was the capricious woman who, only last year, sometimes amusing herself with a mischievous remark, laughed like a child, and then, at the slightest amorous word, fell silent, alarmed and glacial, as if wounded. It was her!

And Dionel, subjugated again, fearful and glad, spoke to her.

As she shook his hand she read in his eyes all the previous pleasures; she was touched by them, but she talked about something else. She had read *Ancient Cities*, and thanked him for having been almost a genius in the reconstitution of a strange, grandiose and vanished life.

But he was no longer thinking about that. All the force of his thoughts was nourishing within him the invisible flower of his amour.

In Psyllene's company he made a tour of the Louvre. Continually, with regard to everything, she questioned him. In order to charm her, he populated the perspectives with picturesque crowds emerging fully armed from his imagination. He visited the ruins with her, explained the mystery that they contained, the occult wealth and the profound philosophy. He evoked an entire civilization. He did much better, for her alone, than he had done a few days earlier for the millions of readers of the journal. He resuscitated brilliant epics. She was amused by them.

Then they left the ruins. They went along dusty paths, between roses and violets, under the azure and the sun.

He expressed to her gradually, in soft phrases, the collapse of his pride. But Psyllene listened without replying.

Then, with a discreet fervor, he read in her, in a low voice, the living poem of her youth and beauty. She became grave and mysterious, but did not reply.

Finally, having become tenderly authoritarian, amorously dominating, he put on that irresolute soul the red seal of a kiss. Immediately, she raised her splendid eyes toward him, vibrant in her entirety, and loved him.

Midday was burning the air.

On the Ganges a light mist trembled, as pale and transparent as tulle.

Outside the gate of the subterranean Western station, a few patient and silent Hindus seemed to be waiting for a prodigy, still distant but announced.

The time went slowly.

Finally, a bell rang; a rumble was heard approaching, and a few minutes later, an entire crowd poured out noisily into the square.

The Hindus, baggage-carriers and vehicle drivers, raced forward, competing for the clientele; the latter, confused, tried in vain to choose between the arms that were offered for their service; the Hindus took possession of luggage, shouted the name of a palace and preceded the strangers at a rapid pace. Quarrels broke out amid the tumult, and then the crowd gradually dispersed through the streets.

Already, no one any longer remained when two young silhouettes emerged from the subterranean station, narrowly enlaced, into the blazing sunlight.

Slowly, they headed toward the river.

There they bumped into a cacophony of shrill offers from merchants of fruits, owners of boats, ferrymen and cloth-merchants, all calling to them simultaneously. Sumptuous sails were hoisted up masts, grating, amid the harps of rigging; red, yellow and green silks were displayed, crackling, in luminous pleats; cherries, almonds, oranges and bananas shone like jewels in large brown hands; there were threats, laughter and growls; and all that noise rose up, overlapping, simultaneously bitter and plaintive.

The young man pointed a finger at one of the sailing-boats; the young woman smiled; they both went down the white steps that led to the bank.

The bright blue crests of the gentle waves of the Ganges, the surface of which had a dark emerald color, splashed and broke along the parapets.

The foreigner called to the boatman; the later inclined a plank above the side of the boat toward the quay, and the two lovers went down.

"Dionel," murmured the dazzled young woman, "look how beautiful it is over there!"

"We'll be there soon, Psyllene, in a moment."

"The water's singing; listen..."

"You'll see what an ancient city is; a picturesque agglomeration..."

"Unhealthy?"

"But fantastic. India is the only country that has preserved its primitive aspect. You'll be able to imagine what Paris must once have been. It will be a beautiful dream that we'll live together."

"Oh yes!"

"Dear Psyllene!"

"How beautiful it is! And bizarre! And vast!"

The sound of a kiss flowered in the tumult of the preparations.

The sail offered its curve to the softness of the breeze, and they set forth. Slowly, the boat glided over the viscous surface.

The racket of the city died down now; all the way to the horizon, in an uninterrupted perspective, the errant crowd could be divined between the buildings, always similar, but it seemed distant henceforth. The silence of the water stifled its cries and appeals into a murmur.

Avidly, Dionel's and Psyllene's eyes searched the scenery in front of them.

Everywhere, a swarming beauty, unexpected, colorful, emerges from both sides of the river; in magical distances, amid heavy shadows, a people is agitating, demented and exalted. Human beings seem smaller there, by virtue of their very abundance, facing their strange work, their staged city, with bizarre architectures in which all the lines collide, and the colors, in wild fantastic harmonies.

In that assembly, formed of temples, palaces, private houses, shops and sheds, nothing is perceptible at first but a jumble of marvels: here, brown towers quit the background in bright enlacements of straight lines, numerous and vertical, which terminate in a crowd of painted sculptures, narrowing their form at the top into a frenzy of shafts and spires, delicately pointed; there, perspectives of asymmetrical façades open and close, following one another with abrupt follies of forms and colors; further away, there are tumults of roofs, in heaps of fruits that are stones and battles that are colors, scaling the skies.

Along the façades the sunlight dances, throwing rainbows and perfumes on to the balconies and overhanging terraces. Ox-carts glide through the heart of the streets, slow and heavy.

Toward the water and plunging into it, all along the banks, life is heaped up, more visible, noisier, more agitated, in broad, massive pale brown constructions, the color of roasted almonds, with frayed corners, hollowed out by numerous stairways, squeezing into the shadow of walls, buttresses and pedestals, extending into profound black corridors like tunnels; and all of that is swarming with Hindu silhouettes clad in silk or rags, cashmere or linen, rich or verminous, but always with a picturesque splendor.

Heavy and poor fishing-boats are lined up against the quays, beautiful in the primitive roundness of their broad hulls, the colored mats laid out between the bamboos, and also their parasol-roofs, the straw of which overflows in irregular tufts. And amid the shadows at every moment, the almost-complete nudity of an Asiatic body looms up like a bronze statue, scarcely draped with a few rags, but with slow and grave gestures, cresset curves and pure rhythms, the head upright beneath the turban, and the lynx-like gaze plunged in the enigmatic dream of that contrast: swarming life and the certainty of nirvana.

At intervals, under the clustered heaps of large parasols, steps rise up to assault the sculpted slopes, on which the most implausible things are being sold.

From time to time, in the rapidity of a slender boat, aristocratic groups glide past, with robes of brown, pink, green or violet silk, beneath turbans. And the water, scarcely rippled by a gentle breeze, rolls its paste of precious gems, scaly here and there beneath the sun.

The boat, impelled by eight light oars, slowly heading upstream, northwards, arrived almost at the extremity of the city. Psyllene and Dionel had remained silent for a long time, ecstatic, devouring the landscape with their eyes.

Finally, the boat came about. The shiny water blinded their curiosity. They took their places behind the sail, glad to find lukewarm shade there, and questioned one another with their gaze at length, amorously. In order to express what they thought, words seemed futile; they admired one another through all the vibrant joy that they had just seen; they felt glad to be alive.

And the oarsmen heard, mingled with the splashing of the luminous waves, the double and fervent murmur of multiple kisses.

VIII

It was already four days since the airship carrying Neick and the French scientists had departed. Berlois, collecting avidly the news that he expedition sent back, furnished the *Western Europe* with important correspondence by the hour. Hardly quitting his work-table, he calculated, in his moments of idleness—slow intervals of fever between dispatches—the chances of his friend's success.

The endeavor seemed to him to be superhuman; it seemed crazy, but marvelous, to seize the steering-wheel of the globe in its course through the abyss, to dare to replace the blind force of the world by the curt desire of an infimal brain. It transported him with enthusiasm, and although, at times, he doubted the possibility of success, he hoped for it nevertheless with all the force of his soul, all his impatience extended toward the imminent moment of glory when science would finally attain the supreme goal of its grandiose destiny.

He thought about that…he thought about it incessantly…and innumerable cigarettes burned between his fingers.

He did not even hear the electric bell announcing Dionel's visit.

The latter, seeing him so distracted and so distant, thought that he ought to reveal himself by means of a burst of laughter.

"Well, dear friend, what's happening?"

"They're all there; they've reached the pyrrilic point and the works are about to commence. But what's the matter? You don't seem to understand. Don't you know anything, then?"

"About what?"

"What! You, his nephew, don't know?"

"Is my uncle…?"

"You don't know?"

"I confess."

"But where have you come from, then?"

"I've been spending some time far from here"

"But the entire world is interested in it…have you been dreaming?"

"I was in love."

This time it was Berlois who burst into laughter. But Dionel was already questioning him avidly.

The story of what had happened during his absence, and above all the incredible and triumphant folly of the departure, raised in his soul the same exclamations that Berlois had previously heard in the resonators during Neick's speech; however, the eventual enthusiasm of the crowd found no echo in the young man. He formulated his opinion clearly, summarizing it in the statement: "Humankind is committing suicide!"

But Berlois protested: "On the contrary, it's commencing its veritable life. The interstellar voyage will be, for us…"

"Death!"

"The total affirmation of our grandeur..."

"We'll die!"

"All our curiosities will be satisfied..."

"We'll die before having quit our orbit! Without having had the time to learn anything whatsoever, without even knowing the joy of the slightest success, we'll die!"

"However, your uncle..."

"My uncle must be mad to propose this infernal adventure, and those who have approved it are blind and naïve!"

"Dionel!"

"But we can still stop him, prevent him from committing this crime. It's our duty. Let's catch up with him."

"You doubt his genius, then?"

"You're defending him? His absurd dreams have intoxicated you to that point? You, Berlois?"

"Listen...!"

"But it's mad, completely mad!"

"Understand that it isn't me alone who is speaking. All the scientists in the world have acclaimed your uncle with enthusiasm and have promised him their support. All the scientists in the world!"

"Imbeciles, rather. Well, let's not waste time. Adieu!"

He left.

At first, reflecting on the means that he could employ, he drew away at a rapid pace, with no precise goal.

Rain was lashing his face; he did not even perceive it. The overwhelming absurdity of what his uncle was attempting was buzzing in his head and casting a dense mist before his eyes. In the depths of that mist he glimpsed the old man who he had previously admired; he represented him vanquished by age, devoid of strength and tremulous, striving toward the criminal goal of his dream in blissful unconsciousness, surrounded by blind but numerous and powerful admirers. Oh, how could he convince them? Stopping the old man would not be sufficient to paralyze their common will, impelled—by what prodigy?—toward this gigantic work of death. What could he do to prevent the triumph of science, equivalent to the murder of crowds, a multiple crushing, the complete and abrupt assassination of humankind? What could he do to save the world?

In spite of his anxious haste, Dionel had directed his steps, without taking account of it, toward the great Montarguis perfumery, where Psyllene worked.

He went around the high stone buildings and headed for the glazed gardens where the necessities of labor retained the object of his dreams.

He went in.

In front of him, in a kind of immense greenhouse, the cubical glass cases reserved for the cultures were outlined in four regular rows. In each of them was a single flower, but of supernatural proportions. Men and women were moving around the glass cases, regulating the play of radiance.

In the distance, he recognized Psyllene. She was slowly turning a large radiator, forming a star of blue tubes and emitting light similar to moonlight, over the face of a glass case. On the opposite face of the same case, he distinguished a smaller red radiator rotating very rapidly and launching something like a beam of fire at the flower. The flower, like all those arrived at the maximum of excessive growth, was about fifty centimeters high and was oscillating slowly on its stem, resplendent with colors and heavy with perfume.

The poetry and mystery of those floral splendors, strangely alive around him, gripped the soul of the enervated visitor. He could not have explained himself the emotion that he felt, but he was dominated by it, and in order to escape that imprecise, but already tormenting, domination his soul needed a refuge.

Soon, he felt the fresh face of Psyllene against his cheek; immediately, his soul felt lightened; a new gaiety dispersed his fears. That was why, recounting the day's news to his friend, he presented it in an aspect quite different from the one in which he had initially imagined it.

As soon as the first words, moreover, Psyllene was rapturous. Neick seemed to her to be a god, for various reasons, of which the principal one was, to tell the truth, his relationship with Dionel.

The latter, in spite of the resolutions he had made a little while before, could not help sharing, gradually, the enthusiasm of his mistress for the audacious conqueror of the day. He certainly conserved, in the depths of his consciousness, the desire to prevent the realization of his uncle's fantastic dream, but that dream, at present, in spite of its apparent absurdity, seemed to him to be beautiful.

So, in spite of the phrase he had hurled at Berlois—"Let's not waste time!"—he wasted a great deal of it, not wanting to quit Psyllene until he had obtained a promise from her to accompany him in the journey he was projecting to catch up with his uncle—a journey that, in his hopes, would save the world, but in his speech, was merely an admiring homage to the man who had announced the conquest of infinity.

IX

"Yaoo…! Yaoo…! Yaoo…! Boldly! Yaoo…! Lower down and further to the right! Yaoo…! Han!"

The metal screeches; a chain falls; with the sound of a gong, the apron of the machine is embedded in the bare ground; the levers stop; the hammers strike; the bolts are screwed in, one by one. Already, from the nearby hangar, the transporter is rising up, in a barely curved trajectory, like a gigantic throbbing grasshopper.

The workmen stand aside. Suspended in the air, the enormous mass advances, directed with precision toward the metallic apron.

Under the grim blackness of its extended wings, around which six helices are vibrating in vertiginous motion, the huge Guilfard coil can be distinguished beside the conductor, inert like a prey between the steel claws of the vice, destined to launch into the depths of the earth, all the way to the mass of pyrriline, a protected current of 80,000 volts.

Neick, who is watching alongside the workmen, counting on the victory, finds the slowness of the approach desperate.

Nevertheless, he is sure of success. Thanks to the protected currents—which is to say, active currents surrounded by a secondary neutral current formed of a beam of Ohl rays—no obstacle can annihilate, diminish or deflect the principal current. In spite of the thickness and density of the earth's crust, the latter will traverse it, bearing afar the formidable realization of its possibilities as easily as light traverses the space between the sun and us, admittedly with less rapidity, but with all the more rectitude and more obedience to human will.

Already, floating in the light, the Guilfard coil is descending; four men rush forward; he transporter stops above them.

Prudently, Neick directs the maneuver; he commands with a precise word, a prompt gesture, and communicates the joy of his pride to all those surrounding him.

The transporter draws away.

The hammers fall again on to the ringing metal, with rapid blows.

The sun, descending toward the horizon, is already caressing the copper and steel angles with red gleams, while the labor is slowly completed.

Finally, the Guilfard coil stands up, framed in the rock, triumphant and scintillating on its broad pedestal. The strip of rocky terrain that advances beneath it in the form of a prow, seems to quiver with delight; the blue air, with a more abrupt fracture, designs it edges; the entire promontory resembles a enormous ship ready to set forth over the waves.

The sea is motionless, however, devoid of splashing: there is dead, stagnant water between the land and the ice-sheet, and the later is still very close, in spite of the recent and multiple conquests of the works.

Several times already, with explosions of thermogenite, the décor of snow and ice had been punctured; several times, a large area of terrain surrounding the hangar had been laid completely bare, and a considerable zone of the atmosphere had been warned, but the cold, a persistent enemy, came back. It transpierced the nerves with sheaves of needles, eroding the effort of the will at its very source. In vain, further thermogenite bombs annihilated its sly power, always vanquished but always immortal; each mass of air whose temperature had been temporarily modified burst like a bubble and was opened wide to the repeated assaults of the glacial wind; everywhere, the crystalline claws and bright teeth of the cold tore at the atmosphere. But the human beings struggled heroically; wanting to master nature, and, tenaciously, they tamed her.

Some distance from the promontory, the fantastic forms of moving icebergs raised seracs with sharp crests and luminous white caps, like innumerable challenges. Neick and his men sensed the hatred of the region, virginal for so long and still forbidden to humankind, accumulating around them, but they had faith that he would be victorious in spite of everything.

Far away, beyond the jagged horizon, other crews were working as fervently as them, extending all their efforts toward the realization of the same single idea. Above the ice-sheet, in the distance, little airships glided from time to time, and one divined, among the blocks of immobile whiteness, the copper cable on which they were keeping watch.

At the other end of the cable, exactly at the terrestrial magnetic pole, a Guilfard coil similar to the one that had just been placed here, ought already to be fixed. Neick was awaiting the certainty of it impatiently, because, once the two coils were connected by the wire, a single gesture would suffice to launch the current underground and to realize the prodigy for which he was hoping with so much fervor.

The work having been terminated, the crew retired to the hangar and waited. Hardly anyone spoke; everyone seemed to be preoccupied with a great dream, the calm hope of which attenuated its exteriorization.

Today was the thirtieth of May, and in a few hours, the country would be entirely plunged into darkness; for about six months obscurity would dominate the entire extent, which already seemed paler and more frightening, with its tranquil horror. Neick was glad to have been able to bring the work to a successful conclusion before the long and sinister polar night, for if there had been any delay, it would have been necessary to work in the dark, and although it was so ardently beautiful, the task would have seemed cruelly disappointing.

The light outside paled; the distances became blurred, as if in a nebulous dream; dusk fell. The airships switched on their electric searchlights, and continued their relentless surveillance.

The hours passed.

Finally, a Hertzian wave caused the Gur hammer to move over the dispatch keyboard; bright stenograms were scrawled in the shadow of a screen. Neick read them, trembling with joy. Thirteen hundred kilometers away, as if before his own eyes, everything was in order. As soon as he wished, therefore, he could give the signal.

The darkness was now complete.

He had the Guilfard coil inspected minutely, and ordered, by telegram, all the crews lined up between the pyrrilic point and the pole to review everything meticulously.

One by one, the responses arrived.

Everything was ready.

Then Neick obliged those who had collaborated with his endeavor—and that rule only suffered the single exception of his friend Lignan, who was at the other end of the cable—to draw away from the apparatus as rapidly as possible.

For a few minutes, the sky was striated with various gleams; the airships, the electrostryges and the lepibolides, opening their large electric eyes, fled.

Shortly thereafter, there was the total silence and bleak void of space.

A strange emotion composed of pride, hope and anxiety stirred Neick's soul so profoundly that he felt himself go pale. For a moment, he remained motionless. Gradually, however, the blood resumed pulsing through his veins; he felt calmer, and, hope completely renascent, he extracted his eletrostryge from the hangar; he examined the motor, the cables and the wings one last time, and then placed it beside the metallic cabin in which the lever destined to launch the current underground was scintillating.

There was also a Naus transmitter in the cabin. In spite of the preexisting certainty of the result, Neick repeated the calculation of the hours; he found the known figure again. In accordance with the difference in longitude, in order for the two currents to depart simultaneously, Lignan had to lower the lever of the Guilfard apparatus thirteen minutes before Neick lowered his.

At the moment, it was eleven twenty-four.

Neick communicated to his friend by telegram the ultimate moment—eleven forty—and repeated his order to depress the lever immediately. Neick had to wait until eleven fifty-three.

The minutes dragged until eleven fifty-two. Neick did not take his eyes off the chronometer.

One more minute.

His soul suspended from the little needle marking the seconds, he counted the time that still separated him from the definitive gesture.

Each displacement of the needle marked in his agitated soul a pulsation of force capable of displacing the universe. He counted: "Fifty-five, fifty-six, fifty-seven, fifty-eight, fifty-nine..."

The lever was lowered!

Immediately, Neick leapt into the nacelle of his electrostryge. The motor roared, but the wings remained motionless. Panicked, Neick doubled, and then tripled the thrust of the motive force; no wing quivered...

He multiplied it further...

Then the bird made a bound, but fell back a few meters away, its wings broken.

While that drama was unfurling, the luminous antennae of a dirigible appeared on the horizon, the form of which was lightly imprinted on the night.

In the nacelle, steering the enormous oblong mass himself, Dionel watched the pale gleam of architectures of ice breaking up the horizons of the bleak expanses of snow.

Psyllene, alone and trembling, accompanied him, and like him sought to discover amid the desolation of that pale solitude the proud host of workers.

Suddenly, a frightful din resounded; an immense flame rose up into the sky in the distance, puncturing its dark crystalline blue with a fantastic red mane; one might have thought that a thousand craters were projecting into the night, in unison, the infernal menace of their terrible howl.

Psyllene, as pale as a corpse, collapsed on the floor of the nacelle, inert. Dionel, quitting the tiller, leaned over her, called to her, and, obtaining no response, seized her in his trembling arms, panic-stricken.

At that very moment, a hurricane seized the fragile balloon ferociously and drove it northwards with savage clamors.

X

The balloon skidded, skimming the ground, brushing the snow...

For a quarter of an hour, without being able to reach it because of its unexpected bounds, three electrostryges had been following it.

Finally, it collapsed.

The rescuers pounced.

Under the torn silk, at the bottom of the intact nacelle, they found two bloody bodies, whose hearts were still beating.

There was a habitation nearby, Psyllene and Dionel were transported there without regaining consciousness; they were laid in large beds covered with soft furs; they were bandaged; then, heavy fir-logs were made to blaze in the hearth not far away from them.

Fortunately, their injuries were not serious. The young man's right arm had been partly flayed, blood had flowed abundantly, but the wound, although large, was neither deep nor dangerous. As for Psyllene, she only had an insignificant cut on the forehead. She was the first to wake up. Without comprehending what had happened, her large eyes interrogated the unfamiliar décor that surrounded her.

It was a picturesque domestic bedroom, with low windows and a large round fireplace, in which logs were crackling. At the back of the room, an ictium lamp was burning, spreading its soft light among the browns of tapestries and the blues of a mosaic, the reflections brushing a few heavy hunting trophies with vivid light. Two men and a woman were there, talking in hushed voices, seemingly paying no attention to her presence.

Psyllene sensed the warmth of the furs around her; she tried to lift herself up, but, not being able to succeed in that, she made an effort to look to her left, searching for the rest of the reality that she divined, trembling between her lashes; but she saw nothing more; slumber, full of imprecise dreams, weighed upon her eyes again.

"I think she moved," sad a voice.

A shadow crept toward the bed, while one of the men called: "Nika, let her sleep! She's still weak..."

But the woman was already examining the invalid, gently pulling the heavy covers over her again.

At that moment, Dionel asked for something to drink. He took from the woman's hands a glass that she offered him, and then, although the gesture made him suffer horribly, he extended his bloody arm toward Psyllene. He called to her, but his voice faded away, like a dull echo, in the silence.

Psyllene did not budge. Then, pale with fear, Dionel straightened; words were strangled in his throat:

"Dead! She's dead!"

His hosts hastened forward, trying to reassure him with soothing words, but he was not listening. With a fixed and dolorous gaze he contemplated Psyllene, whose breast was rising regularly. Slowly, he leaned in her direction, his entire soul trembling with dread and despair.

A few silent seconds went by. Then, mingled with the scarcely perceptible sound of respiration, he thought he could hear the heart that was so dear to him beating. Immediately, his fever eased; he forgot his own suffering. Finally, in an anxious voice, he questioned one of the men who had drawn near: "She's alive! She's alive, isn't she?"

"Certainly she's alive. But be careful; cover yourself up.

"That wound?"

"It's nothing."

"But then…what happened? Where are we?"

"Near Hamga."

"Hamga? What does that mean?"

"South of Wibecq, in Graham Land."

"How did we get here?"

"We found you in the nacelle, over there, near the shore, where the balloon was torn apart."

Dionel shivered; the tragic memory of that crazy course through the air and the vertiginous bounds that, for several hours, had launched the skiff of silk and cord from one abyss to another came back to him. He saw the bounding nacelle again; he heard the whistle of the tempest; he recalled the sheaf of fire on the horizon.

Then, in spite of his pain and his weakness, in spite of his hosts, who tried to stop him, he threw back his covers and, driven by an obsession, headed for one of the widows of the cabin. Without saying a word, he drew aside the curtain and, sticking his feverish forehead to the cold glass, he looked outside.

It was dark: the frightful and lugubrious night that he knew to be six months long, atrociously long, implacable and cruel. He gazed at the plain of snow over which the moonlight was gliding like a silvery mist. He had never seen it so pale.

One of his hosts approached, but scarcely had he darted a glance into the empty desert than he uttered a cry. With a finger, he indicated in the profound blue sky the seemingly-motionless moon. It really was the moon, the suspended mask, wan and sniggering; it really was our dead satellite, that snowy face, that dead face with the ironic expression. And yet—O miracle! O stupor!—its disk had diminished by half.

For several minutes, Dionel stared at it with immeasurably wide eyes; his pale lips were smiling. Without detaching his burning forehead from the moist panes, he murmured a few phrases slowly, like a prayer of gratitude and admiration.

"So he's triumphant! He has taken in his hand the terrible sheaf of the laws of the universe! At the whim of his will, he has broken them! His genius is directing the worlds in space! Already, the moon, obedient to his gesture, is drawing away from our eyes. The Earth is rolling toward the goal of which he alone has dreamed. Glory to his genius! Glory to him!"

The bell of the daily newscast let its pearly trill fall into the silence. Dionel turned round.

On the opaline rectangle, the first text that was offered to his eyes, in enormous letters, were the few words: *Neick, the most illustrious scientist in the world, is dead, the victim of his dream.*

Dionel felt an abrupt shock to his heart, but, straightening his head, he added, in a dead voice pierced by a dolorous pride: "But he triumphed."

PART TWO

I

Over the entire surface of the globe, special works had been carried out in order to ward off the immediate consequences, for the most part dangerous, that would doubtless result from the inclination of the Earth on its axis.

All the observatories had communicated their anticipations to the journals; the population of every country had been warned able he particular probabilities united in its destiny, and humankind entire was prepared for the tragic complement of its triumph.

When the ultimate day had arrived and the Wingallian waves had spread over the entire surface of the planet the order to be read, the name of Neick had risen from three billion breasts with enthusiasm and glorification, in a formidable acclamation, mingled with the craziest hopes.

There seemed, in any case, to be nothing to fear.

It was known that the electric current connecting the magnetic pole to the subterranean mass of pyrriline would provoke a considerable melting of ice, but, the conflagration having taken place at the South Pole and the lands of the southern hemisphere being quite distant from that pole, the ice melt there seemed less dangerous than if, for instance, it had been produced in the Arctic region, so close to the continents That was, in fact, one of the reasons that had led Neick to choose the South, in spite of the greater difficulty of transporting materials there Recognizing his prudence, people had been grateful to him for it; they admired him all the more and had full confidence in the new future that he had opened up.

Already, for several days, his name had been flying from mouth to mouth; the hymn of his glory was vibrating in the motionless sails of ships that had been lined up in ports, behind the formidable shield of immense granite moles. Thanks to Neick, all the oceans had become deserts again, as before the appearance of humans; all the harbors, by contrast, closing their girdling dikes with thick iron doors, were overflowing with innumerable hulls, light masts, sharp prows and heavy funnels the bright sunlit silhouettes of sumptuous metal organisms with a strange life and a mysterious slumber. Facing the sea and isolated from it, human power stood tall, dominating the waves.

From all the shores, however, human beings had retreated. Entire cities had been uprooted, house by house, removed hundreds of kilometers toward the interior of the lands. The savage rhythm of the breath of machines was united with the splendid tremor of a proud joy, young and directed toward the future like a beam of pure radiance. Hearts, like voices, were light and singing. Laughter punctured with multicolored rickets the black grandeur of mechanical breath, and the name of Neick, like a fanfare, bounded through the tumult.

The houses, although displaced, were abandoned temporarily. Great plains, far from the sea and from mountains, had been chosen to await the decisive moment. In savannahs, pampas and steppes, amid the rich fleeces of crops, and in vast areas of bare ground, everywhere was teeming on that last day with the swell of populations. Picturesque groups full of contrasts formed. Scientists in the midst of the crowds explained the reasons for the precautions to be taken and the reasons for their complete faith in the success of the marvelous enterprise. Transports of food supplies, distributing without counting, emptied the immense reservoirs of metallic balloons stopped overhead, and as soon as their provisions were exhausted, departed in search of others far away. Here and there, noisy conversations and laughter burst forth. The crowd populated, with its new and animate efflorescence, once-immobile horizons of fresh verdure and golden wheat.

The hour drew nearer. Early morning for the people of California, bright sunlight for those of Norway, nocturnal for

123

those of New Zealand, simultaneously spring for the inhabitants of the northern hemisphere and almost winter for those of the southern hemisphere, but unique in space, there was the same frisson everywhere, stopping in its solemn anxiety the hubbub of life.

The blood beat forcefully in arteries tightened around innumerable brains: the rhythm of a universal pulsation of a few excessively slow seconds. A fearful silence fell over humankind entire.

The minutes went by like as many centuries, weighing heavily upon the frail beauty of human hopes...

They were still waiting...

Still nothing.

Then, everyone was afraid; everyone acquired the certainty that the moment had passed, and in all minds disillusionment took root. A murmur ran through the crowds, amplifying as it progressed, into an enormous heavy wave dull of shadow and apprehension.

But, caught in the atmosphere like a network of invisible and miraculously serried wires, one phrase was voiced from one end of the world to the other, leaving, at intervals, like drops of blood, the red reflection of its fearful soul, clinging in brief gleams to the blue needles of Nelinso receivers.

The anguish of the multitude was torn into cries: "Neick is dead! Neick is dead!"

From receiver to receiver the news flew, like a bird of light with taut wings, a palpitating richness of vivid crimson; a prisoner here, it lit up a thousand new reflections in the distance, all identical, and, attaching the clarity of its specter to every mast, it traversed atmospheric space like an immense kaleidoscope. Three billion thoughts followed it, and then confronted one another, and there was consternation.

But already, along the coasts of Tierra del Fuego, Patagonia, New Zealand and South Australia, with a thunderous noise, tidal waves such as had never been seen before were rolling. Rocks, capes and promontories were destroyed, carried away, rolled over one another and gradually torn to shreds on the surface of gulfs, where liquid furies clashed, enormous and heavy, like mountains.

Then, among those who saw it, there was unbridled terror.

People killed one another trying to reach the fragile airships for which the hurricane was lying in wait; balloons were seen flying northwards to which veritable clusters of human beings were clinging, suspended from the nacelle, the rigging and he rudder.

Like a gunpowder trail, sinister and demoralizing news spread.

It was said that New Zealand had been entirely engulfed by the waves, that Australia was doomed to the same fate, that the water already extended as far as the Parker Mountains and threatened to surpass their crests; it was said…but what was not said? The true and the false were welcomed everywhere with the same promptitude. In the general disorder, people forgot to make use of telegraphic apparatus, and that was fortunate, for the fear thus remained localized, far from large masses of people. The most important of those were formed, in accordance with the particular reflection of each continent, in the plains of northern Africa, the center of Brazil, North America and the steppes of Europe and Asia.

But the tumult of the waters, with a vertiginous rapidity, launched toward the tropics, inundating the great surfaces of low-lying lands, bowling over obstacles, modifying the configuration of coasts, engulfing islands, destroying ships in ports by the thousand, and sowing terror everywhere with the din of its gigantic force, frightfully unleashed. Nevertheless, the distance covered attenuated its surge, and when the tide reached Senegal and the southern tip of India, it was no longer to be feared.

In the southern hemisphere, however, another danger menaced humankind.

Soon after the passage of the tidal wave, subterranean rumbles were heard. Millions of electrostryges, in order to escape the abrupt hunger of crevasses in the ground, had lifted an entire population into the clouds. The earth was trembling everywhere, and, seeing victims promised to its sly hatred fleeing, it rumbled every more, tensing its age-old muscles beneath the shaken plains, under the twisted plateaus and the high spines of mountains. Finally, the prodigious mass of the Andean Cordillera was seen slowly inclining westwards; with a hellish din, it crumbled, blackening the sky with an abrupt and tenebrous accumulation of dust and smoke, raising its heavy wall like a block of night, heavy, mobile and grim, against the blue palaces where the morning was smiling.

Soon, the wall of shadow was torn apart; trails of lava surged forth in red veins to the massacre of the earth, and spreading the conflagration far and wide. Forests caught fire, crackling, sinister and menacing; at times they seemed to be brandishing above their treetops an entire population of torches; then, suddenly, the wind bent the insolent tresses of the flame under its grim knee and rolled them in thick waves through the sumptuous extent of foliage still intact.

Here and there, humans devoted themselves to opposition. Confident in the fragile musculature of airships, they bounded above the immensity of the furnaces and threw ixilnate bombs into the midst of their frightful red tide. Then, amid the brushwood there were patches of green light. The conflagration, shriveling its blood-colored volutes, recoiled before that other power; in vain its horses reared up, shaking their manes of sparks; those lakes of livid light, fallen from the sky, were insurmountable. Gradually, the flames died down.

Then, throughout nature, there was a quieted rumor, punctuated by dying voices; the whistling of the tempest diminished, lost in the distance like the noise of a crowd, and only a few brief, almost stifled, rumbles responded in the depths of the ground.

Like a swarm of bees, the electrostryges descended again. Humans recovered confidence. The earth no longer frightened them.

Only the murmured threat of a new cataclysm still murmured from time to time on the horizons.

The multitude was calm now.

It was then that, transmitted by Hertzian waves and collected by the antennae of a few electrostryges still suspended in the air, the first news of other peoples reached those of South America.

Departed from Alaska, where it was night at that moment, the telegram gave, without any account of terrestrial phenomena, the first astronomical news recorded. It resulted therefrom that the moon, projected far from our globe, had become almost invisible in space, and that, to judge by the new stars appearing on the horizon, the Earth must have emerged from the plane of the ecliptic.

A "Hurrah!" like a rumble of thunder resounded; people shouted, they clapped their hands; like a hurricane, human joy bounded beyond the bleak horizons, light, enthusiastic and irresistible. The dispatch, continuing its course, was already registered in the distance, among other crowds; it was acclaimed there again.

The name of Neick, in a triumphant clamor, succeeded the applause; then there was delirium; all arms were raised, agitating hats, tools, branches, handkerchiefs, scarves, clods of earth and clothing; and that living forest seemed to be on the march in the atmosphere of the sun.

II

One of the first ships that ventured again into the immensity of the oceans was the great submarine *Riguir*, sent to gather news by the editorial staff of the *Western Europe*.

It was a fine and elegant ship, eighty meters long, with an articulated hull, two rows of fins and a radiumnic engine of the latest Fobliret model. Sometimes, at the level of the waves, it glided like a torpedo, armored with flames and steel; but its own life, organized for operating at great depth, slowed the trepidation of its frantic soul on contact with the atmosphere.

Since the departure, although it was moving in the open air, no human silhouette had dominated it; the purring mystery of its engines made it a sort of conscious and redoubtable monster.

That day, in addition to its ten-man crew, it carried Monsieur Adicourt, the engineer to whom it owed its miraculous existence, Monsieur Birmé, a geologist, Monsieur Junkel, an oceanographer, and four reporters, to wit, Messieurs Aumerx, Langenet, Minn and Berlois.

With the objective of studying the possible consequences of the upheavals produced at the surface of the globe, that small group, brought together spontaneously by the common and generous idea of rendering service to humankind, had embarked in the port of Frega—the former Gulf of Lion—on the morning after the collapse of the southern part of the cordillera.

Cleaving the blue nacre of the sunlit water, the *Riguir*, clad in heroic light, bounded over the mane of the waves like a mad conqueror of fabulous lands. When it had surpassed the Azores, it dived.

Above it, the waves shone for a long time, in seemingly virginal expanses; the horizons resumed the grandiose and unsubjugated aspect of the origins; everything became calm and silent again.

However on the distance indicator in the room between decks where the majority of the passengers were gathered, a needle quivered. From time to time the travelers noted thereon the number of miles traveled.

Only three hours had gone by when they had already reached the coast of Central America.

Adicourt, who had not quit the engine room, ordered an ascension to the surface of the sea. The centrifugal pressure which was two atmospheres in the armored carapace of the vessel, and which served to maintain equilibrium with the exterior pressure of the atmospheric column combined with that of the height of the water, diminished progressively. The noise of the engines was modified; a few flywheels slowed their rotary fury, or even stopped. Others began to turn. The ship climbed, as if lifted up by an invisible force.

When they could finally see through the portholes the movement of the waves and the rutilance of the horizons, the *Riguir* was near the eastern entrance of the strait of Panama. It was alone today in those waters, once so crowded. The sea was beautiful and tranquil; it raised its multiple sensuous breasts in the luminous intoxication of the mild air.

At one of the starboard portholes, Birmé and Junkel were chatting. Before them, bright shores were profiled, suavely enchanting, but over which the crushing certainty of death seemed to be hovering, with a dolorous smile.

"The day before yesterday, all of that was buzzing with human beings," said Junkel, in a melancholy tone. "Behind those curtains of acacias and palm trees, the tumult of active life rose up like a joyous hymn. Today, fear reigns there; silence weighs upon the flowers."

"But tomorrow…"

"Alas! After such a past of joyful pride!"

"It's of the future alone that it's necessary to think. In any case, as soon as the crowds have entirely repopulated these regions, the sea will once again be resplendent with white sails. For centuries, humans have never been more completely victorious! And I'm already rejoicing in the spectacle that will be offered to our eyes by those rejuvenated peoples, proud of their new energies. You'll see that it's an era of splendor that is germinating here!"

The two men fell silent momentarily. Before their eyes the landscapes vanished as the porthole fled, rapidly traveling alongside the wall of the interoceanic canal. They heard beneath them a curt order, and the dull sound of armor plates rotating on their metal hinges.

Before the port-side portholes, each of them registered, by means of precision apparatus, the geodesic particularities of the landscape. Aumerx, Langenet, Minn and Berlois composed for the journal, in an astonishingly rapid fashion, the new relief map of the region.

When they emerged from the strait they turned southwards, but the vessel had only covered a few miles in that new direction when the compass began to oscillate.

"Your charts aren't accurate," said the engineer, approaching Berlois, who was noting at that moment the configuration of the coast they had just quit. "The disturbance of the telluric currents is preventing us from determining our exact position; we're going along the coast at hazard. You can ascertain the approximate design of capes and gulfs, but bear in mind that it's without any precision of longitude and latitude. Even the sun and the stars can't serve us as a basis, and as long as the new movement of the Earth isn't in correlation with a new equilibrium of specific figures, notions of time and geographical measurements will inevitably be false."

Berlois had quit his apparatus. He agreed, and thought about means to attenuate by some discovery the present disorder of his calculations.

"What about atmospheric vibrations?" he suggested.

"They're modified too. Everything that could previously have a value of unity has been subject to the effect of the oscillation, and has become useless. Extraordinary seismic socks have been signaled in Europe and Asia; all scientific theories are crumbling, and the most important of our industries, based almost exclusively on the employment of currents, will already have been arrested."

"But we've been notified in the regular fashion, so the Wingallian currents that are transmitting news to us haven't been deviated."

"Between transmitter and receiver, no."

"But then, the problem is solved; let's establish a system of meridians and parallels formed by those currents; the old frames of geography with thus resume their primitive value, and we'll be able to reconquer the exact sciences one by one."

That proposal, submitted to everyone and approved, formed the text of a dispatch that was sent to the journal immediately.

With the certainty that numerous brains would study the project and would soon render its realization possible, the men of the *Riguir*, while awaiting news from Europe, occupied themselves with other tasks.

First they followed in its capricious meanders a fairly broad arm of the sea that, plunging into the overturned lands, was bristling with new islands and crashing its waves into unknown capes.

On the flanks of sheer mountains, as well as along the waves, amid the chaos of red and black rocks, the tresses of creepers were tangled, still rich in orchids. Palm trees, broken under the weight of avalanches, twisted their elegant foliage amid heaps of granite, or remained suspended from vertical walls, their trunks snapped cleanly, and pouring their generous sap into the thirst of abysms. Here and there, masses of minerals, sumptuously spangled, scintillated in the sunlight and crystallized in pearls of light. In depths of somber vegetation, the nests of eagles evoked by their tattered splendor, full of open claws and bloody wings, the abrupt atrocity of their fall. The cadavers of monkeys, bears, guanacos, alpacas and vicunas were scattered by the anger of the elements, the wealth of furs and the elegance of muscles stilled forever.

Commenting on the tragic spectacle, Birmé, standing with Adicourt, Aumerx and Langenet, recalled in brief and muted phrases the last study voyage he had made to the Cordillera; a kind of religious respect stopped his gestures when, evoking an ancient décor, he pointed at a landslide, a ruin, a precipice or a charnel-house. Berlois, Minn and the others widened their avid eyes and exchanged rare exclamations, but sometimes, they all fell silent, listening to their hearts beat.

The ship having arrived almost at the extremity of the fjord, turned about and veered toward an islet as fresh and green as emerald; one might have thought that a new vegetation had accumulated there of mosses, lilies of the valley and ferns; a kind of spring smiled there; the entire island was nothing but an enormous block of copper sulfate.

The *Riguir* regained the open sea. It doubled a cape of high rocks, traversed a new archipelago and then, having attained the enormous solitude of the ocean, it dived.

There was then an inexpressible joy for Junkel, the oceanographer; a whole world of unexpected marvels surged forth before his eyes, in a strange tumult, in which life and death were confounded in a dazzling miracle of colors. With the motionless and divinely sculpted submarine flora, a swirling multitude of leaves and flowers was mingled, torn and faded but still pretty, scattering in their fluttering of wings and petals al the grace of the atmosphere drawn into the water. Branches still starred with mauve, crimson and scarlet united their sumptuous garlands with the glaucous suppleness of algae. The bodies of dead birds flowered with violent enamels the nacreous backcloth of mollusks.

Palms, ferns, insects and feathers fluttered amid the jewels of submarine life and harmonized with it. Leaves drawn by the currents curled up with the fragile softness of corinthian acanthi; broken wings, in their spinning flight, recalled the murex with the rainbow colors. Dead butterflies floated in the waves like pink and yellow tellins in the green-tinted light of that enchanted land. Gliding through the soft blue depths, helmed in enamel and opening large phosphorus eyes, fish hastened, attracted toward the new shore by the mass of dead flesh. In numerous bands, all armored with magical reflections and cutting through the water with the nervous beat of their fins, they moved in a sly and menacing silence toward the land. Crustaceans followed them, slower but more tragic, opening innumerable pincers toward the foggy distance full of cadavers.

And that living tide, like an army on the march, scaled another, motionless life, in order to reach its goal. Among white and green madrepores, violet jellyfish and the white and pink mollusks, the crustaceans went forth with their oblique gait, heavily, and the fish above them, sometimes breaking up their tightly-knit bands, traversed the compacts group of algae with an undulating motion.

Junkel examined all that, especially glad to encounter a few rare species, and also noting the particular disposition of certain bands of predators attracted far from their place of origin, trying to penetrate the mystery of their collective life.

When the vessel approached the coast, it was soon surrounded by such a cloud of mobile sand that it became impossible to distinguish anything under the sea except for the rapid passage of a few sulfurous fins and the glinting eyes of barely-divined sharks,

The *Riguir* returned to the surface.

A series of green hills extended along the horizon. An immense and tranquil gulf was dormant under the blue sky and impregnated by the tranquil beauty of eternal things. To judge by its general form, however, the shore did not correspond to any line on the map of the world, and that entire gulf had only existed since the cataclysm—which is to say, for scarcely two days. There had stood, for thousands and thousands of years, the imposing and grim Cordillera. The water here was presently profound and calm.

The passengers of the *Riguir* decided to set foot on land. The vessel dropped anchor; an automobile boat was detached from the davits and danced on the water.

They decided to establish a luminoscope on one of the surrounding summits in order to communicate with the rest of the world, and to note, at the same time, the new topography of the region.

After a few hours of marching, the little troop reached the summit of one of the highest hills. Around them, as far as the eye could see, somber forests extended, dense and scarcely interrupted in places by luminous teeth of the sea. In the distance, a snow-covered peak inclined.

"This region has been spared," said Berlois.

"It's quite probable," replied the geologist, who happened to be close to him at that moment, "and even almost certain, that thousands of cubic kilometers of earth and rock have slid, almost intact, into the profound hollows of the primary terrain; only the secondary and tertiary have been disaggregated, and probably, for this location, following a shallow slope, have been uniformly directed westwards; hence the slow collapse of the surface and the general inclination of these terrains in the direction of the ocean. What you see around you is perhaps a landscape that previously existed far in the interior of the continent, at an altitude of two or three thousand meters. Now this same landscape is touching the coast; it doubtless occupies the placement of ancient quaternary escarpments, and its altitude is no more than five hundred meters at a maximum. But what do I see...that red mass down there?"

"One might think that it's a bridge."

"Indeed. Say, Aumerx, pass me your binoculars, I beg you. It seems to me..."

"Here."

The geologist looked, and then exclaimed, in a tone of joyful surprise: "That's what I thought! Look, then! It's the Linarezo Bridge! It really is! Look!"

It was, in fact, the Linarezo Bridge, one of the most remarkable constructions of South America; it was listing at present; one of its extremities even seemed completely twisted, but it really was the gigantic bridge, known to all, the same one that, twenty years earlier, had been erected at the astern entrance of the Andes, not far from Surna, on the great gyroscopic monorail line that linked the two great oceans, parallel to the tropics. Dragged by the land, it had been displaced about three hundred kilometers toward the west, and the hypotheses that the geologist had formulated relative to the slippage of the entire region toward the Pacific were confirmed.

The little troop headed for the bridge.

The village of Surna, previously enlivened by a picturesque life in the shadow of the colossal architecture of iron, was presently crushed between two blocks of the mountain; the houses, for the most part, had been reduced to dust. A few metallic roofs lay on the ground among twisted beams, blocks of polished and sculpted marble, and a thousand objects too small to be crushed in the vice of natural forces scattered there, intact and dolorous, attested by the vanity of their forms and their various utility the minuscule life of civilization.

A penetrating melancholy was emitted by that spectacle; a silence as overwhelming as a mourning weighed upon all souls.

"Should we install the luminoscope?" proposed Adicourt, the engineer, in a low voice.

That was an excellent diversion.

A quarter of an hour later, Langenet leaned over the transmission keyboard of the apparatus and translated into telegraphic language a succinct account of the voyage of the *Riguir*.

When he had finished the description of Surna in ruins, he stopped the emitting current and connected the reception screen to the cirmean needle. Everyone watched.

Firstly there was a dispatch from Mungo in central Brazil, in fiery letters; it announced that the damage caused in that city by the earthquakes was almost entirely repaired. Then came news from Helioville, in Morocco, Kinun, in North America, and Scienville in France. The directors of the *Western Europe* thanked the members of the expedition warmly and promised within two days the establishment of a complete network of Wingallian rays in conformity with the idea suggested by Berlois.

Finally, they learned by means of telegrams arriving from various points that the Urals and the Himalayas had become redoubtable centers of further cataclysms, but that all precautions had been taken and nothing was to be feared for the populations.

Gradually, all that news excited the little scientific committee near the Linarezo Bridge, and the melancholy of the crushed village, although it was so close, vanished in the joy of an ardent and noble struggle of thought plunging wholeheartedly into the sumptuous darkness of the future.

As evening approached, they resolved to return to the *Riguir*, whose black mass was bobbing up and down below them, at the whim of the slow respiration of the waves.

By the time that the first stars were appearing on the horizon, the vessel was already gliding through the opaque depths of the sea, intoxicated by vertiginous speed, toward distant and red southern Africa.

III

When Dionel and Psyllene returned to Europe they found everything there utterly changed. Since Neick's death they had followed the news of the journals with an impatient curiosity, and certainly expected to traverse cities that were partly destroyed and noisy with laborers, but their imagination would never have been able to anticipate the desolation of certain spectacles or the enthusiasm of certain crowds working frantically on the reedification of their endeavors.

The airship that was bring them back first passed over Mega, the richness of which, displayed on the bright plateaus of ancient Spain was dear to their eyes. Before their departure, innumerable golden roofs had scintillated there, scattered in the contemporary fashion amid verdure and covering immense areas with their multiple gleams.

Dionel loved those spacious cities, all on the surface, and contrasted them gladly in his meditations with the high and tightly-packed hives of ancient humanity. Mega, where thousands of ailettes, as light and capricious as feathers had rotated over the houses also had the particular charm, in the eyes of the artist, of concentrating all the value of its life uniquely in the energy of the sun. Those mobile ailettes could be seen everywhere, obedient to light, spreading the mystery of their movement, decomposed in an infinity of mechanical devices; everywhere, like an amber liquid, the sun's rays, captured and domesticated, slid like threads for weaving between invisible but sure fingers; everywhere, heliomotors hummed, aspiring dancing pearls of light from dawn to dusk and transmitting their vibration through fibers and crystals to the metal points whose labor enriched the delicate artistic sculpture of Megalian jewels, universally reputed.

Today, however, the light vibrated in vain, rebounding unused from a few intact houses in the middle of crumbled districts; not one ailette was rotating, and the crystal Gall transmitters remained immobile everywhere; the delicate life of that artistic métier had been completely abandoned.

Nevertheless, the fever of labor was buzzing all around; but it was now a rude and rumbling labor such as the region had not heard and seen for centuries. Everywhere, that reconstruction was hastening; enormous electric cranes were shuddering, with rumbling, menacing, thunderous voices, and human clusters circulating at their bases resembled anxious ants about to be crushed.

The airship passed on.

Huge agricultural machines like insects with long legs and armored mandibles appeared in the distance on hills, in mauve shadow.

"They seem to be alive," Psyllene remarked.

"They are, or very nearly, in my opinion."

"Look at that one to over there the right; one might think it's a dragonfly."

"It's a radiumnic harrow. It goes back and forth without a driver; look how light and pretty it is; one might think that it's about to take flight. And there, between its eyes, which light up in the evening, its radium motor is vibrating mysteriously."

"Exactly where the brain would be!"

"Yes. In fact, isn't that motor, which all its muscles obey, the equivalent of a soul? Isn't its mechanism as beautiful as that of a conscious life?"

"Might it be that our brain also contains a species of radium?"

"Who knows?"

"Look, it's turning now; it's going up the hill and going away."

"Two others are moving along the valley down there..."

The air was calm, without the slightest wind; from time to time, the noise of the rigging mingled a brief and plaintive note with the conversation. The snowy caps of the Pyrenees soon extended beneath the nacelle, and there, in adorable virginal light of the white summits, there was a soft silence, the illusion of an eternal peace.

But Scienville, already visible in the distance, reflected the calm splendor of the daylight in the pride of its metals, and offered the grandiose spectacle of a construction site broader than all the horizons, full of enigmatically motionless black forms swarming with humankind.

The airship descended.

Then, all the silhouettes of machines, which might have been thought initially to be incapable of movement, became animated. Dionel and Psyllene, as well as all the other passengers in the airship, leaned over in order to get a better view. Beneath them, about twenty kilometers apart, were gigantic towers with mobile terraces, bristling with connecting-rods, levers, funnels, concentrating in complex but regular movements the exteriorization of their power. On suspended rails, gyroscopic wagons were going from one to another, with the dull purr of their ebony double flywheels, reminiscent of enormous bees heavy with booty. From one minute to the next the platforms of the towers went up or down noisily, turning and screeching on their steel pivots, or inclined slowly and placidly like the decks of ships.

Further away, on the two banks of a river, high marble walls rose up, several meters thick, retaining the force of the element in their vice; the level of the liquid mass, thus suspended and imprisoned, was elevated some ten meters above the surrounding terrain; on the horizon, a barge retained the water, and an immense, furious cascade could be heard roaring there, tamed in order to serve as the motive force of distant and invisible works.

Then they saw an expanse of savaged land: thousands of houses destroyed and forests uprooted, partly lost in fissures in the ground; and amid the runs, active crowds, willingly forgetful of the past because they were already rich with a more beautiful future. Lost among those thousands of enthusiastic and fraternal souls, however, a few souls were still mourning, for there had been victims here, the earth had swallowed cadavers. All precautions had been taken, as they had elsewhere in the country, but in vain; the possible collapses of mountains and constructions had been anticipated, and the population had dispersed, here as everywhere, into the plains, but abysms had opened up abruptly and closed their frightful jaws again in a matter of seconds, and in spite of the rapid wings of electrostryges and the instantaneous effort of instinct, people had perished.

Thus, from place to place on the surface of the globe, the surge of matter had taken its revenge on the dominant multitude. The deaths were few, but there were some; it was the ransom of the triumph.

The airship carrying Dionel and Psyllene was floating at present above a newly-installed metallic Jevoninan network. Like an immense spider-web it displayed in reflected light the parallel threads of copper, at the junctures of which, on platinum sphere, the blue green and red flames of signals danced. Not far away, electric, radiuminic, hillian and psorial factories were throbbing, proud of their force, raising radiant shadows around them like the breasts of tigers.

Half-hidden by the horizon, the sun was setting in crimson splendor, while the crests of the Alps were outlined clearly in the pale eastern sky. Several telescopes were turned in that direction, scanning the landscape, when Psyllene uttered an exclamation.

In the distance, in the direction of Mont Blanc, she had just perceived a black mass of strange form amid the snow, bristling with tentacles like some monster of legend. At first, Dionel could not explain what it was; intuitively, he divined some new human glory amid that mass of virginal whiteness, without understanding as yet its precise form of its vulgar utility, but he suddenly remembered having read the description of an observatory that ancient people had built here; he recalled the collapse of that fragile structure, and concluded that what he was seeing today was probably a new observatory.

He had guessed correctly. At an altitude of 4810 meters, a marvelous cupola sheltering the most improved astronomical instruments now stood. Thanks to the prodigious machines that humankind now had at its disposal, four days had been sufficient to hoist up to the summit of that incomparable pedestal the materials necessary for its construction, and a few hours to assemble the pieces of the cupola and place the meridionals and equatorials on their complex pivots.

Everywhere beneath the airship, which was flying like an arrow, the activity of populations, in the din of their new labor, attested in its multitudinous frenzy to the possibility of the most fantastic realizations. Everywhere, the tumult of voices, the hammering of implements, the palpitation of fire and the spirals of smoke fusing and rising into the sky like a sublime incense, were audacious, ardent and crazy, the total expression of the human soul.

The light vessel slowed its progress; it was approaching the place where, in fabulous times, the immense flower of stone known as Paris had expanded its prodigious corolla.

Directly above a flat area covered in grass, the airship stopped. The hoist, detached from the nacelle like a boat, descended to the ground carrying four passengers, including Psyllene and Dionel. As soon as they had set foot on the ground, the hoist rose up again, carrying a new traveler.

Those whose journey had ended listened to the sound of the engine throbbing overhead and saw the mechanical bird drawing away in the already darkening sky, gathering speed.

By virtue of a kind of amorous superstition, Dionel wanted to see the Louvre again, where he had encountered Psyllene for the first time. He submitted the idea to her; she was charmed by it, and she interrogated the landscape with her eyes, triumphantly. But there, where they both remembered having followed peaceful paths between fields of roses and violets, they saw a moving spectacle. A panicked crowd, trampling the flowers, was running with gestures and screams toward the very place where their radiant amour had been born.

They ran forward too.

The Louvre had just collapsed, and there was talk of fifty people dead and wounded, buried beneath the ruins.

Already, seven cadavers had been pulled from the rubble and five mutilated bodies still alive. Two crews of workmen manipulating aspirators and dredges were gradually clearing the western part of the ruins, the only sector that had not yet been searched.

Great shadows gliding over the walls were deformed, multiplying tragic silhouettes.

A silent terror now floated over the crowd. Only the magnetism of eyes, attached to the gestures of the rescuers, expressed the thoughts of all, divided between hope and mourning.

Soon, a further four cadavers were extracted; they were frightful, unrecognizable, torn and bloody.

Psyllene hid her face in her hands; then, turning her head, she moved away, running, as if crazed. Dionel followed her, questioning her, trying to reassure her; he heard her murmuring: "Save us! Save us!"

"What do you fear?"

"That! Those cadavers. The blood! Those crushed chests!"

"They're a long way away now. There's nothing but flowers here. Over there is Daxwone's house, clad in wisteria and honeysuckle."

Psyllene was trembling. Her wide eyes, in which the flame of fear still burned, were fixed on a horizon populated by red specters.

Dionel spoke to her softly. One by one, he dissipated her fears, and erased the horrible visions that had formed there from her imagination.

In the meantime, the sunlight set the flowery house toward which they were directing their footsteps ablaze, gradually idealizing the surroundings. The golden laughter of the light seemed to be issuing an invitation to their two amorous souls.

A house of dreams! An oasis of beauty! It seemed to them to be increasingly in conformity with their happiness, increasingly intimate and symbolic...

When they arrived, it was the very Eden of their thought that was harmonized there.

IV

It was not, as they had thought at first, Daxwone's house. They went into it anyway, and were made welcome there. Here, as almost everywhere, for a century, the motto "All men are brothers," a welcoming phrase that had once been inscribed above doors amid florescences, was today profoundly engraved in hearts, and the Prasseno family made it a pleasure to receive the visit of the two young strangers, agreeable to them in every way.

A light meal offered to Dionel and Psyllene with a fraternal amiability broke the slight sheet of ice almost always surrounding the ardent and multifaceted enigma of character between strangers, in spite of the greatest courtesy. With joy and confidence, all of them were soon displaying the richness of their souls, opening the gilded caskets of their past, unveiling the mystery of their dreams.

Monsieur Prasseno was a philosopher; more than anything else he loved scrutinizing the probabilities of the future, but as his guests were attached with a visible avidity to the news—extraordinary, moreover—of the present, he took them into his library and showed them some very curious films. In a few words he explained to them what had happened in Scienville since their departure; with the aid of the films he even reconstituted before their eyes the spectacle of elapsed hours and translated in a dozen photograms the important news from the rest of the world.

It was thus that they were able to witness, in imagination, the perilous ascent of the materials destined for the Mont Blanc observatory. They saw the copper ladders that were to serve as bases for the humming flight of gyroscopes clinging to the sheer walls of rock, dominating the forests, crossing torrents, moraines and fields of snow. They saw the heavy mass of wagons rising up with a vertiginous rapidity. They saw clusters of workmen floating in mid-air, suspended by metallic wings, enormous radiobubbles and giant transporters. At the very summit of the mountain they saw crews rushing, in a swarm of tenacious wills, to assault the ultimate crests and finally leveling them, in order to plant the triumphant pride of iron walls there.

Then Prasseno showed them the reconstruction of the mole of Niga in Australia.

In a prestigious décor quivering with palms, the harbor wall extended, full of broken ships with hulls gaping like over-ripe fruits, losing their torrential wealth like sap. Amid the broken masts and the twisted decks, the armor plating having been ripped away like scales, the foaming waves were bounding. Of the protective mole, nothing remained but an indistinct line, irregular and jagged, at water level. But already, along the quay, dredgers were being set up, taking possession of wreckage of every sort and depositing it in heaps behind them. A host of workmen were carrying out the triage, loading electric trains that were ready to depart. In the meantime, other workmen, on mobile bridges, were bringing the caissons necessary to repair the mole, three-quarters destroyed, under the water. And all of that was vibrant; thousands of arms and thousands of breasts, with exclamations of strength and athletic gestures, realizing what one unique brain had conceived for the wellbeing of all.

A few minutes later, another cinematographic projection reanimated the distant life of Japan. In that country, as in India and in conformity with the customs of antiquity, houses had still been agglomerated, built high and not very solid. In consequence, during the secondary earthquakes, there had been numerous victims; the inhabitants, having no fear, had remained enclosed in their high cities of stone, entire districts of which had suddenly collapsed.

Dionel and Psyllene watched the reconstruction of one of those districts. The work, carried out by night, reminded them of the picturesque scene at which they had marveled on the banks of the Ganges; the play of the light even added an incomparable charm to it. As if in a mysterious enchantment, light and shadow were displaced, throwing from stage to stage, amid the unfinished sculptures and the tumult of builders, mobile dragons, the color of moonlight, against backgrounds of black lacquer, soft drapery bordered by reflections of scintillating enamel. One might have thought that the age-old soul of those strange buildings had suddenly been liberated, and was fluttering anxiously in search of a shelter among human beings.

While contemplating that spectacle, the young couple and their hosts evoked memories or emitted new and interesting opinions regarding that curious land. Madame Prasseno knew it well; she had lived there for several years and could give logical reasons for the apparent eccentricities of the people, both strongly attached to their traditions and highly refined artistically.

While she took pleasure in recounting anecdotes exemplary of what she affirmed, her husband stimulated the interest of the conversation with occasional remarks, redirecting it to ideas of general interest that were familiar to him.

"You'll soon see the proud joy of these populations transformed into fear and hatred," he said. "The future seems to me to be pregnant with menace; and don't forget that it was the scientific aristocracy alone that decided to shift the world from its orbit, and that, by virtue of its monopoly of glory, it now assumes all responsibility."

"What has it to fear, then?" asked Dionel, while Psyllene, drawing away from him with a smile, followed Madame Prasseno toward a few Japanese ceramics.

The old philosopher followed the two silhouettes with his gaze; then, drawing closer to the young man, he continued in a low voice: "A few years from now...but first let's observe that what we called *years* previously, outside the terrestrial orbit, will have a variable value without any signification..."

"Certainly."

"Some time from now, then, our sun will no longer be anything in our sky but a pale and vain star; we shall be plunged in the cold obscurity of interstellar space..."

"But what does it matter? By mans of thermogenite it will be possible to reheat a large enough fraction of the atmosphere; we can also dress, if necessary, in kyrial fabrics; we can easily resist temperatures of a hundred degrees below zero. And as for light..."

"But that's not all. Remember that the seasons will also be disrupted, that there will be abrupt shits in temperature, redoubtable hurricanes, frequent disorders in terrestrial magnetism, in the chemical composition of the atmosphere, in the distribution of the liquid masses on the surface of the globe, in the tides, already subject, since the sufficient distancing of the moon, to the unique influence of the sun, but susceptible to obeying other attractions later. All of that will disturb life, and interrupt human labor. Eventually, the displacement of continents, eruptions of lava, earthquakes, and a thousand unexpected cataclysms will destroy again what people have reconstructed in recent days. There will be a perpetual, demoralizing struggle, and nature will be stronger than us, that's certain."

"We'll struggle. We'll be strong."

"It will be necessary. Before your uncle's departure for the pole, I did everything I could to oppose the realization of his project. Henceforth, it's a matter of being heroic."

"The people we've just seen at work already are."

"But in an unconscious manner. Our superiority over them is in knowing our situation, simultaneously splendid and frightening, Let's fight; let's fight with all our might; but above all, let's make sure that enthusiasm subsists in the hearts of the multitude; it will be our duty to remain calm before those people and to hide the atrocious reality from them, when necessary, with a tranquil gesture and a smile on the lips."

Dionel wanted to respond, but the two women came back, and the old philosopher had already stood up.

"The night ought to be beautiful now," he said, opening a window. "See how bright it is."

Everyone approached and raised their eyes.

The sky was splendid. Already, the ancient constellations were displaced and unfamiliar stars were shining above the horizon.

"And we'll see others, much closer and more beautiful," said Prasseno. As we're traveling through space at a hundred and ten thousand kilometers an hour, the stars will succeed one another in darkness, always renewed, and every night will have the beauty, for us, of an inestimable treasure, accumulated for a long time by the gods and finally revealed to humans."

"What glory and what splendor!" exclaimed Psyllene, enthusiastically. "But you're not saying anything, Dionel. You seem worried? What are you thinking about?"

"I'm dazzled. I'm admiring. The future will be marvelous."

V

For several days an extraordinary animation had reigned in the offices of *Western Europe*. Supplementary crews had been engaged, and two thousand people, on average, were there day and night. All the receivers of news had had to be duplicated; all the machines of composition, transmission and multiplication, functioning relentlessly, were scarcely sufficient to accumulate texts and distribute their three hundred million photograms to the world hour by hour.

From the top of the edifice to the bottom, the phoneteurs, the luminoscopes, the stigraphs and the zenometers were rattling amid the loudness of voices and the vibration of bells. Silent elevators were gliding from each of its forty-five floors to the others, carrying groups of editors, uniting the various tumults. Everywhere, light hammers, fragile levers, slender needles and minuscule wheels were palpitating with artificial life, and fixing figures, phrases curves and light of every color on screens, in frames, on spheres and on sheets of paper. One might have thought that in that colossal tower, from the depths of the earth to the luminous cupola and the sky, all the delicate and mysterious vibrations of eternal matter were coming together, delivering their imprisoned, palpitating and fearful souls into heavy human hands posed on keyboards.

Everything was going marvelously. However, Monsieur Werton, the journal's editor-in-chief, was nervous and anxious. Isolated in the top floor of the building, in the middle of the control room, he seemed absorbed by a dolorous meditation, and his right hand, doubtless beating time to the agitations of his soul, was tapping and scratching the leonine heads sculpted at the golden angles of his armchair.

In front of him, on a small table of pink marble, beside the communication screen, the copper cornet of a microphone was shining.

After an interval of reverie, Werton pressed one of the buttons of the screen with his index finger; then, leaning toward the microphone he asked: "Is that you, Eberignac?"

A voice, as loud and clear as if his interlocutor were in the room, although transmitted from beyond the ocean, replied: "Yes, it's me."

"Hasn't the *Riguir* signaled yet?"

"No, not yet."

"No dispatch?"

"No, we have no news."

"No indication?"

"Nothing."

Werton applied his thumb to another point of the screen, launched the same questions a thousand kilometers further, and obtained the same responses again. He addressed six of his informers. Still nothing. Always nothing.

Then he stood up and paced back and forth, and his bony hands, united behind his back, clenched.

The room in which Werton was pacing was circular; the vault where the daylight was strangely imprecise amid sulfurous yellows and turquoise blues, applied the equator of its hemisphere to a ceiling about a meter high, which measured a dozen meters in diameter. That partition of translucent glass, divided by parallel circular meridians, bore an exact and colored image of the terrestrial globe. At present, only the northern hemisphere was visible, but Werton stopped, placed his foot on a metal bar that emerged obliquely from the base of the wall, near a cleverly dissimulated exit to the floor below, depressed the lever to floor level, and thus caused the cupola to rotate completely. It soon stopped, offering to his eyes, on an illuminated screen, the southern hemisphere of the world.

The divisions of the cupola, each bearing in its frame a mobile and numbered screen, were eclipsed by the screen in question every time news reached the journal relative to one or other of the areas that the divisions of the map represented. At the same time, when communication between the two screens was established, the voice of the microphone announced, in a headline formula, the news registered.

At that moment, only screens 74, 87, 28 and 231 were lowered. As they only covered parts of the map corresponding to continental regions, Werton judged it unnecessary at first to interpret them. Nevertheless, a few minutes later, he established the communication, and the silence was immediately broken by several voices bringing news.

"128: Intense cold"

"31: Volcanic eruption."

"87: New radium deposits."

"74. Florane Bridge completed."

Other information followed:

"198: Work interrupted."

"226: Earthquake."

"164: Eruption of Chimborazo."

But Werton was scarcely listening. He cut off the current to the sphere, and then telephoned his South American and southern Asian correspondents again.

The *Riguir* seemed to have disappeared.

No news of it had been received for forty-eight hours. The last dispatch to reach the *Western Europe*, dated the day before last, had been sent from the coast of Patagonia.

In order to escape the anguish that was already torment-ing him like the certainty of a catastrophe, Werton left the control room. Stopping on the floor immediately below, he experienced a reassuring joy in the tumult. Gradually, the mul-tiple activity of the environment, suggesting new rhythms to his thoughts, brought him back to the clearer and more proxi-mate details of his life; he took an interest in the functioning of the transmitter disks, repaired a broken apparatus with his own hands, questioned the workers regarding the details of their tasks and encouraged them with complimentary words.

Then he went down to the floor of the Wingallian receiv-ers.

There, fourteen large rectangular panels were lined up, placed vertically between copper bars. Numerous stenograms were fluttering on those panels like butterflies of light, imme-diately transcribed by a mechanical keyboard on sheets of cilium recording paper, which a few workers hastily slid be-tween the claws of a rotary machine. The texts were then clas-sified and combined in order to be absorbed by the Gurst multiplicator and dispersed soon afterwards in a new luminous form.

Slowly, Werton went from one screen to another; some-times, he read the latest stenograms transcribed on the pages or examined the regular trepidation of the machines with an attentive gaze.

Suddenly, he stopped, his eyes fixed on the next-to-last screen. His heart beat violently; he had just read the latest dis-patch from Zemgalafo, a small town on the east coast of Afri-ca, signed by one of his friends on the *Riguir*.

When the luminous text had disappeared he had the printed copy handed to him, and read it in a low voice several times. O joy! Adicourt, Birmé, Junkel, Minn, Berlois, Aumerx and Langenet, all his friends, and all the crewmen of the

Riguir, were alive! They were on their way to Europe. In a matter of hours, he would be able to shake their hands.

Happy and impatient, Werton hastened to communicate the good news to all those who passed close to him; for a long time he talked about nothing but the explorers whom he had believed to be lost, and, trying to explain their two days of silence, he formulated the most unlikely hypotheses regarding the dangers they might have encountered in their travels; but those hypotheses only served to augment his joy in knowing that they were safe and sound and getting closer to Scienville by the minute, closer to him. He consulted his watch continually; he would have liked to make he hands advance more rapidly.

As he calculated that a minimum of another two or three hours would go by before their return, however, he strove to distract his impatient mind with serious work. He installed himself at a reception post and registered himself the texts sent from Europe and northern Asia. At the contact of that new order of ideas, he soon recovered the calm necessary to continue what he had commenced a short while before: the general inspection of the labor.

At that moment, his personal correspondence was brought to him. He scanned it rapidly, but nothing among the texts retained his attention. With the tranquil assurance of a man devoted to his quotidian duty, he set forth again.

From floor to floor he inspected the buzzing multiplicity of the machines and the moving tumult of people, all the gears of life and force, from which the prodigious beauty of the superhuman effort—the journal mirroring all the spectacles of the world—emerged continuously. In the feverish and enthusiastic atmosphere of the collective endeavor, of which he felt himself to be an active and useful particle, the hours passed without him perceiving them.

In the meantime, gliding under the waves at a vertiginous speed, the *Riguir* traversed the Indian Ocean, doubled Cape Guardafui, arrived at Suez, entered the Mediterranean and finally stopped in the port of Frega.

Werton was in the hall of the Gann multiplicators when loud acclamations went up in one of the neighboring rooms. He ran to see what was happening.

Seven electrostryges, beating their wings, had just lined up outside the windows and skimmed the grass with their last hops. Outside, on the terrace, Adicourt, Langenet, Birmé, Junkel, Minn, Aumerx and Berlois, emerging from their nacelles, saluted the *Western Europe* with joyful cries. More than a hundred workers responded with hurrahs, and the beautiful summer sun enveloped the newcomers in a light powdered with gold, rendering them similar to gods.

VI

Gradually, the movement of the Earth in space had been modified, and the consequences of that modification slowly became more evident.

Already, the length of the days had diminished progressively over the surface of Europe, Asia and North America while increasing proportionately in the continents of the southern hemisphere. The chill of an unexpected winter gained, by turns, Norway, France and Italy, putting its adornment of frost and snow among the efflorescences of June, strangling scarcely-formed fruits and partly-open flowers with fingernails of ice. The celestial horizon was also displaced. For European observatories the constellations of the zodiac were only visible at rare intervals, and incompletely. Thousands of stars once only visible north of the equator now shone at the zenith of Capricorn.

It resulted from that, in evident fashion, that the Earth, although still conserving its rotational movement, had risen above the plane of the ecliptic and was drawing away from the Sun in the direction of Vega. A new movement of north-south oscillation, the reason for which was not yet known, was troubling the division of days and nights, independently of its position relative to the sun. The dawn, inclining further every day from east to south, also seemed to prove the existence of a more general tilting movement not yet determined.

That morning, as the first gleams of dawn fringed the blue eye of the nocturnal sky with pink lashes, Berlois received a visit from Dionel. The latter, having learned of his friend's return from the first edition of the journal, found him already installed before his receivers, a cigarette in his mouth. The work-room was still solemnly silent; no ticking or ringing troubled the expiring night.

Coming toward Berlois anxiously and holding out his hands emotionally, Dionel was surprised to find him so calm. Had the accident reported in the morning news not happened? Or had the man already been able to forget the horrible adventure of the previous day, full of the tragic fear of death?

Not knowing what to think, Dionel multiplied his questions.

But Berlois smiled. "Yes, we nearly died," he said, "for two days we struggled and battled between the very jaws of the eternal shadow; for two days we were terrified; but fortunately, the vice unclenched; death didn't want us."

"But how did the accident happen?"

"Our error was to venture into that region without resurfacing and without diminishing our speed. As the *Western Europe* has reported, we were approaching the extremity of South America and were already preparing to double Cape Horn when the *Riguir*, then at a depth of fifteen meters, was surrounded by a dense swirling cloud. Our speed was such that even if we had wanted to, it would have been impossible to rise to the surface immediately; a few minutes would have been necessary to stop the propellers, and in any case, thanks to that very speed, we were cutting through the dangerous current as easily as an arrow flies toward its target. The obscurity didn't worry us, but suddenly, we felt an impact; most of our exterior portholes broke; we were almost all knocked over.

"When the first moment of stupor had passed, we observed that water was flooding into several of the vessel's sealed compartments, and that the danger, although not immediate, was considerable. We immediately slid the mobile metal sheets of the armor plating over the broken portholes, and by means of electric pumps we emptied the flooded compartments. Although the propulsion engine was still functioning at top speed, however, the *Riguir* remained motionless. The horror of our situation seemed desperate and overwhelming, but our instinct drove us to act no matter what.

"Thanks to our searchlights we saw in the port side mirrors that the prow of the ship was embedded in a mass of earth with a vertical wall. According to the old maps we possessed, no island or reef had existed previously in that location, but our vessel, planted in the object, was creaking. We reversed the engines, but to no avail; like a coffin, the hull of the *Riguir* seemed to us to be lugubriously narrow; the frisson of fear chilled us. Then, it was atrocious.

"For two days we tried to extract the prow from that accursed soil, which was gradually chewing it up. Finally, we budged. For four hours we were victims of hope constantly mingled with fear; our destiny oscillated between life and death. When it was possible for us to rise to the surface again, when we saw the sunlight again, without yet being able to believe in it…oh, then! How can I express to you what we felt? Our hearts were uplifted, like overflowing cups, all the way to our eyes, and we wept as we shook hands."

"Berlois!"

"Yes, it was like an intoxication of heroism that gave us a consciousness, simultaneously, of our temporary grandeur and our eternal fragility. What had saved us in fact, far more than our personal efforts, was the fortunate circumstance that the mass of earth into which we had been hurled was mobile. As you know, since the great tidal wave that provoked the collapse of the Cordillera, Tierra del Fuego no longer exists; the currents tore it apart, shredded it and scattered it, and it was a fragment of the former island that, dragged westwards, had blocked our path. The same phenomenon has been produced in Australia; enormous masses of earth have slid under water as far as a distance of several miles. Even at the Cape of

Good Hope, a block of three hundred hectares of the surface was detached from the continent and has been transported by the sea all the way to Cap Fria, situated two thousand kilometers to the north."

While speaking, Berlois unfolded a map of coasts newly drawn up by him and his companions. He explained to Dionel the changes in the direction of currents, showed him new gulfs, indicated the locations of vanished islands engulfed capes and collapsed mountains. Interrupting himself from time to time in order to command the new transmission circuits, he launched happily into a maze of reasoning about the probable form of future continents.

During that time the dawn had expanded and the daylight had broadened, but, even though the sky was cloudless, a strange penumbra persisted; first magnitude stars remained visible and without the artificial light one might have believed in the habitations that it was still night.

Dionel, questioned in his turn, recounted what he had seen in the Antarctic region at the moment when his uncle had been killed.

They talked about Neick for a long time.

Berlois recalled how, during the old man's last visit, the latter had begged him to confide his information post to him; he described him precipitating himself with a feverish haste toward the Wirs apparatus, crying to the journal the words that were crazy, but true. An unforgettable day! With enthusiasm, Berlois invoked the grandeur of the genius who, in that room, before the Gann multiplicator, now silent, had suddenly revealed himself to the world in the living apotheosis of his conviction and his theories.

The two friends contrasted their previous incredulity with the present results. Then, speaking about the future, they felt that they were minuscule in the face of the dream realized by that man, whose patiently ardent life and splendidly heroic death they recalled with emotion.

Finally, Dionel took his leave and Berlois continued his work. One by one, frost-flowers crystallized on his windows.

Some five hours went by in that manner, but the sun, already descending below the horizon, stained the pale shy. The days, lugubrious and cold, had diminished their duration by half. Soon, doubtless, as had once been the case at the poles, there would be complete night here, interminable and frightful...

Yes! And the cold! And death!

Berlois could not help shivering as he thought about it.

VII

The days were still diminishing.

Every dawn, more sinister and more belated than the previous one, spread a new anguish in the mute countryside and brushed the silent buildings with more alarming reflections. The increasingly chilly light seemed fearful of touching the earth, crackling with black ice. The last flowers were dead, the rich June foliage had crumbled, and winter, extended over Europe like a monster over a prey, was showing its claws.

Soon, the sun no longer rose over the horizon for more than an hour or two, between long and increasingly dark nocturnal intervals.

Already, fear, like a phantom, was prowling in the darkness, extracting strident cries from oppressed lungs.

Finally, the sun only colored a distant pale horizon, a corner of a forest like an army of skeletons, a motionless shiny pond, a hill with heavy forms, or an anguished river.

Then the night was complete and definitive.

Fear, riding the clouds, bounded from the west to the east, mingling with livid gleams a flying black mane.

Then, everything that remained in humankind of barbaric superstitions, weakness before the unknown and humility before natural forces was revealed.

Women, by virtue of the very delicacy of their organism and the sensibility of their souls, were the first to suffer all the terrors scattered in nature; they were the ones who lent a redoubtable form to shadows, clouds, trees and undergrowth.

They reawakened, in flashes of imagination, legends dormant for centuries in the mysterious grottoes of the night. Workshops of textiles, confection, art and fashion, archives, factories of tobacco aliments, jewelry, hothouses, garden and libraries were all animated, thanks to them, by the invisible but noisy wings of strange menaces, moving translucent specters with blue claws and green eyes.

Habituating to lamplight, human sight was deformed too, and trembled on contact with shadows.

Meanwhile, humans gradually distributed an artificial daylight over the world. Helium lamps, already more numerous than the stars, suspended from wires extended their beautiful globes of light between habitations. New ones were placed everywhere. Like immense spider-webs their networks extended, every larger, under the black dome of the sky, and ripped the darkness from place to place, but they could not join up as yet; their extreme rays, like tentacles, scrutinized the darkness and were lost therein.

During that time, the forms of fear became more precise; the hectic winds that blew over the woods and moaned in the mountains were charged with feverish tableaux by the popular imagination.

In construction yards open to all the sounds of nature, in the various workshops where men and women rubbed shoulders, in factories, among the apprentices and old men, excited imaginations came together in an atmosphere of willful ignorance, full of tragic curiosity.

Already, more terrible stories were being told in lower voices; the artificial logic of civilization gave way, in feeble minds, beneath the surge of primitive instincts, slaves of all terrors; the credulity of some was complicated by a strange hallucination, and there were people who believed in all sincerity that they had witnessed supernatural events that they had imagined in their dreams, or had simply heard recounted.

Some said that they had seen flame-colored dwarfs on the cupola of Hungerwood Observatory, who were dancing around and mewling in the darkness. Others claimed to have recognized, amid the waves of the Rhône, the green dragon that, according to the most widely credited stories, gnawed the bases of the metallic constructions plunging into the river, and many women already avoided the quays and no longer dared to pass over the bridges.

Places once frequented became deserted and lugubrious, simply because a mysterious story had chosen its décor there. It was thus that certain rivers, it was said, carried uninterrupted files of cadavers; it was thus that the grinding of machines, the thunder of hammers and the hiss of flames in furnaces designated certain factories, at a distance as fantastic and terrible animals, devourers of human flesh, which were said to be on the march toward crowds in the folly of horizons.

Soon, several industries confided to the hands of women stopped; the personnel became scarce there and they could no longer be replaced.

Little shadows among the larger shadows, innumerable rustling dresses, populated the night with their furtive steps, their fearful gestures and their perpetual hesitations. They clustered around brightly-lit places, watching the men work, comforted by the spectacle of a activity still insouciant, cheerful and proud, in spite of the legends, beneath the coffin of the sky.

At times, however, when the work slowed down, when a menacing shadow seemed to stop the gestures of the workers, they veiled their faces, uttered cries and fled into the darkness. Sometimes, they were encountered motionless, kneeling down and murmuring prayers at the foot of trees twisted by the hurricane; or they were heard in distant mists, appealing for help, without being seen. And at length, their fear, electrifying the atmosphere, twisting to the point of a shrill grinding the magnetic voices of the wind and the harmonious voices of springs, exasperating the life of spaces and horizons, was communicated to men, troubled their conscience and nourished the seeds of fear there one by one.

News arriving from Asia signaled the same phenomenon of collective suggestion, with its consequences: the folly of crowds and the horrors of massacres; orgies and suicides; and the bewildered flight of certain peoples across the tempestuous oceans.

In Scienville, about a quarter of the population was already demoralized.

In vain, photograms sent by the journals of Africa, Australia and South America proved the existence of splendors still sunlit; in vain the people of the southern hemisphere invited the others of the Earth to come and join them amid the glare of daylight and uninterrupted summer; an entire idle crowd became disinterested, constituting thus for the as-yet-intact strength of the workers of the north a perpetual danger of slow, obstinate and certain demoralization.

The philosopher Prasseno, making an appeal to minds that were still enthusiastic, tried to defeat the evil by example. He traversed the fearful crowds in person, spreading eloquent words of confidence, strength and hope therein. Others imitated him; but the fear gained ground, and even the apostles of will, courage and human omnipotence understood, with regret, that the highest qualities of humankind rested on unsteady bases, and sensed that they were vanquished in advance. They soon had the certainty that the beautiful theories for which they were struggling were irremediably condemned; nevertheless, they elevated them higher, like lighthouses, in order to prolong the agony and spread their splendid and generous light for a little longer over the black waves of society.

In order to save the ensemble of the population, they showed to the discouraged crowds the mirages of the austral hemisphere, full of peaceful beauty; they insisted on the fraternal invitation of distant peoples presently enjoying summer and the unchanging marvel of the light; they engaged people to emigrate beyond the equator, toward those distant countries.

But hatred was already eroding hearts and making their words seem dubious; ever more alive, popular fable, like a multiple enemy with a thousand imprecise forms and a thousand venomous mouths, rushed to assault he truth. Already, the horizon was populated by demons; it was said that thick darkness, heaped up in a wall, barred the roads there, and closed the sky, in order that the humans destined to live could not communicate with those condemned to die.

In reality, a thousand communications still existed. Between the tropics, day and night still alternated almost regularly. There was a real obstacle there—almost uninterrupted violent tempests—but in spite of the danger, ships crossed the equator incessantly, and innumerable telegrams, those transmitted by the vibrations of the ground as well as those confided to aerial waves, passed from one hemisphere to the other. In spite of that, stubborn ignorance substituted its nightmares for all the possible splendors of life, and did not want to listen to anything.

Finally, an event occurred that provoked an exodus. The school of Merimaut collapsed; several hundred children were buried under the rubble.

There was then a general terror in the night; disheveled mothers and half-mad men ran to the place where all their hopes had been concentrated, had lived with adorable gestures, had been elevated by little arms, curly heads and bright eyes looking toward the future.

The darkness was now full of cadavers, full of blood, and full of desperate cries.

The spectacle of the rescue operation was moving and frightful. By the light of lamps and torches, interminably, stretchers passed by, carrying marvelous flesh, kneaded from roses and lilies, but pitilessly condemned, torn apart, twisted and crushed by all the ferocious hatred and all the blind power of death.

Like a trail of gunpowder, the news spread. Many people saw it a sign of destiny.

Soon, on the lugubrious quays, at the edge of the sea, crowds surged, rushing toward boats and departing southwards.

Here and there, a man with a livid face and crazed eyes traversed the crowd with the cadaver of a child in his arms. People made way for him. He went on. But on the edge of the quays, he had to be retained; he would have fallen in the water.

In the dark, descending from the nacelles of airships, emerging from subterranean stations, everywhere, ever more numerous, silhouettes were outlined of the damned, carrying little cadavers in their snowy shrouds.

Soon, all the maddened crowds of Scienville were headed for the sunlit lands. But those who remained, in spite of the strength of their souls, were consternated. For a long time, silence hovered over the landscapes once full of tumult; for a long time, the mourning of the night seemed sinister and menacing.

Eventually, one by one, energies were reanimated.

Labor, movement and life reappeared; a relative calm equilibrated souls; but the wellbeing became more grave; facile joy was dead forever.

The probabilities of the future were discussed. They were full of menace. In vain the philosophers and astronomers tried to find reassuring perspectives therein; the mystery of infinite space was more powerful than their reasoning. In spite of the enthusiasm of past days, the crowd was now anxious. Already the name of Neick was mingled with murmurs of revolt and hatred.

The cold became increasingly intense; even in southern Europe it was necessary to dress in furs and kyrial, exactly like the inhabitants of Lapland. Around workshops and along the roads, reservoirs full of thermogenite were placed, equipped with a special apparatus whose trigger provoked continual explosions of a quantity of heat sufficient to reheat the atmosphere within a radius of two hundred meters.

Many industries having stopped, or only manufacturing what was indispensable, there was available motive force everywhere. It was all employed uniquely for the struggle against the cold and the dark. And as people had the pleasure of vanquishing those two hostile powers, they began to live more intensely again.

The news arriving from other parts of the world, moreover, augmented by contrast the relative happiness of the people of Europe. India entire was dead; its cities, devoured by fire, had framed with flame the bloody orgies of its leaders, still wallowing in the horror of ancient civilizations and adored like gods by a population of slaves. China, whose populations had precipitated, some crushing others, toward the great ports of the south, had seen thousands of egotistical and criminal wills swirling in the waves around departing ships. In Canada, forests had been set on fire in order to struggle against the cold, and all available forces had been deployed to vanquish floods.

As for the countries of the southern hemisphere, they sent more comforting news. In all the cities of Africa, America and Australia, numerous populations united their efforts and realized great and beautiful things; everywhere, the joy of living in the light augmented the audacity and the genius of multitudes.

However, the sun, becoming more distant by the hour in the bright profundities of the azure, was gradually paling; the summer was impregnated with a vague melancholy; the air, perfumed like a fruit, had a new and dolorous charm, divinizing here and there landscapes once harsh or dazzling with new, soft and fragile tints, mingled in delicate mists in suave harmonies, but their languor, infiltrating violent saps, poisoned them. The plants, thirsty for vivid light, were gradually etiolated; the flowers of the lotus withered when scarcely blossomed; some palm trees closed their fans with a chilly grace.

Humankind, happy to live in mild climates, was not yet anxious; however, death was in the air.

VIII

At Mont Blanc Observatory, thirty astronomers, whose teams manned all the observation posts in six-hour shifts, scrutinized the sky, photographed the stars and noted with minute exactitude all the particularities of the life of worlds, the reciprocal attractions and the complex movements of the heavenly bodies wandering in space.

Four great equatorials, turning silently on their axes, fixed their enormous lenses, in spite of the movement of the Earth, on motionless points in the sky. Under the cupola, in a religious silence barely scratched by the clicking of a few items of apparatus, the scientists held their breath, counting the seconds, manipulating micrometer gauges; the figures, lined up and coordinated, took on life under their gaze, and the hours, filling their brains with marvelous realities, seemed to them to be too rapid for what they had to see, to record, to measure and to analyze.

Almost the entire sky was new to them.

The present situation of the Earth in space had modified the perspective of the universe in human eyes, and Vega, for example, which had previously been at mid-height in the celestial vault in June, as seen from western Europe, was presently touching the horizon.

Ursa Major and Minor, Draco, Corona Borealis, Ophiuchus and Virgo, all constellations previously visible and carried by the grandiose movement of the apparent rotation of the heavens, had, in being displaced in accordance with new curves, revealed a multitude of unknown stars. Near Arcturus, for example, three small red stars shone. Their spectra, analyzed, had revealed the presence of sodium, iodine, copper, zinc, potassium and hydrogen, but the exact determination of their chemical composition remained mysterious in spite of everything: numerous brilliant rays, not corresponding to any known matter, striped the enigma of colored bands; but the scientists, repeating the experiments, persisted in their sterile comparisons in the increasing hope of enabling verities to spring forth.

In the constellation of Ursa Major, a new point of light was displacing rapidly, having been recognized as a distant comet whose ellipse seemed to have for its focal point the second magnitude star Merak, at the inferior angle of Auriga.

Two nebular neighbors apparently followed identical curves, and seemed to be comets in formation.

A large nebula had also appeared among the stars of Ophiuchus; it was very similar to that of Triangulum, once visible from September to April, but its spectrum, newly examined, differed from it completely. It was a gaseous mass of spiral form situated some fifty trillion leagues from us, and whose radiance, previously absorbed by the night, had not been detectable until now even by the most powerful telescopes; thanks to the displacement of the Earth, without the few million kilometers traveled by our planet having diminished significantly, the distance separating us from the said nebula, it could now be distinguished with the naked eye. It seemed, therefore, that the obscurity of interstellar space, seen from a new angle, became less opaque: that shadows once thick and impenetrable had become softer, milder and more accessible; and the logical hope of penetrating their secrets, one by one, was already implanted in minds like the pride of victory.

Gradually, too, the night was becoming more translucent. One by one, the stars were acquiring an extraordinary brightness; some formerly classified as second or third magnitude were shining in the new sky as Altair and Vega once had on the most beautiful nights.

Then, as if effaced from the sky by the black hands of night, the nebula of Ophiuchus disappeared, and some time afterwards, the stars paled again. The hypothesis of variable darkness thus seemed to be confirmed. Soon, the astronomers tried to condense the observations related to it into laws, and even established a provisional theory, according to which vague shadows, mobile in space, were propagated in circles around the extreme radiations of stars, like ripples in the surface of water around a point of collision.

They also coordinated new hypotheses concerning the relative size of heavenly bodies and their movements. Newton's law, verified many times, remained immutable in its grandiose philosophy, but was enriched by a few corollaries applicable to many problems of universal attraction.

The results of all the scientific research communicated from one observatory to another, confirmed, amalgamated and completed, suggested new formulas, further research and new discoveries; united in a single enthusiasm, genius multiplied its thought.

Outside, in spite of the obscurity and the cold, the life of the crowds also vibrated with ardent curiosity regarding anything connected with the enigmas of worlds. The sky, in its great ebony cup, offered to souls thirty for infinity the scintillating foam of its constellations, and the Earth, rolling in space, seemed to be quivering with a victorious elation.

IX

The night became more and more beautiful.

Several hours before, in the east, a blue light had appeared, placid and mild, inundating the countryside like a spring morning. All eyes had turned in that direction. The observatories having announced the visible formation of a new nebula, the news had spread, stimulating enthusiasm, and everyone had quit work in order to see it at the indicated moment. On the sea shore, on the mountains and in the valleys, everywhere that there had previously been the murmur of manufacture, the machines had stopped, sounds had fallen silent and, abandoning their tools, men and women had set forth toward the new spectacle.

On the terraces, amid the delicate architectures of palaces and villas, joyful and noisy groups, displacing statues, removing awnings and extinguishing lamps, were already preparing, with hectic carillons of laughter, for a fête in the darkness.

Soon, the perrons and the porticos filled up with a picturesque population, clad in red, gray, green and blue, murmuring, growling and swirling like a wave in a tempest or foliage in a forest.

On top of towers, in the mystery of tall metallic silhouettes brutally outlined against the sky, thousands of gesticulating forms appeared, like gnomes mounting an assault on the heavens.

All the buildings were crowded with people; all the façades facing eastwards, the windows, the stairways, the ladders, the galleries, the architraves, the capitals and the cornices were laden with human clusters.

On the peaks of the mountains, black patches perforated the snow, swarming with the gestures of crowds. On the hills, files of silhouettes, as straight as hedges, were animated by arms and legs. The plains were dotted by minuscule and isolated lives. Down below, in dense tides, multitudes were moving in ragged caravans along the roads.

Everywhere, there were eyes.

Then, slowly, the entire landscape seemed to incline toward the orient, where the blue morning floated; it rose; beneath it, the horizon darkened again, and slid toward the abyss. But a more clearly luminous patch, in the form of a crack, quit the lightly azured mist; slowly, it stretched out in the sky, modifying its contours like swirling smoke, and was then subdivided into three equal parts.

Berlois and Dionel, who were watching from the height of a terrace, leaned toward the crowd, the magnetism of which extended as far as them, impregnating their marrows with a frisson absolutely new to their senses. Certainly, it was not the enigma of the celestial spectacle that could have moved them thus; some thirty hours earlier they had been at the observatory themselves; they had seen the strange light born and grow from there, with emotion, to be sure, but without the nervous irritation by which their entire being was presently disturbed. Something was rising within them, coming from the crowd; their instinct was warning them.

At the moment when they leaned toward that undulating mass of assembled people, a murmur was born therein, faint as yet, but full of occult force, flying from mouth to mouth, clarifying from brain to brain, and thus forming a total emotion, sprung from a thousand various thoughts, a thousand personal emotions, in a singled deflagration of magnetism.

In order to disengage themselves from the present suggestion, the two friends discussed what they had seen the day before and sounded once again the mystery of creation.

Dionel, recalling the crystallization of gleams in space, formulated the hypothesis that, under a chemical action as yet unexplained, billions of atoms might have become incandescent, united in visible molecules, and exercising then, on all the new molecules encountered in space, a chemical or electrical action that rendered them similar, drawing them in their wake, and thus composing gradually, nebulas from which increasingly more-organized worlds emerged.

"That theory," Berlois replied, "excludes the idea of the void; it unifies the nature of space and only allows differences of density and grouping to subsist between the apparent void and worlds. That certainly seems seductive, but is perhaps no more than a clever play of your imagination. I even fear, the ancient philosophers being familiar to you, that you might prefer them to the conceptions of our own time. What you're expressing seems closely akin to what the ancients called Materialism."

"My uncle didn't believe in the existence of the void either."

"But what about Irbanasky, Nozelofem and Becourt?"

"Evidently, they're great philosophers; I admire their works; but in the final analysis, each of them is only valuable because of the logical beauty of his deductions, which only repose on postulations. Since philosophical systems, from century to century, have disputed the illusion of truth, I think that, without being a philosopher and without destroying what exists, one can construct new dreams alongside the old ones."

"Perhaps you're right…but look..."

"All philosophies…"

"Are literature, dear friend."

As he spoke, Berlois indicated, in the middle of the three nebulas, a few white steaks, newly formed, the curves of which seemed to be following one another in a slow rotation, still unappreciable, to be sure, around three fixed points that were still obscure.

"Look," Berlois continued. "The tissues of the fog, in their pale efflorescence. are harmonizing; the light, in places, is becoming concentrated, and what was only a sheet yesterday with a milky glow, when we saw it for the first time above our horizon, is being organized today, slowly and sagaciously; it will be a clear design tomorrow, and in ten thousand years it will become a planetary system."

"That's admirable," Dionel replied, marveling.

"Yes, admirable, indeed. And you're right, a thousand times right, to prefer a dream to a long sequence of reasoning. As we were saying a moment ago, all philosophies are literature, but how superior to all of that is true lyricism! Nature is prodigiously beautiful. What's the point of reasoning? Admire it! Sing its praises! Let's elevate our souls toward it, if we can."

In the shadow, as if in ecstasy, the crowd fell silent.

The blue clarity, gliding along the marble façades, caressing the metallic towers, brushing the waters and the woods, spread a gentle poetry everywhere, extremely moving.

An hour went by in the silence of nature; the creation of a world continued, and like a faint dream, the form of diaphanous image suspended from the enormous vault of the temple of Night gradually became precise, an exquisite flower.

At the centers of the three nebulas, three large, tightly-focused nuclei surged forth, almost as bright as masses of stars...

The bands of white light, scarcely outlined shortly before, were now quite clear, and prolonged in spirals.

PART THREE

I

Continuing its course through space, the Earth, its axial rotation gradually slowing, conserved a velocity of displacement still quite close to its initial velocity.

Through the abysms it rolled, rolled, rolled, and the extent and the duration surrounding it became infinity and eternity.

What did the ancient notions of time and distance signify henceforth for human beings?

However, judging according to the only known unities, about five years had sufficed for it to surpass the orbit of Neptune.

During those five years, the brightness and apparent grandeur of the sun, to the eyes of the inhabitants of the southern hemisphere, had diminished incessantly; the sky around it had darkened slowly; shadows on the earth had extended slyly, finally strangling the last twilight. Alongside the sun, other stars were born; fading into the night itself, it was no longer anything but a second magnitude star. The Southern Cross now dominated the richness of the constellations, and like the glint of a small diamond lost among fabulous treasures, the globe that had once spread its luminous sumptuousness over the Earth drew away, and was no more than a recollection in human memory.

The death of daylight had been very slow, almost insensible; minds had prepared themselves for it tranquilly, the example of the present life of the people of the North encouraging the hopes of the people of the South; and when the night, for the latter, was complete, they welcomed it at first without anguish. For them, the struggle against the obscurity and the cold was facile henceforth; the new procedures developed in Europe assured them victory over nature; without groping, without haste, without surprises, they had labored on the installation of the necessary networks, and when the moment came, they triumphed effortlessly. Other endeavors, too, also based on new methods, were easily pursued.

Helioville, Bazouga and Nieumargue, the three largest cities in the hemisphere, had become extremely prosperous centers thanks to the influx of population in recent years, and there beauty and wealth increased further by the day.

Great observatories had been constructed there. The one in Nieumargue, especially, was remarkable; it was rightly considered as the finest in the world, and some of its rooms seemed constructed by giants. Beneath its cupolas, telescopes a hundred meters long moved with facility on enormous pedestals; the humans whose slightest gesture they obeyed seemed minuscule beside them.

Other marvels had also been realized.

One of them, repeated throughout the world, ensured the protection of vegetal life and multiplied the promise of harvests. Large areas of land had been covered by series of inclined roofs, and cultivation continued thus, in spite of the night and the cold, in an accommodating artificial atmosphere.

Everywhere, a joyful activity reigned. In the cities, where thought seethed, the sciences and arts expanded in grandiose enterprises. In the forests, on river banks and on mountains, bridges, aqueducts and railways were constructed; everywhere, nature was disturbed; mines, canals and tunnels were excavated; the atmosphere was furrowed by winged aircraft and helicopters; the sea was full of ships.

Complete, definitive night did not stop anything.

The space explored outside the solar system enriched the treasure of human knowledge further with numerous striking discoveries, and every time that an enigma was transformed into precise figures and mathematical laws, a delight was added to the happiness of life.

However, more years passed.

The cold increased.

Ships were immobilized in mid-ocean; their prows, although fitted with ice-breakers could no longer succeed in traversing the ice-sheets, henceforth too thick.

On land, labor in the open air became almost impossible; furthermore, the normal reserves of coal became sparse. In order to resist, it was necessary to abandon the usual methods of heating and lighting, and employ the motive forces accumulated by the work in progress for those two purposes.

For some time, all métiers of art and all luxury industries stopped, lending their dynamic value, their currents and their motors uniquely to the production of heat and light. Over the entire surface of the planet, efforts were united in that direction. In the northern hemisphere, already, the cold had claimed victims. In order to struggle against it, it was necessary temporarily to restrict the needs of civilization, sacrifice intellectual voluptuousness and arrest progress.

But the winter became ever more rigorous; it was necessary to vanquish it, to create a new summer, to replace the sun by means of terrestrial sources of heat. It was also necessary, in order to avoid famine, to preserve from death the quantities of plants and domestic animals presently gathered in glazed parks, in the several thousand hectares of the surface routinely heated and lighted thus far. The slightest imprudence in that regard might have consequences that everyone, perhaps surpassing the logic of the reality, believed in advance to be irremediable. That struggle between nature and humankind might last for centuries; humankind was now its own god; and it was on human beings alone that the duty was now incumbent to organize the life of a world whose masters they believed themselves to be.

With a bitter ferocity and an implacable tenacity, winter encircled people, lying in wait for their death-throes, and weighing heavily upon their pride with the clear certainty of crushing it one day beneath its eternal power. Nevertheless, it was the people, at first, who had the illusory joy of triumph. Millions of wills were united; new shafts had been dug and new mines excavated in such great numbers that the supplies of accumulated combustibles were apparently adequate for centuries, at the maximum of necessity.

But that was not the case.

Several generations succeeded one another; the cold only increased; the combustibles were exhausted rapidly; once again, the regular work of the mines was insufficient.

Then, once again, millions of arms abandoned their habitual occupations in order to extract for the ground everything it might contain of calorific possibilities. The last deposits of coal and radium were excavated, peat-bogs were emptied; the search for bitumen, naphtha and oil was extended to incredible depths; finally, hectare after hectare of forest were felled.

But from generation to generation, the dread of a slow death became more general and was transformed into a certainty, into despair. Like the dripping water that hollows out a rock over the years, the obsession of the imminent end of the world gradually wore away all wills. Slowly, society disintegrated.

A new proletariat, egotistical and exasperated, forming the lees of a stagnant civilization, soon appeared in the cities, mingling with the fear of living the savage desire to kill; and that tide of base humankind, lifted by its destiny, clashed with the superior crowds, at first with indifference and then with hatred. Fraternity, the ancient counselor of peoples, no longer existed.

Progressively, life was crushed; the cities became silent, even deserted; all strength, previously dispersed, was concentrated around the social nucleus. The scientific aristocracy, isolated in a few rare gigantic constructions, seemed to lose interest in the bulk of the population. The latter, solely attached to working the earth, was enclosed in the warmth of hothouses. As for the underclass, for a long time it had neglected everything that did not serve uniquely its instinct of self-preservation.

One day, in a port in Asia, a few individuals suffering from cold and hunger took possession of a newly arrived ship heavily laden with European riches. After the pillage, they set fire to it.

Society, risking disintegration under the assault of egotisms, tried to defend itself; it arrested the malefactors and punished their crime by death; but analogous incidents recurred, and became increasingly frequent; evil was born; social laws once engraved in consciences were effaced, humankind became barbaric again; it was necessary to take up arms. Then there were battles, day by day.

As in antiquity, life became prey, fratricidal struggle a means of satisfying all the ferocious appetites reawakened in souls; in the name of their howling hunger, people dared to tear one another apart.

To begin with, hatreds, still imprecise, prowled around the temples of thought; journals, laboratories, schools and libraries, for the first time, were debated and judged; the plebeian crowd, increasingly numerous and ignorant, saw therein, it said, the source of its misery.

In workshops and mines the malcontents united. A few leaders, born of the circumstances, grouped in a frightening sheaf scattered jealousies, idleness in revolt and the vices of an entire menacing society, willfully blind and proud of its folly.

In the shadows, stoking the fires of revolt and sacrificing in advance the crowd obedient to their ferocious egotism, a few bandits calling themselves philosophers specified the grievances, concentrated the arguments, built theories and impelled action, promising everyone individually recompenses that matched the quality of his vices.

Thousands of individuals approved. Then, feeling that they were sustained, the leaders spoke more loudly, addressing crowds gnawed by doubt, long exasperate and hesitant; soon they collided with frankly hostile mass, respectful of the established order and ready to defend civilization.

The plebeian meetings became more numerous and more enthusiastic, the speeches more vehement. The aristocrats were reproached for their disdain for the vulgar; their labor, because it was intellectual, was considered insufficient; the proletarians even discovered therein a cowardly hypocrisy, a retreat from the collective effort. Violent orators designated them angrily to the vengeance of the people as proud parasites of society; they cited examples.

Had not Neick, by criminal caprice, dragged humankind entire into an adventure of which he knew in advance the atrocious price? He had done that for glory, by virtue of ambition and personal interest. And millions of people were dying for him! Had not other scientists, also hypocrites, also dominators, also egotists, in the name of science, crushed under their tenacious pride thousands of lives far more useful than theirs? Had they not made the docile people into a swarm of slaves?

And the need for vengeance, multiplying infamies, added to the realities; acclamations rose up thunderously; and an entire population, thirsty for carnage, showed the fist to the gigantic towers where thought, science and civilization were awake in the night.

Under the influence of a few blindly grim hatreds, class warfare, as in the early days of the world, wrapped in its menace precise wills and consciences already red with future crimes, and gradually crushed under the debris of the social soul ten thousand years of fraternal life.

When the revolt, seething and ready to vanquish, passed from idea to action, it was atrocious and insane.

In the observatories, in the palaces of physics and chemistry, in the studies of engineers and philosophers—everywhere, in sum, where science still assembled its faithful—murder and conflagration appeared. There was a red torrent, a whirlpool of bloody, disheveled shadows with torches and clawed with weapons, gasping with agonies, charged with clamors. Behind ramparts of dead flesh the still-throbbing beauty of the apparatus was attained; their copper, their steel and their crystal was shattered into a thousand pieces. People set fire to the curtains, to the furniture, to the walls; soon, the vaults beneath which retorts, heliographones, neplimeters and telescopes had gleamed were filled by flames and smoke. One by one, the temples crumbled, burying with gestures of religious splendor the heroic accumulation of half-consumed cadavers.

Bleak and silent, night fell once again upon the ruins.

Centuries passed.

Gradually, humans forgot that science had existed.

II

Along the route over which new diadems of stars were incessantly scattered in the blue vertigo of new infinities, the Earth continued to rise above the plain of its former ecliptic in the direction of Vega.

For a long time, already, the Sun and its cortege of orbiting planets, from which it had departed in legendary times, had no longer been distinguishable among the swarm of stars.

An ancient religion, almost discredited, attributed to the gods, the ancestors of humans and the first masters of the Earth, the creation of the sky, the beautiful spangled, grandiose and mysterious dome, profound and soft, simultaneously reminiscent of a gaze and an immense wing. Rotating around an invisible axis constructed by the ancients, it was said to contain the explanation of all mysteries: the signs of fire, strange and mobile, that were seen in the deployment of its heavy, somber fabric, from the zenith to the black horizons, had been assembled there by the primitive peoples in order to give the new races, in a complete tableau, the synthesis of the laws regulating nature. Since then, however, the language of the gods had become incomprehensible; hatred, said the priests, had once separated humans from their own divinity; a few sages strove in vain, by means of meditation, to return to the sources; the crowds abandoned the effort, content to repeat the legends.

One by one, in any case, the sacred verities crumbled.

Already, no one any longer believed in the omnipotence of Neick, the creator of the Earth, nor his descendants, the creators of the heavens. A vague pantheism gradually replaced all that; the unique god, if one had had to be determined, would have been Winter, the synthesis of the world.

It was, in fact, him who, summarizing all known and unknown forces, expressed universal life in the most concrete fashion. He reigned everywhere, as an absolute master, modifying at his whim the aspect of nature, and his origin was inexplicable. He was believed to be without a commencement or an end, and hence eternal. He was even sensed to be hostile, and was feared; unconsciously, all minds, including those of the priests, in spite of the name of Neick and the ancient formulas, addressed all their adorations, hopes and prayers to him. Was he not the true Dominator, the unique Mystery, the sublime Why of creation? Was he not the sole and impenetrable Principle, simultaneously past, present and future, Reason and Omnipotence?

In the white landscapes, the greenhouses and the subterranean habitations where humans took refuge seemed to be oases of wellbeing conquered from the infinity of God. Every day, he was begged to pardon the chilly race that ever-increasing encroachment. Sometimes, with a single snowstorm, he destroyed a town and buried a population.

Grimly, he watched, through the eyes of the stars, those spaces protected by the labor of human beings, those luminous green patches full of an artificial summer, the wealth of animal and vegetal life, beautiful with all the realized desires of a proud and minuscule race. Slyly, he advanced toward those warm paradises the pale crests of his mountains, the sharp blades of his frozen rivers, the thorny bushes of his icy winds: the entire tumult of his wrath.

Already, the human race was decimated. Already, in places, in order to conserve the warmth indispensable to life, light had been sacrificed.

Was he not the conqueror, the eternal Spirit of nature, the master of the world: Cold. Would he not crush, easily, what remained of humankind?

And without haste, in order to enjoy the agony of his victims for longer, he sharpened his claws on the white blades of the atmosphere, on the great smooth surface of the oceans and the scintillating sheets of the ice.

From one century to the next, the landscapes became bleaker. Over the livid angles of the greenhouses, the night extended, silently and softly, the permanent menace of its tentacles of darkness; one by one, the last lights paled; from time to time, the hail, rattling the glass, persisted in long efforts of desertion. However, after each attack, life reacted; flashes and noises, revealing its breathless agitation, still tore at intervals the enormous pulp of the obscurity.

Finally, the hail became rare. The air became dry and cutting.

Habituated to living in that atmosphere of shadow and cold, humankind became less sensitive to winds striated by needles, and more skilled in distinguishing, at a distance, icebergs on the march in the night.

The spangles of the sky, examined by eyes lager and more prominent than those of primitive races, seemed increasingly numerous, and formed in their ensemble a kind of milky fog. The delicate and changing designs of the crystallization of the snow became visibly clearer and more beautiful.

In the covered gardens, the complex tissues of flowers appeared to eyes through the petals. But death, invisible and present, bit the flowers, twisted the clusters of seeds, suppressed all the plants and all the animal races one by one, and threatened humans pitilessly.

For long years yet, humans struggled. It was in vain. Famine, howling and terrible, raised up the multitude of its hideous specters amid the mad distances; the cold fixed humankind with its numerable of feverish eyes, and then drew slowly nearer.

Then, in order to prolong their threatened existence, humans became ferocious again; in order that there would be fewer mouths to fed, the strong killed the weak; thousands of cadavers strewed the ground; blood infiltrated in starry patches into the snow.

For some time, the victors thought themselves the masters of destiny, but they soon became conscious of the absurdity of their hopes. The provisions in the greenhouses were rapidly exhausted; it was no longer possible to replace them; labor became futile in the face of the destroyer, Winter.

However, those who had conquered by crime the atrocity of the present moment wanted to appropriate similarly the probable compensations of the future. Soon, those wild beasts with human faces found themselves hungry again, having nothing before them but continents of ice or the dead immensity of the sea. The first, for long days, looked at one another with suspicion, with hair bristling over their tremulous foreheads, and knives in their hands. Eventually, they raced into the ice in search of cadavers. They killed one another in order to butcher them. When there were none left, they leapt at one another's throats and drank warm blood under the steel of daggers.

In less than a year, those people had almost entirely disappeared.

A few still remained who, living on coasts, strove to live by fishing, but their wretched existence was incessantly menaced, and it was not without battles that they assured themselves of their daily meals. The survivors of the neighboring peoples, attracted by hunger, attacked them as they emerged from their boats. Hideous fleshless and livid silhouettes wandered on all the beaches. Over the smooth black waters rafts glided, laden with huddled shadows and strident anger; everywhere, infernal clamors whistled like the wind, and sometimes, demonic figures clung on to the prows, the fins and the oars of fishing boats, their eyes on fire and their teeth sharp.

And in the night, fringed with high cliffs of ice on every side, the stars shone. All of them were blue, except Vega, which resembled a drop of molten gold in the bitumen sky.

III

A few more centuries went by.

Like a dead star, the Earth rotated in space, incessantly illuminated by the multiple reflection of the constellations.

In the silence of its landscapes, only a few cries revealed the presence of living beings; from time to time, a thickset form with a menacing face, sharp teeth and bulging eyes surged forth, reminiscent of a human being; with a heavy, mistrustful, bestial tread, all terror and ferocity, it approached a raft, took its place thereon, and drew away at hazard over the sea. When a raft came back there were cries, a bounding of numerous cruel animalities, a battle with ax-blows and bites; and those skirmishes of shadows in the snow and the darkness were—O degeneracy!—formed by human beings.

Meanwhile, within indifferent nature, something was happening that might have saved them.

One day, along the coasts of the ancient California, suddenly interrupting their tumult, the human tribes listened...

A rumble of unknown forces, shaking the horizon in the direction of the deserts of ice, toward the interior of the land, tore their marrows with a new frisson. Never in human memory had the silence of winter been troubled in that manner; never had nature appeared so abruptly redoubtable.

The noise continued.

It was as if a caravan of enormous animals, jostling in their passage mountainous boulders, was approaching, powerful and terrible, certain of vanquishing the men of the sea. At the top of the cliffs, a few of them waited, armed with axes, scrutinizing the gray distances with their piercing sight, but not seeing anything emerge therefrom.

For a long time they remained motionless, ready to defend themselves, their eyes watchful.

But nature fell silent.

Gradually, they recovered confidence. They went back to their caves, lit fires there by means of fragments of flint, and waited.

Soon the distant rumbles collided with the echoes again.

Then, gripped by panic, all the human tribesmen ran toward the rafts.

In the meantime, the noise increased, became vast, and multiplied, as if the invisible herd of mammoths on the march had suddenly divided into several columns, preparing to attack from several directions at once.

The rafts drew away rapidly. With a ferocious rage, the humans who had succeeded in piling on to the fragile decks repelled those who came after them.

A continuous thunder was now rumbling in the air, rising toward the infinity of the sky, shaking its dome and stirring the constellations on high, then descending again, encircling the mountain chains with mobile terror rebounding from abyss to abyss, shaking the ground and colliding there with all the powers of darkness.

Suddenly, from the summit of a mountain, a plume of red flames rose up, furious and crackling, punctuating the sky and falling back in a fine rain upon white crests of sierras and the ermine of the plains.

Silently, the humans gazed at that blinding light and listened to the din of lava and rocks rolling out of craters, bounding in space, giving birth around them to clouds of vapor, swirls of smoke and whistling sprays of moving water.

For several hours the earth trembled, and the sky was ripped apart, but no danger approached.

The humans returned to the shore. A few even ventured in the direction of the volcano.

As the flames died down momentarily, ready to leap forth again in abrupt anger before them, even the heroes hesitated; their will oscillated between curiosity and fear. Their conquest was slow, interrupted by flights, prudent retreats and countless hesitations.

After a few days of progressive audacity, a few fell, blinded by the flames and suffocated by ash. The others fled again toward the caverns.

Analogous spectacles frightened not only the populations of western America but also those of certain Mediterranean shores, Iceland, the Azores, the Canaries, Réunion and the Antilles. Everywhere there were volcanoes, columns of fire rose up, surmounted by barbaric capitals and blazing tresses. One might have thought that a single cause had animated them all at the same time, and their cataracts of flames gradually tore apart the accumulated whiteness around their pedestals.

On the flanks of the mountains, torrents of lava descended in red streams, amid golden foam in thick swirls, lifting up amid the torn rocks all along their route a double curtain of high white vapors, noisy and plumed, twisted and magnificent.

With a savage din, the snow was volatilized, under the action of the fire, bracing its new form against the new enemy. The liquefied ice shuddered in contact with motionless rocks, seemingly impregnated by millions of scattered souls; a harmonious life, long imprisoned in the rigidity of its cold blocks, vanquished in the shadow the terror of silence by means of the bounding of its cascades, its pearly vibrations, its voices united in murmurs, in whispers, in prayers and songs.

And, hour by hour, the contact of the flame liberated its torpid forces further; after a slumber of twenty centuries, the water reawakened; the intoxication of its senses thinned out in the quivering kiss of the air; in supple, nervous movements, multiple and varied, it conquered the world, and its soul remembered its ancient and total domination.

Already, on all sides, it was descending from the mountains, undulating through the profound valleys. Everywhere, collapsing before it, the architectures of winter were dislocated, submitted, came to swell its cascades, its torrents and its rivers; incessantly, the rejuvenated power of the liquid element increased; in its radiant glory, it infiltrated from vein to vein all the way to the heart of the earth.

And still the volcanoes rumbled, spitting fire.

The water, expanding in blue sheets over the wide spaces, once entirely white with ice, reflected in the frisson of its mobile surface the scintillation of the stars.

Everywhere, the ice melted.

Slowly, nature entire, modified and vanquished, crumbled and was reborn in new forms, less grim and full of appeased murmurs.

The rivers enlarged, seemingly torpid in their errant good fortune, with soft and heavy waves; but that calm was only superficial; the power of the element, hidden and irresistible, was active.

Soon, the water invaded the last plains; slyly triumphant, its vengeance was now displayed from one horizon to the other, undermining the rocks, the cliffs, the hills, isolated henceforth like icebergs, like islets.

It was a total disintegration.

Entire continents seemed to oscillate beneath water encumbered by ice-floes. From the sky, now completely obscured, cataracts of snow and hail fell. Through the troubled veil of the rain, prodigious masses of cloud were seen bounding, as black as pepper, scarcely punctuated by pale gleams.

And humans, expelled from their caverns, lost in the whirl of the hurricane and incapable of struggling against the currents that agitated the sea, drifted from gulf to strait, from peninsula to peninsula, forgetting their unappeased hunger in the hallucination of fear. Enormous waves lifted and lowered their rafts by turns, threatening every time to drag them into the abyss between their moving masses of obscurity.

In the meantime, boulders, tree-trunks, beams and formless blocks of stone and metal, a multitudinous debris of nature and ancient civilizations rolled in the heart of avalanches, crumbled amid cascades, jostled in the waves of innumerable rivers newly precipitated toward the sea.

On all sides, strange skeletons of disappeared races passed by, somersaulting in the foam. Even flesh floated here and there. Sometimes, human cadavers long buried in the ice glided over the surface of the waters, like frightful phantoms.

And the racket of the craters, more formidable every day, seemed to be shaking the very foundations of the world, beneath the sonorous vault of the lugubrious sky.

To the north, the south, the east and the west, flames surged forth in tragic explosions; mountainous blocks flew through the air. In places, the earth opened up, gaping, and abrupt eddies of waves and foam plunged into it.

Around the volcanoes, the trails of lava, like luminous daggers, stabbed lakes of frozen shadow; in bloody revolts, the liquid element howled there at every new lightning flash.

Thus, for centuries, dislocating the surface of the globe, water and fire, under the grim mobility of their tentacles, crushed with their roaring impacts the centuries-old nocturnal enchantment of the landscapes of snow, bristling ice-sheets and infertile sierras, beneath the pride of the stars.

In that grandiose struggle of the two elements, humankind was merely an atom clinging on to the last melting ice-floes in the tumultuous waves. Swimming marvelously, humans dominated the sea, along with seals, and like them, spread terror among the still-swarming population of fish, crustaceans and mollusks.

In vain, nature growled around them; the tumult of matter no longer troubled their instinct, and the last groups of the human race, developing in a milieu that was, in sum, only slightly modified, finding relatively facile conditions of life there, gradually multiplied and spread out in multitudes over the surface of the world

IV

In the sky, Vega grew larger.

In spite of the humid atmosphere of the Earth, which hid all the other stars, it was easily visible. Through the clouds, the blackness of which its contact made as soft as tulle, its disk seemed as large as a fist, with a mat yellow glow.

Already, at intervals, here and here, its radiance brushed the soil, putting a furtive blondness into it, and, caressing the hills, glided like the robes of goddesses over the snow. Sometimes, scattering over the surface of waters, it illuminated thousands of golden spangles there, but that never lasted for long; thick clouds, sliding in front of the stars, incessantly interpreted the fortunate vibrations of the ether under that new sun.

However, the Earth was approaching it perceptibly.

Already, the successive passages of Vega through the sky, were tearing the fogs more completely and clawing the obscurity of a terrestrial hemisphere in a more continuous fashion during its regular ascension toward he zenith.

Already, for rather long periods, the atmosphere became milkier, more translucent. A kind of pink daylight succeeded the opaque night, rising above the horizon every thirty hours, then thickening, irregularly traversed by vivid gleams, and finally fading away, to be reborn thirty hours later.

The clouds melted gradually; soon, the daylight, sliding without effort between their moving caravans, scattered its arpeggios of light, its scales of pale nacre and its divine and suave harmony, everywhere vibrant with chilly beauty.

At that moment, the Earth was once again three-quarters covered with tumultuous waters. Between the oceans, the rivers and lakes, monstrous with din and seething with foam, a few mountain chains reared up, heavy and imposing, with granite shields and helmets of snow that seemed eternal. A few muddy plateaus, absorbing the radiance, had tones of rust, frissons of great crushed bodies and collapses of warm flesh, colored with tragic, mobile, sulfurous reflections.

For years, the daylight illuminated mute and lugubrious landscapes; Death had passed that way, and the soil, striped with shadow, retained the imprint of it, so profound that it seemed indelible.

At length, however, the plateaus, routinely caressed by the luminous air, dried out. In the meantime, immense sheets of water slid toward the oceans, offering to the splendor of Vega the rude surfaces of continents covered with stones and mud with gleams of copper, ocher and bitumen. The warmth of the light caressed all those wounds with an equal patience, with a soft and radiant hope.

The daylight, rendering the air diaphanous, the waves silvery and the snow scintillating, was triumphant. Thanks to the day, on the slopes of moraines, in the shadow of valleys, and in arid regions strewn with marshes, the enormous fermentation of life was activated.

Tearing the mud, fusing with the interstices of rocks, the prodigious mystery of assemblages of atoms created new forms everywhere.

And over that desolate Earth, which innumerable centuries had struck with the bleak seal of winter; over that accursed Earth, which the cold and the darkness were still crushing with their formidable and mute cruelty, the starlight falling from the infinity of the sky accomplished, in a delicate labor, almost invisible but obstinate, the delectable miracle of spring.

To begin with, little gray patches appeared among the rocks, like flecks of foam, but delicately foliated; they were lichens, which had doubtless been alive for a long time beneath the snow. But the radiance of Vega, posing quivering light upon them, transformed them. Browns, greens and reds were mingled with their gray, and gave their shriveled life a more clearly vegetal form. Their leaves became finer, more elongated and also curlier. Their colors were enlivened.

For several years thus, from detail to detail, they slowly became complicated. Their stems thickened, minuscule excrescences deformed them, grew and expanded; finally, among their flames of intersecting lines, new organs surged: pedicelled antheridia, brilliant archegonia, and then higher stems, at the tips of which mysterious little containers developed in capsules. In each of those containers, a jade colonnette as slender as the shadow of a thread gradually surrounded spores as light as grains of sand, each containing the disconcerting future of a race.

The atmosphere became limpid and warm.

The days, succeeding one another, illuminated by increasingly vivid clarities, were impregnated with a mild, voluptuous warmth extremely favorable to the development of life.

The Earth, slowly reawakened, exteriorized the age-old beauties of its dreams, one by one.

In the great moist plains, plants grew with vertical stems and narrow verticillate leaves; from time to time the wind swayed the pale stems, numerous already and parallel; there was then a mild festival, noisy with tranquil joy, starry with supple foliage.

When the vegetables had attained their maximum growth, they were completed by a yellow plume; spores fell on to the soft ground in a fine rain and multiplied thus, from generation to generation, a host of horsetails throughout the expanse.

Almost at the same time, grasses were born.

In feathers, in tufts, and in light and transparent bouquets, they tickled the atmosphere, brushed the snow and the light, iridescent with reflections, illuminated by pearly humidity.

And everywhere, new species were born, bearing leaves with unknown, strange, sharpened, charming, delicate forms; here there were tangles of twisted stems, there fine and regular tresses.

Thus, on all sides, verdure, mosses and herbs, velvets and silks, jewels and plumes, covered the islands, plains and hills, one by one, and even strove to conquer mountains, rivers and marshes.

Humans recoiled anxiously at its approach. Habituated to the gray monotony of snowy landscapes, invariable under the stars, they believed it to be a danger, and hid under the progressive invasion of that tide of little green things, so multiple and so audacious, so tenacious and so tranquil, and so unfamiliar to them. They observed them for days; tried to make them afraid many a time, in vain; and the thousand little, but charming, beings, by virtue of some profound instinct, forgotten for centuries, put into their souls a kind of unconscious joy. That joy, however, was dominated by the immediate dread of a possible struggle suddenly to be undertaken, of which they, humans, were not certain of emerging victorious. They called the flora the Green Enemy.

In the sky, too, the familiar night, wounded by the golden fist of Vega, frightened them. The brutal intensity of the light irritated their sight. Even the temperature caused them to suffer. And all of that was confounded for them in an exaggerated impression of fear, in a stream of liquid light in which their eyes believed that they could see the color of blood. Vega had received the name of the Red Enemy.

Human beings wandered from island to island. Only the waves, still icy, pleased their life. However, the waves too, shaken by hostile forces, threatened them continually, sometimes throwing them back brutally toward the shore.

On the red and brown soil, among the plants, other glimpsed mysteries had sometimes attracted their curiosity and frightened their vague intelligence. Imprecise but living shadows had fled before their eyes, having brushed their fingers. One might have thought that the soil, in decomposing, had given birth to myriads of larvae, to hideous insects, to an entire swarming fermentation of organized beings.

Humankind, unfortunately amphibious, huddled in fear of marvels. Clinging to their miserable instinct of self-preservation, humans did not understand, and could not understand.

Meanwhile, the spring became more and more beautiful.

Ferns had unfurled their elegant volutes between the grasses and the horsetails. Conifers, with their slowness, had constructed their magnificent green pyramids, as sharp as the wind, and draped the snow of the mountains as of old. Various foliages had heaped up their palmate hands, sharp blades, feathery frissons and rattling medals at the tips of branches. And fluttering above that multiple sumptuousness, butterflies brightened, one by one.

In the sky, sometimes still bloodied by volcanic eruptions, the smile of the azure broadened; even the night became paler; shadow and light suspended the garlands of their contrasts from the ears of the night in delightful harmonies of young tones, mobile opals and light golds.

Sometimes, even in the shadowed hemisphere, the sea passed from grim blackness to blue, green and indigo; in places, it was streaked with silver, scratched with nacre; gradually, it emerged from darkness like a dream, like a luminous palette full of frissons.

At present, the disk of Vega, was larger than that of the ancient sun, and its heat, its light and all its life cradled the Earth like a fortunate and magical breath.

In more than a hundred thousand years since it had quit its old orbit, no similar voluptuousness in space, no similar intoxication in the waves of infinity, had ever gripped the despair of its course. All the fortunate matter of the planet quivered, and that globe, which had once been proud to bear humankind, after having been dormant for a long time, awoke as if in ecstasy.

On all its continents, the marvels succeeded one another. In Asia, Europe, Africa, America and Australia, the vegetation grew, expanding in richness, only leaving bare the stars of lava surrounding the craters. The latter, drunk on force, projected enormous blocks of stone, joyfully, above the clouds, lifted up heavy crimson and scarlet drapes, tearing the air with their demonic laughter. From one Pole to the other, the tides, increasingly powerful, provided a rhythm to the profound poetry of the sea; new currents undulating from gulf to gulf, caressed shores with foam; waves, with the voices of sirens, clashed.

Already, among the rustling of the foliage, innumerable jewels had surged forth like enchanted seashells under the bounding laughter of the light. In clusters and suspended garlands, or rising up one by one toward the blue sky, fresh flesh vibrated: they were flowers. To begin with, like scattered pearls, there were little white, yellow, red, pink and gray dots, scarcely visible. Some time afterwards, those dots grew, became wings, tubes, helmets, claws and stars. Their colors mingled, softened, or burst forth in vivid blues, somber violets and acidic vermilions.

Everywhere, the multiple forms of life were complicated and ordered, gradually climbing the sumptuous scale of successive perfections.

V

As the Earth came closer to Vega, the miracle of spring continued from flower to flower, from fiber to fiber; it enchained new complexities, ingenious, crazy delicacies and innumerable minuscule enchantments one after another.

Then, at length, there was summer.

The horsetails, conifers and larches had been succeeded, firstly, by oaks, beeches, birches and the charms of elms; in turn, maize, rice, vines and mulberries appeared; then there were oleanders, agaves, sunflowers and plane-trees; finally, the entire extent quivered with sonorous foliage and voluptuous shadows, the riot of olive groves, myrtles, orange trees, palms and orchids.

The Earth, now, was no longer anything but a garden.

In enormous clumps, mimosas, magnolias, and azaleas jostled one another. Cascades of violet wisterias put pearly curtains amid the arborescent ferns, iridescent with sunlight; red cactus-flowers burst forth like bloodstains against the backcloth of somber green verdure; fruits hung down from gigantic trees.

In places, forests rose up like sheaves of violent splendor, in the heart of luminous Edens; full of insects, birds, clusters and lianas, they vibrated like lyres under the supple fingers of the wind, and their multiple voices, in murmurs, cries chords and harmonies, laughed and sang, exalting nature and glorifying Vega.

Human beings, alarmed by the luxuriant vegetation of the continents, dared not venture along the rivers; the Green Enemy would have crushed them there by suddenly tightening its arms. Along the gulfs, also, bracing its strength, it seemed to be slyly lying in wait for victims, hidden behind the shield of the sea; it had the patience of those for whom victory is certain. And it changed its aspect endlessly. Here, tangling its anger with the point of a cape, it took the form of a forest plunging roots like fingernails into the torn waves; there, in the sea itself, it set the traps of its nenuphars.

But humankind, ever ready to defend its life, was wary. With large bulging eyes, dotted with glaucous flashes, humans kept watch on the Green Enemy from dawn to dusk. In any case, the danger existed on all sides.

The rocky shores were covered with mosses, seaweed and tenacious herbs; the sandy beaches were bristling with thistles. And everywhere, it seemed that the ocean was retreating day by day. From time to time, under torrents of fire, the horde of trees was torn apart, bloodily, but blocks of terrain crested with ferns were entering resolutely into the waves. Great whirlpools plumed with white vapors sometimes swallowed groups of men and women, and almost always, after those massacres, the bald heads of rocks or mud emerged partially from the waters; for a long time they remained motionless, as if inoffensive, but they were avoided. Open mouths and terrible fangs were divined beneath those skulls, soon hirsute with lichens and reeds.

Among the humans, the habitude of danger and the appetite for adventures had given birth to a few heroes; and often, when the softly curling waves were tinted by the agony of the evening, the swimming slowed, the fishing was interrupted, and they murmured fantastic stories of their exploits to one another.

One day, Bingwal had ventured on to the land. In spite of the hatred of thistles, which had torn his flesh in order to suck his blood, he had been able to reach the forest out there on the hill. There he had seen, in thousands, gigantic motionless serpents raising their heads toward the sky and hissing lugubriously; their eyes scarlet and their teeth white and sharp, they had darted their green and venomous tongues toward him, but Bingwal was a hero; thanks to a magic word, he had vanquished the serpents. Then the Green Enemy had set fire to the forest. Monsters clad in flames had ripped up the horizon and had raced toward the man, clamoring. For a long time he had fought them; several had died under his blows, but new monsters, surging from all directions had incessantly replaced each enemy that fell with innumerable armies. Bingwal was alone; he had been obliged to flee...

Hoff, another hero, hidden under a wave, had allowed himself to be rolled to the foot of a cliff. No longer moving, holding his breath, he had approached a group of murmuring plants closely enough, without attracting their attention, to surprise their secrets.

"It's necessary to kill all humans," one of them had said.

"To invade the sea," the other had replied.

"But how?"

"By sliding under the water like this, without them seeing us, as far as them."

And the plant, sliding toward Hoff at that moment, and suddenly wrapped itself around his legs and his arms, had imprisoned his body and squeezed his throat. Hoff had thought that he was doomed. He made a superhuman effort, broke the plant, which howled in pain, and returned in all haste to his sons, to whom he recounted the adventure.

They accompanied him on his second expedition.

Slowly, silently, they approached the shore where they hoped, the three of them, to be able to vanquish the Green Enemy. At a given moment Hoff went forward. His sons, to whom he had recommended silence and immobility, waited at the place that they judged propitious for the attack. A few minutes went by, interminably...then there was a cry. Almost immediately, a bloody form slid to the bottom of the water beneath them. Hoff was no longer anything but a cadaver. The land had recognized him and had taken its revenge...

Hoya, in the horror of darkness, had surprised the land in its sleep, had conquered it, and had brought back corollas and foliage. Fearlessly, he had struck his enemies with flints, torn their compact host, wrenched his trophies from their hatred.

Hoya was the greatest of heroes. Almost every night, he brought back, with a new dread, a few new objects. Yesterday, again, there was a sort of mauve butterfly, a soft and pale helmet, and a little blue crown with six brown eyes in the middle. But all of that had found death under his hands; nothing was any longer to be feared...

Hoya was the great conqueror, the uncontested leader of humans...there was no longer any hope except in him; his tribe became more numerous every day; everyone brought him, as a sign of respect, a part of his fishing. He accepted everything with a disdainful air, and seemed to be scornful of the cowardice of the number accumulated under the grandeur of his own personality. But the Red Enemy scared him...

That one, in its multiple power, ever increasing, patient and implacable, dominated the world.

By night it made the craters howl. Their flames rose up with prodigious bounds to assault the sky, jostling the gentle and protective shadows and chasing away the millennial beauty of the stars. At every moment, between the stars, from the horizons to the zenith, storms burst forth, lacerating the black velvet of the expanse. And then there was the ride of nightmares, crimson crepitations, the clash of blades and breasts, the horrors of massacre and the terrible shocks of light.

Adding further to the terrors of the night, the daylight, from dawn to dusk, spread a rain of molten gold that hurt the eyes. The disk of Vega, incessantly increasing in size, set fire to the clouds. The air was overheated. Humans suffered from that in their flesh, confusedly; their bodies could hardly tolerate the new temperature outside the water; they scarcely dared quit the waves, even by night. Furthermore, a strange malady, common to the entire race, was becoming increasingly frightful; the thick fur that protected their bodies was falling out; some, who said they could no longer bear it, had a terrible nudity.

Meanwhile, nature, around them, became more and more beautiful. Sumptuous and virginal, luxuriant and unexplored, it blossomed in its savage and indolent joy under the ardent caresses if the new sun looking down on its beauty.

Here, all the way to the blue horizon, there was a violet tide of saffron flowers, with a mild and warm perfume, bearing on its waves the caravels of lilies, begonias, tuberoses and jasmines, all of it seemingly padded by luminous vibrations and transparent mists. There, irises, dahlias, poppies, clematis and honeysuckle were wound in sheaves and scrolls, curtains and bouquets. Further away, pink and light almond blossom, acacias with golden clusters, mauve rhododendrons, golden laburnums and sculpted camellias, as fresh and as pure as the snow, were heaped up in hills of foliage and perfumes.

Clumps of bamboos, as fragile as giant grasses, swayed in the wind. Enormous palm trees, gorged on sunlight, waved their fans with a haughty arrogance.

And from day to day, the spectacle of nature was idealized; the plains, felted with grass and ornamented by corollas, embroidered their marvelous carpet with light and shadow. The plateaus, at dusk, resembled staged palaces, hanging gardens, and terraces garnished with flowery colonnades; and the mountains, draped in foliage and bathed in blue-tinted light, sometimes seemed to be animated by the gentle evening breeze, like mysterious divinities captive in the arms of slumber.

VI

For a long time the days succeeded one another, ever warmer.

Billions of petals fell like rain upon the ground; the grass disappeared beneath their heaps. Sometimes, the wind whipped them up in pink, violet, snowy or sun-colored swirls, superimposing on the nacreous undulations of the saffron-tinted expanse soft blue patches of crushed topazes, rubies and garnets.

And in those whirlwinds of fluttering splendors, insects flew like living gems.

The gardens of the Earth, rich in fruits, were perfumed by amber and musk. Weighing down the branches, golden bubbles, brown cones and green pods formed. In black clusters, grapes mounted an assault on the rocks and shook their foliage the color of lees. Figs, under their parasols of shiny leaves, slowly turned violet.

Bananas, oranges, mangoes and pineapples turned yellow, full of sunlight, in a tumult of verdure still rich in pomegranates, chestnuts, lemons, walnuts and guavas. Under frail branches apples, cherries, peaches, plums and apricots glistened. The undergrowth was full of mulberries, raspberries and strawberries.

To the ancient fruits of all climes and all seasons, new fruits were added pell-mell; and all of them, dense, heavy, swollen with sweet saps and acidic freshness, ripened rapidly, dried out on the branches and fell.

Enriching the humus with their dead flesh, soon decomposed, they saturated the atmosphere with a penetrating perfume, simultaneously acrid and sweet.

And always, on the branches, flowers proudly closed their faded petals again, voluptuously, around their pistils. And new berries always emerged, succeeding the dead flowers, swelling up in the sun in order to die.

Already, heaps of flavorsome fruits were strewing the ground. The trees found a rich sap there, incessantly raising higher the hope of their new efflorescence.

Sometimes, the leaves, appeasing their murmurs, seemed to experience the fatigue of life: yellow, weary, they spun at the ends of their fragile stems, quit the branches, and were carried away by the wind; but they only died one by one; in the place that they had just quit, buds opened immediately, and a few days later they were replaced by fresh tender green leaves.

Then, there were flowers again: young, bright flowers, absorbing the light once more, to form, after a few weeks, other flesh, other bubbles, other fruits.

With an untiring prodigality, nature created. All the vegetation, constantly modified, became both more powerful and more beautiful.

Cedars and baobabs, muscular and triumphant, eventually rose above the forests, and seemed to be twisting the sky with their magnificent arms.

Animal life too, emerging from the wood where it had previously crawled, had risen to a savage and grandiose splendor. In the dark woods, stirring the echoes, roars were sometimes prolonged thunderously.

Tigers, jaguars and panthers slid through the undergrowth, lifting up the foliage there with an undulating rhythm and a prudent suppleness, and then immobilizing, their head on their elongated paws. They lay in wait, in the penumbra full of whispers, for the approach of forms and sounds. Hours went by thus; nothing seemed to be respiring any longer under the leaves. Then, suddenly, a hind or an antelope went by. bounding out of the thicket, one of the kings of the forest, with a hoarse cry of victory, crushed the delicate beast under its striped splendor, muscles with steel and arms with claws and fangs. Blood flowed, inundating the perfumed earth, and the light falling from the dome of foliage put mobile patches on that warm crimson.

The undergrowth, swarming with various lives, belonged to the lion. Sometimes, its superb body, clad in sunlight, emerged from the tangle of branches and creepers, its spine oblique, its head proud, its mane undulating magnificently. Its large eyes, full of calm majesty, scrutinized the horizon slowly. Its mouth, still red with carnage, opened idly in a contented yawn, wider and wider, and then closed again abruptly, with a dry click. The undergrowth belonged to him!

Out there in the florid valleys, herds of anxious and graceful gazelles fled.

On the mountains, on the edge of precipices, goats leapt.

In the air, scraping the silence with pretty sonorous pearls and flowering the azure with their bright wing-beats, the population of birds lived.

Everywhere, life, multiplying its forms, united grace with strength, cruel instinct with beauty, and mingled the joy of conquest with the fear of death. The prodigious mystery, emerged from the battle of atoms, developed in battles. Life created and destroyed, voluptuously, atrociously and marvelously, without pause, without repose and without any visible plan, with a thousand contradictory appearances, always toward betterment, but without reason.

Even in the virgin depths of the ocean, it had developed. The waters, increasingly warm, had seen unknown fish and bizarre mollusks born. Along the coasts, in places once frequented uniquely by humans and seals, other creatures now opened monstrous hungry mouths. Already, new victims served to aliment new existences; numerous humans had been crushed by the jaws of crocodiles. So, no longer able to defend themselves sufficiently, the human tribes had fled at each alert and retrenched themselves on islands not yet invaded by the vegetation, or on rocky shores where plants were sparse.

But the plants had grown and the islands had been covered in moss. Humankind, caught between dangers, had implored the Green Enemy.

Then something truly unexpected happened...

The enemy that had once vanquished Hoff and other heroes suddenly became very mild; without biting, it inclined under the feet of the inhabitants of the sea; with joyful sounds it surrounded with its cool and protective shadows the fragility of naked bodies; soon, by virtue of the exquisite softness of its murmurs, it caused the cruel legends of the past to be forgotten and replaced them with fraternal promises. Humans became accustomed to it; one by one they had touched the marvels of the vegetation. Their curiosity, ever alert, became increasingly adventurous.

But menace and death subsisted everywhere. Every day, before the eyes of humans, leopards pounced on some living prey, tore apart bloodied torsos and fled toward the jungle with the red flesh; in places, at the surface of the water, the triangular maws of caimans opened, and they were often heard snapping shut forcefully, crunching bones, even on the shore.

The nights became more and more frightening. In the darkness, spangled by the reflections of stars, strange forms were outlined. Murmurs, cries, whistles, muffled footfalls, falls of leaves, and the bounds of jaguars or panthers followed one another in various and enigmatic frissons. At the entrances to the caverns where the humans took refuge, eyes seemed to shine amid the mobile leaves. Every shadow was menacing and the silence, even more than the noise, chilled the marrow. A branch suddenly creaking after a few minutes of muted terror reawakened the bitter instinct of self-preservation. The multiple traps of imprecise death were divined everywhere, simultaneously distant and close at hand. Then, in the neighboring cavern, there was the impact of a felled body, a scream, a bloody certainty; the following morning, a human was found torn apart.

Sometimes, storms added their bestial roars to the long nights of anguish, and swept crimson gleams from the sky palpitating under their claws; but that became rare. For some time, the war of thunders had been interrupted on high; longer and longer silences separated their battles.

The air was warm and dry; it burned the eyes and the throat.

The scintillating nights cut out in sharp designs the aerial immobility of palm trees; by day, an ever more intense brightness supported the sapphire globe that extended from horizon to horizon. And the temperature rose, continually, incessantly.

For the humans, that was a torture. It seemed to them that molten metal was viscous in their veins instead of blood, that an invisible vice was squeezing their skull, that a storm was multiplying rapid hammer-blows in their temples.

Fortunately, they did not know thirst.

Habituated to sea-water, their papillae were no longer irritated by contact with salt; its taste had long been supportable to them. Every day, they drank the foam at the crest of the waves and slaked their thirst. Not far away, however, in the dry and cracking jungle, the enervated wild beasts were wandering around dried-up springs. Sometimes, a cry ripped the air, but it was neither a brief cry of agony nor a long roar of victory; here it was a dolorous yelp, there a hoarse howl: always a strange sound, simultaneously full of anger and anguish, but which seemed unfinished, broken between the teeth, as if strangled by death.

Soon, the lynxes and the hyenas emerged from the thickets. Driven by thirst, they prowled in the plains, amid the sumptuous accumulations of semi-decomposed foliage and petals. The trees overhead spread tragic skeletons of bare branches in the flamboyant redness of the sky. Along the streams where a murmurous water had once flowed, the light now illuminated specks of mica in the fine dust, and long lines of cadavers of roe deer, foxes and martens, alpacas and gazelles.

A few storms—very rare, alas—brought a little water. Life was renewed by that momentary freshness. Then two months of desperate drought followed.

The last leaves had fallen; bark cracked; ferns shriveled, with frissons and twitches that rendered them similar to flames; the air, scarcely respirable, had become a coppery yellow, seemingly incandescent.

Then the lions, the tigers and the panthers advanced with a nervous haste, tracing their steps abruptly, stopping indecisively, then resuming with a supple rage their course along the rivers, approaching the sea.

The humans were already at sea.

For days, the carnivorous hordes mingled their savage cries with the indifferent clamor of the ocean. Then the wild beasts returned one by one to the undergrowth in order to kill. Their hunger sated, they licked the ground, damp with crimson warmth, for a long time; immediately thereafter they killed again, but only for the blood.

For weeks on end, not a drop of rain fell.

The burning atmosphere was charged around agonies with myriads of poisoned dust-particles.

Often, by night abrupt exhalations brightened the woods; the creepers, the branches and the trunks, in amber columns, muscular torsions and bewildered gestures, shivered with red reflections and oscillated like torches beneath the sky. From time to time, the fall of a bolide made the immediate menace of fire precise. Sometimes, vast areas crackled under conflagrations, bounding and whistling eddies of force.

During the day, Vega, an immense sun, covered more than half the sky with its disk of flame, prolonging its radiant wrath in cascades of molten copper through the deserts, through the spaces, from abyss to abyss, all the way to the horizon and beyond. Under the crushing power of it fiery will, the Earth gasped.

O luxuriant splendor of gardens annihilated forever! Ephemeral glory of what was!

Everything died.

Everything was devastated, twisted, burned, and destroyed.

And on beds of dead branches, russet leaves and faded flowers, cadavers dried out, skeletons whitened in the sunlight.

Everywhere, the bleak desolation of the expanses, a hundred times more sinister than the horizons of snow of previous centuries, were laden with the remains of life, calcined residues of incomparable marvels.

Everything that still remained of living brings on the planet was now gathered in the green-tinted mists of islets. Mollusks, crustaceans, amphibians, fish, humans and reptiles continued to tear one another apart there, sheltered from the light beneath the tragic sky burned by falling stars. There, nothing seemed changed. Millions of fins continued to beat the water with their regular movements; innumerable phosphoric eyes fixed upon prey that was still similar.

However, if any being had been able to surge forth from the desert of the continents, it would have seen, along the oceanic coasts, the horror of a new cataclysm unfurling.

Under the furnace of the sky, the oceans were slowly evaporating

Already, plains of sand once hidden under the waters were displayed, luminously; algae, sponges and starfish were dying there.

Fogs of white vapor glided over the waves; that was a cheerful spectacle, softly beautiful, exquisite and fresh, but hour by hour and day by day, the consequences became more comprehensible; they were fatal and implacable, as if Death itself, incited against the accursed planet, were inhaling with a ferociously voluntary slowness the last drops of its blood.

Beaches of sand grew wider everywhere. All along the coasts of the Atlantic, like the lips of a wound, the continents bled; around the Pacific, new lands covered with kelp, squamous skeletons, shells and polyps offered their damp surfaces to the ardor of the red sun. A new vegetation—actinias, tubeworms, sea pens, madrepores and jellyfish—tinted pink, green, yellow and violet, emerged from the water and exposed its jewels, similar to flowers, to the sun's rays.

In the vicinity of the Indian Ocean and north-east of Australia, coral atolls were enlarged; the waves, scattering their foam, uncovered them gradually; at present they were little fortresses, preciously constructed, their towers and crenellations looming over the bounding armies of the sea.

Then, at the hazard of the ebbing of the tide, there were strange apparitions of unknown and deformed beings, mysterious and frightening, which came to die in the light, amid other flora slowly revealed.

The waters retreated further and further.

Already, half the ancient surface of the oceans was nothing but a desert of rocks or bare ground. Here and here, under the bright sky, metallic debris the color of rust attested the vanished glory of an ancient civilization. O time that passes! Eternity! O centuries that destroy everything! Those masses of brown shadows once shone in the sunlight. What nature has eroded, bitten and twisted once belonged to the genius of humankind and stood up proudly in splendid organisms. In fabulous times those hesitant straight lines and deformed curves were mathematical boldness and divine grace. Those skeletons of iron, copper and bronze lived, were bridges, towers, dredges, wings and ships.

Alas.

What has become of humankind since?

The sea retreats. From terrace to terrace it descends all the way to the green realm of spider-crabs, hermit crabs and sea-urchins. Its waves, sucked up by the sky, now rise in fogs and in volutes, but the volutes no longer fall back; opaque clouds prolong them, showing in thick curtains hemmed by rosy and yellow radiance, rearing up, mingling their rumps, bounding and galloping toward eternity.

On the edge of the ancient continents, funnels are hollowed out; the sea descends as far as the abysses, and still efflorescences emerge, myriads of animals twitch, agonizing, under the irrespirable gold of Vega.

Already, countless human bodies, vanquished by the torrid air, are lying on the bare ground, on the melting sand.

And still, the waves descend.

Finally crushing under its mortal light the last pride of the last races, Vega covers the sky completely with the vast orb of its fiery shield.

VII

Since it quit the Sun and its moving archipelago of planets, the Earth had traversed space almost in a straight line. From time to time, it had only been subject to a few oscillations resulting from the distant, feeble influences of unknown heavenly bodies.

As soon as it had entered the sphere of attraction of Vega, however, it had obeyed new laws, and slowly, its course had deviated.

To begin with, it had described an immense curve, scarcely sensible, which might, however, have become a closed orbit around the star; for billions and billions of years, a prisoner again, it might have rotated around that new focal point. But its velocity, which had been about seventy thousand kilometers an hour on arrival, had soon increased; the curve of its evolution had also accentuated; at present, it was traveling at an increasingly rapid velocity toward the star itself, following a conic spiral of which Vega represented the summit.

For a long time, all living species had been dead. The Earth was no more than a spinning globe, devoid of an atmosphere, devoid of water. The complex relief of which barely recalled what had once been Europe, Asia, Africa, America and Australia.

Yellow and cracked, the surface of the globe was modified, patched by fire in places. Everywhere, from north to south and east to west, abrupt collapses mingled the massifs of mountains; landslides, upheavals and enormous dislocations of the surface, variously chaotic, brought swells of porphyry, marble, minerals and granite into collision; continually, areas veined by crevasses, crested by new mountain chains, jostled one another in fantastic assaults, often opening gigantic craters in the midst of the tumult. And the attraction of Vega, combined with the somersaults of the central forces of the Earth, distorted the ancient face of the world dolorously beneath the infinite heavens.

For centuries, the Earth rolled, gradually approaching the star. Its velocity had doubled, tripled, quintupled, decupled; the distance to cover was still enormous, but it was diminishing day by day, from one minute to the next. Time, the conqueror of the abyss, guided the vertiginous projectile toward the dazzling globe, the color of ocher, crimson, phosphor and copper, that humans had once baptized Vega, and which, turning for no reason on its axis, was moving for no reason toward an unknown goal.

Finally, the Earth brushed the flames.

Like a grain of dust caught in a whirlwind, it shuddered, spun, leapt, was dragged like a light bubble to the ragged crest of a wave of fire, into amber yellow foam mingled with liquid rubies; sprays of molten gold streaked with blue gleams surrounded it; it crackled, fell into red gulfs, rebounded like a spark. Eventually, it burst, and its matter, volatilized in new light, was lost amid the ancient light, like a little group of atoms in infinite space.

Thus was dispersed, in the luminous atmosphere of a greater heavenly body, what had been a world for humankind.

Paul Gsell: *Wireless Communication with the Stars*
(1930)

I. Folly or Genius?

Toward the end of 194*, a strange emotion began to stir humankind.

A physicist, Barnabé Letord claimed to have communicated by wireless with the planets.

He was an aged professor. At first it was thought that the fellow had gone senile. His first experiments before friends confirmed them in that opinion.

Having created darkness in his laboratory at the Collège de France, he showed them vague shadows on a luminous screen, which passed back and forth, becoming more evident and vanishing without it being possible to grasp their true nature.

"Divine that enigma," he said, with a luminous smile. As everyone held their tongue he declared, triumphantly: "They're beings from beyond the sky." And he added: "Yes, inhabitants of distant planets. Soon, I'll be able to make them less indistinct."

Behind his back, his listeners tapped their foreheads with their index fingers.

In the press, discreet allusions circulated regarding Professor Letord's "daydreams." For some time, it was a theme for delicate mockery. Was the old man "out to lunch" or was he the victim of tricksters?

A few weeks later, in a session to which he had invited the highest competences of the scientific world, he spent a good hour searching, he said, for the wavelength. The dazzling circle of the projector remained ironically virginal. The operator gave the excuse of the great delicacy of the operation and the manipulations, but sniggers were springing forth from the perfidious shadows, when a proud exclamation resounded: "Look!"

Suddenly, on the screen, with a perfect clarity, a troop of gnomes appeared, who resembled humans, but whose fantastic appearance was disturbing. Their enormous skull, which measured at least half their height, was mounted on a very stocky body with thin arms and legs. They resembled the caricatures with big heads that represent contemporary celebrities in humorous magazines.

Those apes were not walking. They were sitting on little wheeled platforms that transported them very rapidly wherever they wanted to go. With a muted sound of continuous rolling, they moved around for some thirty seconds.

Suddenly, the screen became immaculate again.

"Oh! Cut off already!" exclaimed the professor, with some disappointment. "But you know enough now to take account of the facts."

And, switching on the lights in the room, he explained that the hallucinatory race lived on a very distant planet, probably a satellite of Vega.

"Those were," he affirmed, "images that an unknown astral correspondent has just transmitted to Earth by wireless."

Then the scientist explained his discovery. He had succeeded in isolating special vibrations that were propagated throughout the universe with a speed infinitely greater than that of Hertzian waves. He had constructed apparatus to capture them. One day, he thought he had discerned mysterious signals. Suspecting that they emanated from other planets, he had worked hard to test that hypothesis. After countless fruitless attempts and many alternations of enthusiasm and dejection, he had finally collected, by means of a kind of television, precise projections like the one that had just been offered to the audience, and which, without a doubt, reproduced astral scenes. And he had found a means of recording the sounds that accompanied them synchronically.

Naturally, that speech left the entire audience incredulous. "But what authorizes you to suppose," said one, in a mocking tone, "that people from beyond the sky deliver themselves to this intersidereal correspondence?"

"I'm obliged to believe it," said Letord, "since I receive their messages. I suppose that, on many planets, civilization is very advanced and they have already been making use of the astral wireless communication that I've just invented for a long time."

"And these operators send you their radio signal through the immensity?"

"They aren't destined for me; but they're expedited through all regions of space, and I've intercepted a few of them. Soon, I hope to be able to address myself to them in my turn."

The members of the audience shook their heads and exchanged furtive winks. Barnabé Letord had begun to adjust his tubes, cross wires, turn screws and illuminate intermittent light-sources. Then he switched off the lights again and almost immediately, an improbable animal appeared on the screen, the forms of which surpassed in extravagance the most audacious fantasies of Greek mythology and Oriental theogonies, harpies, centaurs, chimeras, hippogriffs and winged dragons. It was a centipede, for it had at least a hundred feet or tentacles, which it was agitating in all directions. Over its body and its limbs a quantity of eyes opened, the furious pupils of which were rolling incessantly. A mouth provided with three rows of teeth in each jaw was hissing with rage and gaping frightfully, as if to grasp an invisible prey.

At that moment, another monster bounded into view, which began to fight with the first. The newcomer was bristling with pincers, spikes and saws, which were not mechanical engines but living instruments like those that certain fish possess—swordfish and narwhals—or certain insects. Whereas those weapons are minuscule in the coleopteran and hymenoptera, however, they were gigantic in the combatant from beyond the sky. Furthermore, like electric eels, it launched electric discharges; but they were much more redoubtable, because they burst forth noisily, attaining the enemy's tentacles at a distance, and the contractions and writhing of those appendages proved the efficacy of the fulminating sparks.

That duel between two apocalyptic beasts, one of which was seeking to envelop and the other in order to pierce it, evoked in some ways the encounters of a retiarius and a swordsman in the Roman arena. It was both impassioning and burlesque, for the whirling of the fleshy arms and the blades, the rolling of the flamboyant eyes and the threats of the distended mouths resembled a delirious parody of hatred—to such a extent that when the scene was abruptly effaced before the denouement of the drama, loud laughter broke out in the room.

"A fine trick!" someone shouted

At first, Barnabé Letord did not seem to understand that remark.

"Come on, what do you take us for?" growled one of the luminaries of the Académie des Sciences

"Confess," then, said another pontiff, "that you're serving us doctored films."

Red with shame, Barnabé Letord protested his good faith in vain.

"Old joker!" sniped one of his oldest friends.

Then the professor got annoyed, seethed with rage, and ended up delivering a magisterial back-handed slap in the face of one of the most jovial jesters.

The slap brought a riposte. There was a fine brawl, in which Letord came off worst, for everyone was against him.

He called his colleagues imbeciles. He shouted them down. Many of them, draping themselves in their importance, declared gravely that high science had just been insulted. Others broke the machines in the laboratory with blows of their canes.

The next day, the quarrel was set before public opinion. In numerous articles, the representatives of official knowledge pronounced against the inventor of astral wireless. They demanded vengeance for his indecent deceit, his insults and his conduct. Charging him with insanity, they demanded that he be retired without delay from his chair at the Collège de France and locked up in Sainte-Anne.

The unanimity of those eminent persons impressed the public powers so much that Letord was immediately interned in the asylum.

Very rapidly, however, a counter-current formed in the camp of free science. There were Letordists and Antiletordists. As always, politics and religion got mixed up in it. The Freemasons, the Zionists and the Republican Left were for Letord, the center and the right against him. In the Latin Quarter, the students, divided into two factions, delivered themselves to pitched battles when they encountered one another at the street corners on the descent from the Montagne Sainte-Geneviève, and there was a hailstorm of jeers, punches and blows with sticks.

Among the newspapers, *L'Espérance, L'Horizon, Le Progrès, Le Mieux-Etre, Tous nos droits, La Torche, Le Brandon* and *Sans dessus-dessous* were Letordist; *La Nation, Cocorico, Rataplan, L'Ordre, L'Intérêt Public, Fructidor* and *Sursum Corda* were Antiletordist.

Each party defended its convictions furiously, without a shadow of proof—for people only fight about what is not demonstrated, and indisputable truths, such as two and two make four, have never excited anyone. In any case, it was not about the sequestered scientist at all, but the advantage each person found in enrolling himself under one banner or the other. That is generally the basis of all the great quarrels that agitate society from time to time.

One of the principal editors of *Tous nos droits*, Jacques Lagité, after having demanded the liberation of the prisoner with extreme violence, had the belated scruple of verifying whether Letord was actually of sound mind and whether he had really made the discovery of which he boasted. He went to visit him in Sainte-Anne, talked to him for a long time, and wrote a luminous article about astral wireless that was reprinted by all the Letordist periodicals.

Two days later, the inventor was released—not because of the article, but because the political party that supported him had just overturned the ministry. Jacques Lagité nevertheless claimed all the credit for the action taken in the scientist's favor.

Barnabé Letord hastened to bring his labors to a successful conclusion, and was served in his final trials by a marvelous stroke of luck. He improved the emissions, which still left much to be desired and succeeded in regulating meticulously the sending of messages to the most distant stars. Even better, responses from certain planets began to reach him.

He also perfected the polychromy of the images that he received, for it is worthy of remark that they were colored like the reality itself.

Those prodigious results were registered by scientific committees that surrounded them with all the requisite guarantees. At first, Letord's adversaries had systematically denied the facts. Then, enabled to participate in the verification, they were obliged to consent to yield to the evidence.

Jacques Lagité, having become the great scientist's best friend, was his spokesman in the press, and signaled each progress accomplished in dithyrambic terms.

France, always belated in recognizing the genius of her children, was forced to admit that of Barnabé Letord when all the other nations had proclaimed it, and no doubt subsisted for anyone. Astral wireless had been definitively invented, disciplined and rendered practical. The ancient dream of all poets and all the inspired had been realized. The appeal of intellect had been perceived beyond the abyss, and the silence of limitless space was finally broken, thanks to a few mechanisms composed of mirrors, cassettes, levers, dials, needles and metal wires.

Intelligence exulted vertiginously toward the infinite. It was about to fathom countless mysteries previously triply sealed. A formidable expectation held the human race breath-less.

II. Lagité Seeks Happiness

Everyone was talking about astral wireless. Everyone was dreaming about it. But Jacques Lagité was talking and dreaming about it more than anyone else. His name—which, by a curious coincidence, had always depicted his character marvelously—had never been as fully justified.

It is necessary to admit that he now had reason to be im-passioned. A specialist in the new invention, he wrote paper after paper, gave numerous lectures, responded to ten tele-phone calls a minute, and maintained a written correspondence with all the countries on Earth. Six shorthand typists he had hired were insufficient for that purpose.

That trepidation on Jacques' part extracted him from his customary reflections, and that was a great advantage, for eve-ry time he returned to himself he fell into the deepest melan-choly. He had tried everything to satisfy or to distract himself. He had educated himself avidly, but, although he was very versatile, his knowledge had little depth. In fits and starts he dipped into Letters, Sciences and Arts, and lost his taste for them just as rapidly. Nothing satisfied him.

He had tried to enrich himself, but in vain. In particular, a company that he had founded to render horse-chestnuts co-mestible had volatilized a considerable fraction of his capital.

He searched continually for happiness; he was, in conse-quence, very unhappy.

One Sunday in spring, Jacques was finishing lunch on a terrace in his small property in Bois-le-Roi, in the company of his young wife Viviane and a friend, Doctor Jean Placide. Young foliage of a delicately acidulated green, cobaea flowers and wisteria decked the arbor where the meal was concluding. The view through a bay overlooked a barrage on the Seine, the waterfall of which, in limpid sheets and foamy eddies, spar-kled with a thousand gold and silver reflections.

The air was very mild and the light divinely amorous.

Naturally, the three were chatting about sidereal wireless.

Jacques said that the velocity of Letordian waves had just been measured by a method similar to the one that had allowed the velocity of light to be calculated. It had arrived at numbers that far surpassed all known evaluations. The vibrations were transmitted almost instantaneously to the astronomical limits attained by the most powerful telescopes. Thus, the distances that luminous rays would have taken centuries to travel were traversed in the blink of an eye by the new radiations. It was to be anticipated that conversations would soon be established easily with all the inhabited worlds.

And Jacques sighed, in a sort of ecstasy. "Then, we shall finally discover the happiness that always flees us!"

Viviane and Jean Placide looked at one another in surprise. The young physician declared that he was, of course, as intoxicated as all scientists by the limitless possibilities of the new wireless, but he confessed that he could not see how it would ensure human beings of happiness.

"Blindness!" riposted Jacques. "Among the myriads of planets, many must be older than ours, and progress presently unimaginable here must already have been realized there. The inhabitants of those worlds therefore enjoy a perfect felicity. And by communicating with them, we shall discover their secrets and we shall only have to borrow their experience to become supremely happy."

Those words had been spoken with a spasmodic ardor.

Jean Placide raised a Havana that he was in the process of enjoying to his lips, chewed it, inhaled the smoke, blew it out in a long blue spiral, and then looked intently at Jacques. "You don't have it, then—happiness?"

"No," said Jacques.

"There are people," Jean remarked, "who don't merit their good fortune. Come on, old chap...happiness? Look around you. It's the exquisite fare that has just been offered to us; it's the mocha worthy of houris, the five-year-old brandy, this cigar, which would make the nostrils of the Eternal fare with delight; it's the pleasure of our conversation; it's the paradisal landscape; it's..."

"I hate rustic meals," Jacques cut in, "but I forgive my wife her whim."

"Oh!" cried Viviane. "I thought I was giving you pleasure!"

"Risking eating caterpillars in the sauce, fearing being stung by a bee!"

"What ideas!"

Jean said, calmly: "Happiness, my dear Jacques, is an adorable woman."

Viviane smiled palely. Jacques was beginning to hate her, because he had ceased to love her.

Stendhal has talked about the crystallization of desire around the little irregularities of a cherished face and body. There is also a crystallization of hatred around the very perfections of a person who has become indifferent. Jacques was now acquiring a distaste for Viviane's delicate complexion, her ash-blonde hair, her violet eyes and her delicate hands. Those attractions were antipathetic to him, because he was sated by them. At that moment he was imagining an amber cleavage, sharp teeth, tapering and combative fingers, everything that delighted him about his brunette mistress of the moment.

Viviane murmured: "He hasn't even noticed my new hairstyle."

"Fluffed up like a Pekinese!" sniggered Jacques.

"It's you who recommended this fashion to me!"

That was true; but it was sufficient for her to accomplish one of Jacques' wishes for him to change his caprice.

He turned toward his friend. "A sad happiness, the one of which you speak! A few poor pleasures for a mediocre sensuality."

"Thank you!" said Viviane.

"Seriously," Jacques went on, bitterly, "How can you expect me to be happy? Our present existence is so flat, so paltry. We experience so many needs, without being able to content them. How many times I have dreamed about the people of the future! I tell myself that they will truly know the joy of living, because they will collect all the fruits of our pains, and the future will have brought them a host of sensual pleasure unknown to us. Exactly what I expect of astral wireless is to procure us immediately the plenitude of satisfactions that I only glimpsed previously for our distant descendants."

"Oh," said Jean, "you truly are Jacques Lagité, always unquiet; you don't repose for a moment in the possession of what you have. Fundamentally, you personify an entire modern generation who, struck by a universal giddiness, flutter incessantly, perpetually running after chimeras and never stop to 'seize the day,' as the old poet puts it. A stupid and macabre jazz-band!"

"Jean is right," ventured Viviane.

"How stupid you are!" snapped Jacques. In his bad mood, he had not measured the harshness of the remark.

Viviane shuddered, closed her eyes momentarily, and seemed to retreat dolorously into herself.

Jacques, who felt guilty, tried to justify himself by means of a worse offense. "You only say things to displease me," he growled.

"Listen, my friend," said Viviane, tremulously, in a low voice, "If I thought that I could render you any happier by leaving you..."

"That's it—you've had enough of me!" he exclaimed, hypocritically.

"Jacques!" she moaned.

"Well, so be it," he said, completely unhinged. "Let's separate."

And as he noticed a tiny spider on the edge of a water-jug, he said: "Look at that!" And he took hold of the crystal and smashed it into a thousand pieces on the ground.

Then, without bidding adieu to Jean, who continued smoking philosophically, he fled. A minute later, they heard the automobile emerge from the garage, and the vehicle carried Jacques toward Paris.

Viviane, her elbows on her knees and her face in her hands, was shaken by endless sobs. She continued shedding tears, and repeating: "The bad man! The bad man!"

Jean stroked her like a child, and with compassionate caresses her ended up saying: "Come on, come on; don't worry. If Jacques abandons you, you won't lack adorers."

She recoiled abruptly and looked at him maliciously through her tears. "I thought you were more delicate," she said.

"But..."

"You're prompt to betray amity. Personally, I'm more faithful to amour."

"How can you love that madman?"

"He's better than you! Yes, Monsieur Epicurean, you savor your pleasures egotistically. That's not enough to seduce me. Jacques gets carried away, but his perpetual anxiety is a rarer quality than your bliss. It attaches me to him. I'd like to soothe it, to calm it. He no longer loves me, it's true, but none of his passions lasts, because he's always animated by a more ardent desire. Perhaps he'll come back to me. Anyway, I love him..."

"I love you too," Jean implored.

She smiled silently. He asked her the reason for that.

"It's a wicked thought," she said. "I'm annoyed by being loved by you, but I experience some consolation in it"

He drew closer to her eagerly.

"La la!" she said. "I tell myself that I'm still lovable, and that Jacques will doubtless perceive it one day..."

He grimaced with chagrin. "He makes you so unhappy!"

"Yes, but I'm glad at the same time."

"What do you mean?"

"I love my suffering, and I wouldn't give it up for anything in the world."

"Viviane!"

"Jean, never talk to me again about your love. Never, you understand! Otherwise, I won't be able to see you any longer. And I'd regret that, for I need your friendship."

With that, she gave him his leave, holding out her hand, which he brushed with his lips.

III. The Planet Venus

Jacques had gone to live with the pretty Cora, his mistress, who painted fans.

Immediately, he had an astral wireless set installed in her home. Barnabé Letord supervised the installation personally, and wanted Jacques to begin a correspondence with the planet Venus, where he had just made some curious observations.

"Venus," he told his friend, "is populated by humans very similar to us. I was astonished by that, because I didn't think that two similar races could exist on two different worlds. But I recalled what Newton wrote: *Natura est ubique sibi consona*. Nature repeats herself everywhere. And since, by the study of spectral rays, science had already demonstrated that the chemical elements of which the Earth is composed are identical in all the stars, I judged it less singular, on reflection, that life should reproduce exactly the same forms on several planets.

"In addition, although astral wireless is in its infancy on our world, we can now make a prediction. We will only ever be able to communicate with sidereal beings who resemble us, more or less, for they alone are in a position to exchange ideas with Earth. Evidently, many species are living in the universe that are not similar to us in any fashion, but it's obvious that we can never know them. Having said that, I'll get back to Venus, and draw your attention to a surprising coincidence. By virtue of a miraculous divination, our astronomers have given Venus the name precisely suited to it, for it really is the planet of Amour."

As soon as the illustrious scientist had got his apparatus working, the public square of a great city appeared on the screen. The houses only differed from ours in their style. The motifs of the sculpture were mostly borrowed from general anatomy. Lingams were employed everywhere, from sideboards to balconies, and from gutters alongside pavements to gutters on roofs.

The men and women of Venus were clad in floral garments of a rather smart appearance.

At a crossroads in the foreground, a young woman prey to an extraordinary excitement was rummaging in her handbag. As at the cinema, the vision was replaced momentarily by the little bag, greatly magnified and held open. It had several pockets, and the main compartment was provided with a small mirror, lipstick and a powder-puff. There was a special compartment for a dainty revolver. It was presumably the current model of all handbags in that country.

A very large feminine hand took possession of the weapon.

Suddenly, the scene reverted to the public square, where the young woman was pursuing a man, firing all the bullets contained in the loading mechanism at him. Her aim was so poor that the bystanders hit by the errant projectiles were falling before her like cardboard figures.

The drama had scarcely finished when a second madwoman fired at point-blank range at another female inhabitant of Venus. The victim had not yet hit the ground when a ephebe, addressing a mute adjuration to the heavens, blew his brains out. Alongside him, a young woman threw herself under the wheels of a heavy truck. And at the same moment, a frenetic couple precipitated themselves from the top of a tower, and the two were crushed on the ground.

"Oh!" said Jacques horrified. "You're mistaken, my dear professor. That is surely not the planet of Amour but the planet of Hatred and Madness."

"Not at all! I've observed it carefully. All those people are in love. That's why they kill and detest one another. There's nothing more usual on the planet Venus. And it's doubtless by virtue of idleness that one of the witnesses of such banal scenes are transmitting them through the heavens. The exasperation of physical desire produces those frightful deregulations. But continue watching. I'll leave you to it."

Jacques saw a huge hall in which a jury of grave individuals was sitting. By the dignity of their features, they were recognizable as wily tradesmen, prudent manufacturers and experienced rentiers. Before them were arranged objects of all sorts that had served to kill: revolvers, knives, hammers, smoothing irons, razors, nails, chipped pairs of scissors, forceps, and even a handkerchief twisted into a strangling cord.

The members of the jury were examining that apparatus in the manner of connoisseurs. They waxed ecstatic over the rare pieces that were not designed for killing, and which only an unbridled passion had been able to transform into deadly weapons.

Then they had the men and women who had employed those instruments enter, one by one.

The president, an old man with a snowy beard, clasped in his arms the first of the murderesses, who had apparently committed the finest crime of passion, and pinned to her breast a golden insignia in the form of a heart in flames.

He shook the hands of the other assassins, congratulated them warmly, and distributed the same decoration to them, but in silver or bronze.

After that, everything vanished.

"My word!" said Jacques. "Some of our juries at the assizes operate in much the same fashion. But if that's the radiant land of Amour, I'd prefer not to live there."

He observed other natives of Venus. They were proud of the wounds they had received from their lovers and showed off their crippled limbs of blinded eyes. They were just as proud of having lost noses in less violent but no less deadly encounters.

It is necessary to add that on that planet, the slightest mark of courtesy that a husband might give to his wife, or lover to her admirer is to offer the other a gallant weapon that cuts through flesh and bone. No wedding-basket is devoid of that durable gift, and no polite liaison without that present of amity.

Lagité had many occasions in the following days to communicate with the planet Venus. He learned to speak with the inhabitants; Letord, who returned, helped him to do that. In fact, the great scientist had just made a new discovery of capital importance. He had noticed that the sidereal beings made use in their interplanetary conversations of the same language, a kind of Esperanto, which had been adopted long before by all the stars linked by wireless.

Barnabé Letord had compiled a grammar and a vocabulary of that language and he had lent them to Jacques, who was soon in a position to interrogate benevolent correspondents on Venus. They gave Lagité a thousand details of the greatest interest regarding their mores.

Naturally, on that world consecrated to Cythera, the women are sovereign. They hold almost all the public employments and only leave a tiny fraction to their male companions. Their conception of social functions is, moreover, very personal. They only install themselves in their offices in order to take care of their beauty.

When taxpayers present themselves at a window in order to acquit some civic duty—to bring money to pay their taxes for instance—the pretty functionaries do not seem to perceive that they are in a hurry. They inspect their pretty faces attentively, in a hand mirror, pout in order to be better able to apply a stick of rouge to their lips, and place the crimson substance with the decision of great pastel-painters.

In the meantime, they slyly address a smile to the waiting citizens; they authorize them thus to be witnesses to their toilet and take pleasure in it—for they have no doubt that they have come solely to admire them, and that the other reasons they invoke are merely futile pretexts. In consequence, they take out their powder puffs and cover up the luster of their noses with the powder. Then they put blue kohl under their eyelids, and unctuous mascara on their lashes. They make use, in fact, of compounds almost the same as the women on Earth, although the names of the products are different.

After heightening their beauty in that fashion they write their amorous correspondence, searching the ceiling with ecstatic gazes for the tender epithets with which it pleases them to gratify their lovers.

When they have finished, they tell the taxpayers politely that the closing bell has just sounded, that they will have to come back the following day in order to hand over their money—and, with a dry click, the close the little copper plate.

Who could complain? They are so delightful?

The women on Venus are not content to be bureaucrats. They fill the most elevated positions and direct all the ministries.

When a jurist, an administrate or an officer or merit wants to deploy his talents he must, above all, please Madame la Ministress; and there is no other means available to him than to frequent that lady's salon assiduously. It is necessary that he spends entire afternoons and evenings here, lying or sprawling on cushions, sipping infusions, digesting cocktails, nibbling ginger-flavored petit fours and praising his hostess on the color of her dress and the excellence of her hair-style.

Those representations of the charming sex have only one design: to make intelligent people waste as much time as they can. The proud refuse to lend themselves to that convention, but they only spoil their existence more surely, since, without the support of women, they vegetate perpetually.

It is appropriate to point out that influential ladies only accord their protection to handsome and passionate mortals. To those, they even permit judicious speech, and while they speak, they observe that they have gleaming eyes. They willingly accept them as lovers, or they seek to procure friends for them in their entourage, for they obtain almost as much pleasure from the amours of others as they own. They tire rapidly of the males they love, and pay no more attention to them thereafter than to the peel of an orange or a laddered stocking. Deprived of the benevolence that they inspired, they naturally lose all their qualities and are no longer good for anything.

The Parliament, it goes without saying, is composed entirely of women, for they have supplanted men in all circumscriptions. One of Lagité's correspondents was kind enough to enable him to witness, thanks to wireless, a session of the Chamber of Lady Delegates.

In the bosom of that assembly, there is gossip, vociferations, lies, slander, strutting and the hurling of insults, exactly as in our terrestrial parliaments, and that it not where their singularity lies. At the very most, one can remark that the adversaries, instead of punching one another with their fists, as they do here, grab them by their hair and rake them with fingernails. What gives a particular character to the Parliament of Venus, however, is the subjects that are treated there.

Jacques witnessed a debate that appeared to be very serious. Should women shave their armpits or not?

Some delegates opined in favor of liberty, but the majority, always tyrannical, turned a deaf ear to that, and in order to attest its power, pronounced in favor of shaved armpits.

After that, they debated the color of stockings for the following month. It was decided that they would be a bright rose color, lightly tinted with tea.

An important debate was sparked on another issue, the solution of which, Jacques was told, would have a profound influence on the forthcoming elections. It was a matter of knowing whether to preserve "combinations," which, in spite of their charm and decency, offered inconveniences, and whether there should not be a reversion to good old bloomers.[12]

---

[12] Although this usage exists in English as well as in French it has fallen somewhat out of fashion, so it might be worth noting that the *combinaisons* [combinations] of the Belle Epoque, which first appeared in the late 1870s and reached the peak of their popularity in the 1890s, were underwear garments that combined the chemise and the drawers into a single garment. They are now rare on the High Street but can still be purchased on line, with the aid of catalogue illustrations that ex-

The Cabinet tabled a vote of confidence in declaring itself in favor of combinations, and obtained a large majority.

At one moment, a report by Madame the Ministress of War with regard to a frontier incident nearly took a tragic tone. That was because Her Gracious Excellence with responsibility for Armaments had a wart on her nose the made her ugly and rendered her bellicose. They succeeded in calming her down by indicating an ointment that would cure her defect, and the war was avoided.

All the parties agreed nevertheless that it was necessary to be careful of national security, and the Ministress was warmly applauded when she announced that she had just entrusted the direction of the General Staff to an individual of universally recognized valor, the famous inventor of a permanent wave.

Jacques conserved some doubts regarding the advantages that would result for humankind of such a progress of feminism. He was certainly wrong, for one or several failed experiments prove nothing, and the flaws they reveal can always be amended.

One day, when he had put himself in communication with Venus, a very beautiful naked woman, with large dark and insolent eyes, shiny and sinewy brown hair, lips demanding amour and a vigorously and supply braced torso, suddenly appeared in the luminous circle.

She nibbled the white flesh of her arms, paraded her gaze complaisantly over her milky shoulders, her firm breasts, her smooth and shadowy abdomen, her divinely pulp, firm and satined thighs, caressed those priceless treasures with her soft

---

hibit their peculiar appeal flamboyantly. The fact that the Venusian Parliament voted in favor of them in 1930 might have suggested to contemporary readers, in spite of the briefly-renewed fashionability in 1920s America of camiknickers, that, notwithstanding the sophistication of their wireless apparatus and their enmity to armpit hair, the Venusians were a little behind the times.

and dainty hands, and invited the entire universe, by way of wireless, to contemplate her.

Jacques, enfevered, uttered exclamations of wonder.

The woman's chamber resembled an immense corolla. The floor was strewn with soft cushions that invited the most attractive games. In the center stood a golden tall pistil crowned with a large fleuron that distributed a soft light. Stamens, also in gold, curved back against the walls, terminating in luminescent incense-containers.

Jacques learned subsequently that flowers, some of which are, among us—contrary to all reason—symbols of candid virginity, rightly symbolize on that world the paroxysms of sensuality. Are they not, in fact, the heady alcoves in which Nature shelters the mysteries of fecundation?

The occupant of the amorous calyx caused the enticing profiles of her loins to veer toward contrasted mirrors; she stood up, lay down and left no one ignorant of her most confidential graces. Then she concealed them, in order to render them irresistible. One might have thought that the she-devil, knowing that she was being watched by millions of desires scattered in infinite space, was striving to stimulate them to the point of fury.

Fascinated and hypnotized, Jacques could no longer take his eyes off her. He had lost all notion of current life. From the first moment, that woman from beyond the sky had taken entire possession of his senses, his reason and his will.

He was on his knees before the idol.

"What does this extravagance signify?" growled Cora, his mistress, behind him.

He did not know that she was there. She had gone to deliver some fans and he had not heard her come back in, so absorbed was he by the plant of Amour.

Surprised, he cut off the communication abruptly.

Ha!" said Cora. "You're feasting on obscenities. You surely have a guilty conscience, since you're not admitting me to your pleasure. This wireless communication with the stars doesn't tell me anything worthwhile, I warn you."

He coaxed her in order to soothe her, but he could not see anything except the other woman. He could scarcely discern the fan-maker before him, and in what she said to him he only perceived an importunate buzz.

From then on, he waited for Cora to go out, and he immediately took advantage of it to invoke his astral divinity. Glad to subjugate him, she had the whim of chatting with him. Jacques knew that she had the poetic name of Gilniz, which, in the Venusian language, means Promise.

Frightfully coquettish, she talked to him about her lovers. An adolescent had committed murder in order to steal a diamond, which he had offered to her. The father of a family, in order to pay for magical garments for her, had gambled his fortune and, having lost, killed himself. In a rivalry that she had provoked, a young captain had challenged his best friend to a duel.

While relaying these tragic proofs of her power, she simpered, smiled and burst into laughter.

Jacques was henceforth bewitched by her, for precisely the same reason that enabled her to reign over so many hearts in the land where she lived. She enslaved whomever she wished because she did not love anyone. Setting her lovers ablaze without burning herself, she refused herself out of cruelty or, if she delivered herself, only did so out of egotism, and was never as distant as when one thought that one possessed her. In sum, she was no closer to those who embraced her than to Jacques, from whom she was separated by an incalculable distance—and she appeared all the more attractive because she was inaccessible.

Lagité no longer maintained any reserve in the expression of his sentiments, and, as it amused her, she responded to him without restraint. At that distance, modesty was not an issue, since no effect could result from the most violent covetousness or the least dissimulated advances.

Naturally, he was careful to cease the conversation when he heard Cora come back.

At present, Promise was playing with Jacques like a cat with a mouse. She blew him impetuous kisses, and with expiring expressions she held out her arms to him recklessly.

"Come on, make a little effort," she mocked, "You'll never reach me, alas!"

He stuck his lips to the places on the screen where his correspondent's suggestions were displayed, and followed in vain the moving reflection of her mouth and her splendid nudity.

Cora surged forth one day while he was delivering himself to that unrestrained pursuit, and howling with chagrin and jealousy, she rushed at the screen, smashed it into a hundred pieces, broke the mechanism and, stamping her feet in rage, crushed them underfoot.

It would not have taken as much for Jacques, who had had enough, to break up with the young woman.

In need then of a domicile, he thought that, in sum, perhaps it would be wise to return to his hearth. He was sure of finding there the independence that the quarrelsome humor of his mistress had compromised. Certainly, he no longer loved his wife, but he appreciated her mildness and her proud reserve. So he went back home.

Viviane, who had been thinking about her husband incessantly, was bathed in tears when she saw him coming back through the window. She mopped her eyes quickly, put carmine on her cheeks to hide her pallor, and arranged her hair with a charming artistry. Then, forcing herself to smile in order that he would not read too much criticism in her gaze and would not be put off by her chagrin, she welcomed him as if he had only been away momentarily.

Well, Jacques said to himself, *she scarcely holds anything against me, and doesn't seem to have experienced any pain because of my absence. And I thought she'd be so unhappy! She's quite indifferent, and has only ever had affection for me.*

That is the way that we interpret, unjustly, the sentiments of people we no longer love.

He reinstalled his astral wireless equipment.

He wanted to become a painter in order to reproduce the features of Promise when she appeared in the screen. He bought canvases, paints and brushes, and became a dauber. At first, he found in that new hobby an appeasement of his eternal fever. Painting was now the sole joy for him. A pox on ink and words, which described so poorly! He no longer touched a pen.

He had wanted to frequent the studio of a professional, but he was told that the less he learned of paining, the more he would succeed in it. Such was the fashionable doctrine; he conformed to it, and painted a portrait of Promise in the nude.

In order to be surer of the resemblance, he strove to paint it on the screen itself, and to superimpose his lines and colors of those to the living image. He had asked Promise not to move, and she had consented to that. But as she was the most skittish creature she could not keep still, and the unfortunate Jacques drew six arms, three abdomens and five thighs. By that sign, the esthetes of Montparnasse recognized genius; but their eulogies did not content him, and he persisted stubbornly in continually recommencing the portrait of his lover.

He scarcely hid anything from Viviane, whom he now believed to be insensible. She learned thus about Jacques' chimerical amour, and that redoubled her sadness, for she understood that such a passion could only lead her husband to despair. And although she judged, rightly, that she was prettier than Promise, she knew that she could never compete with that rival, since she had belonged to Jacques, whereas the other was unrealizable Desire.

IV. The Planet Mechania[13]

Almost at the same time, Letord conversed with his friend regarding the observations he had made of another planet, a satellite of the star Epsilon belonging to the constellation Cygnus

You will doubtless remember that is the course of the stormy demonstration given to his colleagues by the inventor of sidereal wireless, a strange species of gnomes had appeared on the screen.

Since then, Letord had studied the star they inhabited and had baptized it Mechania

That was the new world he designated to Jacques.

"Technology," he told him, "is taken to an extreme there."

"Bravo!" exclaimed Lagité. "I'm sure that the natives of Mechania are friends of veritable progress and do not allow themselves to be distracted, like those of Venus, by the folly of their senses. It's evidently among them that I'll discover happiness."

He therefore put himself in continuous communication with the Mechanians. Their immense skulls remained a cause of stupor for him, and even of repulsion, for some time. He questioned them regarding the origin of that singularity.

The memory was conserved on the planet of a very remote era in which the heads of the Mechanians had almost the same proportions as that of humans, but by virtue of calculating, solving equations, imagining plans for apparatus and de-

---

[13] The name of the planet is rendered as Mécante rather than Mécanie [Mechania] at this point in the original, although it is given in the contents page and in the body of the text as Mécanie; I have assumed that the variant is a misprint, but it is not impossible that the author was establishing a momentary confusion between the mechanization of the society and an echo of *méchante* [wicked].

termining components and resultants, they had developed their mental capacities to such an extent that their brains had been hypertrophied. Their swelling encephalum had exerted pressure on the walls of their cerebral container had gradually forced it to an enormous distention.

By way of compensation, as the Mechanians only made use of machines henceforth for action and locomotion, they had allowed their arms and legs to atrophy, which had become extraordinarily thin. They were constantly seated on the little platforms previously mentioned in regard to the projections at the Collège de France.

Thos vehicles, provided with propulsive organs of great complexity, can move over the ground, in the air, and over water, even diving beneath the surface. When the Mechanians want to launch themselves into the sky, under the action of a spring wings opened above their apparatus. When they want to dive into the sea, two halves of a hull envelop them and form a kind of submarine cortex. Those machines attain prodigious velocities; it is banal among the Mechanians to accomplish a tour of the world in six hours, although the diameter of their globe is three times that of Earth. It is a little pleasure trip to go in the afternoon from the temperate zone to the pole or the equator and come back before nightfall.

Nothing is done except by machines. In apartments, along the walls, innumerable buttons are aligned, which it is sufficient to push in order to enter into communication with all points on the globe. From their offices, the chiefs of enterprises can direct exploitations situated at enormous distances. By means of a simple pressure of a finger, they launch irresistible fluids that light blast-furnaces at the antipodes, transport formidable loads, dig canals and tunnel through mountains—for the Mechanians have domesticated the most monstrous forces for their service: hurricanes, tidal waves, avalanches, volcanic eruptions, colossal molecular energy and even the rotation of their plant.

They are however, far from savoring a universal felicity, and the coin has its other side.

The very aspect of Gronovoc, their principal city, is scarcely engaging. The smallest houses there have two hundred and fifty stories, for materials have been invented that permit very elevated constructions. At the foot of those gigantic dwellings, the widest thoroughfares, impenetrable to daylight and incessantly illuminated artificially, seem subterranean. The rich are lodged at the top of the buildings and benefit from terraces open to the sky. The poor huddle at the bottom.

In that great city the din is stupefying. It is an infernal and perpetual cacophony composed of the roar of engines, the howl of trumpets, the roar of sirens, and the thunder of wheels and crazy helices. And at the base of the cliff, the Babelesque skyscrapers are shaken by a storm of vibrations, trepidations and violent shocks, as if a terrible seismic disturbance were continually overturning the country.

Even when they are at repose in their apartments, the Mechanians are thrown about incessantly, as if on the back of an untamed horse. It is, moreover not rare for those monumental buildings, long undermined and cracked by the universal tremor, suddenly to collapse, crushing thousands of inhabitants.

The air stinks with the fumes of all the factories that surround Gronovoc. A disgusting soot rains down in the streets and, insinuating itself into the most beautiful apartments, soils the precious furniture. Acrid and mephitic emanations catch the throat and provoke tearing coughing fits. The vapors are so pernicious that they even attack stone and steel, and corrode them rapidly. How can the Mechanians resist them? A mystery.

In truth, they are furnished with the wherewithal to breathe. A flourishing industry consists of seeking almost-virginal air in countries that are still nearly new. It is sealed in vast containers and divided into sown and sealed bladders, which are sold very dear to those as rich as Croesus. Pure air is the rarest of goods on Mechania, and is reputed to be the greatest delight because it is beyond price, but the poor cannot enjoy it, and for them, that is the gravest reason for them to execrate the rich.

Another scourge on Gronovoc, and perhaps the most intolerable, is the difficulty of circulation there. The streets and the sky are so cluttered with machines that it is almost impossible to fray a path through them. Mechanians who want to use the public highways or launch themselves into the air on their flying platform have to wait for an opening for hours. The Prefect of Police, Chiappac, has lost his renown as a skillful man for that reason.

At every moment, Mechanians are smashed to pulp in the inevitable collisions. The resulting bottleneck is so complete that vehicles crashing on the ground and gyroplanes blown to pieces on the spot form an indescribable magma in which no vehicle can any longer move.

Thus, the very excess of technology renders machines completely useless.

Outside the cities, the spectacle is just as desolating. Nowhere are woods, meadows, rocks and rivers to be seen. Everywhere, forests have been razed in order to make way for factories, quarries and mines. Everywhere, running water is imprisoned in mill-races, pipes and turbines, from which it only escapes filthy and noxious. From chimneys, forage wells, hideous slag-heaps, suspended chaplets of blackened skips, antennae, gigantic gangling cranes and inextricable tangles of steel beams and metallic cables, the whirlwinds of humming engines dishonor the earth and the sky.

In a few places, Mechanian engineers, in order to ward off the regrets of poets, have substituted for trees, which could only perish in the midst of that chaos, masts bearing zinc leaves painted green.

As he collected that information, Jacques felt his enthusiasm cooling. He followed a great sporting event, that of the Eight Days. For a week, the Mechanians circled their planet indefatigably in ultra-rapid aircraft. Some of them effectuated as many as fifty complete tours in twenty-four hours. By night, the fulgurant headlights pursued one another through the sky, transmitting, so to speak, an incessant illumination.

Loudspeakers continually promised a bonus offered by a manufacturer of a vaseline or a laxative to the fastest execution of the next two or three circuits of the world. The lure of recompense provoked momentary vertiginous rivalries of speed. It was then that crashes between competing airplanes occurred, and mortal falls. But no one attached any importance to those futile incidents. With the aid of a sort of large spoon, the formless debris of the victims was scooped into an *ad hoc* receptacle and the fantastic round dance did not pause for such trivia.

The person who was proclaimed the winner of the Eight Days had completed the tour of Mechania four hundred and thirty times during the ordeal. His record was saluted by a universal delirium of joy on the planet.

Jacques searched in vain for a rationale for that crazy performance.

"It authorizes all hopes," a Mechanian told him, "for it allows the imminent time to be glimpsed when the world can be circled in five minutes."

"But again," said Jacques, "what would be the purpose of that?"

"To beat the record."

"But why beat the record?"

"How can you ask?"

Jacques could not get anything more out of his interlocutor.

He understood then that the machine, after having been the servant of the Mechanians, had enslaved them despotically in its turn.

Caught up by the frenzy of machines, the people no longer had any other ideal than delivering themselves to the omnipotence of their engines. They were no longer acting in order to arrive at a goal or to accomplish a task, but in order to savor a pleasure. Their unique concern was to obey the crazy rhythm of the apparatus that they had invented. The Machine was their divinity, their devouring idol. They enjoyed the bloody dangers with which it threatened them, and like fanatical Hindus having themselves crushed under an enormous rolling pagoda, they continually confronted, joyfully, the horrible death that Machinism reserved for them.

"What lunatics!" Lagité repeated, privately.

It was certain that the Mechanians were unaware of any veritable joy. Not only had they unlearned the most exquisite relaxation, walking on foot, but they had lost the pleasant habit of sitting down together around a table in order to have a meal seasoned with amiable words. They no longer ate, they only swallowed hastily chemical pills exactly dosed to maintain their strength.

They no longer slept either. Thanks to an electrical apparatus applied to the nape of the neck, they eliminated the toxins that accumulated there and procured immediately the vigor that sleep gives us. Like Macbeth, they had "murdered sleep." Of the bath in forgetfulness, the voyage in the lands of the impossible that, after every day, delivers us without annihilating us, the Mechanians had deprived themselves forever, by their own fault.

They had suppressed the night. An artificial sun that lit up above the city every evening and sources of light springing forth everywhere maintained an eternal daylight; but the harsh light of that radiation rendered their large eyes opaque, just as the perpetual tintinnabulation had ruined their eardrums.

And under the pretext of never wasting a moment in sleep, they spoiled their entire lives in disorderly running around.

Their sad existence was darkened even further by a secret terror. The Mechanians were fearful of a sudden catastrophe that would cause multitudinous deaths among them, which might perhaps scythe them all down at a single stroke. They expected incessantly to be swept away in the frightful cyclone of a universal war.

Already, ten years before, that curse had fallen upon Mechania, and the ravages committed by science had surpassed all the horrors of old.

In a matter of hours, asphyxiating vapors, mortal rays and epidemics deliberately spread had destroyed immense populations. A few scientists in the laboratories had sufficed to prepare bacterial cultures, to rotate pegs and to mix venomous substances for entire races of Mechanians to be exterminated.

And as, in ten years, science had made incredible progress, it had its disposal, for evil even more than for good, a few levers whose manipulation would unleash cataclysmic forces, the immediate consequence of which would be to send three quarters of the Mechanians to the other world.

It might be, therefore, that one morning, the leaders of one nation, in order to ensure world sovereignty, would order several other nations to be sacrificed, without warning. That unprecedented crime would be carried out in less time than it takes to dance a foxtrot.

Jacques was not astonished that that lugubrious prospect tormented the devotees of Machinism excessively, and he began to think that almost all the advantages conquered by intelligence had very heavy tributes for a ransom.

He heard mention of a new invention. It was an automatic woman whose author called her the Synthetic Eve. Made in chrome steel and vulcanized rubber, the young woman imitated nature rather faithfully. She was painted pink and dressed in the same way as the most elegant Mechanian women.

Jacques saw her functioning.

By means of a little phonograph that she had in her throat, she repeated, while admiring herself: "I'm beautiful. Oh, how beautiful I am?" Microphones lodged in her delightful nacreous ears corresponded with all the fibers of her body and, depending on what was said to her, she turned her head, talked, fluttered, moved her arms, legs and the rest. If anyone asked her whether she would like rings, bracelets, or lace, she immediately replied: "Yes, yes!" If she were offered a five-string pearl necklace, a dress in the latest fashion, or a racing avionette, her face lit up with a very gracious smile, and she lay down immediately.

Other phrases, on the contrary, such as "Love me," "Have pity," and "Be good," did not produce any effect on her whatsoever. She seemed not to hear them, and did not flinch. That was because she had a platinum heart. Apart from that insignificant detail she resembled the majority of Mechanian women well enough to pass for one. However, those ladies and damsels did not agree, and in order not to disoblige them, the Mechanians told the inventor that his Synthetic Eve would be incomplete as long as she had no soul.

Jacques was witness to another episode that rendered him pensive.

A Mechanian child who was returning with his father from a short excursion of seven thousand kilometers had descended in a public square in Gronovoc. He was gazing at, and sniffing with a keen pleasure, a fragile blue thing that he was holding in his fingers.

At the sight of that fragile object, Mechanians flocked around the little boy.

"Where did you find that?" they asked him.

"Out there."

"How pretty it is! How pretty it is! No jewel offers such variegated hues. And those lines, so softly flexible! And those gentle dwellings! And the perfume of that marvel! One might think that one is inhaling the air of paradise. We've never seen or smelled anything similar. What can it be?"

A white-haired old man who had approached said: "Hang on! Nearly ninety years ago I saw those jewels. They were sometimes discovered then in the vicinity of Gronovoc. But what was it called...? Oh, my wretched memory...no, I can no longer remember."

And Jacques, who was observing that scene attentively, murmured pensively: "The unfortunates! They no longer know flowers."

V. The Danaïde

At no time had Lagité stopped thinking about Gilniz, the divine Gilniz whose name meant Promise and who had set his desires ablaze, but who had been quite unable to satisfy them.

Excruciated by his passion for her, he continued to address incendiary litanies of amour to her, and his obligatorily platonic erethism caused him an unspeakable torture.

In order to staunch his intolerable thirst he was obliged to have recourse to the complaisance of more accessible lovers. He thought that only Venusian prostitution could offer him the intoxication that he intended to demand of it, so he wandered in the little streets that the Faubourg Saint-Antoine confines. Breathless, his temples buzzing, he frequented the popular dance-halls where the girls charge twenty-five centimeters to "sweat one" with their protector.

Although he disguised himself for those adventures, the strange torment of his gaze and his gait denounced him as a stranger to the depths, and the prostitutes, whom he troubled, did not allow him to approach them voluntarily, until he succeeded in making them laugh by executing the black bottom with a parodic rascality. The majority of those who accompanied him into nearby dives, however, disappointed him. None of them realized the kind of frantic ghoul that had been forged in his imagination. The poor creatures lacked all lyricism in their decadence. Not attaching to it any stupor or dishonor, nor any pleasure, they delivered themselves to it as to a monotonous chore; and in the middle of the liveliest frolics they begged, somnolently: "You'll give me forty bullets, my darling."

Jacques quit them without his fever having calmed down.

He ended up, however, discovering one who responded better to his ardors. She called herself La Crépue.[14] Having welcomed many lovers, she had never known amour. Suddenly she was "smitten," and no longer dreamed about anything

---

[14] i.e, "the Hairy one."

night or day but Jacques. He instructed her in the sensualities he desired, and they both savored them frantically.

Lagité strove thus to deceive himself, for in the paroxysm of his transports, it was the woman from beyond the sky who offered herself to his transports. He had even warned La Crépue that he would call her Gilniz at such moments, and she had accepted that whim passively, without understanding it.

But she had a pimp, Grêlé of La Bastoche,[15] and that gentleman thought it very bad that his lady found so much charm in someone other than himself. He did not criticize her for abandoning herself to him, but for enjoying it, and, above all, for tiring herself out. He reproached her for "working poorly" and no longer bringing him sufficient profit. Seeing that neither his objurgations nor his brutalities would bring her back to her duty, he hid one night in the vicinity of the cheap hotel in which the two lovers had gone upstairs. When they came down again, and Jacques had arranged a rendezvous with La Crépue for the next day, Grêlé, who followed him treacherously, suddenly planted a "shiv" in his back. Lagité uttered a loud scream; that saved him, for people came running and his attacker ran away without finishing him off.

After being patched up in a pharmacy, Jacques returned home in an auto.

Viviane had conceived some suspicions regarding her husband's absences, but she had feared knowing too much because, always tremulous with amour, she dreaded that by making protestations she might see Jacques desert the hearth again. When he came back covered in blood she felt, at the same time as a bitter anxiety, the dolor of being cruelly enlightened regarding his crapulous frequentations.

But what could she say?

It was necessary, above all, to help the wounded man.

---

[15] La Bastoche is a slang term for the area surrounding the site of the Bastille. The literal meaning of Grêlé would refer to the victim of a hailstorm, but in thin instance it presumably refers to smallpox scars.

In truth, he was not gravely injured. She cared for him and watched over him. He believed that he had become indifferent to her, and was surprised by so much attention. He explained it as the mechanical solicitude that one shows to a habitual companion.

As a challenge, Grêlé had boasted before La Crépue of having "bloodied the bloke." Panicked, she had first asked for news of Jacques from the concierge of the house where he lived; then, reassured, she had written to her lover to tell him that she would wait for him henceforth in another quarter, in order to put the jealous individual off the track.

As Jacques, without precaution, had left the letter lying around, his wife had found the piece of paper and she had deciphered, disgustedly, the naively ignominious babble:

I miss you, my little man. I've left Grêlé. Come, my Jesus. I'll be very nice. I'll do anything, Your Crépue for life.

How many tears Viviane shed in secret!

Sometimes, she had surges of indignation; she told herself that her honor demanded that she revolt and make violent reproaches to her husband. Then she understood that it would compromise forever the hope of winning him back. She also thought that a delicate individual like him could not wallow for long in that mud, that he would weary of it, and that she would then reap the benefit of his repentance.

In the end, she could not help loving Jacques all the more because he was in peril. And, pretending not to know anything, she drained her chalice while closing her eyes, as children swallow a bitter remedy.

Quickly reestablished, thanks to the cares she lavished upon him, Jacques had returned in all haste to his whore in order to try again to tame his howling desire and forget the woman from the stars. The two lovers testified a new fury of sensuality to one another. But every time Jacques separated from La Crépue, far from experiencing an appeasement, he was, on the contrary, more enfevered.

A profound enigma! Nature, which permits the assuagement of hunger and thirst, does not permit lust ever to be sated. The more humans seek to content their genesic appetite, the more they sense it increasing. And if they cease to obey it, it is not because they cease to desire, but only because they cease to be able to satisfy that desire.

The sculptor Auguste Rodin, one of the great philosophers of modern times, has carved in marble a *Danaïde* that depicts that verity.[16] In vain she strives to capture the ironic wave in her bottomless urn, Breathless, harassed and prostrate, she folds herself up in her martyrdom. In her flesh, the nape of her neck and her spine clenches and twists, her loins stretch as if to burst, her entire body is arched, writhing to implore mercy. But she will draw the deceptive water in vain eternally; the gods will never set a term to her suffering, for their ferocious law wants Desire to be an infinite abyss, which no Ocean can ever fill.

Jacques was now being consumed by the fire he had sought to extinguish, and one might have thought that he had killed the gaiety of his heart.

Viviane, who saw him constantly wasting away, was invaded by a poignant anguish. One evening, he was gripped by weakness, and she thought he was going to die. She summoned Jean. In order to save her husband, she had the cruelty of invoking the amour that she inspired in the young physician. The best of women are ever ready, for the benefit to the man they cherish, to make those they do not love suffer atrociously.

As soon as he had come running, Jean addressed a gaze of comical despair to her, and, with heroic disinterest, he studied means of snatching Jacques from death. After having examined the invalid, he retained an impassivity so constrained,

---

[16] *La Danaïde* (1889), now preserved in the Musée Rodin, was originally intended to figure in a portal depicting the Gates of Hell, but was omitted therefrom and completed independently. The statue is sometimes known as "La Source," translated into English as "The Spring," all that translation does not capture the whole meaning.

and avoid so carefully meeting Viviane's gaze, that she divined a fatal verdict and could not suppress a cry of dolor.

Jean's opinion was that it was necessary to carry out a blood transfusion.

The joy of devotion illuminated Viviane. She would have liked to die for Jacques. Jean was determined to spare her. She reproached him for his scruple as a proof of hatred for the moribund, and the unfortunate physician found it very difficult to resolve such a complicated case of conscience.

After a few days, during which Viviane did not take any repose, Jacques seemed reborn. He had woken up and pronounced inconsequential words. She brushed his forehead with a kiss.

"My darling!" he murmured.

Exultant with happiness, she kissed his lips.

"Is that you, Crépue?" he said, as if in a dream.

She felt a cruel pinch in the heart, and wiped her mouth involuntarily with the back of her hand.

Jacques recovered more rapidly than Jean had thought.

"Are there any letters?" he had asked Viviane as soon as he had recovered consciousness.

She knew very well what letters he meant. With a passably hypocritical air of innocence, she deposited all the correspondence on the bed on which Jacques was lying. He searched feverishly, in vain, for the handwriting of the girl of the gutter. As he scanned the newspapers he had not read, he learned that she had been murdered by Grêlé, who had been caught by the police.

He sighed profoundly, but he did not know himself whether he was experiencing the relief of a liberation or the chagrin of a mourning. We are the last to know our own hearts.

VI. The Planet of the Eighty Senses

Barnabé Letord came to visit the convalescent, and when Jacques admitted the cause of his malady to him, the great scientist told him in a mocking tone: "Such a misadventure wouldn't happen on a certain planet that I've just studied. People there abandon themselves freely to all desires without ever being inconvenienced by fatigue."

"Tel me about that country right away!" cried Lagité.

Still mocking, Barnabé Letord confided to him the necessary indications, the wavelength and the astronomical precisions. Jacques had no greater urgency than to communicate with the new star.

The inhabitants he saw there differed from humans above all by virtue of strange structures they bore on the head. A forest of singular apparatus was planted around their forehead and over the surface of their skull. They were large antennae that resembled those of cockchafers, wasps, amts and butterflies. They made up a dense and high spray of plumes of various dimensions, which affected all forms and all colors, and vaguely resembled the horrific plumage with which Red Indian chiefs adorn themselves.

At first, Jacques mistook those diadems for artificial ornaments. He made allusion to that in a conversation with one named Jozibal, whose amity he had rapidly gained in that planet.

"Are you not inconvenienced," he asked him, "by all those appendices swaying over your head?"

"Not at all. They're as light as air. In any case, we're accustomed to them, for we possess them from birth. They're part of us, and they're indispensable to us for sensation."

"For sensation, you say? Do you not, like us, have sufficient sensations with your eyes, your touch, your ears, your smell and your taste?"

"No, certainly not, my dear Terran, and we're surprised that you can content yourself with so few."

"How many senses do you have, then?"

"Eighty."

"Good God!" aid Jacques. He broached the question that piqued his curiosity most of all: "I'm assured that you never weary of pleasures."

"Rather say that we never exhaust them, for when one of our organs is fatigued or worn out we can replace it with another."

"Oh!" said Jacques, supremely interested. "Explain that to me."

"It's quite simple. When we're at table, for instance, and we feel our stomach getting heavy, it's permissible for us to continue eating for as long as we wish. It's sufficient to substitute a new stomach for the one that is no longer functioning. We unhook one and fit another, and the trick is worked."

"Marvelous! And tell me, is it the same for the other organs from which we derive so much pleasure?"

"Of course."

"What? You dispose of spare parts in your effusions of tenderness and you can prolong your ecstasies indefinitely?"

"Assuredly."

Lagité was jubilant.

As he was methodical and wanted to proceed in an orderly fashion, he first asked Jozibal to enable him to witness a sumptuous feast.

"Nothing easier," said the Multisensitive. "I'll take you via the wireless to the palace of a man named Grimalik. Poor for a long time, he has just been enriched by an unexpected inheritance. He has invited a lot of friends to celebrate his recent good fortune and they're occupied in banqueting."

Jacques was delighted to be admitted to such a joyful spectacle.

The guests had gone to table at midday, and it was evening. The dwelling, of splendid magnificence, appeared to have been edified on the model of the sumptuous porticoes that shelter the patricians of Venice feasting around Christ in the masterpiece of Paolo Caliari.[17] Svelte columns sprang lightly

---

[17] The reference is to the Biblical feasts, most famously *The Wedding Feast at Cana* (1563) and *The Feast in the House of Levi*—originally titled *The Last Supper*—(1573), painted in

239

from the ground, seemed to send one another elegant arches, and delighted to mind by virtue of the fine harmony of their blue, green and pink marble. Along the walls, luminous mosaics representing rural scenes spread a suave radiance, and large bays opened to the vertiginously violet night.

Grimalik had not yet had the leisure to form his taste, but he had addressed himself sagely to excellent artists, who had served him well. Majordomos, virtuosos of gastronomy, had given notice for a week ahead of the menus that were to succeed one another. Immeasurable lists mentioned innumerable victuals, the least of which were so enticing that saints would have damned themselves in order to taste them.

It was agreed that before the end of the first period, the dishes would be announced for the following week, and only the repose that the guests procured in neighboring chambers would interrupt, at the end of the night, the joys of gluttony. According to the regular program, however, the feasting would recommence as soon as the host and his guests were out of bed.

Grimalik, who had suffered from hunger in his youth, intended to take his revenge in that fashion. Having reached maturity, he had decided to remain constantly at table henceforth, and to devote all the minutes of his existence to an immense and unique feast that would only end with his death.

Maîtres d'hôtel incessantly brought extraordinarily delicate dishes that were reminiscent of our shads in the snowy whiteness of their flesh, our gilded pullets, the pink slices of our roast meats, our translucent jellies, our most unctuous compotes, our foamiest brioches and our most brittle marzipans, Wine-waiters incessantly poured Edenic wines and divine liqueurs into the cups.

An exquisite music, with rose up at intervals, maintained mild and cheerful thoughts in the audience.

---

elaborate and sumptuous fashion by Paolo Caliari, better known as Veronese.

When the guests had taken pleasure in the thousand treats of the dessert and the repast seemed ready to conclude, the orchestra, which had just been playing languorous airs, suddenly burst forth with resounding fanfares to announce the beginning of a new banquet,

Then the maîtres d'hôtel made a tour of the tables, presenting the guests with a basket of empty stomachs, as we are offered the bread-basket. The exchange of organs was operated instantly, beneath the waistcoat; and everyone resumed eating, with a hearty appetite

There was a second round of dorados, pheasants, ortolans, roast lamb, puddings, marmalades and, once again, triumphant poultry, succulent meats, ineffable salads, prodigious crusty pâtés, and more miraculous creams, paradisal fruits, fabulous cakes, and so on, without respite or pause.

A few vagabonds whom Grimalik counted among his friends and whom he had been careful not to forget—for wealth had not stunned him—were immediately drunk. For from being offended by them, the amphitryon was moved by hearing them launch coarse sallies and lewd refrains.

"Hey," he cried, "get a grip on yourself, Tobobol, Eat and drink. And you, my old Ralabak, you don't have such a feast when you carry your merchandise on the docks. Don't stint yourself."

The more refined guests savored every dish. They came back to them, delighting in them again, and making signs to the lackeys from time to time to bring the basket of stomachs. Then they plied the fork and raised their cups with a revitalized ardor.

Grimalik was with the angels. His friends were no less happy.

That night, when the sky was tinted pink by the approach of dawn, the company, after eighteen hours spent at table, went to bed entirely satisfied.

And Jacques said to himself: *After all, perhaps that's happiness!*

The next day he found the *bon vivants* almost as radiant as the day before. He noticed, nevertheless, than some of them were attaching themselves less devotedly to eating well and drinking well. By the fourth day, several of them seemed to be bored. They were nibbling. They were not weary, because they could renew their hunger indefinitely, but as they were presented with the same aliments or very similar ones, they could no longer feel an equal contentment.

On Grimalik's orders, the master chefs applied themselves to inventing increasingly impressive dishes. Processionally, to the sound of thunderous marches, they brought monstrous animals on the platforms of gigantic platters with raised arms—a red deer, for example, whose pieces, expertly marinated and cooked, were sown back into its skin, reposed, with its feet tucked under its abdomen, on florid grass, but displayed its antlers nevertheless, resplendent with fine gold. Huge birds that had been stuffed with flavorsome mincemeat and then reclad in their sparkling plumage, displayed their tails and seemed to be preparing to take flight.

At first the guests had applauded those victorious entrances and their appetites had been reanimated by them, but gradually, indifference gained them. They were beginning to lose interest in the interminable guzzling, and with the backs of their hands, almost all of them waved away what was offered to them. After a week, there were defections around the tables.

Bitterly, Grimalik ordered his chefs to diversify their recipes further. He stamped his feet; he howled; he now judged the rarest sauces and the most ingenious sorbets execrable. The principal majordomo protested firmly that no one could do any better. With that, the host threw a truffle purée, which was a masterpiece, at his head. The juice ran over the variegated waistcoat of the officer, who wiped it away in a dignified fashion and resigned. He was replaced by his deputy.

A week later, there was only a small group of faithful adherents around Grimalik, who was holding firm solely as a matter of honor. Soon, he remained alone, bleak and infinitely discouraged. He had changed stomachs frequently, but his servants, in spite of their skill, had proved to be incapable of varying the nourishment sufficiently. And Grimalik, having exhausted all experiments in gastronomy in a matter of days, dismissed his army of cooks. He only kept an insignificant little scullion, and no longer ate anything but very simple foods, like boiled eggs, boiled potatoes and white cheese, because any culinary preparation made him feel sick.

Lagité interrogated his correspondent regarding that adventure, who smiled and told him that it was commonplace on the planet of the eighty senses. That was, for Jacques, a great subject for reflection.

Then, giving another direction to his thoughts, he said: "But what about Amour, Amour?" he cried. "Instruct me, then, as to what it is on your world. After all, if your strength is repaired at will, you're certainly the most fortunate of mortals."

"Oh," replied Jozibal, "you can judge that better for yourself. I'll introduce you to an adolescent and a young woman who are among my friends. They love one another, and it's their first romance. Know that we never raise any obstacle to the testimonies of passion. In that regard, our mores are less hypocritical than yours. You can converse with those tender lovers as much as you please."

Lagité saw the turtle-doves emerging from a boscage.

There was the enchantment of the cheerful season in which, on that world as on Earth, the trees bear more flowers than leaves, and the buds resemble jewels of gold and coral, bursting in order to allow the passage of their underwear, still frayed, the green tips of which powder all the twigs of the bushes joyfully. The little birds indulge in singing competitions. The silver dragonflies cling together in pairs, amusing themselves by firming gallant airplanes with eight wings. The butterflies describe crazy histories in the crystal sky by means of their eccentric zigzags; and on the grass, which the tearful dawn had enriched with diamonds, roe deer and their hinds were bounding, with the odd little white behinds.

Perhaps you will be astonished that the countryside on that star was almost identical to our own, but it only seemed so to the eyes of a human like Jacques. It appeared quite different to the eyes of the Multisensitives, whose sight is very different from ours. We shall explain that in due course.

The lovers who were introduced to Jacques were charming. There was no need to ask them whether they were happy. They never ceased taking one another's cheeks between their ten fingers in order to kiss one another.

Lagité talked to them, but they scarcely had the leisure to reply to him. Getting up at cock-crow, after having spent all night cooing, each of them carried a wicker basket bound with brightly colored ribbons, which contained the jewels they had exchanged.

"Excuse us," they said, laughing, and went back into the boscage.

Jacques told Jozibal that they reminded him of the poetry of Catullus.

"My Lesbia, give me a thousand kisses, and then another thousand, and then a hundred more; afterwards, we'll lose count, in order that no one will any longer be able to know the number of our kisses."

"Well, yes," said the Multisensitive, "that's it, exactly. But your Catullus, with all his prowess, was a braggart, while our couple don't nourish themselves on imagination."

"Oh, the rogues. You'll give me news of them?"

"I won't fail to do so."

The next day, Jacques learned from his informant that, without distinguishing noon from midnight, the young people had embraced continuously.

Other days went by in the same fashion. And Lagité said to Jozibal: "I think that they've surpassed the figure of a thousand."

"I think so too, because, for a week, they've been devoting twenty-two hours out of twenty-four to amour."

On the ninth day they were as fresh as on the first. But they were sulking, turning their backs on one another, and no longer going into the wood. They did not take long to separate.

Surprised by that discord, Jacques asked the reason for it.

"Everything encourages the belief," Jozibal replied, "that the lovers were dissatisfied with one another."

"Did they think that they hadn't given one another enough kisses?"

"If they'd given one another a hundred times as many, they wouldn't have been any happier. It's a fatality of Nature that our desire always surpasses our joys immensely."

"That the fatality in question rules on Earth," said Jacques, "I can understand, for our human joys are brief, but yours…!"

"They are nothing in comparison with our wishes."

Jacques was very disconcerted.

"The disillusionment of that couple," Jozibal went on, "is common to almost all Multisensitives. After a few trials, which demonstrate to us the impossibility of ever being sated, we end up considering physical lust as a lure, and from then on we make the decision only to indulge in it with extreme moderation. We scarcely sacrifice to amour as much as human do, and more often than not we're content to exchange tender words. So when our villagers encounter young people who are impatient, they shout to them, jovially: "That will pass before we meet again!""

Lagité continued to inform himself. He wanted to know what the multitude of sensations were experienced by the inhabitants of the privileged planet.

"First of all," said his correspondent, "the five senses with which you're provided are present to us with an incomparable delicacy."

"Oh," said Jacques, vexed, "I can read without spectacles."

"Pooh! What's that? Our sight surpasses in penetration your most magnifying microscopes. In order to look at minuscule objects, it's sufficient for us to adapt our vision by means of a very slight effort. For instance, at this moment, there's a fly on my table. I can see it as large as an elephant. I'm admiring its eyes with a hundred facets polished like mirrors, in which my window and the sky are reflected a hundred times. Its enormous trunk is extending toward a droplet of water that appears to me as a voluminous and resplendent crystal sphere. And in that droplet, I perceive fish of all the colors of the rainbow. They're innumerable microbes that are floating, swimming, or agitating around them bright tresses of multicolored filaments, iridescent and gilded."

"What enchantment!" said Jacques.

"Even better, with a little more attention, we discover the ultimate mysteries of the infinitely small."

"Truly?"

"Thus, for instance, I can discern quite clearly the smallest molecules of that liquid."

"Bah!" sad Jacques.

"Here's a molecule of water. It's composed of atoms of oxygen and hydrogen, which I can see gravitating continuously like words in the immensity. For me, a multitude of stellar systems are rotating in that droplet."

"You're giving me vertigo."

"We're accustomed to these spectacles. The colors that seem to you to be uniform are decomposed for us at every second into their trillions of vibrations, for we have the gift of noting infinitely fugitive impressions. And as soon as we desire it, Nature entire is to our eyes an endless quivering of prodigiously rapid undulations, which intersect in all directions like the cerulean waves of an opal ocean."

"That's unusual!"

"We can also see a long way."

"I've heard it said that eagles in the Alps soaring a thousand meters in the air can perceive a rat in a furrow."

"Your eagles make me laugh," said Jozibal. "With a little application we can see everything—yes, everything. Our sight, like your Roentgen rays, pierces obstacles that are opaque for you. When I sail on the sea, my gaze plunges without difficulty into the most fearful abysses. I see the blinding phosphorescence spread in the supreme depths by masses of plastic jelly, the prototypes of all life. I see the fulgurations of luminous monsters that pursue one another and devour one another. I see the algae that form impenetrable flexible forests in which supple embroideries, diaphanous fringes and incandescent lace move endlessly."

"How beautiful that must be!"

"My sight traverses the soil of our planet and focuses wherever I wish. Here, innumerable leagues below my feet, is a grotto in which, under fantastic pressures and temperatures, an infinite number of marvelous substances are in the process of creation. It's a crucible greater than all your cathedrals, in which golden lava is bubbling, where sparkling swirls of rubies, torsades of topazes and spirals of beryls are unrolling and stretching out, where arrows of turquoise and sprays of sapphire are fusing, where a single diamond as dazzling as a sun and so colossal that it couldn't be contained in any of your public squares is crystallizing in a formidable furnace of myriads of spurting flames."

"What magical visions!" cried Jacques.

"In the same way, our ears perceive harmonies ungraspable for you."

"One of our ancient philosophers, Plato, said that the Just, after life, will be lulled by the music of the celestial spheres."

"We enjoy it. It's a grave, rather sad melody, sometimes as strident as a burst of ironic gaiety, often as imperious and harsh as the voice of an implacable master, at other times sweet and nostalgic, like an immaterial harp."

"Ah, how I'd like to hear it!"

"Oh, one wearies of it at length, you know."

"But my dear friend, tell me about your other senses."

"Look, for example, at these two little violet plumes that stand up above my ears. Can you see them?"

"Perfectly."

"Thanks to these organs, I can exchange thoughts with the other inhabitants of our plan, no matter what distance separates me from them."

"A sort of natural wireless, in sum?"

"That's exactly it. Instantaneously, it's possible for me to chat with a friend who is at the Antipodes."

"That's very agreeable. You're unaware, then, of the chagrin of absence."

"Hmm. Absence isn't always regrettable. In many cases, one would be very glad to be liberated from certain bores. And you can't imagine how we're sometimes exasperated by feeling our little violet plumes vibrate, agitated by incessant appeals."

"Exactly like our telephone, which renders us enraged."

"There isn't any means of avoiding that tyranny, except to have the two antennae excised. Some of us arrive at that extreme by virtue of aggravation. What else shall I tell you? Other antennae allow us to communicate with animals and permit us to know everything that is happening in their brains."

"That's exciting."

"Not as much as you might think. If you could read the mind of a monkey, a pig or a wolf, you'd probably find it very similar to that of a human."

"Ah!"

"I'd like to describe all our senses to you, but how? The words that designate them in our language are untranslatable into yours."

"At least describe your joys to me."

"They're paltry."

"Truly, it seems to me that you don't appreciate appropriately the marvelous favors with which Destiny has heaped you."

"What do you call marvelous favors?"

"Your eighty senses!"

"Alas, that's a derisory figure."

"If only we had them!"

"You'd lament them, like us. Oh, yes, we deplore every day not being able to grasp anything of the innumerable effluvia with which we're brushed by Universal Life."

"You're very ungrateful."

"Not at all. Think about all the secret forces traveling through space. Can you imagine the fabulous quantity of energies analogous to light, to heat, to sound, that are seething everywhere and from which none of us can profit because the pitiful infirmity of our organism forbids them to us. Try to imagine the inexhaustible sources of mysterious currents that are completely lost to us; and recognize with me that our unfortunate eighty senses are ridiculously insufficient. It's at least a million that we'd need in order to begin to communicate with immense Nature."

"That's true!" said Jacques, struck by Jozibal's remarks. "You're not happy, then?" he added.

"We're very unhappy. Have you not observed the despair of Grimalik and the two young lovers after their vain experiments?"

"Yes, but, to tell the truth, I don't really understand why you don't obtain mire benefit from your precious gifts."

"Think about it. As soon as we make use of them, we want to make more use of them, even more, always more. Well, although those excesses are not fatal to us, as in your case, although we don't risk falling ill or dying of them, they nevertheless fill us with an atrocious affliction. We can multiply the return of sensuality, but our indomitable desire rebounds indefinitely toward higher summits. That is why, as soon as we understand the deceptiveness of that absurd pursuit, we abstain from desire."

You judge yourselves as unfortunate as humans, then?"

"More, because out richer senses allow us to measure more accurately the impossibility of being happy."

Lagité meditated for several days on the planet of the eighty senses. He compared the Multisensitives to humans, his contemporaries, so avid for known or unknown enjoyments, and concluded quite naturally that the frantic search for pleasures could not procure happiness in any fashion—in which he was in accord with all moralists, past, present and future.

While he was thinking, he happened to turn his eyes toward the astral wireless screen, and uttered a cry.

He had just seen Gilniz, his Gilniz, his beloved from beyond the sky, in the arms of an inhabitant of Venus.

The scene was certainly worthy of a great painter or a great sculptor, for the two lovers were young and beautiful, and their couple presented all the charm of a pagan masterpiece. But Jacques had his reasons for not liking that spectacle, and jealousy drew roars from him.

It was certainly by design that Gilniz was showing herself to him in her amorous diversions, for she continually disengaged slightly from an embrace in order to look furtively to the side or over the shoulder of her accomplice, to observe the effect that it was producing on Lagité.

She pushed effrontery so far as to call out to him: "Jacques, I present to you my young friend Varluz."

"Curse you!" howled Jacques.

"Poor Jacquot!" she mocked.

"If only," he added, "you had chosen your partner better."

"For what are you reproaching him?"

"For being ugly. He's a fop with insignificant features, an androgyne with forms devoid of vigor."

Jacques was unjust, but sincere, for we never fail to accuse of bad taste the woman who prefers another man to us.

Gilniz continued laughing.

"But after all," he said, "Why are you imposing this odious vision on me?"

"It's my caprice," she said. "And what use can you be to me, except to spice my pleasure with your impotent anger?"

"I'll die of it!"

"What an intoxication to be loved to the point of death!"

Then Jacques insulted without interruption the woman from beyond the sky, who laughed, and kept laughing.

Planted in front of the screen, he vomited invectives. His fists clenched, his face forward, his eyes bulging, the veins in his neck swollen as if to burst, he launched volleys of insults at the two lovers.

Suddenly, he felt a hand on his shoulder. It was his friend Barnabé Letord.

The professor, who often visited Letord, had knocked on the door in vain, and had come in without further ado. At a glance, he had understood. He began by sagely cutting the communication and advising the journalist to calm down.

Jacques was haggard. It took him a long time to recover his breath and his voice.

"Those," said Letord, "are very deadly emotions. I'm aware of your adventure; you've already told me about it—and I think I might have the remedy for your despair."

"You can cure me?" said Lagité, eagerly.

"Why not? I'll put you in contact with a star whose inhabitants forget everything that inconveniences or disobliges them. In watching them live, you might perhaps lose the memory of your deplorable amour. Then the wireless will have repaired the harm that it has done.

That same day, Jacques entered into relations with the race that the scientist had just indicated to him.

VII. Dancing Planet

The Forgetful do not know any of our troubles.

A great misfortune, in striking us, afflicts us, and we fear its return. They immediately start whistling, singing and dancing, and it no longer appears to them.

Lagité envied them.

To tell the truth, he remarked in the Forgetful strange intermittences of memory. For instance, they recall very clearly the money they have lent, but never the money that they owe. If it is their mistress who is waiting for them at a rendezvous they remember it, but not if it is their legitimate wife. They always recognize their friends who have become rich, but never those who have fallen into poverty. These mental defects are, in sum, rather awkward, because they can generate suspicions as to the quality of their soul.

Dancing, which they practice with so much passion, is for them the great means of procuring forgetfulness. Their choreography, however, is neither amiable nor tender, and Lagité remarked, not without astonishment, that it resembled greatly the kind that is fashionable among us. Away with gentle cadences that lull and enchant! The Forgetful want violent and brutal dances that extract them from reality.

They borrow them from the most abject peoples, for instance, from oxherds who, in their world, correspond to coarse Argentine gauchos. Or they reproduce the vulgar and sinister frolics of pimps and prostitutes. Or again, it is from their most backward tribes, their cannibal peoples, that they request lessons in rhythm. Thus, when they deliver themselves to their favorite pleasure they give the impression of lunatics escaped from their guardians. They shiver, slap their thighs and buttocks, and leap on all fours, or with their legs in the air and heads downwards.

As for their music, it is in keeping. There are no melodious and charming chords, but raucous sounds, the appeals of rutting beasts, the trumpeting, growling, bellowing and gasps of avid instincts, a racket of a menagerie in revolt.

"Exactly like our jazz," Jacques noted, amazed. "In the depths of the heavens, jazz is triumphant, as it is here! How small the world is!"

So, from dawn to dusk, and from dusk to dawn, on that planet, people leap and twirl. It is not only young people who are drawn away by that vertigo but mature people, old men and pregnant women. And it is asserted that some precocious infants even start dancing in their mother's womb. People dance at home, they dance in the street, they dance everywhere. Judges taunting the accused, as is their custom, physicians killing their patients, merchants ribbing their clientele, whores plucking popinjays, and functionaries twiddling their thumbs all dance competitively. Some gamblers wager that they can dance for an entire week, night and day, without sleeping.

Dancing Planet was the name that Letord gave that star.

In order to abolish their memory more completely, the Forgetful also have recourse to drugs. One of them, named the Philosopher, whose acquaintance Jacques made, furnished him with precise information regarding those poisons; and that was a further opportunity for Lagité to observe troubling analogies between Dancing Planet and Earth.

Thus, the Forgetful make incessant use of a white powder called chichi, exactly similar to our cocaine. They snort it, the way we take coke, and then sense a vivid current of air, which, penetrating into their head, empties it of all thought. The pleasure of losing the brain seems prodigious to them, and once they have enjoyed it they can no longer do without it. Chichi takes away from its fanatics appetite, reason, health and life, exactly like our coke. But from the moment that it plunges them into a stupid ataraxia, they ask for nothing more, and they march lightly to the tomb.

Jacques' correspondent cited many other stupefying agents of which the inhabitants of Dancing Planet make continual abuse, and which procure them along with stupidity, a more or less rapid death. Lagité commenced from then on seriously to doubt whether that race was a model to follow.

The Philosopher told him that in reality, forgetfulness was not a sovereign remedy for all evils, and in that regard he told him the instructive story of a young Forgetful woman.

Her name was Riri. She had large forget-me-not blue eyes, a slightly turned-up nose and fleshy lips like twin cherries; and she smiled incessantly.

Her mother, named Valnou, had died tragically a few weeks after bringing her into the world, and Riri had been brought up by an aunt. When Riri had grown up, that aunt took her into a charming little wood near the city and said to her:

"Try to remember what I'm going to tell you. You see that rural dance-hall. It's there that your mother met your father. They danced together, after which, the good Valnou, whose head was spinning a little, came to repose with him on their flowery bank of grass. She told me that herself. As she was tired, she went to sleep and she had an enchanting dream.

"She thought that the god of Amour took her in his arms and that, flying away with her, he took her on a beautiful excursion above these woods, ponds and hills. When she woke up, it was your father who was holding her in an embrace; I owe it to the truth to recognize that she took great pleasure in it.

"Until you were born, your father remained your mother's good friend, but when you were born, he left her, without anyone being able to discover what had become of him. And Valnou came back here to shed burning tears. One day, on that little bridge over there, she threw herself into the river and drowned there."

"Oh, Aunt," said Riri, "how right you were to bring me to this fatal place. I'll come back here often, in order to preserve the memory of my mother's sad example, in order not to fall into the same error."

Ad she did, in fact, come back.

She met a young man there, who complimented her on her beauty and offered to take her to the nearby dance-hall.

"No," she said. And, by telling him the whole story of Valnou's disgrace, she made him understand that it was futile to persist.

"On the contrary," he said. "You can dance with me, since the dire fate of your mother will retain you on the slope of error."

That reflection seemed luminous to Riri, so she danced; and then her head spun, and then she went to rest on the grassy bank, and then she had an exquisite dream, and then she gave birth to a little girl named Titi, and then her lover abandoned her, and then she drowned herself.

"And that," said the Philosopher, is where forgetfulness leads.

"Is that adventure true," Jacques asked, "or have you invented it?"

"It's scrupulously exact," replied the other.

"It seems marvelously symbolic. Fundamentally, your story of Riri is the story of all the generations that succeeded one another on Earth as well as on the planet, for the Forgetful."

A few days later, the Philosopher said to Jacques: "You know that a terrible war ravaged our planet only a few years ago..."

"What! You too!" said Jacques. Is it necessary that from one end of the immensity to the other, the same horrible catastrophes are renewed? But go on..."

"In one of our capitals," said the Philosopher, "An Unknown Soldier was buried under a majestic triumphal arch..."

"Ah!" said Jacques. "Exactly like us!"

"And this is what has just happened. The other morning, near that arch, passers-by gathered around a former combatant dressed as if he had returned from the trenches, with his cape torn, stained and dirty, his cap staved in, and his boots and trousers caked in mud. His face was the color of ash, with a short beard pricklier than the shell of a horse-chestnut. His eyes were burning with fever in their sunken orbits.

"In a hoarse voice he said to the people surrounding him: 'I've risen from my tomb.'

"They decided that he was mad. He went on: 'I'm the Unknown Soldier.'

"They shrugged their shoulders and left him, going on their way. But now, people are talking about him. I've just met him, wandering over one of our battlefields, where there was the greatest massacre. I want to show him to you, and for you to hear him via wireless, with the aid of an apparatus I take with me when traveling. And in order for you to understand what he says, I'll translate it for you into interastral language."

"I'm obliged to you," said Jacques.

On his screen, a mountainside was projected. Venerable fir-trees had once shaded that landscape, but the hurricane of shells had striped them all of their branches, sliced, shattered, and uprooted them, turning them upside down.

A tavern served as a rendezvous for the tourists that had been attracted, at first, by the history, and who continued to come out of habit, but who could hardly remember the recent tragedy.

Some young women were talking a walk while waiting for poultry that was being prepared with their intention to finish roasting.

"From this viewpoint," a guide said to them, "you can see an area where at least two million soldiers were killed." He pointed out a nearby clearing. "In that narrow space alone, at least two hundred thousand combatants died."

"Why tell us that?" murmured the darlings. "It isn't cheerful."

And their companions added: "It's necessary not to talk about the war any longer; it's boring. Let's have lunch."

Thy feasted, therefore, in the open air, and the champagne corks popped joyfully.

Then, to the sound of a vielle[18] and a bagpipe, they organized a hop on the very spot that the cicerone had pointed out to them. They needed to stretch their limbs, agitated by the wine. One dancer stumbled over a bone that was sticking out of the ground, and nearly fell, but her dancing-partner caught her, and no one took any notice of the negligible incident.

Suddenly, parting the bushy branches of two decapitated fir-trees, the Unknown Soldier loomed up on a rock. He stood there for a long time, impassively, his arms folded, and no one paid any attention to him. He was emaciated and cadaverous; his gas-mask surmounted the long thinness of his face like a monstrous dome. His waxy skin was stuck so closely to his cheekbones that he might have been mistaken for a death's-head.

---

[18] The elastic term *vielle* was originally applied to a kind of lute, and then to a hurdy-gurdy. It seems to be used here to refer to an accordion.

On the height of his stone pedestal he seemed enormous. A phantom of all those whose bones blistered the soil, he lowered the heavy gaze of the past upon the present.

He cried: "Are you not ashamed?"

Through the fol-de-rol of the music, a young woman heard him. She perceived him, and stopped instantaneously as if changed into a statue of salt, her arm extended toward the apparition.

Those who were around her followed the direction of her hand with their eyes, and were immediately petrified. Communicated from one to another, the immobilization rapidly gained the whole assembly, including the musicians, who interrupted their tune at the measure they had commenced.

All of the stared at the Revenant, and stood there, his eyes dilated and his mouth open.

Suddenly, as one of the witnesses of the scene fled, howling with fear, all the others, seized by panic, dispersed in the blink of an eye. They ran all the way to the horizon without looking back. Even the tavern-keeper and the dish-washer, one throwing away his white cap and the other her dish-rag, ran downhill recklessly to the plain.

As for the Unknown Soldier, grim and not deigning to say a word to the Philosopher, who had been left alone with him, he resumed his way of the cross through the folds of the terrain fertilized by the blood of his brothers.

The newspapers of Dancing Planet related that episode in a few words. The journalists were only astonished that a lunatic had been left at liberty.

Jacques asked his correspondent to continue to give him news of the Unknown Soldier, and the Philosopher promised Lagité to attach himself to the specter's footsteps.

Two days later, immense forges appeared on the screen, filled with a volcanic rumble of machines. In an enormous hall, axles were rotating relentlessly, which activated innumerable transmission belts, connecting-roads, levers, pistons and endless chains.

On aerial rails, carts were moving rapidly. Gigantic steel cylinders were suspended from metallic cables, which, having been brought thus to powerful machines, were subject to a quantity of transformations. Borers hollowed them out, emptied them and turned them into tubes. Under the bite of irresistible scrapers, steel chips were detached and twisted regularly into long, glittering spirals, reminiscent of strange curls of hair.

The tubes were fitted into one another, engaged in thick hoops that circled them, bound them and gave them a formidable solidity.

At the end of that cyclopean manufacture, which required the efforts of an army of workers and the expense of incalculable treasures, cannons of ten, twenty and thirty meters with terrifying mouths were lined up, their interior mathematically rifled: artillery capable of hurling enormous shells extraordinary distances, the explosion of which would disembowel the most massive ramparts, sink marine leviathans instantaneously, raze towns and asphyxiate entire peoples.

Under hangars with infinite and desolating perspectives, projectiles, interminably arranged, were classified in accordance with their height, their width and their destructive properties.

Before those frightful threats of massacre was a group of important individuals, who were strutting, leaping and frolicking. They were the directors of the factory, flanked by military men, governors and diplomats belonging to several nations of Dancing Planet.

One statesman, speaking to his foreign colleagues, said to them flippantly: "Dear allies, thanks to these toys, of which we're making such an abundant provision for you and for ourselves, I think that we're in a position to pulverize all our enemies."

The Philosopher was listening to them, and spoke to them with authority. By what entitlement was he there? A mystery—but as each member of the audience thought himself to be alone in not knowing who he was, he was allowed to say whatever he wished.

"It seems to me," he observed, "that we might have employed our time better since the last war."

"What war?" asked the Forgetful.

"The one that left twelve million dead ten years ago."

"Oh, yes…," they said.

"Consider that it was with toys exactly like these that the admirable result in question was obtained."

"Indeed," conceded a diplomat.

"Are you not of the opinion that it's necessary henceforth to find another way to regulate relations between peoples?"

"Another way?"

"Yes. For example, an unshakable agreement of all nations, a decisive resolution no longer to deceive one another, to associate equitably in all their enterprises, to submit without reserve to a jurisdiction agreed by them in advance to resolve all their disputes. Would that sage organization and that reciprocal confidence require much more intelligence, effort and sacrifice than the unlimited accumulation of all these diabolical engines?"

"Aha!" said the Forgetful. "You're a pacifist."

"Is it not our primary duty to want peace?"

"Undoubtedly, undoubtedly," replied the diplomat. "And we ourselves, in a large number of debates, conferences, congresses, committees, consultations, conventions, sessions, meetings, commissions, colloquia, determinations, deliberations, communiqués, motions, memoirs, conclusions, communications, suggestions, leagues, societies and international groups, are gradually elaborating the code of the peace."

"Well, is that code ready?"

"Not yet, but we've signed a pact."

"Ah! Will it suppress war."

"It puts it outside the law."

"Words! Does it let it live?"

"Evidently."

"You haven't accomplished anything, then?."

"Such is certainly our opinion. And that is why our governments continue to arm themselves to the teeth."

With that, a general cried: "Universal fraternity—what a chimera!"

And everyone agreed: "War is a necessity."

"Beneficent!"

"No progress without war!"

"Blood is the fecundating dew of all civilization!"

Chatting animatedly, the Forgetful had turned their backs on the rows of shells.

One of the diplomats concluded: "This will always be the ultimate reckoning." He turned round abruptly in order to indicate the munitions.

But his arms fell back, and his companions were as petrified as he was.

As if he had emerged from the ground between the nearest projectiles, the Unknown Soldier was standing there, sinister and hallucinatory, as he had appeared on the accursed mountain.

Again, he cried: "Are you not ashamed?"

The amazement of the official personages did not last long.

"Oh, it's the madman," said one of them, "the famous madman that the newspapers have mentioned. Inoffensive, after all."

And they drew away, laughing...

The next day, Jacques saw a pretty house in the suburbs of a great city on Dancing Planet. A low fence surrounded the little garden appended to it. Sitting on a bench, a robust woman was knitting. She had scarcely passed thirty, and, plump and insouciant, she seemed happy.

In a pathway, the master of the house, red-faced with large bulging eyes, a thick neck and a pot belly, was making two young boys of twelve or thirteen, provided with model weapons, perform military exercises.

"Present arms...! Quicker! Mark time...! Present arms! At the double! Up! Up...! At ease! I ordered: 'At ease!' Good

God, what dawdlers you are! If you don't shape up, you'll never be able to kill anyone. What good will you be if you don't even know how to use a rifle? Have you no courage? Don't you love your fatherland? If you love it, it's necessary to hate all foreigners, it's necessary to learn to kill, to kill quickly, and to kill abundantly. That way, your nation will be able to crush other peoples and enslave the world."

The Unknown Soldier had just come to lean on the fence.

He listened, he looked and he condemned with the concentrated anger of a judge confronted with a nameless infamy.

Addressing the woman, he said: "Wife, do you recognize me?"

She raised her head instantly and was shocked to perceive him.

"Who are you?" she said.

"The dead man."

"The dead man?"

"Yes, your husband."

"What?"

"I've risen from the tomb in order to see what's happening."

She sat there, open-mouthed.

"This is your lover, then. I remember. He was our neighbor, While I was in the trenches, he was under cover. I remember. When I was on leave, I noticed something shady between you. Yes, already, while I was with the martyrs out there, you were cheating on me..."

Incapable of turning her eyes away or articulating a word, she wondered whether she was dreaming while awake.

He went on: "Now he's eating your widow's pension, and, being a chauvinist, like all those under cover, he's stuffing the heads of my kids, training them for slaughter. That's how our death has served!"

The lover questioned the woman, dully: "Who is he? Do you know him?"

"No," she said. "It isn't him, since he's dead—at least, they said so; but no one ever knew what became of him."

261

Suddenly, an old cat that was curled up on a bench near his mistress, warming himself in the sun, stretched himself, saw the phantom and leapt on to his shoulder with a single bound, rubbing himself tenderly against his bushy beard.

"Ronronni!" said the Soldier. "My old Ronronni! Animals have better memories than people."

"It's him! It's him!" cried the woman. "A ghost! A ghost!"

And she fainted.

The lover had run into the house. He came back with a revolver, which he aimed at the Soldier. "Get away!" he howled

The other did not budge.

Two detonations rang out.

The Specter did not shudder.

"I hit him, though!" growled the shooter.

"One can't kill the dead," said the Specter.

The lover threw away the revolver and fled.

"Adieu, lads!" said the Soldier to the children, who were bewildered and nailed to the spot. Then, slowly and heavily, at a pace that scraped the road, he resumed the route to the city. Blood was flowing from one of his sleeves and tracing a thin continuous red line on the ground.

Behind him trooped poor people who were already mature, or even old. An irresistible power was impelling them. They had made war and, alone among the Forgetful, they retained a vague memory of it.

They murmured: "It's the Unknown Soldier. He said so and it's true. Let's follow him. He'll speak to us."

The Phantom went all the way to the triumphal arch. As he drew closer to it, his march became more leaden. He appeared to be climbing Calvary. His companions matched his dolorous tread religiously, advancing with extreme slowness. They were all as distressed as he was. And that ascension was so poignant that no one thought of impeding it. The police limited themselves to channeling the fantastic cortege and containing the curious on the sidewalks.

When the Soldier arrived under the arch he saw the Memorial Flame dancing ironically, and by pressing a spring, he extinguished it.

"Lie!" he growled. Then he cried, furiously: "Forgetfulness is a crime!"

And, lying down on the slab, with his hands joined, as if he were a recumbent stone figure on a Medieval sepulcher, he expired.

In the crowd, some said: "He's gone back to sleep. It's necessary to lift the slab in order to lay him in his coffin again." But when night fell, the cadaver was taken away. When he was undressed, it was perceived that he bore two fresh wounds, in one shoulder and the arm.

Lagité interrogated the Philosopher: "Can you explain that enigma to me?"

"It's not my responsibility."

"Do you believe in ghosts?"

"No. I can imagine several keys to the mystery—but so can you, I imagine. Choose the explanation that pleases you most."

"Have you not remarked the extreme resemblance of your planet to the Earth?"

"In fact, people forget there almost as quickly there as they do here, and it's for that reason, without a doubt, that among all the worlds, ours are the most backward."

"I thought for a moment," said Lagité, "that Forgetfulness might procure happiness."

"Do you still think so?"

"Certainly not—for, although Forgetfulness effaces painful memories, it perpetually brings back misfortune and deprives us of the divine benefits of experience. Au revoir, Philosopher."

"Au revoir, Lagité."

VIII. The Star

Jacques was thinking again, somberly, about his ferocious lover from beyond the sky when he saw the face of an inhabitant of Venus appear on the screen.

He recognized him immediately. It was Varluz, the lover he had seen with Gilniz.

"What do you want with me?" he cried, angrily. "I hate you. I don't want to see you. What evil joy leads you to torment me? Disappear! Disappear!"

"Monsieur," replied Varluz, who knew that Frenchmen address one another thus, "I don't mean you any harm. On the contrary, I feel sorry for you."

"Keep your pity. I don't want it."

However, the other spoke so softly that Lagité ended up consenting to listen to him.

"Gilniz," said Varluz, "has wagered that she can drive you to suicide within a week."

"I'll enable her to win her bet."

"You're mad!"

"She's so beautiful that she's worth the sacrifice of my life."

"No, she's a rather vulgar woman, and there are many among us more beautiful."

"Why do you love her?"

"I did love her, I don't know why; but I no longer love her, and, having possessed her until the point of distaste, I see her now as she is."

"Youth, charm and intelligence," said Jacques, "she has all the graces; she's incomparable."

"What an error!" said Varluz. "Out of compassion, I'll tell you the truth. At a distance, Gilniz seems exquisite to you, and it's true that she was once quite pretty. But at close range one sees the commencement of goose-feet, wrinkles in the forehead and creases in the neck, an unfortunate down on the chin and hollows in the shoulders. She fights those defects with an arsenal of unguents and incessant massages, but she has to do a great deal to dissimulate the erosions of time."

"You're calumniating her!"

"I'll call upon one of my friends, who is here, and who was Gilniz's lover before me. For you must suspect that, at her age, she has had several"

"Gilniz is a ruin," the friend affirmed. And they both continued, speaking alternately:

"Gilniz is ugly."

"Ignorant."

"Stupid."

"Nasty."

"Hateful."

"I believe you're sincere," said Jacques, "but that's because Heaven has overloaded you and rendered you very difficult by giving you the most adorable women in the universe."

"Not at all," exclaimed Varluz. "Your women on Earth are infinitely more beautiful than ours."

"Oh, nonsense!"

"I swear to you. Very recently, my friend and I have chanced to see on your Earth a marvelous woman whom we've named the Perfect."

"Bah! Describe her, then."

"Impossible!"

"Try, though."

"We'll certainly remain far below the model," said Varluz. "But since you beg us, here it goes: her eyes launch lightning flashes."

"They're very soft," said the friend.

"She's robust," added Varluz

"As light as a butterfly," the friend contributed.

"Melancholy."

"Very jovial."

"Can't you agree, damn it?" said Lagité.

"We are," said Varluz. "It's because the most opposed merits are conciliated in her. She's sometimes this and sometimes that. I love her for certain qualities, my friend for others, for we're both madly smitten. Oh, how we envy you for respiring the air that bathes her and treading the ground that bears her!"

Lagité was beginning to love her too, so communicative was their ardor. "You assure me that she's more desirable than Gilniz?"

"A thousand times!"

"I beg you to make your portrait more precise," he insisted.

They told him that the terrestrial woman was blonde, of medium height, that her voice and her laughter were enchantments, and that, without any doubt, a host of mortals must kiss the traces of her footfalls.

That final hyperbole orientated Jacques' imagination.

"She's a film star," he said.

"We don't know, but it's possible."

"Where have you seen her?"

As they were about to respond, the communication was suddenly interrupted.

Lagité swore like a Templar.

He made countless attempts to resume the conversation, but he did not succeed; the apparatus his correspondents were using was probably defective.

It was necessary for him to make a decision.

Surely she's a film star, he thought.

By dint of repeating that, he eventually put a name to the conviction: "It's Ellis K. Pittsworth. I'll wager that it's her. Doesn't she respond in every way to the description? More beautiful than Gilniz? In truth, they ought to know, since they live near Gilniz. But in that case, that's the cure for my folly. I love Ellis K. Pittsworth, I adore her, and I want her."

Such was the soliloquy to which he delivered himself.

He had never encountered the celebrated American star, but he had seen enough of her in the films in which she appeared to place himself in the number of her fans.

One of those cinematic romances, above all, had triggered the delirium of crowds. It was a weepie entitled *The*

266

Vengeance of Amour. Ellis K. Pittsworth played the role of a certain Miss Rosalind, a completely insensible young woman. Rosalind was triumphantly seductive, but she remained deaf to all the pleas of her adorers. It seemed to her that amour was degrading; she did not intend to submit to it at any price, and wanted her heart to remain proudly free.

A quantity of suitors filed through her home. Rosalind's parents welcomed them sadly, for they were only too well aware of their daughter's arrogant humor. Sometimes, they risked intervening with her in favor of some suitor provided with great merits, whose success they desired keenly, but she always blocked her ears. The number of desperate actions caused by her disdain was uncountable.

One young millionaire had laid all his wealth at Rosalind's feet. He had offered her a marble palace full of fabulous marvels, statues by Phidias and Praxiteles, paintings by Raphael, Titian, Rembrandt and Watteau, priceless jewels, books and manuscripts calculated to drive the most ostentatious bibliophile mad. Rosalind had declared: 'I don't care about your palace, or you.'

To which the amorous fellow had replied: "If you don't accept it, I'll burn it."

She had contented herself with shrugging her shoulders. Immediately, he had set fire to the sardanapalesque accumulation of treasures and had hurled himself into the blaze. Naturally, the film reproduced all the phases of the tragic holocaust. Many other lovers similarly dismissed by Rosalind had sought and found death. It was their espousal with death that gave the film an irresistible attraction and kept the public breathless.

Before the eyes of the impassive Rosalind, a champion racing driver who adored her took part in a contest and drove his machine at such a fantastic speed that his intention to kill himself gave rise to an intolerable anguish. In his bolide he overtook the vehicles of his competitors with a temerity that wrenched exclamations from the spectators. Suddenly, the inevitable accident occurred; the demented auto escaped from the track, bounded into the air, fell back at an enormous distance and turned a dozen horrifying somersaults before immobilizing definitively. Then, by a tragic hazard, the stretcher carrying the frightfully mangled body of the champion passed in front of Rosalind, whose face did not betray the slightest emotion.

Two aviators who loved one another like brothers and who had had the misfortune to fall in love with Rosalind at the same time had decided, after having endured her refusals, to die together. At an altitude of five thousand meters the two heroes of the air smashed their apparatus voluntarily in a frightful collision, which left a long wake of flames as they fell.

The description of the other catastrophes with which the reel of film was packed would be tedious. Let us limit ourselves to noting that Rosalind's scorn put a frightful end to a mountain-climber who scaled perpendicular walls vertiginously and then fell into a bottomless precipice, a navigator who launched himself on to a furious sea in a frail boat, and an animal tamer who excited his wild beasts to the point of devouring him.

Those suicides were so well imitated that nothing revealed the trickery, and the public had gooseflesh. Finally, the tearful mother of a young man came to beg Rosalind not to refuse her child: a vain intercession; the young man killed himself, and his mother after him. But, in order not to belie the title of the film, Amour avenged himself, and Rosalind expired under the revolver of a final lover, who then turned the weapon against himself.

That deplorable tissue of ineptitudes had enjoyed a success with stupid crowds all over the world to which masterpieces of thought and fantasy had never been able to aspire. And it was thus that Miss Ellis K. Pittsworth had conquered star status among the most dazzling stars of the United States.

Lagité had no doubt that she was the extraordinary woman designated by the two inhabitants of Venus. The penchant that she already inspired in him suddenly increased, and he did not attempt to put a brake on it, since he hoped that it might be a distraction for his unfortunate passion.

Giving Viviane the pretext of a journalistic investigation, he therefore set forth for Hollywood.

There, he succeeded fairly rapidly in being introduced into the little group who frequented Miss Ellis K. Pittsworth, and had himself introduced to her.

To tell the truth, the star was a creature as puerile and mediocre as she was vain. She had commenced by selling flowers in the city of Cinema; a director had noticed her, made her his mistress and had confided the principal role in the famous *Vengeance of Amour* to her, and the star had been launched in order to launch the film. An incredible debauchery of publicity had been unleashed in favor of Miss Ellis. Surprising stories had been told about her. Her dresses were woven from the feathers of hummingbirds. The water of her baths was made up of dew collected by a multitude of servants from odorous plants. Her favorite dish was the tongues of nightingales. She had had a barman to whom she was attached invent a cocktail that bore her name, and in which all know species of alcohol—which is to say, exactly three thousand six hundred and fifty four—were expertly mixed.

These items of information, trumpeted at great expense by all the newspapers in the world, had created a prestigious popularity for Miss Ellis. From that moment on she had become an idol drunk on incense. She no longer listened to any but the most absurd caprices; and by virtue of a phenomenon often observed among cinema artistes, she identified with her role, even in real life. She affected with regard to her fervent admirers the indifference of Miss Rosalind, and pushed indifference as far as barbarity.

One of her fantasies, above all, had produced an effect of terror on public opinion.

She had invited an amorous young man who had pursued her with entreaties that would have moved any other woman to comparison to come to contemplate her at her home. "But before then," she specified, "prove the sincerity of your pas-

269

sion send me your oath in writing to look me full in the face and not to turn your eyes away from me for at least a minute."

The other had sworn something that seemed to him to be so simple and had hastened to the nocturnal rendezvous she has assigned to him.

He had passed through rooms in which a profound obscurity reigned, through which he had been directed by invisible guides.

Then, suddenly, he had been pushed into a room of which Miss Ellis K, Pittsworth, standing on a pedestal, occupied the center. She was constelled by an infinite number of jewels, which were electric lamps of a prodigious intensity. Above her forehead was a resplendent diadem formed by several juxtaposed suns. It was an apparatus as powerful as the maritime lighthouses with the moist distant range.

Miss Ellis closed her eyes. When she was told that the adorer had entered, she commanded him: "Look at me for a minute, an entire minute; I order that it should be verified.

He was so madly in love that he agreed to submit to that extravagant demand. He believed that he could support the glare of the fulgurant light. Operators equipped with dark glasses followed the second hand of the clock. Half a minute had not gone by when the amorous young man cried: "Blind! I'm blind!"

Then she cried, sniggering: "He hasn't kept his oath, since he can no longer look at me. Throw him out."

Such was the woman, the perverse child, that Jacques Lagité proposed to conquer.

She, of course, allowed him to sigh without taking any pity on him. She only seemed to be more desirable. Every day he discovered new seductions and found more grace in the attractions she refused to him. But he remarked, dolorously, that she showed herself more merciful with regard to a very rich man, Arthur W. Ricklin, the Chewing-gum King.

Ricklin seemed to have at his service a genie from the *Arabian Nights*. All that Miss Ellis desired, everything that she seemed to covet with a glance, everything that she wished for idly while yawning, was instantaneously granted to her: jewels, twelve-cylinder autos, luxury animals, palaces, estates and insensate fêtes.

Lagité nourished a furious jealousy with regard to the Chewing-gum King. He was afflicted by not being as rich.

When he expressed his regrets in that regard to a young American named William J. Burkle, who practiced astral wireless as ardently as he did, that confidant sketched a smile and said: "My dear Monsieur Lagité, I've been in communication for a few days with the Planet of Gold. Come and see me at my home. You'll see what sort of happiness the inhabitants of that star have.

"Oh," said Lagité, "if I had their good fortune, I'd be immensely happy!"

So saying, he went to Burkle's house.

IX. The Planet of Gold

Scarcely was he there than the apparatus, tuned in advance, projected the image of a city whose appearance struck Jacques Lagité with surprise. The houses, the passers-by, the pavements, the vehicles and the trees were so shiny that one could not look at them without blinking. Reflections sprang from all sides, intersecting, filing the air with myriads of flashes.

"You're in the land of Gold," the American said to Jacques.

"What a strange spectacle!" Lagité murmured. He added, in a low voice: "It's terrifying!"

An instant later, he was talking to an Orian to whom Burkle had introduced him, whose name was Bassadec.

"I can see," said that person to Lagité, "that you're eager to know about our way of life."

"Indeed," said Jacques.

"Many of your peers," said Bassadec, "Are ecstatic about the substance of which we're made. I can assure you, however, that it isn't pleasant to be made of gold."

At that moment, Burkle manipulated his wireless apparatus so that Bassadec's face occupied the entire screen. It was a repulsive vision. Bassadec looked like one of those men coated in metallic powder who pretend to be statues at fairs. He was sticky with gold. But what caused a frisson was the sight of his gold gums and tongue when he opened his mouth, and, above all, his eyes. Instead of being limpid, like ours, they were both opaque and radiant, like the back of a golden spoon. The golden pupil, marked by a slight round bump, moved from side to side without letting and thought or sentiment filter through.

Bassadec continued: "In truth, there are on our planet, as on your Earth, things and being who are not made of gold, mortals on veritable flesh, animals, plants and fruits that are natural; but they're only found far from our cities. A certain number of us, known as 'gold-handlers' possess from birth the deadly gift of transforming everything they touch, and even approach, into the resplendent metal."

"That's quite bizarre," said Jacques. "Our ancient Greeks imagined a fable of which your words remind me. They related that King Midas had received from a divinity the favor of turning everything into gold."

"Well," said Bassadec, "in our country that power is a reality. Here there are many King Midases. I'm one of them myself."

He was interrupted by a golden domestic who came to announce a visitor. Bassadec said to Jacques: "It's a young cousin that I'm about to welcome. She has always lived in the country. She often writes me exquisite letters, and I know that she's adorably pretty. I asked her to come. It's my dream to marry her, for I'd like to found a family. I authorize you to witness our first conversation."

The young woman came in. She was not made of gold; she resembled the most charming women on Earth: pale blue eyes, a complexion of almost diaphanous freshness; her lips were not thickened by rouge like those of our elegant women,

272

but their soft crimson revealed the attractive purity of her blood and her tenderness.

On seeing her, Bassadec seemed transfigured.

For an instant, his hard gaze seemed to become profound, and translucent.

Then something frightful happened.

As Bassadec contemplated her, the azure of the young woman's eyes changed progressively into an opaque yellow color. It was a sort of leucoma that, born in the center of the pupil, expanded to invade the entire eyeball. Soon, the entire surface of what had been the celestial liquid of tears and laughter solidified like a lake frozen in the course of a harsh winter.

Bassadec's features expressed a poignant dolor. He moved his face very close to the young woman, as if he wanted to capture there a living light that was withdrawing forever. And his own gaze, momentarily softened, was covered with a new gleaming armor.

"The golden leprosy!" he cried.

Now the golden tint was spreading from the woman's eyelids to her cheeks, and all of her face. Her smile, initially as caressant and as aerial as a dancing ray of sunlight, mutated into a hypocritical and fixed grace.

"A golden smile!" murmured Bassadec, sobbing.

"What's the matter, cousin?" she asked him.

"Oh," he said, hiding his face in his hands. "I love you…and I'm very unhappy."

"I don't see what's so sad about that. I love you too, my cousin, and if you wish, my happiness will be yours."

Raising his head again, he put his arm round his cousin's waist and tried to give her a kiss; but the young woman's lips had just acquired a splendor of newly-minted coin.

He sighed: "A golden kiss!" And, relaxing his embrace, he said, bitterly: "Forgive me, I'm suffering…"

"I can see that, and without being able to explain your chagrin, I share it."

She thought that she ought to express compassion, and addressed soothing words to him, as if to an invalid. He remained silent.

Then she said: "Look; you're making me cry."

He looked again. In his cousin's eyes, two metallic pearls condensed, grew, slid over the edges of the eyelids, and swelled into thick, sparkling, heavy, droplets that rolled down the cheeks.

"Golden tears!" said Bassadec. He added: "I need to be alone."

When she had left him, he said to Jacques: "Now you know what the golden leprosy is, the terrible contagion of our planet."

Jacques was still anguished.

Bassadec went on: "Our scientists affirm that it commences with the hardening of the heart. From there it reaches the eyes, and then the entire body."

"It's certain that I no longer envy you," said Lagité.

"You've just seen what becomes of the women we love: golden statues. Even those who say that they are our friends have a heart of metal As soon as they frequent us our gold flows over them, their gaze is veiled and we can no longer read their souls. The most envied possessions—houses, châteaux, domains—as soon as they fall into our hands, lose all the charms with which art or nature has adorned them and no longer reflect anything but the glacial radiation of gold. No sooner have we admired a beautiful painting than it is converted into a uniform sheet of gold. Our greedy majordomos only serve us extremely rare and complicated dishes, which are transformed as soon as they appear on our table. Oh, the indigestible nourishment! How fortunate you are, you who can regale yourselves with salads and good vulgar wine!"

Jacques felt sorry for him, and asked: "What are your occupations?"

"To a host of worthy fellows we offer wind, fog or smoke, and they come running in a host to give us their petty savings of golden coin in exchange."

"That's a simple métier."

"Not as much as you think. It's not always easy to see smoke. It's necessary to shout very loudly, to run out of breath and become hoarse on the steps of the Temple, where that merchandise is offered. Between gold-handlers, we fight rude battles. Bold competitors succeeded in depreciating our stock. Then the clientele demand their money back. If we can't return it we're dishonored and we have to blow our brains out." Bassadec took a pretty little golden revolver out of a drawer. "You see this plaything. It's loaded. I always have it within arm's reach."

"What a frightful threat! It's paying very dearly for the privilege of piling up a lot of gold coins."

"I ought to admit that a number of my colleagues abstain today from shooting themselves in the head. They prefer to live, and the judges send them to nurse their sick honor in an establishment called the Santé."[19]

"Very good. But what do you do with your gold coin?"

"We fill strongboxes buried in our cellars."

"A singular happiness!"

"We count our wealth repeatedly. We congratulate ourselves when we observe that it surpasses that of our rivals."

"Good. But there are always people richer than you."

"Indeed," Bassadec admitted. "That's our continual torment. But the richest among us dreams lamentably about becoming even richer."

"Are you never happy, then?"

Bassadec reflected for a few seconds. "No," he said, "never, since we lack amour. And when I die on my treasures, my despair, you see, will be to search all my memories in vain for a single gaze of a sincere lover."

---

[19] In the early twentieth century La Santé Prison, built on a site where there was once a sanitarium, was the principal place of criminal detention in Paris.

"Poor rich man!" sighed Lagité. But he added within himself: *Which doesn't alter the fact that if I had so much gold, it would be easy for me to conquer Ellis K. Pittsworth.*

At the same moment, someone came to announce that the Chewing-gum King had hanged himself from a tree in one of the estates that he had given to Miss Ellis. He had committed suicide because he had learned that the star was cheating on him outrageously with a boxer names Elias Mokololo.

Lagité welcomed that news with chagrin. He deplored the fact that Miss Ellis had not chosen him as an accomplice to betray Arthur W. Ricklin. *Why*, he wondered, *is she smitten with that pugilist? Is he worth more than me? Am I not infinitely more seductive? To prefer a negro to me!*

That thought no longer quit him.

His friend Burkle, whom he saw again a few days later, was struck by his sadness and asked him the cause.

Jacques told him, and exclaimed: "If only I were a boxer! If only I were an athlete!"

To which Burkle replied mysteriously: "I want to offer you a spectacle that might perhaps distract you." And taking him home with him, he placed him in front of the sidereal screen again.

X. Sporting Planet

Jacques saw a crowd at a crossroads.

In the foreground, a strange being was standing. He had a small head, a low brow, immense legs, strong thighs and powerful calves; he was cleaved all the way to the chin. He was the inhabitant of that star who had entered into correspondence with Burkle. His name was All-legs. Very obliging, he willingly translated into sidereal Esperanto the conversations going on around him. Lagité understood without difficulty what the members of the crowd he was observing on the screen were saying.

There were many individuals there just as extraordinary as All-legs, although very different. Some of them were remarkable by virtue of enormous fists much more voluminous than their head—fists that could stun an ox with a single blow. Others possessed massive biceps, like stout oak branches, which knotted as they flexed, rounding out and selling into formidable globes.

All of them, however, had a skull as flat as those of reptiles and fish.

Jacques widened his eyes as he looked at them.

A number of the natives of the planet had neither biceps, nor fists, nor thighs, nor calves, and were scarcely visible, so paltry were they. But they were neither the least active not the least strident. They were running in all directions, shouting and vociferating, apparently prey to a delirious excitement.

"Tomorrow is the great day," they howled. "Thanks to Bruto, we're sure of winning. To our nation, victory over all the others! Hurrah for Bruto! Bruto is our pride, Bruto is our glory. What science in the attack! What artistry on the defensive! What a glance! What energy! What valor! Bruto is the thunder and the lightning! He's a hero! He's our savior! He's the flower of our blood, the supreme effort of our race! We put all our hopes in him. All our destinies repose on him. Oh, Bruto, Bruto, our noble, our prodigious, our divine Bruto!"

"Who are they talking about?" Jacques asked "This celestial Bruto they adore is doubtless a great general? I think they must fear an invasion, and are expecting the salvation of the fatherland from him. My word, I'm dying of the desire to make his acquaintance."

"Nothing easier," replied All-legs.

And following that amiable correspondent, who was equipped with a portable wireless apparatus, Jacques penetrated into a vast and luminous hangar.

Important people were running around there as feverishly as the crowd in the public square.

The attention of all was magnetized by a central point toward which All-Legs slipped, with some difficulty, through the close ranks of the audience.

Suddenly, he said to Jacques; "Well, here's the individual you want to see."

Lagité found himself confronted by a large ape, a frightful gorilla: jaws ignobly heavy and jutting, a broad snub-nose which seemed to have been indefatigably and implacably hammered; prominent eyebrows bearing the traces of terrible blows that that broken them in several places. The eyes, in the depths of hollow orbits, were blinking like dying flames. The bestial muzzle was ornamented by a forest of russet hairs that rendered him even more hideous.

Lagité looked at the ape with some impatience.

Where, then, is the magnanimous Bruto?" he asked

"In front of you," said All-legs.

"What! This gorilla..."

"...is Bruto, our great boxing champion."

"I don't understand."

"Your friend Burkle hasn't told you what our planet is, then?"

Burkle intervened. "My dear Lagité," he said, "I wanted to let you discover the planet of sports—Sporting Planet, where athletes are kings—for yourself. Bruto, the gorilla you're contemplating, is the object of general fanaticism in this country because he's fighting tomorrow, according to what All-legs tells me, a gorilla no less massive and no less ugly than himself, named Poussah, the champion of another people.[20] They're disputing the royalty of boxing. Over the entire planet, you won't find a beggar, a toothless old crone or a street-urchin with a shit-stained shirt who isn't impassioned by that fight. The people whose gorilla triumphs will be proclaimed the foremost of all, and the one whose gorilla is beaten will suffer a mortal humiliation. Now you're informed."

Stupefied, Jacques continued to observe the gorilla, especially his hairy fists, which were as large as valises.

---

[20] A poussah, in French, is the name of a figurine with a rounded base, which rights itself automatically if tipped over, like an American "Bobo doll."

Bruto seemed anxious. Furtively, he reached out toward a flask, but before he could grasp it, his trainer had snatched it away, crying: "You know very well that a champion doesn't have the right to be thirsty without the authorization of his manager."

A moment later, Bruto dropped his paw on a basket of fruits that happened to be within his reach. The trainer pulled it away rudely.

"You know very well that a champion doesn't have the right to be hungry without the authorization of his manager."

"Truly," said Jacques, "That's a king less free than a slave."

Suddenly, Bruto gave signs of the most intense delight. He had just perceived, in the midst of the people present, a little she-monkey who, opening her mouth all the way to her ears, addressed the most provocative of smiles to him. He ran toward her, jostling everyone in his passage, and there were hectic caresses, ardent clashes of muzzles and passionate purrs of tenderness.

The trainer spat out an oath. "Who let that female in? I've strictly forbidden the door to her."

And, calling acolytes to his aid, he bounded forward to snatch the gorillette away from Bruto.

They had a great deal of difficulty doing so. The gorilla held firm. Sometimes, a wild anger was legible in his eyes, sometimes a poignant supplication. He would rather have died than be separated from the little she-monkey. But nothing could soften his torturers. They loosened his arms by force and, in spite of his desperate groans, they expelled the object of his amours.

"You know very well, though, Bruto," the despot concluded, severely, "that a champion doesn't have the right to without the permission of his manager." With that, he ordered: "Let's get to work!"

Then an imposing fellow came to plant himself in front of Bruto and landed a volley of punches methodically on his muzzle. The gorilla submitted to that martyrdom almost without a peep.

That's called *soaking it up*,"[21] All-legs specified.

The huge ape's muzzle was tumefied. From time to time he uttered a muted plaint, and moved backwards

"Bruto!" cried the manager, furiously.

And the gorilla repented, offering himself again to the avalanche of blows; his poor face was swollen with bruises.

That barbaric exercise lasted a full quarter of an hour.

"How much compassion Bruto's face inspires in me!" said Jacques.

The next day was that of the Bruto-Poussah match.

In the eighteenth round, after a ferocious combat, Bruto reckoned with his adversary.

Each of them was in a state as bad as the other. Bruto's head, shoulders and chest were nothing but a crimson mass. His shredded muzzle left his broken teeth visible. One of his eyes was buried beneath a swelling over his cheekbone; the other, having been torn out, was hanging from the orbit like a huge bloody billiard-ball.

"Victory! Victory!" howled the unbridled crowd. They scarcely had time to wipe Bruto's face. His adorers seized him in haste and perched him on their shoulders. All-legs followed them with agility.

From all the crossroads, all the streets and all the houses the multitude rushed toward the victor. Living whirlwinds incessantly unfurled around him, and his escort had a great deal to do to prevent him from being crushed. The city, the nation and the world were seething with an overflowing joy.

---

[21] The French *encaisser*, employed at this point in the text, has several meanings, but with regard to punches it means taking a beating or handing one out. It could, however, also be construed to mean "boxing" in the straightforward sense of putting something in a box; the covert *double entendre* is probably intended.

Four hundred inhabitants of the capital perished, stifled. One of them, who emerged from his swelling dazedly and seemed not to understand anything, was snatched up by the turbulence, knocked down, trampled flattened and reduced to pulp. It was learned that he was a great scientist who had discovered a short while before the unique formula to which all the laws of nature were obedient. At the very moment when he had been torn apart, his mind was doubtless concentrated on an equation that would have opened up new and infinite horizons to science.

The people, informed of that loss, consoled themselves immediately, considering it as the utterly negligible ransom for the immense delight caused by the victory of the national ape.

Bruto's bearers continued to swing him around through the tumultuous popular effervescence. Suddenly, the gorilla escaped them. In spite of the lamentable state of his eyes, he had discerned his gorillette in the midst of the crowd, on the arm of a puny little fellow, who was kissing her without restraint.

Bruto had reached the couple rapidly. The panicked gorillette tried to flee; the champion tried to grab hold of her. At that moment, the little lover, so pitiful, of whom it seemed that Bruto ought only to make a mouthful, rapidly opened a long, sharp cutlass, which he plunged into the champion's side all the way to the hilt. And the emperor of all past, present and future boxers fell, stone dead.

"What good did it do him to be so strong?" concluded Jacques, philosophically.

All-legs, detaching himself from the crowd, resumed the conversation with his terrestrial friends.

Jacques asked him whether Bruto would be regretted for a long time on Sporting Planet.

"Oh," said All-legs, "nothing is forgotten as promptly as a champion. I was once the champion runner. Who remembers?"

"At least," said Jacques, "in the epoch of their glory, the aces of sport savor the ineffable joy of deploying their physical strength magnificently."

"Not at all; for instead of building our muscles in order to render our life more agreeable and more useful, we waste our entire life building muscles." He went on: "We're never happy, you see. A frightful anxiety eats us away incessantly. We run fast, but we always want to run faster, and we tremble constantly that a rival will snatch our record away from us. But what annoys us most of all is the abandonment in which we're left when our vigor declines. I, All-legs, once so acclaimed, counts for no more today than an old wheezy horse. And it's the same for all the old kings of the stadium or the ring. If they dared, they'd sent us to the abattoir."

Jacques shook his head in a melancholy fashion. "It's certain," he said to Burkle, "that I wouldn't want to live on Sporting Planet. However," he added, "I know a boxer on Earth who is happy. That's Elias Makalolo."

At that moment, someone came in to announce that Elias Makalolo had just been beaten in five seconds in San Francisco. Apparently, his little fêtes with Miss Ellis had harmed his fitness considerably.

The next morning, when the defeated boxer presented himself guilelessly at the star's residence, she had him thrown out.

Who was delighted? Lagité.

He recommended putting forward his amorous candidacy obstinately. No less obstinately, Miss Ellis dismissed him, but always with teasing remarks that retained Jacques rather than putting him off.

While he was agape with idolatry before the star, she became madly smitten with a certain John La Blague, a cinema actor, an utter imbecile who ordinarily had the employment of a buffoon.

"My God!" lamented Lagité. "Why am I not a cinema artiste, then?"

He exposed that ambition to the star herself, who suggested treacherously that he present himself to a director in order to assume the most reckless roles—for example, leaping from a moving express train, entering into a burning building, or going over Niagara Falls.

Convinced that he would amaze the beauty thus, he did not hesitate to follow her advice, and was accepted.

Miss Ellis became increasingly cheerful, and promised herself a rare delectation in watching him kill himself before her eyes.

It was at that moment when Viviane arrived on America. For several months she had not received any letter from Jacques. Suspecting that a new danger was menacing him, she resolved to fly to his aid. Without warning him, therefore, she came to Hollywood and, adopting a false name, she carefully avoided meeting him.

She learned that he was courting Miss Ellis with an unfortunate perseverance, and that the star was amusing herself with him as with a marionette.

She understood that her husband's life was at the mercy of a caprice of the scatterbrain in question, and she was even more convinced when she was informed of the audacious exploits that he had promised to accomplish on signing his contract as an artiste.

As she was very good herself, she could not imagine fundamental malevolence, and thought that he simply desired to move Miss Ellis. She therefore paid her a visit and spoke to her naively as a sister. She told her how much she loved Jacques, how much she was suffering, and begged her to cease her inhumane games with him.

The star let her finish, and then, with the closed face of a disdainful doll, she said: "Madame, your husband is only one of the most obscure of my millions of admirers, and I scarcely discern him at my feet. Play with him? He's too indifferent to me. If you value him so much, you ought to take better care of him. Take him back, please. It's the greatest service you could do me."

Viviane asked her to excuse her, and above all not to reveal the step she had taken to her husband. The star made no response. And when she saw Lagité again she hastened to say to him in a honeyed tone: "I've had a visit from your wife, my little Jacques."

"My wife?"

"Yes, your wife, Viviane. She's in Hollywood. She came to confide her subjects of complaint to me. How can you render such a sweet creature unhappy? It's necessary to take pity on her, my little Jacques, and not to see me anymore. I promised her formally to detach you from me, and I no longer want your homage. I'm sacrificing it to the tranquility of your charming wife. Go find her, my little Jacques. Go on. And make her happy. She deserves it. Forget me. Adieu, my little Jacques. I authorize you to kiss my foot."

Lagité had gone pale with rage, and remained nonplussed. He asked where his wife was. Miss Ellis possessed that information, and gave it to him.

Lagité ran to the hotel indicated. Scarcely was he in his wife's presence than he said: "Why have you been to see Miss Pittsworth? What need do you have to interfere in my sentimental life? You had proved sufficiently that you didn't care about me. The separation scarcely cost you. We had each organized our existence apart. It was a tacit convention with which you seemed comfortable. And suddenly, out of idleness or malfeasance, you come to trouble an amity that is very dear to me."

Viviane tried to interrupt him.

"Jacques, Jacques, my dear Jacques, don't you know that I still love you, that I never stopped loving you? Jacques, Jacques, my dear Jacques, I've only ever acted for your benefit. I no longer even think about myself. I've acquired the habitude of suffering! But I don't want anyone to cause you to die. You're letting yourself be led astray. Don't you know where you're being led? I wanted to save you from yourself."

"If I've gone astray," said Jacques, "that doesn't concern anyone but me, and I beg you not to occupy yourself with me

284

any longer. Return to Europe. I no longer want to see you here."

Viviane went on: "Jacques, Jacques, I love you. Jacques, surely you'll thank me some day for having warned you. Surely you'll recognize that I'm obeying an immense tenderness. Jacques, my Jacques, look at me. Jacques, try to reflect for a moment. Try to get a grip on yourself..."

He turned his gaze away from her willfully, clenched his fists, ground his teeth, and growled impatiently: "Will this last long?"

"Look at me one last time," she said, "since you can no longer tolerate me."

He consented to make her that gift.

He saw Viviane's eyes bathed pitifully with tears; he saw her lips trembling and extended toward him, against all hope.

This wife's expression was so dramatic that, without him being conscious of it, a sort of revelation of amour took place in his mind. But that did not last for more than a second. He remained immobile and harsh.

Quickly, in a low voice and a heart-rending tone, she said: "Adieu, Jacques.

"Adieu," he said, dryly.

She left.

A few days later, in New York, Jacques was shooting his first big film with Miss Ellis K. Pittsworth.

The principal episode was to bring the emotion of the spectators to its paroxysm. In the scenario, the hero followed a ledge a few centimeters wide along the façade of a skyscraper at the height of the forty-fourth floor. Then he made an enormous leap through the void in order to launch himself into a bedroom whose window was open. He rejoined his lover thus, without anyone being able to suspect the vertiginous route he had taken.

That role had been reserved for Jacques, and that of the lover for Miss Ellis.

It would not have been difficult to fake the scene, but the star, by means of her promising smiles, piqued Lagité's boldness. She succeeded in making him request himself that the terrifying prowess be accomplished veritably. By means of plunging views, they would impose on the public the certainty of witnessing an acrobatic extravagance, implausible and yet real. And that conviction would give the film an inestimable price.

Jacques signed a paper in which he took full responsibility for his crazy stunt.

An extraordinarily high building was found in New York, which fulfilled exactly the conditions of the film. The narrow ledge and the window separated from the neighboring wall by a distance that only a champion long-jumper was capable of crossing seemed to have been designed expressly to respond to the intentions of the scenario.

At the appointed date the artistes and cinematographers were projected by the elevator to the forty-fourth floor. The operators posted themselves above, below and on all sides.

Then Jacques steppe over a sill and placed both feet one in front of the other on a thin projection. He stuck his back against the concrete wall that descended vertically all the way to the causeway a hundred meters below. In the sudden silence of all other sounds, the *tac-tac-tac* of the recording apparatus was unleashed. In the depths of the abyss, Jacques could see large streetcars, autobuses and vehicles without number reduced to Lilliputian proportions. The passers-by were no more than busy ants and the drama that was beginning to unfold up above could not even attract their attention, so distant were they from it.

Fifty meters below Lagité doves were circling, and their flight caused him to experience an impression of vacillation. He noticed a group of children at the very foot of the wall and wanted to shout to them to move away, for he feared that he might fall on them, but his voice choked.

A cinematographer began to chide him without mildness: "Get on with it, then! Play your role, damn it! Think about what you're doing."

Jacques stiffened, and began to walk mechanically, easing along the façade. He reached the angle from which he had to jump. It was absolutely necessary that he make a leap, because there was no room to turn around to return to his departure point.

He could never understand why, at that moment, his memory evoked the infinitely sad face of Viviane. Directly opposite him, but at a distance that seemed insurmountable, he perceived Miss Ellis, who was addressing a strange smile to him. The star's eyes were shining with a strange joy, and fascinated him. Her hands extended toward him and her fingers were trembling, as if to attract a prey.

The cinematographer who had admonished Jacques shouted again: "Go on, then! Jump!"

Jacques could no longer detach his gaze from Miss Ellis's eyes

And suddenly without him understanding how it happened, he found himself launched into space.

The extremity of his feet came down on the sill of the window he had to attain, and one of his soles slipped on the stone corner, but the other held. He had a frightful sensation. Miss Ellis who, according to the scenario, was supposed to help him, made use of her extended arms not to help him regain his equilibrium but to push him back into the void. Jacques' knees received the shock of those perfidious little hands, which, while appearing to help him, tried, on the contrary, to throw him to his death.

Making a supreme effort to lean forward, he remained for a quarter of a second—which is to say, an eternity—wondering whether he was about to fall into the room or outwards into the gaping void.

Then his will-power, perhaps violating the law of gravity, pushed him into the room where the star was.

He rolled on the parquet, but got to his feet immediately. And, closing the window abruptly, he took Miss Elis by the arms and held them tightly against her body.

"Slut!" he shouted, in her face.

She laughed spasmodically.

Then like a boor, for he had lost control of himself, he rained a magisterial volley of blows over the shoulders and back of the American woman. She protected herself as best she could with her hands and arms. Jacques seemed to relieve his quivering nervous tension thus. As for Miss Ellis, she did not seem overly upset by the adventure. Letting the storm pass, she limited herself to moaning: "Sorry, sorry, Jacques, Jacques, my little Jacques."

It even seemed that the rain of blows had produced the beneficent effect of a cold shower

When he had duly corrected her he took her, with no further ceremony, on the carpet. To tell the truth, she scarcely resisted, and started to sigh ecstatically: "My dear Jack, my love, my little Jacky!"

Then, at the first relay, she looked at him tenderly, as if to beg for further caresses, and she repeated: "Jacky, Jacky, little Jacky."

Lagité thought: *What, then? That's all it was? And it's for that that I was breathless with desire for so long? I thought she was so attractive, but she's insipid! I thought she was so beautiful, but she's vulgar! I thought she was so intelligent, but she's stupid!*

And without saying a word, he left.

He returned to Europe.

Viviane, who had preceded him there, had taken literally recommendation that Jacques had made to her no longer to appear in his presence. She had rented lodgings. of which she had not sent him the address.

As soon as he was in Paris, Lagité received a communication from the star Venus.

It was Varluz and his friend who were telephoning.

"Aha! There you are!" Jacques said to them. "I congratulate you for having informed me so well. I found her, your unequaled woman. She was the most repulsive creature of whom one could dream."

"Who are you talking about?"

"The woman you indicated to me, the American star Miss Ellis K. Pittsworth."

"We never signified her to you. We know her well, for so much renown surrounds her that we wanted to see her on our screen. But we judged her insignificant. No, no, dear Monsieur, the Earthwoman who seemed to us so beautiful, and who certainly is..."

"You've seen her again?"

"Yes, very recently."

"Where is she?"

"In Paris."

"In Paris you say?"

"Yes."

"Where?"

"Rue..."

Once again, the apparatus ceased functioning.

"Thunder!" howled Jacques. "Always cut off when I'm expecting a capital revelation. One might think that Destiny is playing with me."

He grumbled and raged, and tried every means to renew the conversation, but in vain.

Once again, he was prey to a frightful pessimism.

In the course of the conversation he had with Professor Letord he exhaled his irremediable bitterness.

"The happiness I seek," he said, "flees me incessantly. Recently, I thought I'd discovered amour down here. What a disappointment awaited me! All our dreams of felicity, when I see them realized in the planets, appear to me to be ridiculous. And since our wishes, even when they're fulfilled, can't bring us any contentment, there's no doubt that the universe is very badly made. I'm beginning to believe that nothing is as it should be, that everything is topsy-turvy, and that it would be necessary to change the world radically to render existence acceptable."

"In that case," said Letord, smiling, "I have what you need."

"How?"

"I'll introduce you to the Topsy-Turvy Planet."

"What star is that?"

"A world in which everything works in the opposite fashion to this one. Perhaps it will please you."

XI. The Topsy-Turvy Planet

Jacques saw then the most bewildering spectacle that astral wireless had yet contrived for him.

On a road he saw a horse harnessed to a cabriolet, identical to those of our countries. The horse was trotting and the cabriolet was rolling; but it was not the animal that was drawing the vehicle—it was the other way around. The vehicle was going backwards and pulling the horse at a good speed. The occupants of the carriage had their backs turned to the direction in which they were going. One of them, who was holding the reins, reached out from time to time to deliver strokes of the whip to the animal, which was lifting its legs alternately and running backwards with extreme celerity.

Recovering from his stupor slightly, Jacques asked: "Where are they going?"

"Apparently, where they desire to go," replied Letord. "What is certain is that they're going briskly."

Lagité agreed.

He saw an express train that was traversing the countryside. The train was similar to outs, except that, like the cabriolet, it was going backwards. To be sure, that happens among us when a locomotive is hitched behind wagons and pushes them, but in the topsy-turvy world certain details indicated that the locomotive was functioning in a fashion exactly opposite to ours.

Thus, the smoke, which on our world escapes in thick clouds and dissipates in the air, after having floated for a few moments in a long trail, was flowing in an inverse direction. It gradually formed in the air, became a gray cloud above the train, then caught up with the engine, amassed in thick swirls and was suddenly engulfed in the funnel with a tumultuous violence.

When the train came very close, in the brief moment in which he was able to observe the platform of the engine, Jacques saw, not without amazement, that the stoker was drawing pieces of coal out of the furnace, which were extinguished, and which he threw into the tender in the aspect of large black lumps.

"Where is that train going?" Lagité asked.

"It's going," said Letord, "to the station that, here, would be that of departure, and on that planet is that of arrival."

Jacques took his head in his hands in order to prevent it from bursting.

"It's necessary to do that," said Letord. "Fundamentally, the trains on that world depart and arrive as they do here, more or less regularly. What is backwards on Earth is forwards there. And that's the only difference; perhaps it's not very sensible."

The professor had naturally given the natives of the planet in reverse the name of Retrogrades. For some time already he had linked himself in amity with one of them, named Edaramac, and they had frequent conversations.

Let us note that when the Retrogrades want to translate their ideas into sidereal Esperanto they always begin their words at the end. It is on that condition alone that they render them comprehensible to their correspondents on other worlds.

Edaramac kindly offered to allow Jacques to witness via wireless the birth of an old man.

Lagité and Letord then found themselves in a cemetery in the land of the Retrogrades. A large audience was stationed around a crypt occupied by a coffin covered with a great many sheaves of roses and lilies.

The undertakers moved aside the heap of flowers, lifted the heavy bier on to their shoulders, and walked backwards to a hearse, on to which they loaded their burden. After that, the crowd formed a long procession behind the plumed vehicle and started walking backwards toward the dead man's domicile.

The hearse followed them, slowly and solemnly, still going backwards, in the fashion of the land.

The body was taken up to the mortuary chamber. The undertakers unscrewed the coffin, took the dead man out and laid him in his bed.

Then he uttered a profound sigh. He started crying like a new-born baby, opened his eyes to the light, with difficulty, closed them again, and then opened them again.

Jacques thought aloud: "In truth, whether one starts life at one end or the other, birth and death have no more difference than an entrance door and an exit door."

Edaramac told him that the resemblances were, in fact, considerable. And for Jacques' instruction, he indicated many others.

"Isn't that old man who has just come into the world similar to your babies? No hair, no teeth. He can only eat pap. He doesn't talk; he babbles. His intelligence is unsteady. He's a child. He has no more sex than a baby. Women serve him, while caressing him, according him an indulgent and protective solicitude. They rebuke him when he's dirty and when he's demanding; they repress his tantrums.

"In accordance with the natural laws of our planet, he'll rejuvenate as he gets older. He'll take several years to become a vigorous individual, an active and enlightened person, important in the State. He'll maintain himself for some time in that fortunate situation, Women will address engaging smiles to him and treat him as a conqueror. He'll make them suffer and take pride in being tortured by them. Then he'll rejuvenate further. He'll become a veritable child; his consciousness will weaken; he'll no longer be able to talk; he'll eat pap again, and women will spank his bottom. One day, in a warm bedroom, he'll enter his mother's womb, and nine months later, he'll return to the nothingness from which he emerged."

"I can see," said Jacques, "that on your world, as on ours, one goes from impotence to impotence and from oblivion to oblivion, savoring few brief and feeble joys in the interim."

"That's it exactly," replied Edaramac. He went on: "Our public life is also very similar to yours. We go from one war to another, passing through a peace that is always too short. Or, if you prefer, we go from one bad peace to another bad one, passing though atrocious and impious wars."

"Absolutely as we do," sighed Jacques.

"Our civilization," said Edaramac, "of which we are proud follows almost the same curve as yours. We depart from a profound darkness that you all decadence and we shall end up, I believe, in another night no less black, which you call primitive barbarity. Your progress, by an exactly opposite route, borrows the same trajectory and goes, like ours from nothing to nothing."

"That's true," said Jacques.

"However," said Edaramac, "on observing you closely, I'm obliged to think that we are more favored than you are."

"Why?"

"I've learned that among you, life becomes harder from day to day. Your produce gets incessantly dearer. In order to eat, drink, sleep and pay for the smiles of courtesans, you constantly spend more; and you always have to furnish more labor, always make more effort, in order to procure what is indispensable to you."

"That's only too true," said Jacques, afflicted.

"Here, on the contrary, everything is better arranged, and our products are less sophisticated than before. I've also heard it said that in your cities, it has become very difficult to find lodgings. There are not enough apartments there, except for the rich, who don't flinch at paying extravagant sums to proprietors. We once suffered from that nasty encumbrance, but it has ceased now; there are few among us who don't possess their dwelling, and the others pay modest rents for the habitation of their choice.

"From one year to the next, our existence is less feverish and less unsteady. We no longer know the bustle that once rendered the streets of our capitals impracticable. We are getting rid of inventions that were very dangerous, like the airplane and the automobile. We are giving ourselves the charming pleasure of traveling in carriages throughout peaceful countryside and savoring exquisite cuisine in our village inns, and excellent vintage wines."

"Alas," said Lagité, "how far that time is from us!"

"I also know that morality is declining in your countries, that criminals are incessantly becoming more audacious, that even your children are committing murders, the accounts of which in your newspapers make the hair stand on end"

"You're well-informed," said Jacques.

"Here," said Edaramac, "those horrors were once frequent, but they are becoming rarer, and we observe with pleasure that our society is heading toward the reign of Virtue."

"So much the better for you," said Jacques. "In sum, it would be in our interests to imitate you sometimes—which is to say, to live backwards."

"Pardon me," said Edaramac, "but it's you who live backwards and we who live forwards.

"Perhaps you're right," said Jacques, "and I'm too courteous to contradict you."

The conversation was left there, and Jacques said to Letord: "Fundamentally, in spite of certain temporary superiorities, the existence of the Retrogrades is too similar to ours for me to desire it. Backwards or forwards, life is as detestable in one direction as the other."

After that session, therefore, Lagité returned home more desolate than before. A bell rang on his wireless apparatus. It was the inhabits of Venus, Varluz and his friend, once again.

"Ah! Finally!" cried Jacques. "You can say that you've damned me. Lord God, may your apparatus function! Repair it once and for all! Now, quickly, quickly, the name of the wom-

294

an whom you consider to be the most accomplished creature in the universe, and whom you have nicknamed the Perfect."

"Her name?" said Varluz. "She hasn't revealed it to us. She consents to talk to us in order to distract herself, but she's so reserved and so discreet that she hides her name from us."

"Her address too, it goes without saying?"

"Yes," said Varluz, "but we possess it, for we were in communication with the person who occupied the same apartment before her. It's in Paris, forty-four Rue de Rennes, on the fourth floor.

"Very good," said Jacques. But in order for me to recognize the Perfect reliably, repeat to me what she looks like."

"Adorable! Adorable!"

"That's understood, but tall or petite?"

"Tall," said Varluz.

"Petite," said his friend.

"Ah!" said Jacques. "Always this discord! Are you talking about the same woman?"

"Certainly," said Varluz. "Only, for myself, I like tall women and he likes petite ones. At such a distance, everyone sees his divinity in the aspect that seduces him the most."

"You told me that she's blonde?"

"Yes, like gold," said Varluz.

"Like ripe wheat," said his friend.

"She's blonde, that point is established. The color of her eyes?"

"Blue," said Varluz.

"Maroon," said his friend.

"Damn it!" said Jacques. "You're odious, with your contradictions. Anyway I'll run to the address you've given me."

"Be careful," said Varluz. "There's another woman with her constantly, a friend that she cherishes with all her soul, and who lives with her."

"Damn!" said Jacques. "I don't want to make a mistake. Give me a portrait of the friend...but you're going to tell me black and white again. I'll compare the two women myself, and I'll quickly discern the more beautiful."

"There's no mistaking her," said Varluz.

Jacques thanked them and set forth at a rapid stride. He climbed four floors of the indicated house, and without seeking a pretext under which he could present himself to the mistress of the apartment, he rang the doorbell.

The door opens.

Who does he see?

His wife.

Very surprised, she allows the radiance of a boundless joy to appear on her face. She is on the point of saying to him: "Oh, my dear husband, you've searched for me and you've found me!"

For an instant, he is struck by the extraordinary transfiguration of his wife; then he says: "What! You live here?"

Immediately, the flame that has just illuminated Viviane is extinguished. "Didn't you know?"

"No," says Jacques, and remains nonplussed.

"Why have you come, then?'"

He looks at her with increasing embarrassment. "Don't you share this apartment with a friend?" he stammers.

"Yes, with a young Englishwoman, Miss Pearson."

"Oh! Can you describe her to me?"

"Certainly. Thick golden blonde hair..."

"That's it. And the color of her eyes?"

"Maroon."

"I was sure of it. Can I see her?"

"No, she's in London at the moment."

"Can you give me here address in England."

She noted it down on a piece of paper and asked him: "Do you know Miss Pearson?"

"Someone has told me about her."

"Would you like me to write to her?"

"No thank you. Common friends will take charge of introducing me."

"So be it."

"Au revoir, Viviane. Excuse me for having disturbed you..."

"Jacques, Jacques, it's not..."

He had taken her hand and, without thinking about it, had retained it in his own. There is sometimes a secret will within us better than our own.

Suddenly, he got a grip on himself again, and, releasing Viviane's hand, he retreated toward the door. He was not very proud of himself. On tiptoe, like a thief, he escaped.

He resembled a somnambulist who follows a path between obstacles without seeing them.

The following day he was in London, outside the house in which he expected to find Miss Pearson.

He asked the porter for her.

"Miss Pearson?" said the man. "Don't you know?"

"No..."

"She was run over by a tram yesterday."

There we go, thought Jacques. *It was written that I would never know the most beautiful woman in the universe.*

He returned to Paris.

"Still as dark?" Letord asked him, when he saw him again.

"In truth, your topsy-turvy planet wasn't of a nature to cheer me up. And since that sorry experience, nothing has reconciled me with life. Well, I've ended up suspecting that it's me who is incapable of savoring the pleasures of existence. I suppose I don't have enough intelligence to discover the beauties of creation. Perhaps if I were more intelligent..."

"You think, then, that intelligence procures happiness?" Letord interjected.

"How do I know?"

"Well, my dear friend, I'll conduct you via wireless to a land inhabited by beings whose brains are the most luminous and the best constructed. They know everything at birth. They foresee everything and forget nothing. It's sufficient for them to see a cause to divine its most distant results. They're the Sages.

As usual, he turned screws and handles, and said: "Here's the planet of the Sages."

XII. The Planet of the Sages

Jacques saw two lovers in a park from a tale of enchantment.

It was dusk. Light breezes swayed clusters of roses the festooned an arbor like cassolettes of incense. For the crown of an elm, a nightingale launched its plaint into the golden sky, which seemed to be weeping diamond tears. The long, thick grass, from which hundreds of downy moths were rising, enchained the footfalls of the couple and invited them insidiously to lie down. The male retained his companion, drew her against him, implored her, and sought passionately the sensuality of the chalice of her lips.

But she turned her head away sadly. "No," she said to him, "no. It would be folly to make the voyage to the land of blue dreams tonight..."

"But..."

"Oh, my beloved, don't you know what the fatal effects of our amour would be? Can't you foresee them, as I can?"

"I love you. I love you and I don't know anything else. Every note the nightingale sings is a kiss fluttering toward you; every frisson of the nocturnal breeze is a caress that envelops you; every star, every rose is a counsel of amour. Don't refuse so much joy!"

"Is it necessary that desire blinds you? The woe of which I'm apprehensive is doubtless distant, but I can see it; I can see it with the bitter certainly that the privilege of being able to read the future clearly gives us. If you testify your amour to me here, I shall have a son who will be our joy to begin with. He will grow up, he will be handsome, he will have as much courage as intelligence. At twenty-five he will marry a young woman worthy of him. But alas, it's in this very park that the cruelty of Fate will be attested. Our son, conceived in the ecstasy of this evening, will be as sensible as we are to the enchantment of this exquisite location. At the end of a heavy summer day, he will stroll on this lawn with his wife. They will come to sit down in the shade of that elm, already so majestic, and which, in twenty-five years, will be immense. While they are intoxicating themselves with kisses, all their sagacity will vanish for an instant. They will not pay attention to the rapid approach of a storm. And lightning, striking the tree, will kill them instantly."

The lover looked at her with terror.

"What despair we will experience," she said, "on learning of the death of those cherished children, scythed down in their radiant beauty, snatched from our infinite tenderness! What frightful regrets for our old age! Oh, my beloved, do you still want a pleasure for which we will pay later with such suffering?"

"No, certainly not," he said, sadly.

Then, sagely, close to one another but carefully avoiding any contact between them, they returned home and put off until another day the effusions of their amour.

At that moment, Sufar appeared; he was Letord's correspondent on the planet of the Sages. He was the one who had hidden a recording apparatus in the grass in order to permit Letord and Jacques to follow the conversation of the lovers.

"What do you think of that couple?" he asked Lagité.

"The lover is a mere fool," said Jacques, "unless he's lost his taste for such an annoyingly far-sighted woman."

"Don't think that she was talking nonsense," said Sufar. "All that is strictly accurate."

"Well, it's a great calamity to perceive such distant disasters; and I believe that one would never sacrifice to amour if one calculated its consequences in that way."

That same evening, Sufar took our two friends through the streets of the capital of the Sages. Many natives of the land were standing with one foot in the air, like storks sleeping with one leg raised. Lagité asked what that signified.

"To satisfy your curiosity," said Sufar, "you're going to hear one of those whose attitude astonishes you. Here is one of my relatives, who is standing outside his mistress's house."

He approached the individual in question, who was talking to himself out loud.

"Ought I to go up to see my little friend No, because she'll ask me for a pearl necklace, and if I give it to her, she'll have other demands, which will end up putting me on my uppers.

"Should I go home? No, for if I break it off with my mistress, chagrin will trouble my head, I'll administer my affairs badly and I'll run to disaster."

Sufar left him to his irresolution and said to Lagité: "All the other Sages that you see here on one foot are stopped in the same way by insoluble alternatives."

They went to see one of his friends, a great industrialist. He was at his work-table, pen in hand, his arm in suspense. And, much like the other, he was talking to himself:

"Should I sign this letter to accept a larger metallurgical order? Yes, or else a competitor will supplant me, and won't take long to ruin my enterprises. But no, because, worn out by excessive labor. I'll neglect my wife, who will cuckold me, and her treason will overwhelm me with dolor and drive me to suicide."

Sufar extracted him from his reverence and said to Jacques: "In all our dwellings, Sages remain thus, with a hand or a foot in the air."

"What a people!" said Jacques.

The next day, Sufar enabled Jacques and Letord to witness a Council of Ministers. He had greased the palm of one of his cousins, an usher at the palace of the Presidency, who had dissimulated an apparatus in a corner of the room.

Against the wall, on a platform, they perceived a beautiful statue of a naked woman whose gaze was meditative and forehead high but whose legs and arms had been cut off at the level of the torso. Lagité put off until after the session asking Sufar what the image represented.

The Ministers examined several important matters

Should a new city be built at the mouth of a certain river?

"Yes," said Their Excellencies, "for that port is indispensable to our national commerce."

"No," they said, a moment later, "for in fifty years, to the day, according to ineluctable previsions, there will be an earthquake in that region, and the city will be entirely destroyed."

Conclusion: nothing was decided.

Another question: should they found a colony in a certain territory rich in future promise?

"Yes," said the Ministers, "for it's necessary to direct out there the surplus of the metropolitan population."

"No," said the same Ministers, "for that colony, in sixty years and six months, will excite the jealousy of a neighboring nation by its prosperity, which will take possession of it after a murderous war."

Conclusion: nothing was decided.

A third question: the great coquette of the National Theater had broken her contract and was performing on another stage. That caused some scandal, for among Sages as among fools, the actions and gestures of the princesses of the comedic gambling-den impassion everyone.

Ought the capricious individual be constrained to respect her contract?

"Yes," said the Ministers, "for the example of her rebellion is fatal."

"No," they said, immediately thereafter, "for the sly fox is very well in with several members of the opposition, who will bring down the government."

Conclusion: nothing was decided.

After which, the session was concluded and Their Excellencies retired, very satisfied with themselves.

Jacques did not know what to think He interrogated Sufar about the statue devoid of arms and legs.

"Oh," said his correspondent, "she presides over all our meetings and assemblies. She's the image of our wisdom: a head to reflect, but no legs with which to walk or arms with which to act. A long time ago, we recognized that extreme meditation is the sworn enemy of action.

"Possibly," said Jacques. Then, addressing Letord, he added: "I think that among the Sages, the only joys are those of intelligence. They're doubtless so intoxicating that they must console people for any affliction."

"I believe as you do," said Letord.

"It's necessary to question Sufar, who knows everything, on that subject. He'll be able to reveal to us the radiant perspectives of wisdom, and we'll be content."

"That's right," said Letord.

Sufar told them that he was ready to respond to them regarding the most arduous questions, and Lagité began by asking his opinion regarding the principal theories of terrestrial philosophy. "Our Greek Sages," he told him, "are famous. Plato affirms the God, who is infinitely rich, has espoused the extreme poverty of the world, and that all appearances are born from their marriage."

"Pooh!" said Sufar.

"Aristotle declares that Divine thought is the idea of a thought, and that that is sufficient to make the world turn."

"Bah!"

"Plotinus believes that God allows all creation to tumble from his loins and then to climb back toward him."

"Your Greeks were terrible quibblers," said Sufar, "with a great deal of impertinence."

"The English," said Jacques, have excelled in morality. Bacon, Hobbes, Locke, David Hume, Berkeley, Bentham, Stuart Mill and Spencer esteem that individual interest is confounded with the general interest, and that it's necessary to work for the public good, because that is what returns the most to the individual."

"Your English are accountants," said Sufar.

"Spinoza," said Jacques, "has reduced God to being nothing but a gigantic theorem in geometry."

"That's not so stupid," said Sufar

"Leibniz has declared that God has created an imperfect world because, if creation had been prefect, it would not have been distinguished from the creator."

"Your Leibniz absolves Providence very lightly of all the evil that one observes in the world."

"Kant says that Necessity rules the world but that humans are nevertheless free, because they choose their character themselves before birth."

"Bizarre!"

"His disciples, the Germans Fichte, Hegel and Schelling, seek the first principle of all things. Fichte believes that he has found it in the Self, to which the Non-Self is opposed, Hegel in Being, which is opposed to Non-Being, Schelling in the Subject, as opposed to the Object. And each of them extracts the entire Universe from his formula, as a consequence. As for their compatriot Einstein, he enslaves the world to a single force: inertia."

"Your Germans want the great All to behave in a Prussian manner."

"The Frenchman Descartes opines that our will can manipulate as it pleases within our brains the little pineal gland, and thus direct the animal spirits that accomplish all our actions. Maine de Biran claims to prove our liberty by means of our sentiment of effort. According to Bergson, the material universe descends a slope, Life climbs up it again and, thanks to their liberty, humans climb that slope faster than other living beings."

"Your turbulent Frenchmen," said Sufar, "are insurgent even against the discipline of Nature."

"Meyerson, another French philosopher,[22] proclaims that nature is essentially unintelligible. In order to understand it, it would be necessary to return it to unity, but that is impossible, for it is frightfully diverse and changing."

"Ha ha! Your Meyerson isn't an idiot."

"The American pragmatist William James recommends Christian belief as the one that has the best usage in contemporary life."

"The American, if he could, would put God in a tin can," said Sufar.

"But what do you think of those systems?" Lagité said.

"Almost all of them are full of falsity. How do you expect your feeble reasoning to adapt to the infinite complexity of the world? The Universe, in its progress, doesn't care what you think and won't yield in the slightest to the petty rules of your understanding.

"Even we, in spite of our sagacity, only see a little more clearly than you. In all probability, the word is ruled by a capricious and extravagant will, which seems to amuse itself with the games you call hide-and-seek and blind-man's-buff. Hiding from the creature, it cries; 'Cuckoo!' It imposes on us the law of seeking it with eyes blindfolded, groping at hazard. What is disconcerting is that it takes pleasure in that puerile amusement.

"Dear inhabitants of little Earth, take it from the Sage who is talking to you: life is just a trick of a mocking Demiurge. It would be much better if nothing existed."

"In that case," said Jacques, "why don't the Sages seek to destroy themselves?"

"That's because destruction is still action," said Sufar. "That desperate resolution would have many repercussions. Our abolished race would probably be replaced by others that would be worse. That's why we continue to live. But we re-

---

[22] Émile Meyerson (1859-1933), born in Poland and educated in Germany, was naturalized as a French citizen after World War I.

duce out existence almost to negligibility. We only eat, drink and procreate just enough to perpetuate our species, and no more. We act as minimally as possible; we think. On which note, I wish you much pleasure."

And he took his leave of them.

"They're not light-hearted on that world," Jacques murmured. "Truly, the philosophy of that Sufar has given me a chill in my spine. Anything rather than such a wisdom! I prefer to be poor in spirit.[23] I'd have more chance of being happy."

"Perhaps," replied Letord, smiling, "and I can even enable you to make the judgment. Come back tomorrow and I'll show you the planet of the Poor in Spirit."

"Decidedly," said Jacques, "one can never catch you at a loss."

XIII. The Planet of the Poor in Spirit

The following day, Jacques, punctual at the rendezvous, saw people in the streets of a city whose faces were radiant.

Gross jowls, double and triple chins, florid complexions, large red ears, wide mouths, ecstatic gazes and comfortable paunches: in sum, they had all the attributes of perfect contentment. Even those who chanced to be thin seemed raptur-

---

[23] The original has *pauvres d'esprit*. Because the word *esprit* can mean "mind" or "intelligence" in French, as well as "spirit" what Jacques is implying by contrasting his desire with the intelligence of the Sages is that he would rather be unintelligent, but the French phrase, like its English equivalent, is famous by virtue of its use in vernacular versions of the gospel according to Saint Matthew, in which Jesus says that the poor in spirit are blessed because theirs is the kingdom of Heaven. The author also seems to have in mind during the next chapter Christ's assertion, via Matthew, that the pure in heart will see God.

ous. They were laughing angelically, singing, and dancing rather than waking.

"Good!" exclaimed Jacques. "These people aren't downcast."

Letord introduced him to one of the Poor in Spirit, bursting with delight and obesity. "This is my friend Nirup," he said. "He's going to tell us the secret of the universal felicity distributed over this planet.

"It is," said Nirup, with a sigh, "that we possess certainty."

"Certainty, you say?" said Jacques, eagerly.

Nirup shaped a profound affirmative nod of the head.

"Doubtless you've searched for that certainty for a long time?"

"Searched?"

"Yes. I imagine that your scholars have worked hard and studied a great deal before discovering it?"

"Don't talk to me about scholars!" said Nirup. "We despise them. We glory in being as ignorant as carps."

"But then..."

"We draw the truth from a big book that fell from the sky thousands of years ago."

"What?" said Jacques. "What is written in such an ancient book can still be applied to all present circumstances? Does it contain solutions to all the new difficulties that emerge, and all the questions that modern science poses?"

"I've already told you that science is of no importance to us," said Nirup. "But everything is in the big book. Everything!"

"I'd have more confidence in a new book," Jacques opined, "in which the concerns of the present time are reflected."

"You don't understand anything," said Nirup. "The older a book is, the more confidence one can have in it."

At that moment, the enthusiastic songs resounded of a cortege that was passing in a neighboring street.

"Ah!" said Nirup, with a manifest sympathy, "those are worshipers who are going to see Him."

"Who is Him?" Jacques asked.

"Him, Him! He has no other name. Him! Oh, Him!" Nirup rolled the whites of his eyes and seemed inundated by an ineffable voluptuousness.

"But in sum," Jacques said, "tell me about this Him that you idolize."

"He's our benefactor," said Nirup, "and our king. And he only shows himself to him, the Poor in Spirit. The mortals of other planets would like very much to see him. It's their dearest ambition. But he's obstinate in hiding from them. At least, he only permits them to see him via astral wireless. We alone enjoy the signal privilege of possessing him in our midst."

"Can you enable us to know him?" asked Letord.

"I consent to that," said Nirup. "Let's go to his palace."

A few minutes later, Letord and Lagité saw a dense crowd that filled an immense room sustained by high columns. In that nave, which resembled a sanctuary a fabulous luxury reigned, but in dubious taste: sky-blue vaults strewn with stars, statues that were gilded or painted in loud colors, garish paintings, stained glass with the insipid translucency of syrups and candied fruits.

The audience was waiting silently at the foot of a triumphal golden throne, which was unoccupied.

Suddenly, a brightly-clad chamberlain appeared. Organs launched forth squalls of harmony. And on the royal throne, the individual summoned by all the prayers of the crowd took his place. It was the Him of whom Nirup had spoken.

Letord and Lagité had not imagined him as he was.

The sovereign of the planet of the Poor in Spirit. had the appearance of a fat well-to-do bourgeois. Like the majority of his subjects, he was red-faced and stout, with a long white beard: a debonair aspect that was nevertheless belied by false gleams that traversed his eyes, of different colors.

With a single movement, the members of the crowd had prostrated themselves, face down, and they maintained that attitude for some time. Then they put themselves on their knees and modulated hymns to the glory of their monarch.

"How beautiful he is! How beautiful he is!" they repeated. "How good he is! How wise he is! Happy, happy, a hundred times happy are those he governs with so much mildness! Long live Him! Long live Him!"

And the songs alternated with ovations.

"They're really treating him like a God," said Jacques to Letord. "And yet there's nothing divine about him. Don't you find him rather vulgar?"

"Yes, indeed," murmured Letord.

Him quit his throne, and with a generous condescension he passed through the ranks of the multitude in order that they could contemplate him at closer rage. Jacques thus had the opportunity to observe him more closely, and he found him even more disquieting. Beneath the feigned bonhomie of that powerful individual he discerned a sort of knavery, a perfidious cruelty.

He questioned Nirup about the monarch's habits.

"Very simple, even rustic," Nirup replied. "He's passionate about horticulture and possesses a splendid orchard. Of course, he doesn't like people stealing his fruits, That's a trait of his character. He's a good father, but he prefers his apples to his children, and condemns marauders to death pitilessly."

"That's frightful," said Jacques.

"What do you expect?" said Nirup. "One takes that for granted. Otherwise, an excellent heart."

Him had emerged from his palace and, as was his custom, he wandered through the streets of his capital.

As he passed by, everyone cheered and bent their knees.

He went into a dwelling of poor appearance, which he had already visited on previous days. It was his pleasure to visit thus, unexpectedly, his most modest subjects as well as his highest dignitaries.

He climbed a humble stairway and headed straight for the small bedroom where a child was lying. The parents followed him to the bed. They fixed Him with the suppliant gaze of a whipped dog.

"Our darling is a little better," they said, in a whisper.

Him smiled benevolently and, as he had done the day before and the day before that. He put his forefinger on the head of the poor child, sternly.

The child woke up then. His eyelids opened immeasurably. His eyes fluttered with a panicky rapidity. His lips trembled. His hands were continually agitated under the covers. His eyes, tipped backward, seemed to want to flee torturing visions, and he uttered a long hoarse plaint.

The sovereign lifted his finger.

The pain immediately ceased, as if by a miracle, and the child sighed, appeased.

The king, still paternal, replaced his index finger on the forehead of the invalid. The signs of an atrocious suffering reappeared immediately. The infant howled. The modulations of his scream had the effect of his parents of a red-hot iron turning back and forth in their bosom. The paltry body stiffened, braced, and contracted.

Something infernal was happening in the brain of that unfortunate little being, that no living being would have been able to imagine, because such an exasperation of dolor was the very entrance to annihilation.

And with a last savage cry, the supreme breath was liberated. In an ultimate convulsion, the child slumped on his side; the index finger of the sovereign accompanied the head inexorably in that displacement. Finally, the body was immobilized.

The parents sobbed, with great heaves of their curbed shoulders.

Him said to them: "That's done it!" And he smiled again.

Then, an insensate scene unfolded. The parents knelt down, took the hand of the sovereign, covered it with kisses and stammered: "Thank you! Thank you! How good you are to have killed our child! You're too good!"

Now, they too were smiling through their tears, and repeating: "Thank you, thank you."

Other witnesses who had come into the room with the king made a chorus with the parents: "Glory to Him! Glory to Him!" they clamored. "Everything that he decides is perfect! If he had cured that child, we would have blessed him. But since he didn't want to, we bless him all the same. He's always right. The suffering that he distributes so abundantly is much preferable to joy. Suffering is the supreme felicity. Glory to Him! Glory to Him!"

They went out with the sovereign, toward whom the actions of grace of his subjects rose up without discontinuity through the streets.

Lagité and Letord looked at one another without saying a word.

The king, continuing his march, went into a second house. A young mother was in the course of giving birth to a child there. Around her there was a joyful expectation, nuanced nevertheless with some apprehension. The husband was proud of having created life. He was already puncturing his dear wife offering her breast to the nursling and forgetting her dolors in the rapture of maternity. He saw her in advance appealing by means of gentle baby-talk to the intelligence and tenderness in two little flowers of light.

However, she was lamenting, and breathing heavily, and the midwife was striving to encourage her with comforting words.

The sovereign appeared.

Among the people present there was the same blaze of confidence as there had been in the house of the little invalid previously.

Him approached the body agitated by a cruel swell and placed his broad hand thereon. Instantly, it was as if the young mother froze. She uttered a feeble groan and became inert,

"There!" said the king. He added, speaking to the husband: "Your son will live."

"Oh, thank you, thank you!" said the father. "How good you are! How good you are!"

And again the noisy demonstrations of gratitude erupted.

"That woman has ceased to suffer," they said. "Glory to Him! He wanted the life of the mother to serve as ransom for that of the child. Blessed is he! Blessed is he!"

Lagité leaned toward Letord's ear and said to him, with alarm: "But what is this sadistic madman? He scares me. And what is this people who magnify him for such sins?"

The sovereign, nodding his head, went on his way.

He made a third halt and went up to another dwelling. There, a young mathematician was gasping. He was in an armchair near the window, enveloped in blankets. Within arm's reach, on a table, were sheets of paper covered in formulas. An old man, his professor, was standing beside him.

On that planet, where study was disdained, the two scholars loved one another all the more because their mutual affection compensated them for the general indifference.

The invalid had taken the old man's hand and was looking at him sadly. He was desperate to complete a great discovery toward which his precocious genius was guiding him.

"I would have needed another week," he said.

"But you're going to live," said his friend, turning away in order to hide his tears.

The king, who had remained on the threshold momentarily, advanced toward them.

"Save him!" said the professor. "Save that prodigious intelligence!"

"You believe in my power, then, scholar?"

"I will believe in it."

Without responding, Him placed his hand on the breast of the moribund genius, whose head inclined over his shoulder.

"It's over!" said the sovereign, challenging the dead man's friend with an ironic glance.

Overwhelmed, the old scholar remained silent,

As for the worshipers of the king, they resumed their dithyrambs:

"Long live Him! Long live Him! That young mathematician was a genius, it seems. Our king has condemned him. He has

311

done well. Perish all scholars, all geniuses, provided that Him is triumphant! From Him, we accept everything with joy! Let him test us, let him torment us, let him inflict upon us and ours the most refined tortures, let him crush us! So much the better! Glory to Him alone!"

And they sang until they ran out of breath.

"They're happy, it's undeniable," exclaimed Lagité. "They are even the only happy mortals that we've observed thus far in the planets. But away with such a happiness! They're truly too poor in spirit!

So saying, he cut the communication, without even saluting the bloated and blissful Nirup.

XIV. A Celestial Crash

After that further disappointment, Jacques had fallen back into his hypochondria.

He was dreaming more than ever about his Gilniz.

He forgot about everything the inhabitants of Venus might have said against her. And since it was impossible for him to love the terrestrial woman whom his correspondents claimed to be marvelous, it was toward Gilniz that his exacerbated desires were redirected.

He had, however, sworn not to think any more about his mistress beyond the sky, and he had kept that oath for a long time.

Suddenly, though, after a brief internal struggle, he evoked the apparition that haunted him on the screen, and Gilniz smiled at him.

"Ingrate lover," she said, "why have you neglected me? I'm so stupid, that I think about you incessantly. Oh, my beloved, what an unspeakable dolor it is not to be able to respond to your desire!"

Strangely enough, she seemed sincere. Was she? Perhaps by caprice, during the moment when she was speaking.

And the bewitchment immediately recommenced. Jacques now saw Gilniz every day; he seemed irresistible condemned to that folly.

The astral wireless itself, however procured him a diversion of sorts from his amorous torment; for that invention, the prodigies of which were enfevering the entire world, suddenly brought its devotees the most anguishing surprise that it had yet contrived for them.

From a distant star, a prolonged, persistent, painful signal reached all the receiving posts, which was translated by sonorous appeals of an unusual timbre and by extraordinarily sinuous flashes.

It soon became clear that it was an immense cry of distress launched into infinite space: a sort of intersidereal S.O.S.

Letord was the first to identify the planet from which the heart-rending request for help was coming, it was Phi in the constellation Canis Major. Without delay, he invited Lagité to witness his observations.

The astronomers of Phi had just acquired the certainty that in a short time their globe was about to collide with satellite number three of the star Omega. The pulverization of the two spheres would be the infallible result.

As soon as Barnabé Letord had put that news into circulation, all the wireless enthusiasts of the Old and New Worlds adjusted their apparatus, in order to witness the imminent tragedy.

The catastrophe was no more distant than thirty-five days. The astronomers of the threatened planet had indicated by means of calculations of an unchallengeable precision the exact minute and second at which the collision would occur.

It goes without saying that the inhabitants of Phi gave their globe another name. They designated it by the word Grul, and for them, the satellite of Omega was the star Lap. That is what we shall call the two heavenly bodies in our story.

The prediction of the scientists of Grul had initially been greeted with skepticism, but the ruling class had not taken

313

long to believe it, and the masses had soon sensed that it was a matter of an irremediable condemnation. In any case, Lap, which had previously had a small diameter, was growing continually. Now, everyone could take account of that increase with the naked eye, without any recourse to astronomical telescopes.

The race in peril found itself almost in the situation of a paralytic who, placed on a railway track, can see an express train growing in magnitude on the horizon. The scientists of Grul addressed themselves fearfully to their colleagues on other worlds and asked them whether anything could be attempted—but they only obtained, as you can imagine, evasive responses or nonsense.

Barnabé Letord had wanted to make contact with the inhabitants of the other star that was about to perish. He had succeeded, not without difficulty.

In fact, while the inhabitants of Grul resembled humans closely, the population of Lap was composed of veritable monsters, only a few of which were capable of employing wireless.

The professor of the Collège de France remembered perfectly that during his earliest experiments he had chanced to communicate with Lap. He had even collected the famous apocalyptic image that his colleagues had accused him of having composed by trickery.

In pursuing his investigations, he also learned that the monsters of Lap were the products of hybridizations unknown anywhere else. Any species coupled with any other, and fabulous types were born in consequence: fish with human heads, like the Oannes of Babylonian legend, winged lions like that of Saint Mark, sirens, harpies—in sum. all imaginable fantasies of genesic power. Some of those creatures enjoyed a highly developed intelligence, but they were rare.

The interest awakened throughout the universe in the frightful adventure, therefore, generally turned away from that pandemonium in order to concentrate on Grul.

That was a world of very advanced civilization. The greatest geniuses in the various orders of knowledge had realized innumerable inventions there, which had suppressed all physical servitudes. High Science reigned uncontested, and life was an enchantment.

As soon as the conviction of an imminent end was imposed, however, all activity stopped. Merchants closed their shops. The population, soon hungry, broke down the doors, and the majority of the merchants who defended their property were massacred.

If the consumption of products assembled on the planet and ready to be utilized had been methodical, it would have far surpassed needs until the fatal hour. But a frenzy had taken hold of all the inhabitants, and they stimulated one another mutually to stuff themselves with victuals. Like filthy rodents that, with a single bite, poison the most precious products, they delved at hazard into crates and barrels, and after the few extractions they made, they abandoned the remainder to putrescence.

The very spectacle of that plunder gave them the idea that everything would soon run out, and like insensates they hurled themselves upon one another to dispute the booty, murdered one another, stuffed themselves, and then, stuffed again and dead drunk, snored in the wine and the blood.

Famine became rife about a fortnight before the denouement, and battles around the almost-exhausted aliments became increasingly ferocious.

Jacques, at Letord's house, followed those lamentable scenes, thanks to the scientists of Grul, who continued relentlessly to solicit the illusory aid of all the thinking brains in the entire universe.

"What desolation," cried Jacques, "to think that a few weeks ago, that people was perhaps the wisest and most fortunate in infinite space! With what incredible rapidity the varnish of civilization that covers the primitive savagery of the most polite society cracks!"

The attention of the two friends was attracted by episodes of another sort. The approach of the end suppressed all restraint of instinctive impulses. Young people of both sexes contented one another mutually at crossroads, like animals, without anyone raising any obstacle. Mature women cajoled schoolboys brazenly. Incests were committed before the eyes of everyone, and the sight of those aberrations, far from scandalizing the witnesses, suggested to them the firm design to imitate them.

Only ten days remained. Lap, which appeared in the nocturnal sky like an enormous bomb enveloped by a metallic gleam, was visible even by day, and exercised a frightful obsession upon those who raised their eyes.

Rich people who, at the first news of the catastrophe, had amassed choice food supplies, gathered in the domain of one of them. It was an area as large as a small province and renowned for the enchantment of its landscapes. A magical palace stood in the midst of age-old forests. The master of the abode invited his friends to continual rejoicing there. And at first, the fêtes were rather well ordered. An orchestra executed passionate tunes that procured an aphrodisiac ecstasy. Couples spread outside the sumptuous dwelling beneath the opaque foliage and sought the numbing of the senses there.

On the sixth day before the deadline, however, the musicians, besieged by the common haunting, produced so many false notes and discords that they could not continue playing. And the lovers whose gallant conversations had been interrupted by frightful silences ceased to madrigalize. As they headed for the thickets they forgot that they were together and went back separately to the château.

It had been forbidden ever to make allusion to the horrible terminus, but no one succeeded in being distracted from it. Repeatedly, one of the condemned pronounced in a loud voice the number of days that separated them from death. Growls of anger greeted that reminder, and the importunate individual was thrown out of the gates of the estate.

In spite of that severity, a young poet started to howl: "Five days! Five days!"

He climbed on to a platform on the golden balustrades and repeated his cry from there. He was told to shut up, bombarded with cups and crystal vases, from which he took refuge behind columns, and which fell back and shattered into a thousand pieces on the mosaics, in the midst of the oaths of those they struck. And he, driven by a Dionysian delirium, resumed his refrain:

"Five days! Five days! That's all that remains to you. Employ them well. Into those few hours concentrate all that the years of your life promised you. Intoxicate yourselves with so much amour, wear yourselves out with so many enjoyments, that in five days your vigor will turn into decrepitude, your blond hair will turn white, your eyes will tarnish, your heart and your blood will finish blazing, and Death, thinking to surprise you in the spring of your youth will only scythe down ice-cold old men."

Then he put his arms around two young dancing girls and they staggered away in their embrace.

Suddenly, his orgiastic excitement took possession of the entre audience. And as, in the kennels, the first bark unleashes a furious din, a colossal roar of salacity resounded. It was a gigantic exhalation of desire, with which spasmodic laughter, songs, hiccups and demented clamors were mingled.

That little society, which, among the elite of the land, had once represented the rarest distinction, was precipitated without restraint into an unspeakable debauchery. Madmen and madwomen bowed their heads together over large alabaster vases filed with wine and drank avidly, like animals from a pond; then, all garments torn away, they appeared in a furious saraband of nudity that undulated through the enormous palace, over the pavements of the halls, along the marble stairways, the thresholds of doors and the steps of perrons. Masters, musicians and servants were now confounded, and the baseness of certain valets set the tone for the bacchanal.

When no more than two and a half days remained, many of the guests were dead of excess. Others were so sated by lust that they remained inert. Only a few got up, staggering, in order to drink more, to eat scraps steeped in wine and fall back among the sprawling nudities, scattered pell-mell.

Very few of them were conscious of what was happening when a barbaric rumor filled the surrounding park and a mob of vagabonds irrupted into the château with the violence of a muddy inundation.

The intruders were innumerable and sordid, faces leaden with fatigue and striped by scars, with meager and blackened flesh that their tattered rags rendered visible. It was the populace, who, having dilapidated the provision of the towns, had spread out into the country, where they exterminated the peasants in order to feast on their flocks. The rumor had run around those bandits that fabulous provisions had been heaped up in the château where the orgy had been unleashed.

Armed with billhooks, pikes, pitchforks, clubs, cutlasses and axes, they had formed a compact column in order to head for the goal of their brigandage. The first to enter the palace hurled themselves upon the women, murdered the guests and rushed upon the food and the drink. The rich scarcely defended themselves, so exhausted were they. In any case, any struggle was vain against the multitude of the invaders. Other vagabonds followed incessantly. They continued to kill, to guzzle and to swill; they choked the unconscious women under constantly renewed assaults; then they massacred one another in order to snatch shreds of victuals; they paddled, slipped and rolled in the blood that streamed in cascades over the steps, over the flagstones, along the walls and all the way to the distant pathways of the park.

Finally, they set fire to the edifice, and the flames devoured, in a matter of seconds, the accumulation of marvels that the greatest artists had created.

None of those sinister visions escaped Letord and Lagité. For, in the same way that in our most treble battles, reporters are always to be found of an inconceivable temerity, heroic transmitters on Grul never ceased to circulate and collect for the wireless testimonies of the lugubrious destiny of the unfortunate planet.

"Frightful! Frightful!" repeated Jacques. And again he meditated on the short time that had been required for barbarity to efface so many centuries devoted to the triumph of intelligence.

Other information, however, proved to the two friends that all thought was not dead on the star in question. Among several scientists of Grul a supreme preoccupation had been born. Since they could not save themselves, they wanted to transmit everything that they had discovered. They communicated their latest endeavors feverishly to their colleagues on other worlds. As in conflagration one hastily wraps the most precious objects in blankets in order to throw them out of the windows, they launched into the sky all of their magnificent knowledge. They dictated word for word certain treatises in which their noblest doctrines were condensed, and adjured the worlds not to allow any of it to be lost.

In their principal city, Professor Gasbi, the director of the Central Institute, had organized a service informed the universe hour by hour. It was a matter of consigning for future science a rigorously objective aspect of events. The messages were numbered carefully.

No. 34839, second day of the third week of the twelfth month, midday. The collision will take place, as everyone knows, tomorrow at eleven hours, ten minutes and twenty-three seconds. Presently, we are only separated from it by twenty-three hours, forty-nine minutes and thirty-seven seconds.

Lap is clearly visible in broad daylight. Its apparent diameter is one meter thirty.[24] *The contours of its shores can*

---

[24] Author's note: "To minimize complication, we are translating into terrestrial units the measurements of length and time employed by the inhabitants of Grul."

easily be discerned. That observation permits us to resolve a question that has divided our scientists. The ridiculous thesis of Professor Bono on the form of the continents of Lap was completely erroneous. It is that of Professor Gasbi that is correct.

No. 234840, thirteen hours. A few details regarding the activity of our Institute. We have to deplore the dejection of many of our collaborators, who, dominated by an anxiety otherwise excusable, are no longer interested in our studies.

Young Doctor Rilu is pursuing his magisterial research on immortality. He believes that he has found henceforth the principle that will assure living beings of a perpetual existence. In order to bring the discovery definitively to a conclusion, he will devote himself to one last experiment.

Other various items of information were accompanied by live pictures. All the wireless enthusiasts on Earth, like the populations of Grul, saw Lap increasing in size from moment to moment. They remained amazed by the calm physiognomy of Professor Gasbi and the ardent labor of Doctor Rilu.

On the morning of the last day the following message was received:

No, 34897, third day of the third week of the twelfth month, eight o'clock in the morning. The gravitational effects of the approach of Lap are beginning to make themselves felt. On Grul, the weight of objects and living beings is diminishing. Plates thrown into the air with a moderate force rise easily to a hundred meters and fall back slowly, without breaking

Professor Gasbi, wanting to verify the new conditions of weight personally, has just made, in spite of his age, a leap of thirty meters in height in the courtyard of the Institute.

A short time afterwards a communication was sent from Lap by one of the rare intelligent creatures inhabiting it. It was a disconcerting vision.

The monsters of that planet, tormented by an apprehension that even overtook the unconscious beings, were agitating desperately. Long serpents with multiple feet were delivering themselves to strange contortions. Enormous fish, with a thrust of their caudal fin, were springing out of the sea and launching themselves into the air through the liquid mountains that they lifted up with themselves. Beasts bristling with spikes, like gigantic porcupines, were making disorderly leaps, colliding with one another, howling and fleeing in all directions. A panic terror had taken possession of that entire hideous race, whose violent and futile efforts to escape destruction rendered them pitiable nevertheless,

And the dispatch of coded messages from Grul continued:

No. 34940. An indescribable panic is observable in all living beings. The inhabitants of the city are running around at random in the streets, colliding and resuming their route without following any direction.

Animals are giving evidence of the same disarray. Little birds are flying into walls and falling in front of cats, which neglect to seize them. Reptiles, rats, dogs and wolves, meet at crossroads without the enemy species seeking to harm one another.

No. 34941. Five past eleven. The panic of intelligent beings and animals has suddenly turned into a kind of torpor. All of them are still, lying down flat on the ground, seemingly paralyzed.

No. 34942. Six minutes past eleven. Remarkable instance of the persistence of the genesic instinct.

At the same time as that announcement was formulated, visible on the screen, in the midst of the mortal torpor of nature entire, was a young couple perfectly indifferent to everything that was happening. The two lovers, sitting on a bench, were exchanging ecstatic gazes.

No. 34943. Seven minutes past eleven. The hindrance of breathing is becoming intolerable. Lap is invading the entire sky. One can distinguish forests, rivers and lakes.

No. 34944. Eight minutes past eleven. Monsters recalling species long extinct on Grul are falling from Lap on to our planet.

No. 34945. Nine minutes past eleven. Darkness is falling progressively with great rapidity. Our city will be at the exact point of impact of the two globes.

At that moment, one saw again, in the gloom, the couple of young lovers. They were saying to one another: "Forever!"

And they took one another in a frenetic embrace.

No. 34946. Ten past eleven. Doctor Rilu will make a communication to all his colleagues in the universe.

Then, by the light of a lamp, the face of the young scientist appeared, transfigured by joy, and he was heard to say: "I have just discovered the secret of immorta..."

The phrase remained incomplete. Everything was eclipsed.

Jacques and Letord looked at one another. A frightful anguish prevented them from speaking for a long moment.

"When three hundred years have gone by," said Letord, finally, "our astronomers will observe in that part of the sky a sudden and colossal conflagration. The formidable impact of the two planets has certainly developed so much heat that the two spheres have immediately been converted into flaming gas. A prodigious blaze must now be illuminating that region of space."

"And that's what has become of the admirable civilization of Grul," said Jacques. "That cataclysm is, of all our astral experiences, the one that discourages me the most. Until now I had conserved a vague hope of finding happiness on the planets. I haven't discovered it anywhere, but it seems to me that the inhabitants of Grul were close to it. And behold the atrocious irony! In the blink of an eye, by virtue of a stupid whim of fate, all the long efforts of one of the most intelligent races have attempted in order to be happy have been annihilated."

"Oh, my dear friend," said Letord, "such stellar encounters are very rare."

"Agreed," said Jacques, "But whatever the delay accorded to planets might be, all of them must perish."

"That's possible."

"At least, all of them will cool. And on all of them, life will end up being extinguished, along with its chimerical promises of happiness."

"That's certain," Letord agreed.

"That, then, is the condemnation of all faith in the future," said Jacques. "Oh, I don't know why I'm avid to see one of those worlds where life is agonizing. There must be a bitter need in me for suffering, for the vision does me harm. But I'm avid to learn, and perhaps the satisfaction of my desire will compensate me for my dolor. Have you discovered one of those planets, my friend?"

Letord did not reply.

Then Jacques said, with an extreme vehemence: "My friend, my friend, I want you to give me that spectacle."

"I hesitated to propose it to you," said Letord, "But I am of the opinion that Science bears within itself the appeasement of all our sadness, and you have always been so passionate for the Truth that you will be able to support yet again looking it in the face."

XV. The Last Couple

At a further rendezvous at Professor Letord's house, Jacques saw on the screen a country whose aspect caused him a constriction of the heart.

A snowy mountain dominated an immense icy extent: there was winter everywhere, but not, as for us, a cold season in which the pulsation of life continues to beat, when rivers flow beneath the ice and when the sap remains moist in the heartwood of trees. On the planet that Lagité was looking at, the land and the water were definitively as hard as marble, and death reigned implacably. It gave the evident impression that henceforth, no effluvium of spring would ever soften that rigidity.

There was a torrent there that was precipitating from the heights, but its disheveled cascades were forever immobile. They hung down in weighty sheets, in heavy vitrified draperies, and the foam no longer swirled in the gulf, but had been solidified for centuries to come.

From the summits, the sea was visible in the distance, but its great angry waves no longer stirred; it was nothing but an infinite disorder of enormous pieces of ice. It was deducible that before being fixed in that hard eternal chaos, the liquid masses of the Ocean, still free, had risen from the most profound of its abysms in many revolts against the crystal cope whose ice had ended up oppressing them. And in the configuration of those colossal and bizarre asperities, the prolonged struggles of movement against an endless slumber were recounted.

Now, even in its deepest declivities, the Ocean no longer formed anything but a single block, as dense as granite.

A perpetually livid, although very pure, sky covered that desolate landscape. The sun of that aged universe no longer had the strength to illuminate its planets. It rose redly in space, and its surface was striped by the moving shadows that pass over a semi-consumed hearth.

At the first glance, no inhabitants could be seen.

However, on the indications of Letord, who had already explored that land by wireless, Jacques distinguished, in a rocky fissure in the flank of the mountain, two torpid beings next to a dying fire.

They had a vaguely human appearance, except that their spine was curved toward the ground and their emaciated faces revealed a mortal lassitude. They were clad in the skins of polar bears, the snowy color of which was confounded with the general hue of the region; that is why it had been difficult to discern them.

They were two old people. They only moved with difficulty. The husband had a long white beard; his hands were resting on his knees and he had difficulty breathing. The wife, almost as old, consulted the slightest desires of her companion, and busied herself around him slowly.

She presented the meat that she had cooked to him. She had doubtless taken it from some long-dead animal conserved by the ice with which the cold was dressed. She also offered him the marrow that she had extracted from the broken bone, and insisted that he nourish himself with it. But he refused the food stubbornly. Then he fixed his large dull eyes, in which his imminent end was written, upon his wife.

Sitting next to him against the rocky wall that protected them from the wind, she covered her face with her hands and sobbed.

"I imagine," said Letord, "that they're the last two representatives of a race that, I have reason to believe, was possessed of a superior intelligence."

"But how can these images be reaching our screen?" Jacques asked. "It's not, I assume, that old couple who are transmitting them?"

"Certainly not," said Letord. "But what I suppose is that there is extremely improved transmission apparatus nearby, which was created in the most flourishing epoch of the planet. Those instruments have continued to function, unknown to the degenerate descendants of those who invented them. What confirms my hypothesis is that I've received other images, originating from locations where there was no being endowed with reason. In any case, save for this troglodyte couple, I haven't discovered any trace of life on the globe we're observing. There are neither animals nor plants there. The ice has killed everything.

"Anthropomorphs of the species we can see here must have been the last to resist because they possessed fore to warm them, and also to convert ice into the water indispensable to their existence. But now the fatal hour has come in which they too must disappear, and perhaps we're witnessing their supreme day."

Jacques remained silent, sunk in a profound reverie.

By means of an unexpected effort, the old man had straightened his torso; then, vacillating on his legs, he had clung on to projections in the rock in order to stand up.

His wife, frightened by that caprice, extended her arms toward him to prevent him from falling.

Now, almost upright, he contemplated the plain where his ancestors had reigned in an immemorial past. He allowed his already-vitreous eyes to wander over that empire. His gaze paused and lingered for a long time over the evidence of a very remote epoch.

For centuries, a machine, very reminiscent of our most powerful locomotives had been overturned alongside an embankment. Overturned and corroded by rust, it lifted toward the sky two enormous wheels, the only ones that remained. Doubtless pillagers had often come to borrow pieces of metal from it, for the mantle of snow that extended everywhere had not covered it completely. The rails on the embankment were also visible over a long extent, because the sleepers had been disinterred in many places in order to serve as combustible fuel.

A very ancient seaport displayed its pensive ruins. Disjointed moles, dismantled walls and a crumbling citadel still spoke of a splendor forever defunct.

In one of the basins, the prow of a gigantic ship rose above the ice. That arrogant wreck had triumphed over time and protested against the fate that had enchained it after so much vagabondage through the tempests.

On a crest, something extended that evoked the monstrous skeletons of certain fossils conserved in the glazed halls of our museums. It was the metallic framework of what had once been an immense dirigible.

The old man no longer detached his eyes from it. In the solemnity of his expression, the astonishment was translated that those vestiges had always caused him. He considered them as sacred monuments, and addressed a mute prayer to them.

While he was turned toward the plain, his wife tried to decipher in his physiognomy the ideas that were haunting him. Then, remarking that he was shivering, she tried to reanimate the fire. She picked up a shard of wood; but before throwing it into the flame she kept it in her hands for a moment, and as it was wood with a very hard grain and highly polished, she passed it gently over her cheek in order to feel the caress.

Her husband, who glimpsed that gesture, asked her what she was holding.

So far as Lagité could discern, it was the rounded extremity of an airplane propeller.

"That's surely what it is," said Letord. "Tell me, isn't it strange that intelligence throughout the universe has flowed almost exactly the same stages? It's a verity that I have now registered many times in the course of my research."

Having considered the blade of the propeller, the old man approached it to his lips and kissed it, as a savage testifies his piety to a fetish. All kinds of unconscious reminiscences doubtless remounted in his brain with regard to that relic of such a savant industry.

Then he returned the debris to his wife, which she threw on to the fire without any further respect. And the wing that had transported mortals intoxicated by audacity through the sky served to prolong for a few moments the shivering existence of the last survivors of their once-sublime race.

The old man had directed his bleak gaze toward the plain again. He was seized by a great frisson, which made his teeth chatter. His wife hastily removed the fur by which she was covered and threw it over her husband's. She tried to make him sit down, but he would not consent to it. An obstinacy of grim pride kept him upright. And, as he confronted the great dead city, his almost-opaque eyes were suddenly traversed by a radiant gleam.

The memory of his ancestors, of their power, of their ambitions, of the impetus that had driven them for such a long time to assault the impossible ignited his obscure soul with a single surge.

The flamboyant folly of a species that had shaken violently the doors of all mystery in order to attempt to become divine was concentrated within him for one final time. He raised his arms convulsively toward the somber zenith as if to demand infinite space; and then, exhaling a great cry of distress, he fell to the ground.

His wife, who had leapt forward in vain in order to sustain him, knelt down beside him, lifted his inert head, took his face between her hands, kissed his eyes and called out to him in a heart-rending voice. Then she lay down on his breast and remained there, quivering with dolor.

Letord and Lagité could not hold back their tears.

"She won't take long to follow him," said Letord, "and the planet, depopulated henceforth, will continue to drag in its ironic waltz the ruins of what intelligence once dared, in vain."

"I don't know what effect that vision produced on you, my dear friend," said Jacques, "but it put me to the torture. It seems to me that in contemplating that phantom globe today I've just launched myself in a single bound all the way to the last hours of humankind on Earth, and now I can see with a blinding clarity that the pursuit of happiness, the dream of all mortals, is a delusion. It's a mirage to make humans advance on the harsh road of existence.

"They go on and on toward felicity, the thirst for which consumes them. If they don't have it yet they console themselves with the thought that they're continually getting closer and that, thanks to their hard efforts, their descendants will enjoy it in a distant future. But Nature mocks them so cruelly that it is preparing today the suppression of all consciousness and all life. What good, then, are all the fabulous conquests of thought and its boundless hopes, if all of that must inevitably perish and be buried in icy slumber?"

Letord put a hand gently on his shoulder and said: "My friend, can it really be that, among so many image that have unfurled before your eyes, you've never recognized happiness?"

"Where, then, would I have seen it?"

"Every time a great amour is revealed to you. You've seen it, for instance, when the two lovers of the planet Grul cried: 'Forever!' You've seen it a moment ago when, under the mortal wind, the last woman of the dying planet took off her garment for her companion, who was dying. Believe me; all our hopes and all our dreams might be deceptive, but not Amour, because it finds its joy immediately in itself. Sincere amour is the infinite happiness."

"That's false!" cried Jacques. "That's false! Amour is a damnation! I've tried to love, recklessly. I still love, with an extreme passion, and I'm atrociously unhappy."

"My dear friend," said Letord, "that's because you don't know how to love."

Lagité shrugged his shoulders and, cut to the quick, he quit Letord abruptly.

XVI. The Crimes of Astral Wireless

The astral wireless that was causing Jacques to make such cruel miscalculations was, as you can easily imagine, provoking an extreme agitation all over the world, and no one could yet foresee whether it was bringing our species more profit than harm.

Among the innumerable ideas transmitted by the distant stars, it was the deadliest that humans welcomed with the greatest ardor. They were avid, above all, for inventions applicable to the art of war.

They were of all kinds: for example, extraordinarily improved cannon that sent formidable projectiles incredible distances and annihilated an army in a moment; explosives that, dropped from an airplane, hollowed out enormous craters; liquids that, spread like rain over a great city, disengaged deleterious vapors capable of depopulating it entirely in three minutes...

The governments of our sphere, put in possession of these formulas and plans, judged that the first people to make use of them would exercise a universal hegemony, and strove to procure without the slightest delay the most powerful means of combat. But as means of extermination that seemed superior to previous ones were arriving every day from the depths of infinite space, all the nations continually threw their new materiel on the scrap-heap in order to replace it relentlessly, and everywhere, arsenals filed up with machines that provoked in advance a general terror almost as desolating as war itself.

In addition, the wireless furnished a quantity of recipes for alcohols and stupefying agents previously unknown, which our race set about preparing feverishly, although it had no need of them to brutalize itself.

Were these scourges at least compensated by notable advantages?

In truth, the revelation of very useful prodigies reached our planet continually. People learned, for instance, how to manufacture cheaply an artificial flour better than that of wheat, and splendid fabrics produced by rapid methods that cost next to nothing, Diseases long reputed to be incurable were cured. In brief, every hour lengthened the interminable list of the benefits of astral wireless. But that downpour of miracles did not engender the enthusiasm that might have been imagined.

It is worthy of remark, in fact, that human beings, when they await a discovery, attach much more importance to it than when they enjoy it. Thus, flying through the air was the divine ambition of humans since their origin, but from the moment when aircraft began to traverse the atmosphere, children

330

scarcely bothered to look up in order to gaze at them. It was the same for the marvelous presents of astral wireless. What people yearn to have before possessing it becomes almost indifferent once they have it at their disposal.

It is necessary to add that the majority of these inventions caused intolerable upheavals. People had not had time to adapt their tastes to one innovation when they were already being asked to renounce it and accept other changes. Every social organization was shaken without respite. In the blink of an eye, large groups of laborers became unnecessary, and chemists replaced them. Or, for armies of laborers, builders and weavers, a few technicians were substituted, who obtained the same results by directing ingenious machines.

Attempts were made to train redundant workers for new tasks, but that reeducation required time, and the instability of every profession, with incessant crises of unemployment, provoked a furious exasperation among those who experienced them. They gathered in meetings and formed menacing processions, which the police tried in vain to disperse. Bloody brawls followed, one after another.

And while revolt was rumbling on all sides, war suddenly broke out.

Two countries whose relations had already been delicate for some time, Japan and the United States, delivered themselves more than all the others to a vertiginous arms race. On indications that came directly from beyond the sky, they had constructed many dreadnoughts, torpedo-boats and submarines, of every kind and all dimensions.

One day, a Japanese fleet set forth for the Philippines in order to annex them, and American vessels hastened to find them. A gigantic and frightful naval battle had the Pacific as its theater, the name of which seemed a poignant irony. The incomparable equipment of which the adversaries made us proved its excellence only too well. In less than a quarter of a hour, the two armadas were annihilated.

Riddled like colanders by a hurricane of projectiles, the immense ships sank. Some of those vessels, hit by torpedoes of "the latest model," were reduced to impalpable debris.

In addition, the battle remained indecisive, for it had been equally fatal to both nations. The small numbers of vessels that were still afloat were so badly damaged that their crews could not even think of continuing the combat.

In that infernal encounter, the United States and Japan had just deployed, in order to destroy one another, all the magnificent qualities that they might have used in common for the good of humanity. When their rage had dissipated, the sailors of the two heroic peoples were suddenly seized by an immense respect for one another, and, adding the finest of virtues to those they had dilapidated so sadly, they rivaled one another in generosity in order to save without distinction of origin those shipwreck victims who could be rescued.

The news that spread through the world on the subject of that massacre and the scenes of devotion that followed it excited universal pity. That carnage was judged unanimously to be so stupid and so hideous that diplomatic steps were immediately attempted by the most important neutral nations to put an end to the war.

From that moment on a general conspiracy of minds was formed against astral wireless, held responsible for the slaughter. Moralists, in books, journalists, in their newspapers, politicians at the podium and the populace, in meetings, demanded its prohibition. Only a few scientists demanded its maintenance in the name of their studies—but governments began to wonder whether the interests of science ought to hold in check those of society entire. It seemed that from then on, astral wireless was threatened with an irrevocable suppression.

XVII. The Most Adorable Woman in the Universe

Let us return to Jacques Lagité.

One day, while he was seeking a wavelength in order to communicate with Gilniz, he chanced to perceive the speech of some inhabitants of Venus, and although he did not know them, they entered into conversation with him.

"How fortunate you are," they said to him, "to inhabit the Earth."

"Oh yes," said Jacques, "it's your mania on your planet to envy our lot. If you had any suspicion, however, of the chaos in which we're struggling..."

"It's not a matter of your chaos! You're more than compensated for all your miseries, since the Perfect lives among you."

"That story again! It's already been told to me by two of your compatriots. But the Englishwoman they designated to me under the title of the Perfect died in London, run over by a tram."

"We've never heard any mention of your Englishwoman; what we're attesting is that a daughter of your race surpasses in seduction all the women in the universe."

"Even yours?" said Jacques

"Naturally," replied the Venusian.

Damn, thought Jacques, *here's a new trail to follow in order to break the spell of Gilniz. Perhaps it's finally salvation...*

"You interest me greatly," he said "Tell me everything you know about this mortal woman nicknamed the Perfect, like the other that I couldn't succeed in meeting. In what does her charm consist? Is it in the regularity of her physiognomy, the just proportions of her body or the sovereign harmony of her attitudes?"

"She possesses all those merits," said the Venusian, "but they're the least of her attractions. Her ineffable grace comes, above all, from her heart. Can you imagine a feminine face in which a painter of genius wanted to symbolize the joy of devoting oneself until death to a beloved individual? That's precisely the supernatural light that the Perfect radiates."

"Truly," said Jacques, "you're giving me an extreme desire to seek out this marvel."

"We'll guide you with pleasure," said the Venusian, "although it will be quite difficult. The Perfect is in fact, very mysterious, and has never revealed her name."

Just like the other one, thought Lagité.

"Certain indications," the inhabitant of Venus continued, "lead us to believe that at the moment, she's residing in the south of France."

While describing the landscape in which she was habitually framed he mentioned a large ruined bridge of several stages of arcades.

"Undoubtedly the Pont du Gard!" exclaimed Jacques. And by the details that his informer added, he recognized the Roman aqueduct with certainty.

Immediately making the decision to undertake the journey, he went to beg Barnabé Letord to accompany him. The professor consented to that; and the following day, they arrived at the Pont du Gard by auto.

Jacques was equipped with a portable wireless apparatus.

"What road is it necessary to follow?" he asked the inhabitants of Venus.

"The one that runs alongside the river, upstream of the bridge, on the right bank."

Letord and Lagité took that road, and a few minutes later, they interrogated their correspondents again.

"Are we on the right track?" asked Jacques.

"You're getting warmer," said the Venusian. "A short distance away, there's a small rustic manor. That's where it's necessary to go."

The two friends stopped at the gate of the Château de Saint-Privas.[25]

---

[25] The author has altered the spelling slightly of the Château de Saint-Privat, two kilometers upstream from the Pont du Gard, which was in private hands when the story was written but is now on the official list of historic monuments and open to the public.

"Is it really here that we're going to discover the Perfect?" Jacques asked Venus.

"Yes, you're getting hotter and hotter."

Lagité rang the bell. A maidservant appeared.

"Will you please tell your mistress that the great scientist Barnabé Letord and the journalist Jacques Lagité, passing by the Pont du Gard, would be glad to be admitted to visit the château?" said Jacques.

The maidservant let them into the courtyard, where they sat down on a garden bench. And almost immediately, Jacques perceived Viviane before him, very blonde, gilded by the sun, refreshed by the pure air, quivering with the joy of seeing him again.

"Ah! Jacques, it's really you!"

He could not repress his surprise He was merely careful to translate it with the rudeness that he had testified when he had rediscovered his wife for the first time in Paris. He kissed her coldly, out of simple courtesy.

"Have you been here for a long time?" he asked her.

"About a month. Friends who own this dwelling were kind enough to put it at my disposal for a few weeks."

"Is there no one else with you?"

"At the moment, I'm alone with my domestic."

Then Jacques communicated with the planet Venus again.

"You assured me," he said, "that the Perfect lived in this château."

"Well, yes," said the inhabitant of Venus, "since she's standing in front of you."

"What!" said Jacques. "The woman that is before me..."

"...Is the Adorable, the Unique, the Perfect. Were we wrong to designate her to you as the sum total of all seductions? Oh, the divine woman! We can't weary of contemplating her. What an incredible happiness we experience merely in being able to gaze at her celestial features on the screen! Have you ever seen a woman more exquisite? Anyway, you can

335

confirm our judgment yourself, for as soon as you were in her presence, you embraced her invincibly."

"But she's my wife, imbecile that you are!"

"Oh, that's not very polite!" said the Venusian.

Jacques cut the communication.

Professor Letord covered his lips with his hand in order not to burst out laughing.

Viviane, who had understood, did not allow her thoughts to show.

At that moment a peremptory voice was heard. It came from an apparatus situated in a room whose widow was open:

"Users of astral wireless are required to obey the following summons, by order of all the governments of Earth, interpreting the will of all peoples. By reason of the innumerable scourges provoked by astral wireless, all apparatus consecrated to that means of correspondence is to be destroyed within two days. Contravention of this proscription will incur a penalty consisting of an imprisonment of one year and a fine of ten thousand francs."

"Lord God!" said Jacques, looking at Letord. "That's your invention condemned without appeal."

"I've been expecting it," said the professor. "And the recent calamities that have been unleashed justify the measure all too well. I have no recriminations, therefore."

In spite of her intention to dissimulate her malicious joy, Viviane allowed it to burst forth in the tone of her voice, her bright gaze and the gracious impetus of her gestures as she proposed to the two friends a walk along the banks of the Gardon. They would have all the requisite leisure that evening or the next day to visit the property.

XVIII. A Dialogue in the Socratic Manner on Amour and Happiness

The weather was adorably autumnal.

Under the somber vault of foliage, the crystalline cascades of the river bounded with noisy delight. The strollers, intoxicated by the purity of the air, had the impression of gliding through space rather than walking.

A troop of grape-pickers—a *colle*, to use the regional expression—went past singing a song in the Provençal language greeting the autumn and the grape harvest, and looking forward to drinking the produce. Long carts were transporting the barrels full of opulent grapes, which trembled heavily at every jolt of the wheels.

Viviane took Jacques and Letord to a group of noble plane-trees that shade the Gardon a few hundred meters beyond the Roman bridge. They sat down on the bank.

At that spot, sand forms a golden carpet under the shallow river, and allows its resplendent blondeness to emerge into the sunlight in places. The water, which launches a thousand silver gleams, is so transparent that all the polished shiny pebbles on its bed can be distinguished. The various streams of the Gardon seem to be separating playfully in order to reunite again. Sometimes they hasten in a narrow passage and hollow out a well in which the swirling current takes on topaz hues. Sometimes they spread out lazily and no longer seem to want to leave such an enchanting landscape.

Fishermen were hauling out nets in which numerous carp were wriggling. Naked children were getting muddy joyfully, heaping through the waves.

Viviane said that it made her want to walk barefoot over the sand. And, taking off her shoes and stockings, she amused herself like a little girl refreshing her legs.

Her two companions amused themselves in joining her, rolling to their trousers to their thighs. They laughed when they chanced to slip on a flat stone and the water wet their garments—and Viviane rejoiced in having rejuvenated those masculine souls so laden with cares.

They came back to lie down under the great trees.

Jacques considered Viviane and thought: *So it's her that the inhabitants of Venus judge to be the most seductive of women, the one they name the Perfect. It's true that she's very*

pretty, in fact; and if it were impossible for me to possess her,
how I'd adore her myself!

Then, looking at the scenery, he admired the bell-tower
of a distant village. He remarked on the vaporous blue color of
the village.

"My dear friend," said Barnabé Letord, "that shade is indeed delightful. But you never change. It's always necessary
for you to turn your gaze toward the horizon. It's that alone
that attracts and delights you. However, that azure village, if
we went there, would seem much less beautiful to you than the
place where we are."

Jacques stated laughing.

"For myself," Letord went on, "I can't imagine that we
could find a more vivid pleasure anywhere than here. I could
believe myself transported into the famous landscape by Nico-
las Poussin in which shepherds are gathered around a tomb,
deciphering the inscription that summarizes all terrestrial joy:
Et in Arcadia ego."[26]

"I understand the lesson," said Jacques. "You're criticiz-
ing me for never collecting the happiness that is offered to me.
But how can I? My fantasy always seeks superior joys further
on."

"Well," said Letord, "if you've never encountered happiness, it's precisely because you've always looked for it too far
away."

"Bah!"

"Well, yes. You've pursued it all the way to the moon
and the stars."

"Alas!" Jacques murmured.

---

[26] The painting in question, one of two with the same subject,
also known as *Les Bergers d'Arcadie* (1637-38) has become
much more famous since the present story was written, because of its association with modern myths of Templar treasure and the Holy Grail. The significance of the epitaph [rough-
ly, I also exist in Arcadia] has been much debated.

"To tell the truth," said Letord, "your misadventure is that of the majority of men. One could believe that they set out expressly to be unhappy, for they only ever desire what it's impossible for them to obtain. Take note that even if they realized their dreams, they wouldn't be happy. Every wish, as soon as it's granted, loses the prestige that caused it to be confused with happiness, and it's replaced by others, even more painful and torturing."

"Oh, how right you are!" said Lagité. "But what can one do, then? What can one do to be happy?"

"Love," said Letord.

"Yes, that's your anthem," said Lagité, laughing. "Love! But you, my dear professor, who talk so well, what are your amours?"

"Science!" said Letord, proudly. "I love her with a fervent amour. It's the passion that counts. I also love my fellows, and for them, I would gladly give my life."

"I know that," said Jacques, suddenly becoming serious again. "It doesn't alter the fact that you did them a bad turn by offering them astral wireless."

"Oh, my friend," said Letord, "every discovery is very good or very bad, depending on whether it is employed for good or for evil. If humans have made poor use of my invention, I can't do anything about it!"

Lagité shook his hand silently.

With new force, Letord affirmed: "It's necessary to love."

"So be it!" said Jacques. "But what proof is there that amour procures happiness?"

"It is happiness itself. Amour—by which I mean disinterested amour, that of true lovers in whom all egotism is abolished, the amour of the scientist and the thinker for their mission, the amour of the humblest mortal for his quotidian task, draws its intoxication from its own ardor. And all of life is only made to furnish us with pretexts for loving! Our destiny has no other meaning.

"If we ought to labor relentlessly for our brethren, if we ought to aid them incessantly, to render their existence less harsh, if we ought to struggle against their suffering, relieve and suppress it, it's in order to show them our love. And from that we extract immediately an immense happiness, because amour, once again, experiences all its joy in giving itself.

"What does it matter, then, if we fall into the grave one after another? What does it matter that nations pass, that our very planet is condemned to perish? At every moment, humans are free to love and to be infinitely happy. At every moment they are free to enjoy a sublime melody in the concert directed by Amour. You know full well, my friend, that good musicians, when playing a beautiful symphony, put all their artistic sensuality into every note that they cause to vibrate. In the same way, in life, when it is Amour that orchestrates its chords, every minute is immediately filled with a limitless felicity.

"But I'm losing myself in the clouds. I'm only talking about devotion to science and love of humanity. I'm forgetting that I have a listener who certainly represents amour under a less solemn and more tender aspect."

"Well, my dear Monsieur," said Viviane, ever jovial, "evoke for us now the pleasures of lovers."

"You're making fun of me," said Letord. "That isn't the affair of an old professor. However, I accept the challenge. These benevolent trees and this merry water are listening to me favorably, as the plane-tree of the Ilissus inspired the words of Socrates and young Phaedrus. Or rather, it's you, my dear Madame, who are going to instruct us, for I want to interrogate you. Isn't it true that people name amour sentiments very different from one another, and even opposite?"

"Oh, certainly," said Viviane. "There are vile and filthy amours, and others that are celestially blue."[27]

---

[27] Socrates makes this argument in the *Phaedrus*, but Letord, in setting out to elicit it from Viviane, understandably leaves out other aspects of the Platonic dialogue, including its homo-

"Isn't it true that amour shouldn't be confused with desire?"

"You're going to make me blush. Desire, naturally, accompanies veritable amour, but amour doesn't always accompany desire, which is often—how shall I put it—that of a bitch on heat."

"Isn't it true that, without amour, physical desire is incapable of procuring happiness?"

"I don't know," said Viviane.

"I can guarantee it," said Letord, "and I'll tell you why. It's because desire occupies the entire soul, which is infinite, violently, and the satisfactions that it seeks are always finite; they are, therefore, only ever a very small contentment for insatiable demands."

"That seems just," said Viviane.

"Veritable amour, on the contrary, already finding all its happiness in itself, enjoys an infinite plenitude."

"I'm sure of it," said Viviane, ardently.

Letord darted a sideways glance at Jacques, whose gaze was following the fleeting water, and he concluded: "The happiness that so many of us seek so far away is very close to us. It's within us. In order to discover it, we have only to love the beings who need our love."

"It's beautiful, what you say," murmured Viviane.

"My dear Madame," said Letord, "it's even more beautiful to feel it. And what is entirely admirable, what is sublime, is the heart of a noble woman who continues to devote herself in secret when she is repaid with ingratitude and neglect."

Viviane stiffened momentarily. Suddenly, she hid her face in her hands and burst into tears.

And Lagité, leaping toward her, clasped her in his arms. He was weeping too. He hugged her, and gave her endless kisses.

"Excuse my rambling," said Barnabé Letord, flippantly.

---

sexuality and the fact that Socrates characterizes love as a species of madness.

Through her tears, Viviane addressed a smile of gratitude to him.

They stood up.

It was now evening. Passing over the river again on the monumental bridge, the eternal witness of so many ephemeral existences, they took the road of return. And as the air was cool, Viviane took off her scarf, involuntarily, to cover Jacques' shoulders.

Lagité remembered the frozen planet where the last woman had made the same loving gesture in favor of the last man.

Barnabé Letord preceded the lovers, and repeated in a cracked voice a line from the grape-pickers song: "Cut the grape, and have a good time!"

They went back inside.

Jacques, a disciplined citizen, smashed his astral wireless apparatus.

"It is, however," he cried, "the instrument that enabled me to discover the Perfect." And he underlined those words by giving Viviane further kisses.